The World Between

THE WORLD BELOW BOOK FOUR

VIVIENNE LEE FRASER

Also in this Series

The World Below
The Minotaur's Maze
The Unseelie Court

For all of you who have followed Pris, Snake, and Percival on their journey so far.

World Below
World Between
Wyld Woods
Wizard Council
Melliores
Essendore
The Capitol
Avondale

CHAPTER 1

In The Shadow of Dragons

Lights flicker in the distance, illuminating the shadowy trees lining the path as I follow Eleanora and Eugenia to Wyld Woods village. Their sharp whispers and the beat of dragon wings are the only sounds breaking the stillness of the night.

I resist the urge to watch Snake leave. Although my witch companions are two of my oldest friends—and we are talking centuries here, not decades—I feel alone without Snake.

Perhaps because the past few weeks, he and the elven princess have been my constant companions. *Ah, Pris.* I replay the vision of her falling in battle and another of her being swept away by her dragon, Am'ratha. I hope she is all right. She has to be. I will not countenance any other outcome.

Ours is a friendship forged in adversity. Perhaps that is why I feel so hollow. Or perhaps it is because being with them helped me remembered who I was—no, who I am.

Ellie and Genie are pulling ahead, their longer legs covering the distance to their house more quickly than mine. It hurts that they have not noticed I am not with them.

Their disregard sparks a flash of anger. For years they pushed for me to do more, to be a part of their plots and plans for the World Below. Well, I am here now.

My fists ball up in frustration. I take in a couple of deep breaths before forcing my fingers to relax. Returning to myself is new, and my friends were not there to witness it. It is not up to them to make space for me to join them; it falls on me to remind them that I am a force to be reckoned with, and that I will help them defeat Bernais and his elven cohort.

I am *the Percival*. The Percival who helped rid the world of the blight. The Percival who worked with the gnome Drow to prevent the use of transformation to punish lesser creatures ever again. This is who I am, and I should live this.

'Ellie, Genie, wait up,' I call into the night.

The two witches half turn and wait for me.

'I'm sorry, Percival,' Ellie says. 'Genie and I have to hurry back. A leader of a group we hope will join us in the fight against Bernais and the faux council he has set up is stopping by.'

'*We* need to be back for that,' I correct her, my voice firm.

Her eyebrows rise, and she sends a sideways glance towards Genie, a smirk playing on her lips.

'About time, Percival,' Eugenia says matter-of-factly. 'Then *we all* must make haste.'

Is it as simple as that? Have they been waiting all this time for me to stop being a cat and remember that I am a sprite with a voice?

As we reach the outskirts of the village, we take the left-hand fork in the road and head towards a rambling house built in the shade of an enormous oak tree. Even though we don't venture into the village itself, we can see that the streets are eerily deserted for this early in the evening.

Genie follows the direction of my gaze and places a hand on my shoulder.

'We have much to catch up on, my friend. Given the current state of political unrest, creatures are reluctant to leave home after sundown.'

Before we reach the house, the door opens, spilling light out in a welcoming arc and illuminating the figure of the woman who is my second mother.

'Hello, Percival. You have made it safely. Welcome home.' Seraphina's voice is warm as she greets me. 'Daughters, Gregor is already here. He hasn't much time before he travels to the World Between.'

Seraphina stands aside, allowing us to enter before her. While Ellie and Genie remove their cloaks, she studies me. 'You look like you have been in the wars, young creature.'

'That is an understatement. I literally had to fight my way past dwarves to the portal at Loch Ness to get here.'

'Would you like me to organise a bath for you?'

In the past, I would have killed to bathe and change into a clean set of clothes from the store I leave here. Gregor is the most powerful witch of his generation, and he is also the leader of a group of young people challenging the existing order in the World Below. The new Percival is going to attend this meeting.

'No, thank you, Seraphina. Perhaps later on. I will join the others for now.'

She inspects me silently, her eyes black pools of concern. 'Something is different about you tonight, Percival. We must speak after Gregor has gone. In the meantime, would you like some tea and something to eat?'

My stomach gurgles and Seraphina laughs. 'I will take that as a yes.'

'Yes, please,' I say as I follow Ellie and Genie into the living room. Seraphina retreats to the kitchen, leaving both doors open, something she does when she wants to hear what is going on.

'Eugenia, Eleanor. I was worried I would have to leave before I had spoken to you,' a young man says as he rises from a chair by the fire.

Genie waves a hand at him, gesturing for him to remain seated. 'If we stand on ceremony, we'll be here all night, Gregor.'

The young man relaxes back into his seat and runs a hand through unruly auburn hair. 'Is it safe…?' He glances my way as his voice trails off.

'You've met Percival before,' Ellie says, sitting on the sofa opposite their guest, and Genie joins her.

'Yes, of course. But normally….' Again he does not finish his sentence.

'Yes, yes,' I say impatiently. 'Normally, I am the cat on the sidelines. Tonight I am the sprite taking part. Do you have a problem with that?'

Gregor's eyebrows are not the only ones in the room to rise at the brusqueness of my words.

'No, of course not.'

'Good.'

I take a place on the sofa opposite the fire, close to Genie. Soon after, Seraphina comes in carrying a tray with a teapot, mugs, and some slices of fruit cake.

When we are all seated, drinks and food distributed, Gregor begins.

'I came here tonight via the Capitol. When Bernais took control of the city, many students ended up stuck, unable to go home. Some of us made it to the World Above before they placed a barrier on the portal. We've been returning in small numbers via the mountain gate in Essendore.'

He pauses to sip some tea. 'I would not have stopped here, except I had to wait for permission to join my friends in the World Between.'

Everyone else nods their understanding except me. This is not right—creatures do not just ask for permission to enter the dragon realm.

'What do you mean you are going to the World Between?' I ask.

Everyone turns my way as if I have said something strange. Then Ellie's eyes flicker with understanding. 'Of course, you were in the Unseelie Court when the Capitol fell.'

'I was.' I lower my eyes as a twinge of betrayal tugs at my heart. Ellie was one of the creatures who had plotted to send Pris, Snake, and me to the Unseelie Court. Hurt though I am that she had not let me in on the plan, that is a discussion for another time.

'Let me bring you up to speed,' Ellie says. 'The university has always encouraged liberal thinking and challenging the status quo.'

'It is the way of the young,' I agree, wearily hoping she will get to the point soon.

'Well, Bernais and his new council took exception to their protests and declared them, and some of the more radical protestors in the Capitol, outlaws.'

'That *is* surprising, but it does not explain how the dragons are involved?'

Gregor leans forward and places his now empty mug on a side table. 'The dragons have offered us sanctuary while the monarchy is under dispute.'

I massage my forehead. This is a lot to take in. Dragons

do not take sides in our internal politics. They were clear that they could only assist Pris, Snake, and me when we were actively working to help Queen Ariana so she could restore the proper flow of magic between the worlds. Had things now become so bad that they have no option but to intervene? And what does that mean for our future?

'I see what you are thinking, Percival,' Seraphina says, 'but you are wrong. The dragons have not taken sides. They are only offering sanctuary for those outlawed by a government the dragons do not consider legitimate. If Bernais's faction is successful in overthrowing the queen, then the dragons will withdraw their offer of a home when they accept Bernais as king.'

My weary lids droop closed. I have only been gone a few weeks. When had this all become so complex? Or was it always, and I just had not noticed?

'Percival?' Seraphina places a hand on my arm. 'You are clearly tired. Your room is prepared. Perhaps it is time to sleep.'

I force my lids apart. 'It has been a long day for me, and there is much I need to tell you all, but that can wait. However, I would like to know what Gregor came to tell us before I rest. He did not choose to wait here by accident.'

Gregor nods. 'I came to warn you that we are going to attack the Capitol. We have to do something before the elitists become intrenched and definitely before they take over the palace. While the Queen's Guard holds out there, there is still some hope we can oust them.'

No one speaks. Effie and Ellie share a look that suggests a lack of surprise.

'You are not the only ones thinking this way,' Genie says. 'Ellie contacted the Wizard Council, and, while they will not support any action we take, there are some who will abdicate from the order and help our cause.'

'If you send word when you are ready to move, we will join you and bring all the strong magic users we can muster,' Ellie adds.

'And what about the other creatures?' Gregor asks.

I stare from my witch friends to Gregor and back again. Are they discussing what I think they are—civil war?

'Some local communities are already calling a muster. The Wyld Woods village and sprite representatives are meeting tomorrow. We believe they will also agree to join the muster at the base of the Essendore Mountains,' Seraphina tells the young witch.

'Those of us who have fled the Capitol, or have come back from the World Above, are ready whenever you are,' Ellie says. 'The only creatures we have not heard from are the elves and gnomes from the villages within the Wyld Woods. They never accepted the rule of the Crown family, and as Magnus Baaronson has left them to their own devices, they probably do not feel they have a stake in this fight.'

Gregor shifts in his chair. 'Can we win without their support? What if all the greater creatures decide to opt out?'

'Then that will make your position all the stronger when we win,' Seraphina says dourly.

'His position?' I ask.

'Gregor and his rebels want to use Bernais's takeover to upend society. They want to support inter-creature marriages and restore lesser creatures to equal status in society,' the witch protector of the Wyld Woods says, her tone sour enough to turn milk.

'But Seraphina, I thought those were your aims as well,' I say.

'They are, but I believe those rights need to be won through the court, not on the battlefield.'

'What would you have us do, Mother? Sit back and wait for Ariana to retake her rightful place and hope that is enough to stop Bernais?' Ellie asks.

'Or would you rather we stop him before he gets started?' Genie presses.

I have clearly opened a can of worms that I should have left closed.

Beside me Seraphina huffs. 'Bernais and Magnus would destroy our realm. They have no interest in seeing magic restored, although they might change their minds when there is no more magic for them to use. However, I would rather not see war in our land.'

'That is not within our control, Mother, but in Bernais's. He has had a taste of power, and he will not let go unless we force him to,' Genie says somewhat sadly.

Ellie stops refilling her teacup. 'It is like this is the last stand of the conservatives. If they don't grab power now, they will lose everything because the forces for change are getting stronger and challenging their privilege.'

Seraphina folds her arms and leans back in her seat. 'You are right—this is necessary, but I still do not want to see creature fight creature.'

I stare into the fire and wonder what is becoming of my home. Can I really do anything to save it from destruction?

⚬

Someone's in my room. I'm immediately fully awake, holding still, listening. Beside me, Pris's body is nestled into mine, her chest gently rising and falling. There isn't much space in the single bed, but it's worth the discomfort to have her this close to me. I bury my face in her hair, the scent of her washing away the loneliness I'd felt at our distance when we were in the Unseelie Court.

'Ugh,' she groans as she tries to turn over. This is the noise that woke me. There isn't an intruder after all.

Before our reunion last night, the Dragon Queen had used her magic to heal Pris. I pull Pris closer as I remember that reunion, then mentally shake myself—*focus, Snake Fieth.* Although she is outwardly fine, her body will need a lot of rest to recover, and we certainly had not spent the early part of the night doing anything remotely restful.

There is another bed in our room, but I don't fancy the idea of crawling from the warmth of our shared nest and moving over there. I have a better idea. Not far away from our room is a bathroom containing a tub filled with naturally warm springwater.

I slip from under the covers, making sure not to let any of the cool air disturb Pris, then pull on some loose trousers and grab my shirt. Pris rolls into the warm patch I've left, snuggling deeper under the covers. For a moment I consider climbing back in beside her, then remember she needs to sleep.

The bathroom is free, and as I sink below the gloriously warm water, I stretch and allow my body to relax. Percival is with Eleanor, Pris is safe, and the injury she sustained as we battled to reach the World Below is healed—I am done for the moment. I am so tired of being ready to react to the next thing the World Below has to throw at us. It is so liberating to be safe.

The tension of the past few weeks seeps from my shoulders as my body floats free. From the time I found out the Bad Fairies had taken my mother to the World Below to face trumped-up charges of illegally profiting from magic, I have been on one quest after another to get her back.

It started with convincing Pris to come with me to save her own parents from the same fate. First, we found our way to the Midnight Ball in the World Below, and then Bernais hoodwinked us into accepting a noble quest to bring back what was in the middle of The Minotaur's Maze. We reached the centre to find Queen Ariana locked in stasis, and we were duped into going to the Unseelie Court to petition their king for help. After all of that, we still don't have our parents back, and rescuing them will now have to wait until we save the world.

I duck under the water again, trying to block everything out and just be in this moment, but I can't. Once I might have been able to forget about my commitments, but not now. The journey Pris and I took to get here has taken its toll, and I am no longer the gnome I was—hell, I'm not really a gnome at all. What a revelation that was, finding out my grandmother was an elf, and that my mum being half elf was why Bernais had really arrested her.

Unable to hold my breath any longer, I break the surface of the water and shake my head, trying to clear my thoughts. There is no value in rehashing the past few weeks. What matters now is how we move forward.

Unlike Pris, who is being nudged in a direction she doesn't want to go, no one is manipulating my actions. I can't rescue my mother, and though I will always help Pris, I need more than in my life than supporting her. Just what that will look like... goddess only knows.

I push myself from the bath and towel myself dry before dressing in the clothes provided by the outlaws. They are a little crumpled from being discarded on the floor while Pris and I greeted each other, but they will do for now.

Cleaning the bathroom to make it ready for the next creature takes a couple of minutes, but it wakes me up. I pop my head into our room, but Pris is still asleep. There are voices down the other end of the hallway, coming from the communal room sitting at the hub of the cave complex. Joining them is an option.

I pass several doors before hiding in the shadows of the common room opening. The creatures there are deep in conversation, and I don't want to interrupt anything personal. A mixture of creature races circle the fireplace in the middle of the room, most of them relaxing on large cushions. It's difficult to believe these creatures are being hunted simply for wanting to change things. Just as I can't believe that in the week Pris and I were at the Unseelie Court, so much changed in the World Below, and all because Bernais Baaronson is now the self-proclaimed Chancellor-Soon-To-Be-King. He and the councillors he hasn't dismissed are intent on returning the world back to a time when elves were supreme and every creature knew their place.

'I don't want to live in the Unseelie Court just because I love Gregor,' Verona Coronas is saying as I force my attention back to the group around the fire. She is the only creature I recognise, and I'm surprised she's with the outlaws, as her father is one of Bernais's staunchest supporters. 'But I will if I have to,' she finishes.

Stepping out of the shadows, I decide it's time to give them an update about the events in the World Above and the Unseelie Court.

'I'm afraid the Unseelie Court is no longer an option,' I say, and everyone's attention turns my way. I suck in a breath to calm my nerves. *This is no different to singing to a room full of strangers.* 'In order to protect the Unseelie Court from an attack, we had to place it in magical stasis. The

World Above will need to produce an awful lot of magic before anyone can cast the spell to bring it back.'

The room falls deathly quiet, and the atmosphere is so tense, you could cut it with a knife. The fire hisses and crackle as I wait for someone—anyone—to respond.

Someone across on the other side of the fire laughs, 'Good one, mate. You had us going there.'

I don't know what to say to that. It is a fact, but I can't prove it, and I'm too mentally exhausted to debate the issue.

'Snake, come and join us,' Verona says, smiling her encouragement as she waves me over.

I'm grateful for her save, but I'm uncertain if I want to be here now. Verona moves over to make room for me on her oversized cushion. I accept her invitation and sink down beside her.

'Do you feel up to telling us what happened in the Unseelie Court?' she asks.

I don't think I'll ever be able to bring myself to share the story of how I helped wake a giant, stole its magic, and put an entire court to sleep in order to prevent it being destroyed forever. Or describe the soul-destroying revelation of betrayal just as we were fighting our way back to the World Below.

I find myself fixated on the fire, regretting not having returned to bed. Then again, if I don't help these creatures understand that there is no Unseelie Court to offer them refuge, who will?

I begin at the beginning, with the queen needing King Maddox to help her cleanse magic. I tell them about the king grieving because attacks on the Unseelie Court killed the love of his life. Then I tell them about the battle that has already begun in the World Above. I don't tell them I worry there will soon be a battle in the World Below; admitting that out loud will make it too real.

'If we can't go to the Unseelie Court, then we must stand and fight here,' Verona says, and many around the fire agree with her.

'If the king and queen restore magic, we can cast the spell to bring the court back. I'd rather go there and forget about this backwards realm,' the girl beside me argues.

'Yeah, even if the queen is back in charge, nothing will ever change while the elven lords rule their fiefdoms as governors,' the boy across the fire adds.

How long have the creatures in the World Below felt like this? To me, the creature realm has always been a place with unfettered magic where creatures don't have to hide their abilities. On closer inspection, there are as many problems here as in the World Above.

'We will never have a better opportunity to change perceptions than this. If we help Queen Ariana put Bernais and his followers back in their place, then she will have to listen to us,' Verona argues.

I close my eyes as the debate rages around me. Suddenly I'm overcome by a bone-deep weariness as the past few weeks catch up with me, and I'm too tired to take part in the discussion. As my mind drifts off, a thought worms its way into my subconscious, pulling me back from the edge of sleep. Should these creatures achieve their goals, they can marry whomever they wish. In the world they want to make, there will be room for an elf and mixed blood gnome—Pris and I would have a chance, and that is worth fighting for.

Princess?

The insistent voice interrupts my dream. Ignoring it, I focus on Snake, his arms around me, him leaning in….

Princess!

Why are we always interrupted just when things are getting interesting? No, wait. We—

Princess, I do not need to know that!

My eyes fly open. Was I just about to relive Snake's and my reunion for Am'ratha?

Yes, you were. And thank the Mother I reached you before you did!

I sit up, rubbing the sleep from my eyes as I note the absence of another body in my bed. The place Snake occupied is cold, so he's been up for a while.

Princess, please focus. You must get ready to fly to the Minotaur's Maze.

I'm still searching the room for signs of where Snake disappeared to, so it takes a moment for my bonded dragon's words to sink in.

What? Why?

I was not given a reason. As soon as it is light, I am to take you to the Maze. That is all I have.

The Minotaur's Maze? Really? My memories of that place are not particularly fond, and I have no desire to head back there. What would happen if I refused to go?

That would not be a good idea. The Dragon Queen wants you there, and it is best you never find out what would happen if you did not go.

Sometimes it is disconcerting to have someone able to speak directly into your mind, let alone read it. And it's even more off-putting when they deliver information with a thread of dread that leaves you reeling.

I will be ready.

After last night's physical activities, I need a bath. I hope I have time. It's hard to tell because there are no windows inside the dragon's guest caves.

Throwing off the sheet and colourful woven blanket, I swing my legs over the side of the bed, wincing as I force myself upright. The Dragon Queen may have healed most of the damage done to my body from the magical blast I received, but my side is still tender.

Moving slowly, I retrieve my clothes and shuffle towards the bathroom. The corridor is empty, but voices drift down from the common room, so I either slept for a short time, or I was out for the count and it's morning already. I quicken my pace, not wanting to keep Am'ratha waiting too long.

The warm water is bliss. I slide back, allowing my hair to stream out behind me. It's still disconcerting to see it white instead of its natural black. I guess my eyes changed from brown to blue when I arrived here too. I trace my fingers round the slightly pointed form of my left ear. Although I can feel the touch, the shape does not register as belonging to me. I'm still not used to changing into elf form every time I leave the World Above.

My change in appearance makes it difficult to deny who I am now. I'm no longer the girl about to embark on a family holiday before starting university. I am an elven princess who is part of a strange, magical world. That's not strictly true. I am not a part of this world. I am part of the royal family who governs the World Below.

No longer relaxed, I sit on the ledge running round the edge of the pool. All my recent problems come back to the fact my mother is the niece of the queen. That means I'm actually in line to become ruler of the Seelie Court in the World Below. Worse still, the Dragon Queen will bump me to the front of the line if Queen Ariana doesn't get better soon.

No, I don't want to go there. If I accept my fate, I'll have to give up ever having a normal life—and I'll probably have to give up Snake. My body tingles at the memory of last night. We had waited so long, and it was so worth the wait.

If only we could spend some more time together… but I've been called away again. Will I always have to put duty first? Is this my life now?

I lean my head back against the lip of the tub and stare up at the ceiling. If only I were back at home in my bathroom with its white tiles and fluffy purple towels. Everything in the dragon's guest quarters is grey and spartan. Still, it's amazing to have a real bathroom in a cave. How did the dragons do it?

Magic, of course. Everything here is magic.

If someone had told me a few months ago that magic was real, I would've thought they were nuts. And that's exactly what I thought when Snake told me. Even when I used magic to make my first flame, I still couldn't quite believe it existed. Then Snake and I stepped through a doorway to the World Below to attend the Midnight Ball, and there it was—a magical world straight out of a fantasy story. If I hadn't physically changed when I stepped through that door, I would probably still be denying I belong here.

I shake the water off my hair and force myself out of the bath, no longer able to relax. If the World Below had been a revelation, the Unseelie Court had been a bombshell. My parents had hidden the World Below from me, but they had also kept the fact that my father's brother was Maddox, King of the Unseelie Court.

I roughly dry myself, almost like I think I can rub away my parents' betrayal with the towel. I can't. Nor can I wash away the fact they brought me up believing it is my duty to contribute to society and to make the world a better place.

Argh, it's so frustrating. The sense of obligation they instilled in me means I couldn't ignore it when I was asked to help Queen Ariana and the Seelie Court. It's also why I'm getting dressed so I can do the Dragon Queen's bidding now.

Oh my god, have Mum and Dad been preparing me for my royal duties all along?

The thought burns like acid in my stomach. Have they really been that deceitful? I'd like to believe they haven't and that they have good reasons for what they've done. Perhaps I should reserve judgement until they have a chance to explain themselves.

I pull on the linen trousers and shirt given to me when I arrived, plait my hair, then quickly tidy the bathroom. Our room is still empty, so I wander down the corridor towards the voices.

Feeling unsure if the bunch of strangers will welcome me, I search for Snake. I find him curled up asleep beside a petite platinum blonde creature who looks vaguely familiar. Was she at the Midnight Ball?

'My father's as big a hypocrite as any of them. I mean, look at the size of me. There is no way an elf would be this short if there wasn't some creature-mixing somewhere in our past,' the girl says. 'So why's he so against my being with a witch?'

At the mention of her father, I study the elf closely. Those sharp eyes and the sardonic quirk of her lips transport me back to the house in London where Giles Coronas, the elf who later spoke against my mother at the Midnight Ball, attempted to talk me out of finding my parents. Snake is sharing a cushion with Gile Coronas's daughter, Verona.

My chest tightens. The two of them seem so comfortable together. Jealousy is not something I'm used to feeling, but here it is, rearing its ugly head. Before I can do anything stupid like act on it, Snake's eyes blink open, and he groggily searches the room. He spies me and jumps to his feet, startling his pillow mate.

'Pris.' He's by my side in seconds, worry twisting his face. 'I left you to sleep. I figured you'd need it for healing, and after, you know....' As his voice trails off, his face flushes. He takes his hand in mine. 'Come join us.'

I resist his pull. 'No, I can't. I've been called to the Minotaur's Maze.'

He stops in his tracks. 'Why?'

'I don't know. Am'ratha just said her queen would be upset if I refused.'

Snake's lips quirk into an almost smile. 'You still thought about not going, didn't you?'

'For a moment. I'm tired of feeling like a piece on a chessboard. I'd like to stay in one place for a while.'

Snake slips his arms around me, and I snuggle into his shoulder. 'I'd like us to be together, too, and I keep saying we will be soon, but—'

'Unfortunately, in these times of unrest, romance must wait.' The voice comes from behind Snake, and I untangle myself from his embrace to find Verona Coronas smiling up at me.

'Sorry to interrupt, but we've had a dragon messenger arrive. They asked us to kit you out for flying. I'm Verona, by the way, and you're Priscilla?'

'Pris,' I say automatically, that little worm of jealousy writhing in my stomach.

The elf smiles with a warmth I'm not able to return. 'Yeah, Snake said you prefer that. If you come with me, there's a surprisingly good clothes stash in a cupboard in the dining room.'

I reluctantly let go of Snake and follow the girl. Snake trails behind as we go through a curtained archway into a room containing three long wooden trestle tables with benches down either side. The smell of sausages frying distracts me for a moment, and Snake nudges me forward. On the other side of the tables is a large cupboard stuffed with gear.

'Where did all this come from?' I ask.

Verona rummages through a shelf and hands me some moleskin trousers and the softest white woollen jumper.

'Most of us arrived with only the clothes on our backs. So, the dragons made a run down to the villages in the Wyld Woods, asking for spare clothes. Do you have boots?'

'Yes, they're back in the room.' I hold the clothes up, wondering whether they'll fit.

'They're magical, so they'll do fine,' Verona tells me matter-of-factly. 'Snake, are you going with her?'

'Umm, I don't know if I've—'

'He wasn't expressly invited,' I tell Verona, before placing a hand on Snake's arm, 'but if you want to come....'

'Do you want me to come?' he asks, and it's the perfect response.

'Of course I do,' I reassure him. 'But it is the maze, and if you haven't been invited, then, we don't want to upset the Minotaur.'

'So it's probably better if I stay here?' His eyebrows rise in a question, his tone all too eager.

The sigh escapes before I can suppress it. I understand his reluctance, I'm not looking forward to meeting Aeron again either. This is yet another thing I must face alone when I would rather have Snake with me. 'I guess so.'

Drawing me near, he gently kisses my hair. 'I'll be here when you get back.'

'What will you do while I'm gone?'

'Sleep,' Snake says as another male voice chimes in, 'Help us prepare to march on the Capitol.'

Our attention shifts to the doorway, and we discover a tall creature with dark auburn hair standing there. In the blink of an eye, Verona was by his side and then in his embrace.

'Gregor, I wasn't sure—'

She stops mid-sentence as the creature bends down and kisses her as if there's no one else in the room. My little worm of jealousy does a deep dive of shame as Snake leans in and whispers, 'Gregor was stuck in the Capitol, and Verona was worried something horrific had happened to him.'

'Why?' I ask.

'Because he's a leader of the creature rebellion.'

I make myself busy folding my clothes, wondering how I'm going to get past the reuniting couple to get changed, when Verona turns in Gregor's arms.

'Hon, this is Priscilla Crown and Snake—'

'Fieth,' Gregor finishes. 'Percival told me you'd be here, although he said you were injured, Princess.'

'Pris, please,' I tell him.

Verona turns to me. 'How about we organise you some breakfast while you go get changed? She has been called away by the dragons.' This last is directed towards Gregor.

Snake picks up my clothes and prepares to follow me.

'She won't have time for you and food, Snake,' Verona says.

Snake glances at me, and I'm caught between wanting to spend as much time with him as I can and wanting to eat.

'I'll be quick,' I tell him as I take the clothes and slip between Gregor and the door.

CHAPTER 2

Posturing

Crossing through the now empty common room, I pull back first one, then another treated leather curtain blocking the cave entrance, making a gap big enough to glimpse the rising sun turning the sky pink. I rush to get changed, waiting a beat for the clothes to adjust to my size, before returning to the dining room. As I enter, the smell of a cooked breakfast sets my stomach rumbling. Sending a quick prayer to whoever is listening not to send Am'ratha until I've eaten, I scan the room for Snake.

Creatures crowd around two of the tables, eating, talking, and laughing. Snake, Verona, and Gregor are at the far end of the third table, separate from the other creatures, who are casting curious stares at them. I slide into the empty seat beside Snake and serve myself from the platter of food on the table.

I take a mouthful of the steaming cup of coffee someone thoughtfully left for me, and groan in pleasure before wolfing down some sausages, eggs, and mushrooms.

Letting the food settle, I notice quite a few of the creatures are watching me.

'They know who we are,' Snake whispers. 'We've become kinda famous.'

I cover my mouth before I snort out coffee. 'In a good way, I hope'

A wry smile appears on Verona's face. 'In an iconic "we'd follow you to the ends of the earth" kinda way.'

I almost choke again, and she laughs. 'Aren't you pleased about that?'

I turn halfway to check out what's happening behind me, and some of the other creatures shift position, pretending they weren't staring at us.

Leaning towards Verona, I ask 'Why?'

Her chuckle is low and throaty. 'Because you stood up to Bernais Baaronson, and you went on a quest and met the Minotaur, and you're in love with each other. It's the stuff of songs and epic novels.'

'It's what?' Snake splutters, and I say, 'We're just friends.'

Verona and Gregor share a look that screams, 'Can you believe these guys?'

Under the table, Snake squeezes my hand. If ours is a love story, and we haven't had time to figure that out, then I'm certain neither of us wants it to be such a public one.

'Stop teasing them, Verona. From what I've heard, they've been through a lot, and it's not over yet,' Gregor says.

Verona's face turns serious. 'We've all suffered, Gregor, and we're all risking so much. That's why it's so important to remember why we're doing this—so you and I and Snake and Pris can decide whether we want to be together, not have some outdated and restrictive set of laws tell us who we can love.'

Verona is so intense. She clearly feels deeply about this and it makes me wonder how many other creatures feel the same. However many, it's comforting to find someone else who is passionate about change in the World Below.

Clapping breaks out from the tables behind us, and Verona colours, perhaps unaware of how her voice has risen. Gregor hugs her. 'If our little movement has a heart, it's you, Verona.'

'We have the heart and the brains. What we need now is a leader we can rally around, someone to inspire us,' Verona says, looking expectantly our way.

'What?' Snake forces out while I'm still searching for words.

'No, you can't mean us,' I finally say.

'No one here knows us,' Snake adds.

Verona smiles and leans closer to us over the table. 'No, but they know *of* you, and they know what you've risked, and that is even better.'

'Man, I'm pleased you're on our side,' I blurt out, in awe of Verona's cool, calculated approach.

Gregor grins with obvious admiration, 'I know, right?' He turns to us. 'In all seriousness, we do lack inspiration, and we're going to need it because I want us to join up with the other groups opposing the new council and help them take back the Capitol.'

It's like someone has thrown a bucket of ice water over me. After fighting the dwarves to get here, the last thing I want to do is walk into another violent confrontation, let alone a full-on war.

Under the table, I grip Snake's hand, wanting to feel the comfort of his touch.

Snake whispers, 'Pris, are you okay?'

I'm far from okay, but I can't find the words to express how I feel right now. Squeezing Snake's hand as if I'm clutching onto a life raft, my eyes find Gregor's and I beseech, 'There must be another way.'

'If you have any ideas, I'm all ears. The last thing I want to do is lead my friends into battle against trained soldiers.' There is a heaviness to his words that convinces me this is not a decision he's taken lightly.

'Can't you wait for the queen to make good on her promise to rise from her sickbed and reunite the country?' I ask in desperation.

Gregor studies me with such intensity, I have to resist the urge to squirm. 'Do you know something I don't? I mean, my contacts at the palace say no one has seen her for some time. They fear she is dead.'

'She isn't dead,' I blurt out as Snake says. 'It's more complicated than that.'

Snake lets go of my hand and leans forward, lowering his voice, 'Please, this is just between us. The queen exhausted herself trying to keep magic flowing. We convinced King Maddox to help her even though his court has been under attack, but it will take time for the two of them to sort things out. Surely we can wait until then.'

I school my face not to react to Snake's words which, although aren't strictly lies, skirt the edge of truth. Maddox and the dragons must wake the queen before they can restore her health, but that makes little difference to what we're asking Gregor to do.

'The Elven governors have sent most of their forces to the Capitol. They have control of the council and have imposed martial law. The only reason they haven't overrun the palace is that the Queen's Guard stands strong there. However, once the palace falls, so will most of the resistance to the new council,' he says.

'I don't understand how the conservative faction got enough votes to remove Elias as Chancellor,' Snake says.

Gregor barks out a laugh. 'Oh, that was easy, and a politically genius move. Bernais brought forward a resolution to have the wizards removed from the council, stating that, although they hold themselves apart from the rest of witch-kind, they are still witches and so should not have separate seats. Of course, the dwarves and goblins jumped at that because they've long complained that witch-kind had six seats to everyone else's three.'

'But how could that pass?' I ask. 'If there were six witch votes, three gnomes, and Elias, that should have passed 10 to 9.'

Verona grimaces. 'Unfortunately, wizards couldn't vote on a motion about them.'

'Oh,' Snake and I say in unison.

'Yes. And it gets worse,' Verona continues. 'Once the wizards were removed, a dwarf brought forward a resolution stating that, as gnomes are lesser elf-kind, then the same rules should apply to them. That passed, and the elves then controlled the council. They appointed Bernais Chancellor, and the queen was not there to object.'

My stomach churns, and I worry my breakfast might make a reappearance. Two simple resolutions were all it took to change everything in the World Below.

Beside me, Snake balls his fists. 'Our race is hundreds of years old. Sure, we were once elves, but we have evolved and flourished as a separate race.' His voice rises in protest. 'We have lost our voice and our identity in one fell swoop.'

Gregor nods sympathetically. 'I understand your anger, but that is just the tip of the iceberg. By limiting the council to elves, witches, goblins and dwarves—'

'Elves and their cronies are running the World Below,' Snake finishes.

'And any chance of lesser creatures joining the council has been pushed back hundreds of years,' Verona adds.

How can this happen? Surely their constitution has checks and balances to prevent these sorts of decisions. 'I don't understand how they can get away with it.'

Verona grimaces. 'Unfortunately, you're thinking like I used to, that things here work similarly to the World Above, but they don't. It is up to the Crown, or its representatives, to ensure there is fairness and justice for all.'

'It took generations for the queen to give the council decision-making powers,' Gregor says. 'Initially, the council were simply advisors to the Crown, and the monarch would choose three from each of the greater races. Queen Ariana's mother turned the advisors into councillors who could suggest changes to the laws of the land. She then allowed the greater races to choose who represented them and expanded the council to include wizards.'

Gregor cups his hands around his mug and stares morosely into his drink. Rubbing Gregor's arm in a comforting gesture, Verona picks up the narrative.

'Things changed again under Queen Ariana. The witches proposed that the gnomes should join the council, and a single vote passed it. At that point, there was an even number of councillors. Queen Ariana decided the Chancellor was to have a deciding vote when the council was tied.'

'My family speaks of this as one of the greatest days in gnome history, and perhaps even in the history of the World Below. Elves treat gnomes as lesser creatures, and many thought this change would pave the way for other lesser creatures to join the council,' Snake finishes up.

'And in the last couple of days, Bernais and his cronies have rolled back centuries of change,' I say, as disappointed by their actions as the others.

Gregor bangs the table with his fist. 'Oh, we will fight this. But first we must prise the Capitol back from the conservative's grasp. Did you know, when I left, they were rounding up insurgents and throwing them in prison?'

My gaze flies to Snake. What about his family? And the witches? Eleanora and Eugenia had been working with the witch representatives on the council. Snake's eyes widen in fear as they meet mine.

'Don't worry, Snake, your father got your family to the palace. The witches refused to take a role in the new council, and they warned senior gnomes and witches in time for them to either flee the city or take refuge in the palace.'

Snake's worry lines ease as he replaces fear with resolution. His eyebrow rises in query, and I nod. He doesn't have to ask for my support, but I'm pleased he still considers us a team.

'I'll join your fight, but only as a foot soldier.'

Verona turns to me. 'And you, Pris? Will you join us?'

I take in the creatures around the room and Verona's hopeful face. I so want to say yes, but I promised the Dragon Queen I would take over Queen Ariana's duties if she didn't recover. If I hadn't, she might have agreed to acknowledge Aunt Adina's line, which would see Bernais seize not just the chancellorship, but the Crown.

Snake drapes an arm over my shoulder, and I lean into him. 'She can't. She is the only one who can prevent the dragons from acknowledging Bernais's claim to the throne. Her first duty is to make sure that doesn't happen.'

It sounds like a copout. I want to fight, and I'm more capable at fighting than Snake. Honestly, he'd be better with the dragons than me. He's way more diplomatic. If only we could reverse roles.

Am'ratha interrupts. **Princess, I am waiting.**

On my way.

'I reckon your battle is the tougher one.' Verona chuckles. 'I've met your aunt in the court of the Dragon Queen.

She is very keen to see her son on the throne. Watch your back, and your front, with that one.'

'I've got to go,' I say reluctantly, taking one last gulp of coffee as I stand up.

'We'll talk more when you get back,' Gregor says.

Snake follows me out of the dining room and pulls me to a stop when I get to the treated leather curtains leading outside.

'Be safe,' he says, brushing his lips against mine.

I want him to hold me, but I fear if he does, I'll be tempted to stay.

'You too. And don't start any wars before I get back.'

His lips quirk into a lop-sided smile. 'I'm not promising anything.'

Snake leans in and touches his forehead to mine. I close my eyes and relish this moment of togetherness. Drawing in a breath, I squeeze his hand before I force myself to break the connection—I'm not great at goodbyes.

Am'ratha perches on the ledge outside, her purple scales glinting in the morning sun and her yellow eyes sparkling with humour. *Oh, this is going to be a fun trip.* I climb up her leg and nestle in a comfortable spot on her neck.

You have made the most of your short time here, my dragon friend says.

I don't know what you're talking about.

Our bond is different. You have mated.

OMG, is nothing sacred? And what does she mean by mated?

Ed'rathe will be pleased. He can request to bond with your mate.

Woah, hold on…. Back up there a mo. Snake and I are… close, but we're not mates.

Wow, how backward this place is if sleeping together means you're mated.

It is not about physical relations, Princess, it's about the bond between creatures. Surely you can feel the change.

I'm not talking about this—at least not with you. It's between Snake and me.

I should have guessed that my bonded dragon would feel obliged to weigh in on what happened last night. However, one night together does not a relationship make. We haven't talked about things between us yet, so I'm hardly going to discuss anything with Am'ratha.

Can we just get going? The sooner we get there, the sooner we can return.

Am'ratha humphs her displeasure as she pushes off with her powerful back legs, and I'm thrown backwards. I grip on to her scales as Am'ratha flies towards the snow-capped mountains of the World Between, then banks and comes back full circle.

What are you doing?

Before we go to the maze, the queen has decreed we must complete the bonding rites.

Sorry? What? I thought we *were* bonded.

Am'ratha snorts. Clearly we aren't actually bonded, but how was I supposed to know? I'm learning this as I go.

So, tell me, what do we have to do?

I am sorry, Princess. I sometimes forget no one has schooled you in the ways of an heir. We were granted permission to bond and given time to get to know each other. Today, the Dragon Queen asked me if we were ready to declare our bond before the ancestors, and I said yes. I hope that was all right?

There is a smidgeon of doubt in Am'ratha's question, which surprises me. This is clearly a big deal for her. As I believed we had already bonded, I can hardly object.

Yes, Am'ratha, it was the right thing to say.

I'm certain I sense a relaxing of Am'ratha's muscles beneath me, then she drops down below the cloud line and lands almost immediately on the ledge of a cave. As she folds her wings, a wave of hot air wafts over me.

Where are we?

The cave of the ancestors. You must stay on my back, as no creature can ever set foot on the ground here.

Okay, I say as Am'ratha drops her head and waddles into the cave.

If I thought flying on a dragon was difficult, maintaining my seat on her neck is near impossible as she makes her way through the cave entrance. I'm concentrating so hard on staying put that I almost lose my balance when Am'ratha stops moving. When I've regained my seat, I take the time to get my bearings and to appreciate the importance of this place.

Delicate crystalline stalactites hang from the roof that are so long, they must have been millennia in the making. They sparkle in the glow of the sconces around the walls, giving an ethereal air to the cavern.

The cave itself is awe-inspiring, but it is nothing to what rests in the centre of the floor. Surrounded by a colourful array of sleeping dragons are hundreds of silver, white, and gold eggs sitting in the glowing embers of a fire.

The eternal fire of life, Am'ratha explains.

Where are the ancestors?

They are here. When a dragon passes, a new egg appears. When an egg is ready, it hatches, and we are born.

I've been struck speechless very few times in my life, but now is definitely one of them. Am'ratha has brought me to the heart of the dragon world, and the honour not only steals my voice, but it takes my breath away.

What now? I ask.

We wait.

Wait for what?

As I finish speaking, I know what it is I have to do; what I have to say—it is as though the ancestors are placing the words in my head.

Great ancestors, we come before you to declare our sisterhood and that henceforth we will support each other as family. We will care for our brothers and sisters and the magical world to the best of our abilities until our dying breath.

We say the words together, and it takes less than a minute, but I know the weight of that declaration will remain with me for the rest of my life.

No doubt if I'd had more time to think this through, if I'd had some idea of what I was committing to, I would have stressed over whether or not to complete the bond. However, this way is perhaps easier.

As we leave the cavern, I lean down and hug Am'ratha. **Sister?**

Yes, we are sisters. But do not think that means you can take advantage of me.

The laugh escapes my lips as we reach the outside ledge.

Never, I tell her. **I feel....**

I trail off because I really don't know how I feel or what this means for my future. On the one hand, I have made a commitment to the World Below in a way I never have before, yet my mother made the same commitment and left this realm behind. Oh, and Adina must also have sworn the bonding oath, and look at how she behaves.

Do not overthink it, Princess. Now that you

have made the bond, the bond will tell you if you are acting contrary to your oath.

So, I simply carry on as normal?

Of course. Just do what you believe to be right.

It can't be that easy.

The bond works on intent. If the ancestors believed your intentions are bad, then they would not have given us the words of the oath.

Oh. I don't know whether I find it disturbing that the ancestors assessed me without my knowing, or whether I think it's cool that magic works in this way.

Come, it is time to journey to the maze.

As Am'ratha pushes off and her wings beat, I can't help but think there should be a more dramatic ending to such a spiritual event. Then again, perhaps that is more of a creature or human perspective. The dragons seem to take all these amazing magical things in their stride.

Once we're above the jagged points of the mountain range encircling the dragon stronghold, the chilly air fingers its way under my clothes. Am'ratha banks, then flattens out.

Soon after we have left the mountains behind, the landscape turns orange and gold, and the breeze brushing my face turns balmy. I pick out the Wyld Woods to my left and the walls of the Minotaur's Maze to my right.

Beyond the maze, I can almost make out the forest that kept Snake from me so he could meet his great-grandparents. That seems so long ago, but it has only been a few weeks.

Leaning forward, I wrap my arms around Am'ratha's neck, suddenly needing something solid to hold on to. So much has changed over the past months, and it doesn't look like it'll slow down anytime soon.

I close my eyes and block out the world, turning my

thoughts to Mum and Dad. If what Gregor said is true, they aren't in any immediate danger, so long as they have the Queen's Guard to protect them. In fact, they're safer than everyone else in the World Below because creature kind will soon face off in a civil war.

If I had a choice, I'd be back there with the others, plotting revolution rather than joining the establishment and supporting a regime I don't believe in. This is not who I am, but it's who I have to be until I can get someone else to take over.

Blowing out my frustration, I hug Am'ratha again. At least I am not alone in this. I have her, and I have Snake. They have my back. And, hopefully, I still have Percival.

We are almost there, Princess.

I want to bury my face in my dragon friend's neck and hide. Below lies more strangeness, more responsibility, and there's no one there with my best interests at heart.

I am here. I will look after you.

But only if you can without displeasing your Queen.

Am'ratha snorts a chuckle. **I will not let anyone hurt you.**

I guess that's something.

Am'ratha circles towards the ground, and I straighten in my seat, blanking my expression to one of cold confidence, unwilling to let anyone else see how tired and disheartened I really am.

· ·ᴗ· ·

The sun slips through the gap in the curtains, falling across my face and forcing my eyes open. I can no longer feign sleep. The presence I sense in the room shifts in the chair as I roll over. Nathanial, an elder from my home grove in the Wyld Woods, stares unblinkingly at me.

'Percival, good, you are awake. Seraphina sent me to ready you before everyone arrives.'

Forcing myself into an upright position, I rub a hand over my face. 'Everyone?' I ask, frantically trying to remember why creatures would come here today.

'Yes—the local leaders attending the meeting to discuss what we are going to do about the unrest in the Capitol.'

A thought forces itself through the fog clouding my brain. The lesser creatures want to fight, to start a war against the armies of the ruling fae. Fear keeps me still as I contemplate how many might die should we fight. Our side has the numbers, but they have the trained standing militias. They also have the will to go to any extreme to win.

'Are you all right, Percival?' Nathanial asks, resting his elbows on his knees. 'You have gone quite pale.'

The sprite elder's concern touches me. I have missed him.

'I am… fine, Nathanial.'

He cocks a bushy grey eyebrow, and it slips under a fringe of almost white hair. *My uncle is old.* The thought hits deep. When had that happened? He is so old that he should be back in the grove, enjoying his last years, not here preventing a war.

Preventing a war? Is that what the sprites will do? Work to stop bloodshed and, when they cannot, retreat to the grove and wait out the violence?

'Yes, fine,' I say, although we both hear the lie. 'I will ready myself and meet you downstairs.'

Nathanial does not move. 'Your brother is here.'

I grin, my mood lightening. *Wait, he should be at the grove, overseeing the mourning of my father—preparing everything for the last farewell.* If he is here as our spiritual advisor, then things must be worse than I thought. Emrys's being here is a clear sign the sprites see recent events as impacting their well-being and security.

'And Nisha is with him.'

His words hit me like a punch. 'What? Nisha's here?'

To see me? No one else knows I am in the World Below.

'She is here to represent us at the meeting.'

I'm surprised—both by the fact that Nisha agreed to come and that we are old enough to represent our kind.

'Thank you for letting me know, Nathanial.'

Nathanial stands up to leave, then pauses. 'The witches want you to be a part of this meeting, and I can under-stand why—you have been involved in their machinations for years. However, I must make it quite clear that you do not speak for the sprites.'

His words are another blow. Nathanial has never treated me any differently since my punishment made it impossible for me to return to sprite form. That he should say these words to me now. Betrayal is not a strong enough word to describe my feelings.

'Oh, I see.' I fail at disguising my hurt.

Nathanial's face softens, and he takes a step closer, 'I have not spoken clearly. Sprite-kind chose us to represent them. We did not foresee your being here, so you can have no official role.'

'I understand,' I say, although the familiar old feelings of rejection and shame wash through me. It is so much easier to believe I am unwanted and unworthy—to assume the worst. Nathanial clears his throat, pulling my attention back to him.

'Also, it occurs to me your direct involvement in recent events means you can paint a bigger picture, one that includes all creature-kind. That is why your input will be valuable today.'

I *am* wanted, maybe even needed. The spectre of my own inadequacies releases its hold on my heart, allowing me to breathe again.

I swing my legs around. 'I guess I had better get ready, or I will not be attending, let alone representing anyone.'

Nathanial nods. 'Of course. We will wait for you downstairs so we might walk to the meeting hall together,' he says before letting himself out.

Before getting up, I ensure the door is closed. Someone has laid fresh clothes at the end of the bed and brought a bowl of water and a towel, which are on the dresser. I place my hands on the metal bowl and speak a warming spell, then give myself a quick wash, allowing the water to cleanse away the last of my hurt feelings.

The clothes are black, the only colour I have worn since my transformation into something not quite sprite, but they are from the World Below. The trousers are moleskin, the shirt linen, and the fine jumper I pull on over top is woollen. Someone has cleaned my black boots, and I pull them on gratefully. All clothing in the World Below is spelled to fit the wearer, even shoes, but a new pair of boots is never as comfortable as ones that have been with you for some time.

Checking myself in the mirror, I grimace. My hair has grown and is a little messy. I take a moment to imagine my hair shorter and draw in some magic. My scalp tingles as the strands shorten and my hair tidies itself. *Perfect.*

I could lie to myself and say that I always take pride in my appearance—and I do—but I also cannot bear to have Nisha see me disheveled. Since we bonded, I have put my mate through a lot, including spending years away from her. Now that I understand her belief we can have a life together regardless of my not being a full sprite to be true, I want to make a good impression on her.

Voices drift up from the living room, and I attempt to calm the butterflies flitting in my stomach as I descend the stairs. I am always excited to see Nisha, but this time I am also wondering why my healer wife, who rarely leaves the grove, has done so now.

My hand hovers over the door latch, and I attempt to catch a little of the conversation before entering. The stout wooden door filters everything into indistinguishable murmurs. I take in a breath as I press down on the latch and push the door open.

Genie greets me as I scan the room for Nisha. 'You're finally here, Percival. We can leave.'

She swoops past me, followed by Ellie, who squeezes my arm in a gesture that I perceive as support before exiting. Nathanial follows last, leaving two creatures standing in the middle of the room.

Emrys, my brother, and the new spiritual leader of the grove since our father's death, steps forward and pulls me into an embrace. 'It is good to see you so well.'

I return his hug, but all the while, my eyes are on Nisha. It is almost surreal to see her in the human form she dislikes taking. How graceful and fragile she appears, standing with her hands clasped in front of her. Her liquid black eyes hold mine while I finish greeting Emrys.

My brother releases me and follows my gaze. 'We shall talk later. Nisha, we have very little time before the meeting starts.'

Emrys's message is obvious—do not take too long. He leaves Nisha and me alone, firmly shutting the door on his way out.

She holds her hands out to me, and I step towards her.

'I did not expect you to be here,' she says as she clasps my hands.

Resting my forehead on hers, I breathe in her essence. 'Is it a pleasant surprise?'

She pauses before answering. My mate has never found it easy to lie, nor is she practiced in the arts of demurring.

'It is neither good nor bad, Percival. Or perhaps I would be more accurate to say it is a little bit of both. I am always happy when you are with me. However, having you here may divert my focus from effectively representing our grove.'

I press my lips to her hairline and whisper, 'What is it you are here to do?'

She pulls away from me and straightens her back, her countenance stern. She is such a warm person that it is easy to forget the rod of steel that runs through her.

'Percival, please do not ask me what the grove wants. I am not your spy or your agent. What I have to say today may run contrary to your beliefs, but it will be in our community's best interest.'

I run my hand down her arm in what I hope is a reassuring manner—it is hard to tell, as we have never spent long enough in each other's company to build the level of unspoken communication other couples have.

'Nisha, I am proud that you are here for our kind, proud that you have stepped forward. I will do nothing to compromise your work. This day we will both need to be true to ourselves and our beliefs, but I hope that does not lessen our bond.'

Nisha blinks slowly, considering my words. 'We have disagreed on many things in the past and that has not happened.'

I send her a smile that is tinged with sadness and regret. The distance between us is the result of my decisions. I want to rectify that, but does she? After years apart, I know who I am and that I want to be with her, but I cannot expect her to simply fall in line. I must work to win her back.

Holding out my arm for her to take, I say, 'Perhaps we can find some time to spend together later—we have much to catch up on. However, for now we should join the others, or they may leave us behind.'

Nisha slips her arm through mine and remains beside me all the way to the meeting hall. I walk a little taller with her by my side. When we arrive, she leaves me to join Emrys and Nathanial.

The tables, which are usually reserved for banquets and weddings, have been repurposed for this meeting. Someone has pulled them together to run the length of the rectangular room. Wooden chairs stand down either side with name tags in front of each one.

Genie walks along the sunshine-dappled floor in front of windows looking out over the town square. She takes a place at the top of the table beside a giant of a creature, his face obscured by a bushy brown beard. Thomas Mulligan, Wyld Wood Village's Head Creature, and head, too, of the dwarves here, bangs a gavel, and the creatures in the room take their seats.

On the right-hand side, facing the windows, are the lesser creatures—the sprites, brownies, pixies, and dryads. Opposite them are the representatives of the greater creatures—the dwarves and goblins, witches and gnomes. The seat beside Ellie and her mother, Seraphina, is vacant. They must be waiting for a third witch.

Although the creatures are greeting one another, the air in the room is tense, as if each group is poised to do battle. Politics in the World Below have not encouraged creature unity, but I hope they can over-come this antipathy today.

There is a row of seats on either side of the double entry doors, and I choose one on the lesser creature side of the table. I have just made myself comfortable when Thomas Mulligan calls the meeting to order and begins.

'We can wait no longer. We must start if we are to finish before any of the fey in residence at The Manor realise what is going on and send the guards out.'

The room falls silent, and the dwarf gestures for Genie to start.

'Good morning, all. We have an update on the Queen today, thanks to our friend, Percival.' She pauses as everyone turns my way. I lift my head and sit a little taller as I meet every gaze before they return their attention to the head of the table. 'King Maddox arrived in the World Below yesterday. We hope he and the queen will join forces and begin repairing magic once they have dealt with the threat to our govern—'

'I apologise for being late, but I ran into a couple of old friends, and I insisted they join us,' a voice booms from behind me, carrying to every nook and cranny by force of magic.

I do not need to turn around to know that Mandor the Wizard has entered the room—he must be the third repre-sentative of witch-kind. However, I am interested in finding out who he has brought with him. Shifting slightly in my seat so I can watch the party enter the main hall, I let out a gasp of surprise as Drow and Heart follow Mandor in.

Once Pris is gone, I no longer have the stomach for breakfast, but I've no idea what to do with myself. The refugees are limited to the guest cave for the time being, as dragons don't like creatures wandering through their realm, so I'm stuck inside. The cave itself only has two accommodation corridors, a common room, and the kitchen/dining area, so I can't really go exploring here either.

A few creatures have drifted back to the common room and are sitting round the fire pit chatting, so I drop onto a free cushion and listen while I wait for Verona to finish eating. Perhaps she can help me find something useful to do to pass the time.

'I appreciate this is an opportunity for us to force change, but I'm not sure a physical revolution is the answer,' the small elf girl to my right says.

'If you were as committed to forcing change as the rest of us, then you would fight,' a burly dwarf boy says with a sneer.

The girl rises to her feet and stares down at everyone. Her intense blue eyes are so like Verona's, I wonder if they're related. She places her hands on her hips and sneers right back.

'You write me off because I'm an elf, and because of that, you assume I can't be as committed to change as all of you. You're like children playing at revolution. The reason I believe we're not ready to fight is because we have no plan for after. If we completely overthrow the current government, we'd best be ready to rule—and we aren't.'

She turns on her heel and strides away.

'Johan, that was cruel,' another girl says. 'Orissa's parents threw her out when she defended Verona and Gregor. She could have stayed quiet and lived a comfortable life, but she is every bit as committed to change as the rest of us.'

'And she's not wrong,' someone else continues. 'We don't have a plan for after, and we don't want to pull everything down with no idea of what we will replace it with. That would be worse for creature-kind than what we have now.'

The cushion shifts as someone leans down and whispers close by my ear, 'So, what's the answer?'

'What?' I ask, turning to find Gregor crouched beside my cushion. 'I'm not a part of this. I have no experience living in the World Below.'

'True, but everyone has a view on the future of creature-kind, no matter where they live. And I'm not asking you to fix it single-handedly. I'm simply asking for your opinion.'

I stare at the flickering flames of the fire, fully aware of what Gregor is doing. If he draws me into the debate, I'm more likely to become their figurehead and rally everyone behind the plans for war. I answer him anyway.

'Life doesn't have to be all or nothing, Gregor, and it doesn't take a revolution to change things. If I were in your shoes, I would see Bernais and his followers as the principal threat because they represent a step backwards. You can't fight on two fronts, so I would consider working with the Queen, perhaps leveraging her need for your support to have her agree to a programme of change.'

Where did that come from? I'm not normally a political person. Perhaps spending time with Pris has rubbed off on me.

Gregor stands up and stretches. 'I didn't know gnomes were mind-readers.'

'We're not. Hold on, is that what you're planning to do?'

Gregor gnaws at his lower lip for a moment, and I get

the impression he's trying to decide something. He studies me intently, like he's weighing up how much to trust me.

'Come with me,' he says, turning to leave the room.

I follow him down the corridor opposite the entrance. It also has bedrooms coming off it, but there isn't a bathroom at the end like there is down our corridor. To the left is a dark passage that smells slightly sulphuric, and to the right is a curtained doorway. Gregor pulls back the curtain and ushers me inside. I step into an almost empty room about double the size of the bedroom I shared with Pris. There's no furniture, just a few large cushions arranged around a small fireplace set into the opposite wall.

The curtain swishes closed behind me, and Gregor gestures for me to sit. Nestled between two of the cushions is a tray with a teapot and cups. Gregor clearly intended us to talk, no matter what I had said.

When I have a mug of tea in my hands, Gregor begins. 'What do you know of creature history?'

My brows draw together. This is not what I was expecting. 'That's a broad question. Although we all learn about the same events, I think our creature race colours our understanding of it.'

'Of course.' Gregor sweeps a hand as if brushing away my comment. 'Let me clarify. How much do you know about creature history and the origins of magic?'

'Oh.' I place my cup on the floor and run a hand through my hair, attempting to dredge up lessons from long ago. 'Well, let's see. Dragons produce most of our magic. Some of it seeps through to the World Above and the World Below. Taking care of the environment and growing things supplements magic in these realms.'

'Well done.'

I'm surprisingly pleased by his praise.

'What about the waning of magic?'

This is easier to answer, not only because the history is more recent, but because I've always been interested in magic in the human world. 'In the World Above magic began declining as Christianity took hold and witches were persecuted. The Industrial Revolution, which saw more and more people leave the countryside for cities to work in factories, followed this. With fewer people working the land, and even fewer remembering the old ways to care for it, there is little magic left there.'

Gregor nods for me to continue.

'I knew little about the World Below until recently. As I understand it, magic bounced back after the blight, but lately the flow of magic between the worlds has become sluggish, and I guess we're using more than we're creating.'

Gregor nods. 'You have the gist of it. I have a book in my room on the history of magic and magic usage in the three worlds which I think you would find interesting.'

Is he kidding? I'd love it. Before all this adventuring, my plan had been to study physics and how it affects magic at a university in the World Above. Apart from music, this is what I am most passionate about.

'Let's go back a little further,' Gregor continues. 'Long ago, the three realms were separate. We each produced our own magic and kept to ourselves. When the ways between worlds opened, the dragons were worried some of their kind would force dominion over weaker creatures, so they cast a binding spell, keeping dragons in their own world, and have always limited who can come and go in the World Between. However, to ensure no one tried to sneak in to take magic, they allowed some of their store to flow through to the World Above and the World Below.'

'And that led to the Bargain of Dragons,' I say.

'Yes. The Dragon Queen summoned the most powerful magic wielder of each generation to step forward and form a bond with a dragon. Then the two would help channel magic into the flow between the worlds.'

'I thought it was the king or queen who was called to serve.'

'Back then, the World Below had no monarch. It was several separate territories, each with their own leaders and laws. A contest was held every fifty years to choose the next creature to bond. The elves consistently won every competition, which granted them a degree of power over other creatures, and they eventually held the leadership of most of the territories. Then, one family line showed most able, and our monarchy was born.'

I lean forward, fascinated by this new view of history. It explains a lot.

'What about mages and witches in the World Above?'

Gregor blows out a breath. 'Okay, the quick version of the history of the human world closest to ours, which maps onto Great Britain and Ireland, is that for generations, mages chose which of them would bond with a dragon. When the persecution of witches became a thing, mages and witches went underground. It became harder and harder to find magic wielders of sufficient ability to keep magic flowing.'

'If I have this right, originally a creature in the World Below and a witch in the World Above bonded with dragons to keep the flow of magic going,' I clarify. 'Did that change when the elves took the Crown?'

Gregor grins. 'It did indeed. Many creatures objected to the new monarchy, and especially to them imposing one rule of law on all creatures.'

'The first of those were the elves who didn't want the Crown family taking control,' I say.

'I should have known you'd be all over the gnome history. Unfortunately, the Crown family were too powerful, and when they won the battle, they restricted the amount of magic their enemies could access, creating gnomes.'

It hurts to have the birth of our race talked about so casually. The humiliation of serving the elven race since that day to earn back what is rightfully ours sours the stomach of every gnome.

It's also odd to be reminded that had the Queen not fallen ill at the Midnight Ball, my family would no longer have limits placed on our use of magic. Then Bernais would have less to complain about because my half-elf, half-gnome mother would have been more acceptable. A little ball of anger stirs in my gut. We are not lesser than elves because of our ancestors' actions. Nor should anyone treat my mother and me differently because we are mixed race.

I don't want to dwell on these thoughts, so I change the subject.

'There were other creatures who decided not to confront the elves directly, and they left the World Below to set up the Unseelie Court in the World Above.'

Gregor nods. 'Go on.'

'From that day on, the dragons allowed the monarch and their heir in both courts to bond with dragons to maintain the flow of magic between the worlds. Is that why we have people like Princess Petunia and Princess Adina bonding with dragons? Is it because they were heir to the throne at one stage?'

'Yes, that is exactly why,' Gregor confirms. 'And here ends our lesson on creature magic.'

Although I already knew most of these events, the new way of viewing them has my head spinning a little.

'Hold on, creatures keep magic flowing in the World Below, and the King of the Unseelie Court has taken on the job for the World Above, so what happened to human magic users?'

'There are very few people able to use magic in the World Above today, and much of their lore was lost when magic users went into hiding during the witch trials.'

'Wow, it must have been horrid to have an entire culture wiped out,' I say.

Gregor's lips twist into an almost secretive smile. 'That's the common history in the World Above. The story told in the World Below is different.'

Eager to learn something new, I urge him on. 'So, what really happened to human magic users?'

'Well, some of them had found a way into the World Below. The witches who arrived here were essentially refugees and had no place in this realm. Fortunately, the sprites and dryads offered them a home. They were used to dealing with all kinds of magical creatures in the World Above, so of course they became advocates for creator creatures in the World Below.'

'Creator creatures?'

'That's what creatures who tend to the environment used to be called. We call them lesser creatures now because they can't wield a lot of magic.'

'That is so cool. So, if witches came from the World Above, are they creatures or humans?'

'We have been here a long time, and we have assimilated into the culture, but yes, we are essentially human.'

Wow, and I thought I had problems.

'Is that why the conservative elves hate witches so much? Because you're not creatures?'

'It depends who you ask. Some of them dislike us because they hate humans, and some of them dislike us because we are as powerful as them—some of us more so.'

My head is spinning. 'Can I just clarify? Now that we

have elves seizing power in the World Below and rewriting the rules to suit them, creatures who disagree set up the Unseelie Court.'

'Exactly. Then we have the ways closed between the worlds to consolidate elven power, which causes the blight here and the Dark Ages in the World Above. And magic has never been the same. And that's a potted history of magic in the Worlds Above and Below'

'Hold on, how do the creature villages in the Wyld Woods fit in? They're mixed communities and they follow their own rules.'

'Since they keep to themselves, no one bothers too much about them. There is just one more piece for me to fill in,' he says, 'and this is not a part of history that is often shared beyond my kind. When witches came here from the World Above, we could wield magic at a similar level to elves. In return for sanctuary, we agreed we would put no one forward to bond with a dragon.'

I can't believe what I am hearing. 'You're saying you agreed never to challenge elven superiority?'

'Correct. But it gets worse. Witches have a tradition of studying and developing the use of magic, and that didn't change when we came here. Add this to the fact that magic in the World Below is richer and runs deeper than in the World Above, our people soon began to develop spells and use magic in a way elves never could.'

My eyes are almost popping out of my head. 'You mean witches are stronger than elves? Why don't you all just take over?'

'Our original agreement. Any witch wishing to study advanced magic must leave the World Below and make a magically binding promise to never challenge the leadership of the Seelie Court.'

'And that's why witches formed the Wizard Council?' I

ask. Mandor, the wizard who'd helped us enter the Minotaur's Maze, had given up his life with Eleanora to join the Wizard Council.

'Yes.' Gregor stares into the distance. 'We have such a wealth of power, and we can never use it because once a wizard breaks that basic rule and challenges the Crown, everything they have learnt since taking the vow is ripped from their memory.'

'That's harsh.' I can't imagine what it would feel like to have years of learning gone. 'Can't they just bind their magical ability like the elves did to the gnomes?'

Gregor's laugh is harsh. 'As you already know, it is possible to reverse that spell. Once wiped, a wizard's memory is irretrievable. Also, no one has ever triggered the spell, so we don't know how much of a wizard's memory is wiped. It may just be their knowledge of magic, but it also might be their life experience until that point.'

After Gregor finishes, a heavy silence lingers in the room. Finally, I state what is now all too obvious. 'So, basically, what it boils down to is elves acting to keep elves in power.'

'Of course.'

'I can't believe Queen Ariana or Princess Petunia would be a party to that,' I protest. 'Well, not Princess Petunia. She did defect to the Unseelie Court after all.'

'Perhaps she isn't part of it, but her sister definitely is. To her credit, she's made some minor changes, but she's not had much support from those who hold the balance to her power—the council and the regional governors.'

'I can't believe I'm defending her, but she's spent a lot of time trying to sort the flow of magic.'

'True, but the rise of elves and the failure of magic are linked. She should put as much effort into ensuring we produce more magic and use less.'

This is blowing my mind. It all goes so much deeper than we ever thought. There's too much to take in, too many problems, and no straightforward solution. I close my eyes and attempt to pull my thoughts into some sort of order.

'What I don't get is what could Queen Ariana do to make sure we produce more magic?'

Gregor's eyebrows rise. 'That's a fair question. Let's see. Take a dryad—a tree spirit. They take in magic from the world and feed it to the trees they tend, and in return the trees spread even more magic into the world.'

'Yep.'

'When we cut down trees, there are fewer trees to create magic. If we planted more trees that would help, provided we planted them in the right places. Because dryads and sprites don't do so well in villages and towns, trees planted there are not tended properly and produce no magic.'

'But if we set up groves for sprites and closes for dryads, they could live in villages,' I suggest.

'Exactly, but we're not even having those discussions. Meanwhile, greater creatures continue to use magic with abandon, while creator creatures are finding it harder and harder to work.'

I bark out a laugh. 'So we're caught in a vicious circle.'

'Yes, one that will only get smaller and smaller if Bernais and his friends strengthen their control over the world.'

I run my hand through my hair, trying to sift through everything I've just learned. While I understand why magic is failing, and also why Pris and I, being from the World Above, might see things differently with all the climate change debates, what I don't understand is what Gregor expects me to do now.

'Gregor, what do you want from me?'

He starts as if the question is unexpected, and then he grins. 'What I'd hoped was that you'd be so overwhelmed with compassion, you'd say, "Gregor, I'll do whatever you ask to fix this".'

I chuckle. 'If you think I can do anything to fix something this thoroughly broken, then you're madder than a box of frogs.'

'True, and I might well be.' He sinks back into his cushion, his gaze drifting to the fireplace. 'Part of me *was* hoping I'd inspire you to help. Our world is being stifled to death. We have one lot of leaders who want to smother it more quickly, and the other lot is moving so slowly, it'll suffocate before anything changes.'

'You have inspired me, but I don't know what I can do to help.'

'To be honest, I don't know what any of us can do. We're all so young, and we have no clout, and there aren't many of us. Yet, if we sit back and do nothing, we won't have a world to live in by the time it's our turn to run it.'

Gregor's despair is a heavy weight. Pris and I were aware something much bigger was happening in the World Below as we ran around trying to save our parents, but until now we hadn't had time to stop and find out what was really going on.

Now that I know, I almost wish I didn't because how can I sit by and do nothing? Equally, I can't see what one person can do to change any of this. I slump back on my cushion, the weight of the world now squarely on my shoulders. And that was what this was about. I turn and stare at Gregor, and he nods, the ghost of a smile on his lips—he knows he has me now.

'It was Verona's idea. She said anyone who went to so

much trouble to rescue their mother wouldn't be able to walk away once they knew what's at stake.'

Dammit. I can't leave, but I'm tired of being manipulated. If I'm to take part in this fight, it has to be on my terms.

'I won't help overthrow the government, nor will I manipulate Pris or her position to help us. What I *will* do is help you forge an alliance with Queen Ariana's court, if that is the path you choose to take.'

Straightening in his cushion, Gregor pins me with an intense gaze. 'And will you help our leaders formulate our demands?'

'I… I'm not a politician or….'

'Think about it, please.'

Before I can refuse, the curtain rustles, and Verona pokes her head through the gap. 'I thought you two might like some fresh tea and sandwiches for lunch.'

CHAPTER 3

A Slow March to War

Mandor's footsteps echo as he strides the length of the room. All eyes follow his progress except for mine. I watch my friend as the husband who foreswore her for a life of study takes the spare seat between her and Seraphina. Ellie's face is blank. Only her eyes betray the tumult of emotions she is feeling.

Their living apart for the last few centuries was no more their choice than it was mine to live as neither sprite nor man. We had all suffered the consequences of disobeying the council. Although Ellie had married again —more than once and had children—she'd only taken mortal lovers. I believe that was because no one could dislodge Mandor from her heart.

Mandor places a hand on Ellie's shoulder, and she raises her eyes to him. I cannot see what passes between them, but the wizard takes his seat moments later.

'Pleased you could join us,' Genie says somewhat tersely.

Mandor bows his head towards Thomas and Genie. 'My apologies for the tardy arrival, but now that I no longer have access to the wizard's source of power, I can only take one creature with me when I portal. As I thought you would want to hear from both my guests, it took us a little longer to get here.'

Heart and Drow remain in the doorway while Mandor speaks. The wizard motions them in, and as he does, he notices me sitting in the back. A smile brightens his face, taking the harshness from his next words. 'Perhaps I shouldn't have bothered, since Percival likely has more current news than we do.'

I force myself to acknowledge Mandor's greeting. When everyone's attention returns to the front, Drow and Heart move into the seats beside me.

'Did I hear correctly? Has Mandor renounced his wizard status?'

Drow leans past Heart to better see me. 'Hello to you, too, Percival. And yes, Mandor, as well as about half of the wizards, have renounced their affiliation and have joined the other creatures readying themselves to march on the Capitol.'

'So there really is going to be a rebellion? Who are they intending to fight? The council or the Crown?' A knot of fear forms in the pit of my stomach as I wait for their answer. 'And how come Mandor still has his memory?'

'The Wizard Council refused to take part in this battle even though they have a lot at stake, so some of their number renounced their positions. Because of that, they are cut off from the wizard's pool of magic,' Drow says.

'But who are they fighting for?' I ask.

'The Crown of course. They can't renounce their vow, which means they have to fight for the leader of the Seelie Court or lose their memories. Now, if you two would stop nattering, I want to hear this,' Heart hisses just as Nisha stands up to speak.

I miss my mate's first few words as my head spins with worry. It is a good sign that the wizards are joining the fight, but they will have to walk a fine line if they are to retain their abilities—and their minds. With their help we increase the likelihood of removing Bernais, but if we topple the government and court at the same time, the backlash could devastate the ex-wizards.

'…and I speak for the sprites from the Wyld Wood Grove. We creatures prefer peace to war, but we are prepared to fight for change in the World Below… provided that change bencfits *ull* creatures.'

The table erupts as almost every other delegate's voice rises either in support or disapproval of Nisha's words. She does not let the dissent cower her, and her poise makes me proud.

Thomas Mulligan holds up a hand. 'Come now,' his voice booms, 'if we carry on like rabble, we will be here for an age.'

When the table has quietened down, Thomas turns his attention to my mate. 'Nisha, you must be aware that we as a committee do not favour overthrowing the Crown.'

Nisha's head drops, and I worry she might sit down. She does not. Instead, she raises her head and studies every greater creature on the other side of the table. 'Ever since the council formed, we have allowed you greater creatures to play politics while we so-called lesser creatures have tended to the lands, and the air, and the water. Look where that has brought us…Magic is disappearing from our realm, and we are on the brink of war. We sprites have had enough of standing by while others destroy our world. We want a say in our future.'

Pride wells inside me as Nisha speaks for our people and expresses what is inside my heart. The dryad to

Nisha's right rises. Their voice is low and melodic when they speak.

'We dryads of the Oaken Stand say we have had enough of the distinction between the creators and users of magic. Our world needs all our skills and talents, and we all should be a part of the government.'

The delegates alongside Nisha murmur agreement, while stony silence reigns opposite. A brownie delegate stands up, followed by a pixie. The brownie, a young male, speaks first.

'We came expecting that we would have an equal vote here and that we will have an equal vote once we have ousted the current council.'

Heart leans back in his seat as Drow sits forward, and we wait for the next creature to speak. There are a number of private discussions, but no one speaks up. I contemplate whether I should.

This issue is the very one Drow, our friends, and I fought for when we were younger. Lesser creatures had understood that the blight had to be stopped at any cost, while the council were more worried about the political fallout of reversing their decision to close the ways to the World Above.

It is Thomas Mulligan who speaks next. 'I.... We may agree in principle, but I am not sure exactly what we are agreeing to.'

Mutterings on the greater creature side of the table increase, but before they raise an objection, Mandor says, 'I believe what we are agreeing to is that we do not want Bernais and the current council to continue to hold power. The problem is, we can't agree on what changes we want after that. If my summary is correct, then let's move on and leave the details for later, as we have much to decide.'

'Yes,' Thomas Mulligan agrees. 'A good idea. After this

meeting is over, those of you who are interested in hammering out the details of this accord might form a group led by… umm.'

'How fortunate that I brought one of the eminent lawyers of our generation with me,' Mandor says, rescuing the dwarf. 'I am sure he would love to spend time drafting an agreement. Although this will be the first formal agreement in this war, I do not believe it will be the last.'

'A show of hands?' Thomas Mulligan asks.

A few hands are slow to rise, but the vote is unanimous. Drow sits back, a smile splitting his face. As Genie calls the meeting back to order, I catch Nisha's gaze on me. I nod my encouragement, hoping she senses my admiration. Her cheeks colour, but she raises her head a fraction and straightens her spine before turning her attention back to the meeting.

Over the next half an hour, I listen to the debate, which is way less emotionally fraught now that they have sidelined the most contentious issue. I am so weary that I find it difficult to maintain focus, and my mind wanders, only to be brought back as the group hits another bump on the road. The dwarf contingent are on their feet, ready to walk away. It would be a disaster to lose such ferocious fighters.

'We are here because we believe the elven stranglehold on our land should not continue,' their leader says.

'Your representatives were happy to take their side on the council,' the brownie leader heckles.

The dwarf reddens, but he stands strong. 'Our brethren in the city have forgotten their roots. They are nothing but hired stooges for the elves. We in the country prefer our independence, and many will be happy to see the council fall.'

Others around the table nod their agreement. If they are in concert, why the disagreement? What have I missed?

Drow rises to his feet. 'If I may?'

No one hears him.

'Silence!' Seraphina does not appear to move, but her voice fills every nook and cranny in the room. The response is immediate.

'Drow, do you have something to add to the… discussion?' she asks.

'Thank you, Seraphina, I do. As I understand it, this is a problem essentially of who we are fighting—our immediate foe or the entire system. In our hearts, I think we would like to choose the latter, but we then strike a problem. And our problem is one of capacity.'

'Capacity? We're talking about fundamental issues with how our world is run,' the leader of the dwarves says, puzzlement crossing his face.

Drow grins. He is enjoying this debate. 'Should we choose to enter as a third party, we will fight not just the regional militias, but also the kingdom's most skilled military unit, the Queen's Guard.'

'We can take them all on,' one dwarf brags.

'Huh.' The laugh slips out, and I immediately wish it had not, as everyone turns to stare at me. Not so long ago, I would have wilted under such scrutiny, but not now. I glare at the dwarf.

'We will have numbers, it is true, but we are not soldiers, and we don't have military discipline. To fight a battle on one front will be tough enough, but on two fronts….'

'Not to mention,' Genie adds, 'there is a balance in the world to respect. Who knows what will happen to magic if we descend into all-out war for months on end.'

'Does that mean we should not fight?' Nathanial asks.

'I didn't say that. Fighting will damage our world by using magic as well as by taking creatures away from creating it. The shorter the war, the less damage there is. What we don't want is a prolonged war that might leave our world in a worse state,' Genie explains.

The leader of the dwarves leans his fists on the table, and I fear our words have fallen on deaf ears. 'If we just oust the council, nothing changes. What is the point?' His shoulders slump, and he sinks back into his chair.

'Not to mention, we wizards cannot fight with you if you are working against the Queen and the Seelie Court,' Mandor adds.

'Well…,' Drow starts, his eyes still twinkling, 'there may be a way. If we take on the council on the Queen's behalf, we have leverage. I believe if we produce a list of demands in return for our support, we have a unique opportunity to force change.'

'A nice idea,' one of the goblin says with a sneer, 'but all of this started because no one could get access to the Queen.'

'We might have a way.' Drow's eyes lock on me.

'Do we?' I ask, somewhat bewildered.

Genie raises her eyebrows. 'I don't believe *we* do, Percival. I believe you might, though.'

My heart skips a beat. I *did* help the Queen out by bringing King Maddox here. She might grant me an audience when she wakes up. Can I do it?

Everyone is watching me. I find Nisha in the crowd. Her presence exudes empathy, and I'm embarrassed by my uncertainty.

'We each have our role to play, Percival,' she says, her tone encouraging.

Thomas Mulligan slaps a hand on the table. 'I propose we expand the remit of the group working with Drow to extend our alliance agreement to include a proposal for the Queen. We will offer to fight in support of her if she will agree to our requests for changes to be made.'

When no one disagrees, Thomas Mulligan continues. 'Moving on. Can the designated military leaders stay here and work out logistics? We must consider how to move creatures into position and keep them concealed until we are ready to attack. Mandor, can you join them and work out how many of your witches we will need for this?'

'I can,' the witch says.

Crash! The doors beside us swing open and bang against the wall. A young dwarf enters, shouting, 'The guards are coming.'

'Break into your groups,' Thomas Mulligan shouts.

'Planners to the tavern,' another voice adds.

'Medical and support to mine.' Seraphina's voice carries above the noise of shuffling papers and chairs scraping as the creatures ready to leave.

Nisha joins the witches as they depart through a side door.

Mandor hurries over. 'Drow, those of us wanting to work on the agreement for Queen Ariana are also heading to the tavern.'

Drow rises to his feet and follows Mandor as he exits through the doors beside us. Heart and I wait amidst the chaos. Through the window, I see that the sun is high in the sky. We are soon alone in the empty hall.

Heart pushes himself to his feet. 'Well, old friend, it seems we are surplus to requirements. Shall we head to the tavern? I could do with a pint of ale.'

'Shouldn't we be doing... I do not know... something?' I ask.

His face turns serious. 'Once things wind up here, we will be busy. I will go into the Wyld Woods to canvas the villages for support, and you will go to meet with the Queen.'

I rise, then Heart's words sink in, and I sit back down. 'Wait, you're going home?'

Heart's mouth breaks into a crooked grin. 'Yes, imagine that—I'm going home.'

'Well, this is turning out to be the oddest of days.'

'To the tavern for some Dutch courage?' Heart asks hopefully.

I shake my head. 'Sorry, Heart. Much as I enjoy your company, I want to make sure Nisha can find me when she's done.'

He claps a hand on my shoulder. 'And you'll want a sober head for that conversation, too, no doubt.'

'Indeed. Let's go back to Seraphina's. She will have food and ale, and maybe we can be of some help.'

'Okay,' Heart says, and I lead the way out.

As I open the door to the street, two young guards bowl through. They don't even stop us to ask what we are doing here. If they're who Magnus Baaronson has left to police the village, we have nothing to worry about.

After weeks of being on the move and having Pris and Percival with me, I thought it would be relaxing having time for myself and absolutely nothing to do. Perhaps it would have been if everyone else wasn't busy doing something. In the end, boredom gets the better of me, and I make my way to the kitchen and offer to help with dinner. I'm not much of a chef, but I can peel a potato with the best of them.

After answering an initial flurry of questions about Pris's and my adventures, the cook and his helpers forget about me. As it turns out, working in the kitchen is a great way to hear what's going on in the worlds. This must be why spies work as hired help.

I hand the full pot of potatoes to the head chef. He passes me an empty one. 'If you could fill this also. I hear we are to expect some refugees from the Unseelie Court for this evening's meal.'

I almost dropped the pot. 'From the Unseelie Court? I thought they were all locked in stasis.'

The brownie scratches his head. 'Some escaped. From what I hear, a few are camping out with our main forces—of course, I can't tell you where they are—loose lips and all that. Some leaders are coming here for the big meeting tonight.'

I place the pot on the bench and begin peeling. The dwarf working beside me is busy making some sort of pies, so I'm careful not to take up too much space as I get back to potato peeling. She nudges my arm. 'I heard it was mostly servants who escaped. They made it to the Birmingham gate.'

'They had to go there because the dragon's closed the Loch Ness one, no doubt,' I say.

She nods as she crimps a crust. 'The renegade wizards secured the Birmingham gate for us because it comes out close to their sanctuary. It's a good thing they did because the gate to the Underground Ballroom exits in the Capitol—'

'Which means it's under elven control,' I finish for her.

'Yep.'

'Renegade Wizards? You're having me on, right?'

She laughs. 'No, I'm not. Some of the Wizard Council

decided they could not sit this out and renounced their vows.'

The potato I'm peeling slips from my hand and tumbles across the bench. 'You're kidding. I didn't know they could even do that!'

'Nope. Not kidding, and apparently they can.'

'Wow' is all I can manage after that as my brain tries to process the enormity of this news. It simply can't. Massive changes are happening in the World Below, and it's so chaotic that I can't see where it's all heading.

'Have you heard anything about the creatures who attacked the Unseelie Court?'

'Nope. Only good thing is, they'll have to head south in the World Above to get here, so our forces have a one, maybe two, day advantage.'

'But that will fly by. Our enemies are mustered in the Capitol already, and we are still trying to recruit. If only the ex-wizards could portal more than a person at a time,' the chef says.

'I sincerely hope you're not discussing tactics in here,' a familiar female voice says from the doorway.

'Susan!' The chef drops his ladle and rushes to throw his arms around the elf.

'Steady there, George. I still need to breathe.'

The brownie apologises and lets go of Susan. 'We thought you were lost,' he says.

'I made it out of the castle before the stasis spell took hold, along with many of the servants.' She catches my eye and shoots me a smile. 'See, Snake, it all turned out okay in the end.'

'Did any guards get out? It sounds like we could use a few trained soldiers in the coming days.'

'Why Susan, I'm so happy to see you,' Susan says sarcastically, and I bark out a laugh.

'Of course I'm pleased to see you. I can't imagine what it would be like to be held in stasis. It's just….' I drop the potato and peeler onto the bench and suck in a breath. 'After all that effort, all that energy and planning, we were duped. Giles Coronas and Grossman Green didn't commit any of their forces to the castle, and Dinian had been feeding them information all along.'

Susan steps around George and crosses the distance between us before placing a hand on my shoulder and giving it a quick squeeze. 'We did the best we could, Snake. I heard from Petunia how dwarves ambushed you at the Loch Ness gate and how we were double-crossed by that slimeball Dinian. We couldn't have predicted that. At least the castle is safe, and King Maddox is doing what he has to do. All *we* can do is regroup and move forward.'

Her words, meant to soothe me, don't quite work. So many thoughts and worries curl their way through my brain, but I can't grasp hold of them. I'm so weary, I'm beyond thinking. As I slump against the bench, she drops her hands and gives me a little nudge with her elbow to make some space for herself before picking up the peeler and dealing with the potato.

'How's Pris? I heard she was injured?'

'She's fine. The Dragon Queen healed her.'

'Really?' Susan grins. 'That must have been awesome to watch.'

'It probably was, but I didn't get to see it.' My voice comes out all sulky, but I'm finding it hard to feel anything but exhausted.

Susan plops the potato into the water. 'And where is she now?'

'She was summoned to the Minotaur's Maze after breakfast, and I haven't heard from her since.'

Glancing at me, Susan radiates sympathy, and I can't

bear it. 'She has her duties, no matter what she and I might want.'

'She does,' Susan starts, her voice tentative, 'but they don't need to control her life.'

I drop my head, not sure how to answer that. The closeness between Pris and me is so new, and after last night, I still have a lot to process.

'Anyway,' Susan says, 'you haven't told me where the others are. I assume King Maddox went directly to the maze.'

'Yes,' I answer, relieved at the change of subject. 'Euphemia went with him. Susan, what's happening with the others in the World Above?'

She stops peeling and studies me. 'Petunia was warding her home and preparing to come to the World Below with some of the unit that guards the Loch Ness gate—she may even have arrived for all I know. Most other creatures, my sister and her family included, have hunkered down, waiting for this to all blow over. A few realise the significance of this battle and have returned home to right the balance of the worlds, but most don't even know anything is going on.'

'The balance of the worlds?' This is the first time I've heard that phrase.

Susan runs a hand through her hair. 'Interrupting the flow of magic is not the only thing that might throw the worlds out of balance. Extreme social change and war can do that too.'

'If that's true, then why aren't all the creatures from up there down here?'

Susan releases a long breath. 'Most creatures have become so distanced from our home, they have forgotten the teachings. If you weren't here now, would you even have any idea there was something amiss?'

I think back to my life in London. I'd be busting my butt and saving like mad to start uni next year, and I probably wouldn't have even thought about the World Below unless my uncle Earth mentioned it. And I wouldn't have paid much attention to what he said anyway.

'No, perhaps not. Are you here to fight?' I ask.

'I'm here on behalf of the refugees from the Unseelie Court. We want our court to be returned to normal, but we can't ignore what's happening in the World Below either. If the Baaronson faction remains in control, the Unseelie Court will always be under attack. Besides, maybe it's time for genuine change, and that is something worth fighting for.'

George clangs some pots onto a work surface. 'Too right it is. It is time to remove these divisions. Time we were all treated equally.'

The dwarf on the other side of me snorts. 'As if that will ever happen.'

'It won't happen if we do nothing,' George responds.

Picking up another peeler, I help Susan finish up the pile of potatoes, leaving the other two to their bickering. Less than two months ago, my life was pretty normal. I had work, and university, and a future. Now I'm caught in the middle of a civil war I hadn't even known was brewing in a realm I left as a baby.

As is always the case, it is more complicated than that. My family are major political supporters of the Crown and Pris is herself a Crown, which places them on one side of this conflict. My mother and I are mixed race, which puts us on another. The only side in this triangle I don't have a stake in is the conservative elven faction. This is one of those times I wish I'd never tried to save Mum.

Then again, if I hadn't, I'd never have met Pris, and I would never have fallen in love with her. I stop mid-peel.

Hold on, that's a leap. I shake my head. When had that happened? When had attraction and friendship developed into something more?

'Snake? Snake?'

'Sorry, Susan. I missed that.'

'You were miles away. I asked if you were coming to the meeting tonight? Verona mentioned you joining their group.'

'I might come, but I haven't decided. Pris and I have been on the go for so long, and I need some rest.'

Susan's shoulders visibly relax at my answer.

I give her a suspicious glare. 'Why do you ask?'

Susan leans in close to me and whispers, 'With your being so close to Pris, you want to be careful about making any political alliances. You might inadvertently end up putting her in a bind.'

I'm stunned. 'I don't make my decisions based on our friendship,' I say through gritted teeth.

'If it were simply a friendship....' Susan extends her hands, palms upwards.

'What Pris and I are to each other is nobody's business but ours,' I hiss. 'Just as what I do, or don't do, is my decision, and—'

I was about to say it wouldn't involve Pris, but that would be a lie. I really need some alone time with Pris so we can figure out how we navigate this minefield together. What I wouldn't give for a mobile phone about now. *Hold on, there might be a way to speak with her.*

'Susan, I've got to go.'

Susan's eyes widen in surprise, but I don't give her a chance to object. Moments later, I'm alone in my room, sitting on the bed Pris and I shared last night.

Ed'rathe, are you there?

I tap on my leg as I wait for a response.

I am, Noble One.

Phew.

Are you able to relay a message to Pris for me and then wait for an answer?

I really shouldn't.... Is it urgent?

It's urgent for me, but would the dragons think it was important enough to bend the rules?

Not if she's going to be back here tonight.

She will not be.

It would have been nice if someone could have told us that this morning.

Then, if you could pass a message on for me. There is a meeting here tonight. They want me to do some things, and I need Pris's input.

There is a hum in my head, something I'd not heard before. Then Ed'rathe comes back. **My cave mates say a brief message should be all right.**

Okay. Tell her the resistance wants me to fight with them. I believe in what they are doing, but I can see problems for her if I do this.

No.

No? You mean no, you won't send the message, Ed'rathe?

I mean, no, you cannot join in the fight with the rebel group. You are the Heir Consort, and that is not appropriate.

I'm the what? I splutter.

You and the princess have bonded, and so you are now her consort.

Bonded? Is this because we.... I trail off, not wanting to discuss what happened last night with my dragon friend.

Oh, no. Physical relations have nothing to do

with it. Something happened between you last night and you started to form a mate bond.

What the hell? A mate bond? Like Percival and Nisha? Is that even possible? It wasn't unheard of, but it rarely occurred between greater creatures. Political alliances commonly formed the basis of their marriages.

If we *had* partially bonded, that would explain my deeper feeling for Pris, but hell, we hadn't had a chance to even discuss things between us, and now this?

Can you please just send the message?

Done.

My head thrums, and Ed'rathe is back.

The princess says things *are* moving fast. If you can put off deciding what to do until you two can speak, she would be pleased.

Thanks, Ed'rathe.

You are welcome, Noble One. Now, make yourself presentable, and I will be at the door in a few wingbeats—the Dragon Queen wishes to speak with you.

You're joking.

I most certainly am not. Indignation laces Ed'rathe's words.

The Queen? What does she want with me?

I'll be there, I mutter as I pull out my clean questing clothes and change as fast as I can.

Bloody hell! I'm about to meet the Queen of Dragons.

⌣

Am'ratha drops into a courtyard behind a mansion in the centre of the maze. Last time I was here, I was so drained,

I was in no position to appreciate the grandeur and magnitude of the Minotaur's residence. Now, as I slide from my dragon's back, I take it all in. The cream stone dwelling is impressive. The morning sun picks out shadows in windows half hidden by balconies in the upper two stories and throws the arched walkways circumnavigating the ground floor into shade.

A figure emerges from a side door. As she approaches, Am'ratha lowers her head and says, **Al'kyla has summoned me.**

Al'kyla?

Queen Ariana's bonded one. She needs my magic.

I'll come with you.

No, Royal One. With someone as exalted as Al'kyla, she must invite you into her presence.

I blow out a breath of frustration.

All right, but if I'm not supposed to help, why *am* I here?

I am sure they will reveal the reason in good time.

How do dragon's do it—remain so calm, and so obedient?

I was brought up to put community first.

Stop reading my thoughts!

Learn to shield them!

The good mood flying always brings evaporates, and I concentrate on suppressing my irritation. *Honestly, I'm going to come out of this whole thing looking ten years older than when I started.*

I take a couple of calming breaths. **Will you let me know if you hear any news from the Capitol or from the World Above?**

Of course.

Am'ratha waddles round the side of the building.

When her tail is no longer visible, I redirect my attention to the creature who arrived to meet me. Standing just below my shoulder, she is wearing a simple knee-length black dress with white cuffs and collar and has a white apron tied around her waist. Is she a brownie?

'I am Xia, Your Highness, and I am to escort you to your rooms.'

'My rooms? I've only come for today. Perhaps you could take me directly to Queen Ariana, or even King Maddox will do.'

A slight flicker of shock passes over her face so quickly, I almost miss it. Was it because I asked to see the King and Queen, or because I questioned her orders?

She gives nothing away. She simply turns on her heel and walks back towards the building. Short of remaining outside, I have no option but to follow her.

Leading me, she takes me into a corridor through an open door. The whitewashed wall reflects the sunlight and my eyes struggle to adapt to the dark windowless space. My guide's feet click on the terracotta tiles, and I have to rush to keep up.

The corridor ends, and we enter an atrium that opens up to the sky. Skirting the fountain and gardens in the middle, our path takes us up a flight of stairs, then round the first-floor balcony. Xia stops in front of a set of double doors and waits for me to catch her up before opening them to reveal a large, opulent room in calming blues and creams.

A semicircular sofa dominates the space, giving anyone seated there a spectacular view of the desert through the open patio doors, and I can just make out the wall of the maze at its edge. To my right is a dining table laden with fresh fruit, nuts, and pastries. To the left is a set of three doors—this is definitely a guest suite rather than a reception room. How long do they expect me to stay here?

My guide gestures with her hand towards the sofa. 'If you will make yourself comfortable, I am sure someone will be with you soon.' She closes the doors behind her as she leaves.

I've not long had breakfast, but there is little else to do, so I head for the table. After loading a plate with fruit and pouring a coffee from a carafe, I take my snack out onto the balcony that runs the width of the room. Tucked behind the door is a wrought-iron table and chairs. Once seated, I close my eyes and allow the sunlight to warm my face.

The place is eerily quiet except for the occasional trill of birds and the rustle of leaves as the breeze stirs them into action. The lack of other creature sounds is unnatural, and I feel isolated and alone. Panic pricks at my skin.

Shaking my head, I try to relax and dispel my anxiety. I concentrate on enjoying my coffee while nibbling at the food. All too soon, the sun drenching the balcony makes it uncomfortable to remain here. I take my dishes indoors and place them on the table.

A quick circuit of the room reveals nothing to distract me. I open the doors to see that they hide generic double bedrooms with a bathroom between. They would not look out of place in a hotel. I flop down on the sofa and stare up at the ceiling. What on earth am I doing here?

With a grunt, I push myself to my feet, pad across to the entrance, and fling open a door. Before I can put a foot outside, a dwarfish guard in the Queen's livery steps into my path.

'May I help you?'

'You can let me out,' I snap.

She folds her arms across her chest. 'I'm sorry, I can't do that.'

My heart rate increases. How was I stupid enough to become trapped here? Forcing my fears down, I draw myself up to my full height, which is slightly taller than her, then arrange my face into haughty princess mode, 'Am I a prisoner?'

The guard isn't fazed. 'No, Princess.'

'I'm so sorry,' apologises a familiar voice. 'We have so many guests, and we are not prepared for this.'

The brownie who showed me to the suite appears as the guard steps away. 'I thought you might get bored while you waited, and I did not know….' Her voice drifts off as she hands me a basket.

Taking it, I peek inside. There are a couple of books, some wool and needles, what looks like it might be embroidery, and a large box that rattles in a way that suggests it might contain puzzle pieces.

I'm not here to knit!

'Someone summoned me here,' I say, hating the whine in my voice, but feeling too aggrieved to do anything about it. 'I could be with my friends doing something useful. Do you know who called for me and when they will actually appear?'

An apologetic facade appears on the brownie's face, intended to empathise and neutralise my irritation. 'I believe it was Al'kyla who requested your presence. There is….' She draws a breath. 'Things are happening, and I'm not sure I can talk about them. Someone should be here soon.'

She bobs a quick curtsey and disappears as the guard closes the door in my face. I glare at the solid wood, debating whether to let my temper loose on the bulky guard. Hoisting the basket up my arm, I step back from the offending door. One thing I have learnt from my time around creatures is that you have to pick your battles wisely, and this one isn't worth the effort. I curl up on the plush sofa and reach into the basket.

Pulling out the books, I study the cover of the top one —*Tess of the D'Urbervilles.* Yuck. I didn't like it at school, and I doubt I'll like it any better now.

Oliver Twist. Who chose these? I guess at a push I could read this.

Oh, what's this? Wilkie Collins's *A Woman in White.*

I pop the other two books back and place the basket on the floor. Curling up against the arm of the sofa, facing toward the window, I open the novel and start reading. I'm about a quarter of the way through the story when my eyelids droop. I've spent so much time rushing here and there these past few weeks, I can't remember the last time I could sit and do nothing. My body is certainly appreciating the chance to relax.

Sometime later, I force my eyes open. The sun has changed position, and I'm covered by a blanket. My head feels a little heavy, as if there's some sort of pressure building up behind my forehead. Blinking a couple of times, I allow my eyes to adjust and find them drawn to the figure sitting at the other end of the couch, *Tess of the D'Urbervilles* in his hand.

'Pris, you're awake,' the Minotaur's deep voice rumbles, and I resist the urge to leap to my feet and take a defensive position.

The last time I saw him, he'd tried to kill us. He then took part in the subterfuge that sent us to the Unseelie Court. Although this is his home, he was the last person I expected to see here.

Staying alert, I force myself to say politely, 'Aeron… ah… how, um, nice to see you again.'

CHAPTER 4

Life Lessons

The book on my lap falls to the floor as I sit up. The Minotaur grins, his smile revealing his prominent lower tusks.

'Princess Priscilla, the pleasure is mine. I thought I would join you for lunch, given everyone else appears to be too busy to spare us any time.'

I swing my legs to the floor and glance behind the half man, half bull to find the table has been cleared and is now set for two people. Aeron stands up, his black trousers and a white shirt emphasising his massive muscular form. While they hide most of the hair covering his body, they cannot conceal his hooves or that he has the head of a bull.

He holds out his arm, and I rise, resting my hand in the crook. This is so bizarre! I have visions of *Beauty and the Beast* as the Minotaur of myth and legend escorts me to the dining table, where he takes his place at the head, while I sit to his right.

When we're settled, he reaches out and rings a small bell. Seconds later, Xia enters, pushing a trolley. She serves a soup course and leaves us alone.

I groan with pleasure as the spicy soup hits my taste buds, and my stomach rumbles as I crack the crusty bread to soak up the liquid my spoon can't reach. When the edge of my hunger is dulled, the absurdity of the situation hits me anew, and I question why I'm here with Aeron rather than with one of the two creatures who came to assist the Queen.

'Aeron, where are Euphemia and my uncle?'

Aeron places his spoon down and dabs daintily at his mouth with a napkin before answering. 'The Witch Protector of the North and King Maddox are still working with Al'kyla to heal the Queen.'

'If everyone is busy, why am I here?'

Aeron runs a hand through the course, stubbled hair on his head. 'I believe it is because the Dragon Queen wanted you trained to work with King Maddox at restoring the magical flow.'

'Oh.' That makes sense.

I eat a little more before my skin tingles, alerting me to the fact Aeron is watching me again. I pause and raise a questioning brow.

'You are happy to do that?'

I blink twice, then stop myself from saying, 'Of course I am.' Instead, I inquire, 'What am I missing, Aeron?'

'You are here because the Dragon Queen worries that Queen Ariana won't recover. With your mother in the middle of a potential war zone, the Dragon Queen wants you to take on royal responsibilities.'

Aeron continues his meal, but my appetite deserts me. I place my spoon down and stare out the window, longing to be back in the cave sanctuary with Snake—back where I can be just Pris.

The bell tinkles, and the brownie appears, again pushing her trolley. She clears our dishes, then places a covered plate in front of Aeron. As she moves to put one in front of me, I hold up my hand. 'I'm not hungry.'

After Aeron nods, she removes the plate. She tops up our glasses with a chilled fruit drink and sets a plate of flatbreads in the middle of the table before she goes.

'Some heir to the throne I am,' I mutter. 'I can't even get a brownie to follow my orders.'

Aeron snorts. 'Of course not. She has sworn her loyalty to me.'

I pick at the tablecloth. 'I thought brownies were servants. Shouldn't they do what anyone asks?'

'It is so easy to forget that you know very little of our world,' Aeron says as he lifts the cover from his food, revealing a platter of spiced meats, goat's cheese, and some dips. The smell wafting towards me sets my stomach grumbling. It seems my appetite has returned.

Aaron grins and pushes the plate between us. 'Please, share with me.'

'Only if you will tell me what I don't understand about brownies.'

He wraps some of the spiced meats in a flatbread and puts some cheese and hummus on top before rolling it all up and finishing the lot in one bite. It looks delicious.

'Please.' He gestures to the food. As I make a roll, he explains, 'Brownies are house creator creatures. They not only derive income by serving others, they also create magic and strengthen the status of their family as they work. Many unscrupulous masters take advantage of their need to serve, turning their brownies into virtual slaves.'

I nod. 'The strong take advantage of the weak. It's the same everywhere.'

'To protect them, the council issued a decree that brownies in service must sign a magical contract. They swear loyalty to their master, and in return, their master takes care of them, pays them, and agrees on a set of duties. The contract is then assessed by the council and, if it is deemed fair to both sides, they ratify it.'

'And that protects the brownies?'

'In most cases, yes, if the council is diligent. Brownies in my service have a contract saying they do not have to take orders from anyone else unless I ask them to.'

'I see. So the brownies in my uncle's court would have had their own contracts and their own set of duties.'

'I am not sure how things work in the Unseelie Court,' Aeron admits.

I take a bite of the wrap. The pleasure of eating the fluffy soft bread turns into agony as a sharp pain pierces my head, causing me to drop my food on the table.

'Are you all right?' Aeron asks, his voice gruff with worry.

Another wave of something indescribable rolls through the room, and my head pounds in response.

Concern tugs at Aeron's brow, but it is swiftly replaced with a look of understanding.

'Oh dear, they are using an awful lot of magic.'

I massage my forehead. 'This is because of magic?'

'We must fix this. You need to learn to shield against this, Princess. They could be at this for hours.'

'Hours?' I repeat, dismay seeping into every limb as my eyeballs feel like they might explode.

'Close your eyes,' Aeron commands, and I follow his instruction.

'Now, reach out with your other senses. You should be able to make out a sort of dissonance around you.'

'Yes, I can,' I whisper as magic buzzes around me, its sharp edges pricking my skin like hundreds of pins.

'Good, now concentrate on pushing it away from you.'

I try to do what he says, ignoring the increased pain

and using what I already know of manipulating magical particles in the air. I imagine the particles bunching up and leaving a space around my body. They move sluggishly, and then they spring back, sending another wave of pain through me.

Gritting my teeth, I start again. This time I push a little more slowly, allowing the fragments to move and regroup, and then I nudge them once more. Slowly, I create a space around me, and the pain recedes.

'Have you done it?' Aeron asks.

'Yes.'

'Now, imagine a shield of air around your body creating a no-go zone for the dissonance.'

'Okay.' I attempt to do what he says, but as soon as I pull my focus from pushing the particles away to concentrate on my shield, they drift closer, and my head pounds again.

I instantly drop my shield and force the magic away until the pain recedes. This time, I use more power, moving magic further away to give myself a chance to erect a basic shield. I picture the air turning solid like a wall protecting the space around me. Only a little magic seeps back through the cracks in my shield this time, raising goosebumps on my skin. I thrust it away again and strengthen my shield, filling the cracks and adding another layer so nothing can get through. I release my hold a little, testing its stability… and it holds. It is done.

Opening my eyes, I'm relieved the headache has gone, but I'm drained. Aeron is peering at me, his bovine features twisted with concern. I smile at him, and he relaxes a little.

'Well done. Your first shield is never easy. Come, lie down. You'll need to recharge after that,' he says, leading me back to the sofa, then placing the blanket over me.

"You should check your shield frequently and repair it until it becomes second nature to maintain it.'

He returns to the table and rings the bell. When the Xia reappears, Aeron asks for tea and cakes. As the brownie tidies up our meal, he finds a seat on the sofa.

'You arrived in our world with so little teaching and knowledge, yet they want you to stand as heir and take responsibility for keeping magic flowing. It is wrong.'

'Wrong? How?' I ask. I understand my own reservations, but I'm curious to hear his perspective.

'Because you had a life, and they are taking it from you. No one is asking what you want. They all assume what they need from you is what you should be giving.'

Tears well in my eyes. So many people have been telling me I should do what is best for the World Below. It touches me that this creature who hardly knows me is more concerned about how it will affect me. Aeron may appear to be a beast, but the man inside is so much more.

Xia returns, and Aeron insists I drink some tea and eat some of the fruit, while he nibbles on the fruit and nuts from the platter placed on a small side table. The tea clears the aches and pains, but I'm still bonetired. I sink back into the sofa, and Aeron leans back, his hands clasped behind his head.

'What do you think of everything that's going on?' he finally asks.

'Which part exactly?'

'I am sorry, that was rather a broad question. I was there when Fairburn forced you to go to the Unseelie Court not knowing who you were or why it was so important that *you* specifically went. Now you are to become the Crown Princess and save the World Below—a world you didn't even know existed until a few weeks ago. Is this what you want for your life?'

'No,' I say, and it comes from my gut. I follow it with 'But I can't see any other way to stop things from falling into total chaos.'

'Youngling, there is such a weight on your shoulders, and it is evident your parents taught you to do your duty.'

There is a heaviness and sadness in his voice, and it cuts me to the quick. Aeron stares into the distance, his thoughts clearly elsewhere.

'Working out where you fit is the toughest part of growing up. Others see you one way, and they try hard to tell you that's who you are. The trick is to know yourself without being swayed by their preconceptions, or by what they want from you.'

I study Aeron as he speaks. The intelligence and sadness in his eyes are at odds with the face he presents to the world. I have faced a lifetime of scrutiny based on the colour of my skin, both in the World Above and the World Below. It's even worse here because I'm also judged based on my family. Despite how terrible it was, I doubt it compares to what Aeron's endured. As part man, part beast, finding a place to fit in would have been difficult.

'How would you suggest I deal with the Dragon Queen and her expectations?'

Aeron turns to me, his expression unreadable. Then he expels air in something between a grunt and a sigh. 'No one has ever asked for my opinion. How do I answer?'

'You could tell me what you would do if you were me.'

He slowly shakes his head. 'I would not feel right doing that. Perhaps I can tell you a little of my past instead.'

I'm about to tell him I know what the legends say, but I stop myself; maybe it isn't his truth. Instead, I make myself comfortable and wait for him to start.

'Poseidon deceived my mother, who is Helios's daughter, into mating with a bull as part of a power struggle between Minos and the sea god. I resulted from that union.' Aeron runs a hand over his face. 'My family despised me. Not just for what I symbolised, but also for my appearance. In an age where people admired learning and physical beauty, I was a beast—a monster, even.'

The last words are whispered, and my heart bleeds for the pain in Aeron's voice.

'They banished me to the centre of the dark maze, and every nine years, warriors came to fight me. In the months leading up to those battles, they starved me, and goaded me, and tortured me so that by the time the tributes arrived, I was the crazed beast they had been told to expect.'

'Oh, Aeron, that's horrid,' I say. Those details were omitted from the histories I read, and hearing them gives me a whole new perspective.

The Minotaur holds up his hand. 'That was not the worst of it. When my sister fell in love with a man, he vowed to kill me as a display of his devotion. He was a mighty warrior, and I decided to grant him his desire because I wanted nothing more than to end my loneliness and suffering. When he taunted me and boasted he would defeat me and return my head to my sister, I laid down my weapon and told him to run me through.'

Aeron stops speaking and stares into the distance, his face contorted in pain as if he is reliving the moment. I hold my breath, worried he might decide to end his story before it is finished, and I am desperate to hear the rest of it.

'One of his companions stepped forward and pointed out that I was not the beast they had expected, and to kill me would be wrong. I begged them to end my misery. The companion, a centaur, moved to my side as if to defend me. As he did, he talked of a place I would be valued. All we had to do was find a way to get me there. At first I dared not hope his words were true, but he was convincing. Then he and the warrior concocted a plan where the warrior would take back the heart of a beast and claim to have killed me while Fairglade spirited me to the World Below.'

'Fairglade? Any relation to Fairburn?'

Aeron chuckles. 'Yes, he is Fairburn's father. He is ancient now—as am I—but he still visits, and we wile away an occasional afternoon playing chess. The point is, I am here now because he convinced me I am more than my appearances.'

He captures my gaze with his own to drive home the point.

'I get it. I am more than a princess,' I tell him. 'But how did you end up here, doing what you do?'

Chuckling again, Aeron says, 'I had spent so much time alone, I did not feel comfortable around too many creatures. Queen Ariana's mother spoke with the dragons, and they made some space for me on the edge of both worlds. In return for my home, I test the nature of creatures and dragons when they want to travel between the worlds.'

'Are you asked often?'

'When we had more contact with the dragons, yes, I was. In recent years I have not been called upon so much. Mostly I tend to my orchards, read books, and play host when creatures visit. It is a quiet life, but I am not lonely, and I am who I was meant to be.' Aeron rests his hands on his thighs.

I push myself into a sitting position and cross my legs. 'Have you found peace?' I ask.

The Minotaur nods. 'I have, Princess. It has taken time, but, yes, I have.'

I hug the blanket around me. Aeron did not choose to be born or to be treated as a pariah, yet he took a risk and found a place where he belonged and made a happy home here.

Deep down, I'm aware that I can't go back to my old life despite the part of me that desires it. In the past few weeks, I have been manipulated and pushed from pillar to post. I understand why this happened, but I'm done. It would be way easier if I had another option.

'So, my young friend, my challenge to you is for you to decide how you fit into our world. It will be tough, but you will not be at peace with yourself until you do.'

'You're right. It's just, I've been running round so much, I haven't had a chance to stop and think.'

The grin revealing Aeron's ginormous teeth would be terrifying if his eyes weren't twinkling. 'Then perhaps it is a good thing everyone here is preoccupied with bringing Queen Ariana back to health. This gives you time to consider your options.'

My nose crinkles. 'I'll go crazy in this room, just sitting round lost in my own thoughts. I have to move to activate my brain.'

Aeron slaps a hand on his thigh. 'Excellent! Perhaps you'd like to accompany me on a walk around my orchard.'

I leap to my feet, invigorated by the opportunity to do something other than try to fix the problems in the World Below.

Ed'rathe eyes me stonily as I tidy myself after the short ride from the guest quarters to the Queen's Cave.

Is that the best you can do? he asks, huffing on his burgundy scales so they shine.

I didn't exactly arrive here with a suitcase of clothes, I say dryly.

His eyes widen in what might be the dragon version of raising your eyebrows. **You could glamour yourself.**

Glamour myself? I ask, because the idea hadn't even occurred to me.

Using magic for such frivolous reasons is frowned on in the World Above, while in the other worlds, it is commonplace. I turn away from Ed'rathe and reluctantly reach out for magic. I am almost blown off my feet by the weight off it, and I quickly let go. There is so little magic in the World Above that you have to grasp it and pull to use even a little. Here, that tug almost blew me apart.

This time I give a gentle pull and imagine myself in formal clothes. Releasing all but a trickle of the magic to maintain the image, I check myself out. I do look smarter, but I can't get rid of the guilt niggling inside at the frivolous use of magic and the ongoing cost. It lessens somewhat as my mother's voice in my head says, 'Now do us proud, son.' I roll my shoulders back and straighten up, ready now to meet the Queen.

Ed'rathe leads the way into the cave and down a torchlit corridor into an enormous cavern. We stop in the doorway and wait, which gives me an opportunity to survey my surroundings.

An enormous throne cut from the very fabric of the earth dominates the room, and on it sits a dragon, her scales glowing with such intensity, she eclipses every other creature. As if he can read my mind, Ed'rathe sends, **During court gather-**

ings the Queen uses her own form of glamour—one that dulls her light. She is the most powerful being in the three worlds. If she did not hide part of herself, none in the room would be able to bear her presence.**

I wasn't nervous before, but now butterflies flutter in my stomach. I calm a little when we are joined by another dragon and an elf woman. The woman is vaguely familiar, but I can't place where we've met.

Ed'rathe, the new dragon sends, **do you know why the Queen summoned us?**

We should wait for her, Ed'rathe sends back. **Am'nera, this is Snake Fieth, of clan Fieth, and consort to Princess Priscilla.**

I'm about to remind my dragon friend I am no such thing when the elf hisses, 'Abomination! You should not be allowed in the presence of true creatures.'

Her face twists, and recognition dawns, she is Adina, Bernais Baaronson's mother. It takes all my will to not to tell her what I think of her and her narrow-minded family. I will not lower myself to her level.

Am'nera, I am pleased to make your acquaintance. Princess Adina. I acknowledge her with a bow of my head that meets the minimum requirements of respect when meeting royalty—something I know will annoy her, and I have to hold back my grin.

Pris's aunt opens her mouth, no doubt to spurt more vitriol, but a smaller dragon steps between us and advises us that the Queen will see us now. I step closer to the throne, but Ed'rathe holds back.

The Queen did not call for me, he sends.

Without Ed'rathe by my side, I'm even more apprehensive. When I'm in front of the Queen's throne, her power washes over me, which doesn't improve matters. It takes all my strength to hold on to my sense of self as I bow before her.

Welcome to my court, Sneak Thief. I have been hearing great things about you.

My pleasure at her praise outshines my unease at her use of my private family name.

'Thank you,' I mutter.

Young creature, you need to erect some shields, or this meeting will not go as I planned, the Queen admonishes.

Shields? She's reading my mind. I move away a couple of steps and focus on erecting a barrier against magic before returning to my position.

The Dragon Queen bares her teeth. I hope it's because she finds my ineptitude amusing, not because she sees me as a delicious meal. Or maybe it's because she can no longer read my thoughts.

I requested your presence because I heard you are joining our refugees, and I want you to become their ambassador to my court instead.

My mind goes blank, and I struggle to find the words to respond. Adina steps forward.

'Your Majesty, I must protest. There is no precedent for your recognising these… *refugees* as a political entity.' She sneers as she says the word, like it's sour on her tongue and she can barely stand to even speak of us at all.

They are guests in my realm, and I allow who I will at this court. You are only here today as a courtesy—don't make me regret your presence.

'But…,' Adina splutters, 'you can't consider him a worthy ambassador. He… he's not pure.'

The whole cavern falls silent at her words. Am'nera shuffles away as if distancing herself from her bonded princess.

Adina, you are dismissed, the Queen sends, her voice icy as it chills the cavern.

'But—'

Am'nera steps between Adina and the Queen, cutting the princess off as two dragon guards appear from the shadows. The guards lead her out, and Adina mutters in protest every step of the way.

Sneak Thief, I apologise for the rudeness shown to you in my court. It will not happen again.

I'm still searching for words.

Ed'rathe mentally nudges me. **Snake, the Queen is waiting.**

'Um, I don't blame you for Adina's spite, Your Majesty.'

Good. As ambassador, I expect you at the morning court every day. As the Princess Heir's consort, I assign you Ed'rathe to begin the bonding process.

Ed'rathe's pleasure hits me in waves, but I'm still trying to process what's happened here, let alone what's happening between Pris and me. I can't do this. I don't want any of this. I'm not ambassador material, and my bonding with Ed'rathe …. It's too soon too, too much pressure. Finally I find the right words.

'While I appreciate your offer, Your Majesty, I am sure Gregor and the refugees would prefer to appoint their own representative to your court.'

The Dragon Queen's eyes narrow, and she studies me intently before snorting. **Verona Coronas has been doing an adequate job, but as the Princess Heir's consort, this is an appropriate role for you, and it keeps you from doing anything... politically unsound.**

Suddenly the reason for this meeting becomes clear—Ed'rathe and his friends have been doing some manoeuvring behind my back.

'About that, Your Majesty. I think I need to come clean. Princess Priscilla and I have no formal understanding. It would be… a little presumptuous of me to present myself as her consort before we've discussed matters.'

Again the Dragon Queen snorts, and I'm pretty sure that means she's laughing, or at least I hope she is.

Creature relations are so complex. It is a small matter. We can call you Consort- in-Training. Anything else?

Consort-in-Training? What the hell?

Ed'rathe sends a warning. **Snake.**

Is this how Pris feels when others make decisions for her?

Snake, Ed'rathe repeats, this time with a little more urgency.

I don't want to upset the Queen, or be thrown out like Adina, so I say, 'No, I'm good. Thank you, Your Majesty.'

Excellent. Your first job as ambassador is to remind your friends that they cannot launch any activities from their base here. We are happy to provide them with food and shelter while they are homeless, but we cannot support their political agenda any more than we can support Adina's son. We have no desire to become involved in creature politics.

'I will make that clear, but I'm not sure whether they will listen to me,' I tell her.

You have my backing, young creature. They will listen.

The usher brings forward two new dragons, and my audience with the Queen is over.

Without another word, I join Ed'rathe, and he leads the way from the court, a new swagger to his walk.

'Ed'rathe, did you organise all of this?' I ask dourly.

I did not. I merely reported to my Queen that you were thinking about becoming embroiled with the leaders of the rebellion.

I want to be angry with him, but he was only doing what he thought was right. How could he know it wasn't right for me? Hell, *I* don't even know what is right for me.

This consort business has me wondering if I've really thought about what being with Pris will mean for me. She has repeatedly told me how being in line to the throne impacts what she can and can't do, but have I really thought about how, if we're together, that will extend to me?

I care for her. Hell—I'm pretty sure I'm falling in love with Pris, but is it worth letting her being a princess control my future? We really need to talk.

Shall I return you to the guest caves, Noble One? Ed'rathe interrupts.

He lowers himself to the ground, and once I climb onto his back, I lean forward and say into his ear. 'Thanks for what you did. I appreciate it. In the future, perhaps we could discuss things before you take them to your Queen.'

He stretches out his wings, then tucks them back in before turning his head my way so I can see one of his eyes.

Once we fully bond, I will have a little more leeway. However, my allegiance to the Queen and my dragon community must always come first.

His gaze bores through me, and I appreciate he is making a point and that this is the first step in the dance of us becoming a team.

'Of course, I understand. Though if we are to work

together, we need to ensure any actions one of us takes doesn't compromise the other.'

Ed'rathe doesn't move for quite some time, then drops his head slightly in acceptance. **Of course.**

He turns and launches himself off the ledge, making quick work of the leap to the guest caves. He drops me outside before flying towards the setting sun, heading off to goodness knows where. The heavy leather curtain is just falling back in place when Verona accosts me in the entranceway.

'We have company, and they want to see you.'

She drags me by the arm through the main room and down the corridor to where Gregor and I had spoken earlier. He is there, talking to a taller, dark-haired creature.

'Mandor.' The name escapes my lips in a whisper as the other inhabitant of the room steps out from behind the wizard.

'Hello, Snake,' the wiry academic-looking creature says, and I can't help the grin that spreads over my face as I step towards the gnome.

'Drow, you made it below.'

'I did indeed, and not a moment too soon for the state of our realm.' My great-uncle wraps an arm around my shoulder and gives me an awkward hug.

'What are you doing here?'

'I came with Mandor to speak at the gathering tonight. We have much to discuss and much to decide. Will you be joining us?'

'Snake is going to be one of our leaders, or so I hope,' Gregor says before I'm able to answer.

'About that,' I start, then search for the most tactful way to announce my new role. 'The Queen of Dragons wants me to be your ambassador to her court.'

Beside me, Verona barks out a laugh. 'You mean she told you it's your job.'

'I'm sorry, I know——'

'Snake,' Verona interrupts. 'Believe me, it's fine. I'm going to be so busy with logistics and planning, I was wondering how I would fit it in, especially as I can't portal backwards and forwards.'

'But what about you working with us?' Gregor asks. 'I was hoping you could convince some more creatures in the World Below to join the fight.'

Mandor clears his throat. 'We must discuss this, Gregor. Not everyone who opposes the elven elite wants to fight, and we should not force them.'

'And we will need some creatures to stay behind and help the refugees who find their way here.' Verona adds.

'Stay behind?' I ask.

'Yes,' Drow says. 'Those prepared to fight are going to be moving to the main camp over the next few days.'

I let out a breath, and Mandor smiles. 'Let me guess. You have strict instructions from the Dragon Queen that we are not to run a war from here.'

I grin. 'Yes.'

'Are you going to be the Dragon Queen's spy?' Gregor asks in a casual tone.

'I am supposed to report back to her about your activity, yes.'

Gregor's nose wrinkles, then his mouth splits into a smile. 'That means she thinks our rebellion is serious enough to keep tabs on.'

'It's weird that you find that a good thing,' I tell him, and he laughs, breaking the tension in the room—and in me, too, if I'm honest. I hadn't realised how worried I was that my new role would change the delicate balance of the friendships I'd been building.

'Now that everything's sorted, let's get something to eat before the meeting,' Verona says, attempting to hustle everyone out of the room.

As Drow and I make our way to the dining hall, I ask, 'Is Heart here?'

My uncle shakes his head. 'Your grandfather is going to the Minotaur's Maze in preparation to visit his parents. He said if I saw you, to tell you that he will leave tomorrow if you want to join him.'

My last few weeks have been all about duty. Surely I can take a day or so to visit my family. I'd love to get to know Heart's parents, Mender and Keeper, better.

Drow must have sensed my thoughts. 'While he's there, he will meet representatives of the local villages to discuss the rebellion. I am sure the Dragon Queen would see the benefit of your reporting back on that.'

'I'll think about it,' I tell him.

In fact, it was all I could think about during dinner and then again during the meeting. I paid enough attention to make mental notes about the fact that all but a few refugees would fight. Those not prepared to do so would go along and work on logistics. They hoped to use the sanctuary for anyone unable to carry on fighting—which meant those too injured to be of use. I would tell the Queen this when I next saw her.

The moment the meeting was over, I contacted Ed'rathe and asked his advice about joining my grandfather.

The Queen's advisor says that so long as you attend court early tomorrow, I am at your disposal to take you and your grandfather to the villages in the far Wyld Woods. You must, however, agree to report anything you learn to the Queen on your return.

I agree, I send, feeling happy for the first time today. Tomorrow I'm going with my grandfather to visit with his parents. Perhaps being an ambassador will not be so bad after all.

I will fetch you at dawn.

Or maybe it will be, I groan inwardly.

Seraphina casts a "keep-fresh" spell over the leftover food while Heart wipes down the bench and I put away the last of the dishes. He and I have been feeding creatures off and on throughout the day, but now most of the creature representatives from this morning's meeting have finally gone. Outside the kitchen window, the light is fading. Inside, the air is cooling as afternoon turns to evening. It is getting late. Hopefully Nisha will soon be finished.

The kettle boils, and I add water to the teapot before placing the stewing brew on the table. Heart pulls out a chair, and I join him, hoping to catch a few minutes' respite before we are called on to help with something else.

Footsteps drift in from the hall, and I pause, teapot in hand. The door behind me opens to admit Mandor and Drow. Heart half stands to give up his seat, but Mandor tells him to sit. 'We're not staying long. I have to get to an evening meeting in the World Between.'

'Seraphina, they want you in the lounge,' Drow says

She passes him a couple of cups before leaving. He places them on the table before taking an empty seat. Mandor leans against the bench as I pour.

Drow relaxes in his chair as he takes a sip from his cup.

'Seraphina makes the best teas. She swears she doesn't use magic in her mixes, but I don't know.'

'Huh, that's like saying you don't use magic when you brew a potion. If you don't hold the intent in your mind and activate the properties of the ingredients, the potion won't work,' I say.

Drow's eyes widen. 'You mean Seraphina mixes her teas like she does potions?'

Mandor claps a hand on Drow's shoulder and chuckles. 'For such an intelligent creature, sometimes you are quite naïve.'

Drow joins in the laughter, and somehow that as much as the soothing tea helps us relax. It has been so long since the four of us, once almost inseparable, have sat round a table and chatted about inconsequential things. We have not done this since Heart was banished and Mandor was forced to join the Wizard Council. As I sip my tea, I take a moment to enjoy the luxury of our finding this opportunity to reconnect amidst the turmoil.

We do not discuss weighty matters. Instead we catch up on the past couple of hundred years, keeping things light. When the dregs of the tea have gone cold, Mandor pushes himself to his feet. 'Drow, we must leave for the World Between if we are to make the evening meeting with the group there.'

'How come you're doing that?' Heart asks.

'Someone needs to talk to the refugees about what we decided today,' Mandor says. 'And Drow is the best person for that, as he has all the details about the petition to the Queen.'

'And Mandor's going because I need someone to open the portal there and then the one to the Minotaur's Maze after we're done,' Drow finishes.

My eyebrows shoot upwards. 'You're going into the maze?'

Drow nods. 'Yes, we have to if we want to petition the Queen—'

'Who is in stasis,' I remind him.

'If Maddox has done his job, she might well be awake. And it's best to get these things sorted out quickly,' Drow explains.

'Where are you two going from here?' Mandor asks.

I glance towards Heart, who adds, 'And I'm heading for the Wyld Woods and my home. It's past time I reunited with my family. Mandor has some witches spreading the word throughout the villages, and I will help them while I'm there. I may even lend weight to their call for the villagers to join the cause.'

'Oh,' I say, a little jealous of my friends' decisive actions. I should go with Drow to speak with the Queen, but until I have talked with Nisha, I won't be going anywhere. Our previous conversation today has made me realise that, although we may not be moving forward together, it is time we discuss our options and make some decisions together.

'Percival?'

Mandor's voice shakes me from my reverie. 'Sorry?'

'I asked if you wanted Alyce to take you to the maze to visit with the Queen before she takes Heart to the Wyld Woods?'

'When would I have to leave? I'd like to talk with Nisha before I go....'

'Soon.'

As I trace my finger along the woodgrain of the table, wondering what to do, Nisha and Emrys appear, deep in conversation, forestalling my decision.

'Percival, there you are. I was wondering if you wanted to journey back to the grove with me?' Emrys asks.

My eyes are glued to Nisha as my heart pounds in my ears, blocking out the murmur of voices around me. 'With you?' I ask my brother.

'Yes. Nathanial is staying here with Seraphina, and Nisha is going with the witches to Essendore to set up medical support.'

The pain in my heart is so intense, it almost stops beating. Nisha is going away, and she didn't discuss it with me? Even as I remind myself that I have left her on numerous occasions and she did warn me she had a role to play in the upcoming conflict, the hurt runs deep.

As I force myself to breathe, Nisha steps forward and takes my hand. 'If you will all excuse us, Percival and I need some time alone.'

Without waiting for a response, she leads me through the back door and along the path that runs by the edge of the Wyld Woods.

'I see I have hurt you in some way.'

I give her hand a brief squeeze. 'It is not you. It is me. I returned home at the realisation that I've been evading my life, ready to begin anew with you. In the meantime, you have committed to being a part of the opposition to the new council.'

Nisha stops walking and lets go of my hand, then turns to me, sadness written on her face. 'Oh, Percival. Your timing….'

I smile wanly. 'I know. As Snake would say, "it sucks."' I take her hand. 'I was proud of you today. You have so much to offer, not just to our grove, but to the creature world as a whole. I am here to support you in whatever you do. It's just… I do not know where I fit into your life.'

Nisha leans in and touches her forehead to mine. 'You belong with me, and, after this is over, we will be together.'

We stay there, our energies mingling, our spirits reconnecting, until the sound of the door opening behind us breaks the spell, and I reluctantly pull away.

'Emrys is going to the grove to ready the sprites for war. He would certainly appreciate your help,' Nisha says as we slowly wander back to the witches' house.

I shake my head. 'I must earn my place back in the grove, and now is not the time for that. It is more important that I talk with the Queen as the committee asked.'

Then another thought strikes me. I can do more than convince the Queen to sign this agreement. In this changing world, Queen Ariana will need new advisors, and at least one of them should be a lesser creature. Why shouldn't that be me?

'Percival?'

'I'm sorry, Nisha, I was thinking.'

'I asked if that was the best use of your skills, given your connections. If you are serious about accepting who you are, you need to recognise that you have a lot of influence in the higher realms of government.'

I turn my eyes back to her, surprised by her words and their closeness to my own conclusions. Can Nisha read my thoughts? I had heard of bonded couples being able to do that after many years together, but Nisha and I had not spent enough time in each other's company for our bond to strengthen that much.

'Do not look so shocked. You are connected to some of the most powerful non-elves in our realm. You should work with them.'

I chuckle. 'I was just thinking that I will present myself as an advisor to the Queen when she awakens.'

Nisha's lips spread into a smile. 'Perfect.'

Before we step into the light spilling from the kitchen door, I pull Nisha to a stop and turn her to me, then wrap my arms around her and hold her close, as if I am imprinting the feel of her onto my brain. 'I will miss you,' I whisper into her hair.

'Are you two ever going to come back inside?' Heart's voice booms into the twilight.

I suck in a breath, then reluctantly let Nisha go as Heart and Emrys join us, followed by a young witch.

'You took so long, Mandor and Drow left already,' Heart informs us. 'I've been talking with Drow, and he's going to see if Snake wants to come with me to the Wyld Woods. Alyce here is about to take me to the Minotaur's Maze to wait. She'll come back and get you.'

'Percival, you're not coming back with me?' Emrys asks, sounding dismayed. 'With father so recently deceased and Nathanial staying here to co-ordinate things, I could really use your help at home.'

His request is genuine, and I know he believes that I could actually help him. However, he forgets that there are still many sprites who have not forgiven me for the anger I brought down on them from Magnus Baaronson when I spread blight to his property, then challenged him in the Queen's Court. I have much to make up for before they will accept me back.

I draw my brother into a hug and hold him tight. 'Emrys, you know I would come with you if I thought I would be any help at all, but I think I can do more for sprite-kind working with the queen.'

I feel his gasp rather than hear it. 'You raise yourself too high.'

Taking a step back, I hold my brother's gaze. 'No, Emrys. These are creatures I have known all my life, and they have accepted me for who I am. It is time I encouraged them to extend that acceptance to all sprites. My only regret is I did not see that sooner.'

Nisha moves to my side. 'This is his role, Emrys. Let him do it.'

Emrys's head swivels from me to Nisha, then back again, his lips pursed. Then his face softens, and he looks me directly in the eye as he says, 'Perhaps, yes, this might still be as father saw.' He hefts a pack over his shoulder and includes everyone in his farewell. 'Until we meet again, may we all be successful in creating a better future for our fellow creatures.'

He drops a hand on my shoulder. 'You may not believe it, but the grove is still your home, Percival, and we all miss you deeply.'

Tears well in my eyes as I watch my brother make his way into the forest. With that parting sentence, he has hit at the heart of my worries. I send a prayer to the Mother Tree that I will earn my place back in the grove soon.

Heart breaks the moment. 'Right, Percival. Are you ready?'

'No, not quite. Just let me say my goodbyes and gather some things.' I make my way past him and into the house.

Eleanora is standing by the stove, waiting for the kettle to boil. She looks up, and I suspect that she's only making tea because she wants to catch me.

'You're not staying, are you?' she asks, tears glistening in her eyes.

My heart is heavy. For so many years, she has cared for me, championed me when I have not valued myself, and encouraged me to be more than the recluse I turned myself into. She must have known all the time that when I came out of my self-imposed exile, I would leave her.

'No. It is time.'

She takes my hand in hers. 'My friend, you and I both know it is well past time. Where will you go?'

'I am heading to the maze,' I tell her.

'Good. Ariana had better listen to you.' Her face is fierce.

'How did you—'

'Oh, Percival, Ariana herself has wanted you to talk to her about the life of sprite-kind ever since she met you.' Ellie wipes the tears from her eyes.

I want to hug her, but she will not thank me for making her cry harder.

'There is a pack ready and waiting in the hall, I bought some of your things from Wimbledon. My girls are on their way here to take part in the coming war—except for Mae, who is staying behind to look after the children and creatures who have not come to join us.'

'Is she to be the new Witch of Wimbledon?' I tease.

'Temporary Witch of Wimbledon.' She winks, then waves me off, 'Go grab your things. You don't want to keep everyone waiting.' She sniffs and smiles.

When I return with the pack, Ellie is making the tea, her back turned to me. I know she will not like a long goodbye, but I cannot simply leave.

'Ellie, there are no words I can say that will express how grateful I am for the years you allowed me to indulge myself. You are the best friend anyone creature could ask for.'

'It is what friends do,' she says in a tear-choked voice.

I place the pack on the floor and close the distance between us, standing patiently beside her.

Finally, she turns, bends, and hugs me. 'I didn't think it would be so hard when you left. We have done so much together...'

'And we will do so again,' I tell her as I squeeze her. 'Take care, and do not do anything reckless.'

I step from her embrace and walk away, aware there is nothing and also so much more to say.

Nisha waits by the door. In her face I find understanding and love, and it almost undoes me. My years of cat life were so much easier than this, and yet, they were also so much less.

Clearly aware of my fragile hold on my emotions, Nisha touches my arm and says, 'Stay safe, and stay strong.'

I nod. 'Until we are together again.'

With that, she disappears inside, leaving me with Heart and Alyce.

Taking a couple of deep breaths to steady myself, I force myself forward. 'Right, let us be on our way.'

CHAPTER 5

Taking a Stand

The ex-wizard, Alyce, transports me to an internal courtyard in the Minotaur's palace, narrowly missing dropping us in the water fountain as we land on the rim. I quickly jump down, and she disappears almost instantly to pick up Heart. Before she returns, a figure joins me.

'Percival, I did not think to find you back here,' Fairburn, the Captain of the Queen's Guard, says.

'You mean after you tricked us into going to the Unseelie Court while refusing to tell Pris about her family connection to the King?' I ask tartly, but I'm too heartsore to put any genuine anger into my words.

The centaur shifts uneasily, his hooves clattering on the tiles. How had I not heard him approach? He must have used magic to hide his hoofbeats.

'I promised her parents I would allow them to tell her about her family.'

Fairburn, although honourable, should have known that sending Pris to the Unseelie court without warning her of her grandmother's presence or that the King was her uncle would lead to problems.

'How is the Queen?' I ask, changing the subject.

'Maddox, Euphemia, and three dragons are with her. I am told it will take time to reawaken her. Then more time to cleanse her body of the poisons she has taken on for the good of our realms.'

There is a touch of sadness, and maybe a little fear, in Fairburn's voice. I study him from under lowered lashes. He seems more attached to the Queen than he once was—more attached than a Captain of the Queen's Guard should be. The Queen's husband died long enough ago for them to form a close friendship—or even something more. I refrain from comment; what goes on between them is their business.

'Are we talking hours? Days? Weeks? There is a war brewing—one the queen herself could stop by making an appearance and taking control of the situation.'

'Percival, do not be disingenuous—the Baaronson faction has gone beyond falling back into line once the Queen is better.'

His words ring true, but there is a large part of me that wishes it were otherwise, that there was a simple, non-violent solution to the impending war that is building. And still another part of me is aware that our realm needs a shake-up if lesser creatures are to gain our rights.

Once my friends and I were so passionate about change, we had put our futures on the line. Princess Ariana was there with us—back when we fought the blight. Our future Queen believed, as her sister did, that all creatures are created equal—although she was nowhere near as passionate about putting her ideas forward. As heir to the throne, she had to walk a tight political line.

Despite his attachment to the future Queen, our friend

Allard had gone with Mandor, Ellie, and Genie to test out opening a gate to the World Above. The rest of us stayed behind to cover their absence. Upon their return, the council imprisoned them. Drow eventually freed three of the four—everyone except Mandor. Someone had to be held responsible, and their leader was their scapegoat.

However, we only realised the extent of our trouble when Magnus Baaronson attacked us, dispersing us and preventing us from causing any further trouble.

Using an old statute against inter-creature relationships, Baaronson had Heart banished to the World Above. After being convicted of treason, Mandor was saved from execution by Professor Xander from the University, who spoke on his behalf. They offered him the option of life imprisonment or joining the Wizard Council. Ellie had begged him not to choose prison, but he believed Drow would find a way to free him.

Unbeknown to Mandor, Drow was feeling the failure of not being able to save me or Heart, and he had left the World Below for the Unseelie Court. Euphemia had already taken up her position as Witch Protector of the North, and she offered to introduce him to the King.

In the meantime, the council appointed Ellie and Genie to positions in the World Above. Although it broke Seraphina's heart, she sent her daughters off with her blessing. She had worked with Magnus Baaronson for long enough to realise they were safer away from home.

Although Ariana's support of us weakened her position at court, she insisted on marrying Allard, which might have been what saved him from punishment. As for me, I had returned to my home, the grove in the Wyld Woods, to lick my wounds. I tried to fit in, but I was still angry about my treatment.

Finally, Nisha had taken me aside and suggested that I

might be more useful helping Ellie settle into her new position in the World Above. After a while I agreed, and I'd arrived on Ellie's doorstep with a letter from Mandor and curled up in Ellie's lap as she read it out loud.

My Darling Ellie,

You told me I should choose to live my life over rotting away in prison. I have followed your wishes, and I am with the wizards.

I have done what you asked. Now I ask you to do something for me. Live your life. Do everything we talked about doing—have a family and build a dynasty.

I will always love you, and one day, I hope we will meet again as friends.

Mandor

Drenched by Ellie's tears for the life she would never have, I had shared her grief. Together we helped each other with our losses, and we built a life in the World Above. Although we kept our connections with the World Below, our passion for change had slowly died.

When Ariana was crowned and took her place on the throne a hundred years ago, we'd hoped this might be our time again. She had started out with a great deal of promise. Then Allard died in a hunting accident, and something died inside our friend. Without her husband by her side, she became afraid to rock the boat lest it sink.

We understood her reaction, and we did what we could to help her. In the end, she lost faith in herself and left more and more of the day-to-day ruling to her Chancellor and cousin, Elias. This left a power vacuum that Bernais was more than happy to fill. If we had come back and helped Ariana earlier, would we have been able to avoid all of this?

'A song for your thoughts?' Heart's voice draws me from examining my guilt.

My head snaps up to meet his eyes. For a moment I'd almost forgotten where I was, so lost was I in my memories. I am in the Minotaur's home… and there's Fairburn talking with Alyce.

I offer my old friend a sad smile. 'I don't think they're worth a song, Heart. Besides, who would want to hear a lament for our lost ideals and the time we wasted getting ready to challenge everything that is wrong in our realm?'

Heart chuckles. 'Wow, Percival, if I had known you reconciling with Nisha would do this to you, I would never have pushed you into it.'

'Percival, Heart,' Aeron rumbles from behind us. 'Have you ever considered that the reason creatures enjoy such a long life is to give us time to come around to doing the right thing?'

Aeron joins us by the water fountain as Heart says, 'Perhaps, but it may also be so we have time to repair our mistakes.'

The Minotaur's laugh comes straight from his belly and soothes my heart.

'Percival, I was not told you were coming. I am having a room prepared for you, but in the meantime, I have a young princess who has been here since early this morning and would probably appreciate the opportunity to spend some time with her friend.'

'Pris is here?' I ask somewhat redundantly.

'She is. Up the top of the stairs and to your left—the room with the guard outside the door.'

I pause.

Heart raises a brow. 'Go ahead. I may have to wait some time for Snake before I leave.'

He does not need to tell me twice. I am up the stairs in the blink of an eye. The guard opens the door, revealing a pacing, pale Pris. She eagerly turns as I enter the room, then, perhaps seeing it is just me, her shoulders slump.

'I am sorry. Were you expecting someone else?' I ask, a little hurt by her reaction.

'Oh, Percival, I didn't mean to be rude.' She takes a step towards me, and for a moment, I think she is going to give me a hug. When she doesn't, I side-step her and make my way to the sofa in the middle of the room.

She joins me, and there is a smile tugging at the edge of her lips, as if she knows I rushed here and that I am pleased to see her alive and well.

'You look good, Percival.'

'Better than you do,' I say, concern for her gnawing at my gut. 'Are you not fully recovered from your injuries?'

'Yes—well, almost. It's just....' She runs a hand across her forehead as her brows draw downwards. 'It's just I felt a change in the air, and I'd hoped....'

She walks over to the window, and the light nighttime breeze ruffles her white hair. Now that she mentions it, something is different. I allow my natural barriers down and find the air is heavy with magic—healing magic. Has this been going on all day? A single glance at Pris, who is unaccustomed to defending herself against such enchanting accumulations, shows that it has. That she is not unconscious on the sofa suggests Aeron has taken steps to ensure her safety.

As I rebuild my walls, the magic drifts away, which suggests that the creatures with the Queen are no longer using it. *Is that good or bad?*

Pris stiffens before turning to me, her eyes bright with

unshed tears. 'Am'ratha says the Queen is waking.' Pris staggers towards the room's central sofa and collapses onto it. 'She is alive. I don't have to be Queen.'

'You do not have to be Queen? Who said you needed to be?' The words escape before I can bite them back. 'What have they been doing to you in the day or so that we have been apart?'

So, this is what having the stuffing knocked out of you feels like, I think while another part of my brain recognises that Percival is working himself into a fury on my behalf. I mentally shake myself and focus on answering Percival's question.

'The Queen of Dragons said I was the next in line to the throne, and, should Queen Ariana not recover, I would have to step up.'

Percival raises himself to his full height, which isn't much over four feet. 'How dare she! What about your mother?'

I lean my head back against the sofa and stare at the ceiling, unable to rouse the anger or the fear that kept me keyed up all day as I waited to find out my fate. A voice inside my head niggles, saying, *It might still be your fate,* reminding me that I'm still in the line of succession and the Queen waking has merely delayed the inevitable.

Percival crosses the distance between us and takes one of my hands in his. 'Pris, what is it? You have gone over all pale.'

I rouse myself for long enough to answer. 'I might not have to be Queen now, but I might have to be someday, if only to stop Bernais Baaronson from taking the throne.'

Letting go of my hand, Percival stands in front of me. 'Why don't you tell me what has been going on with you since you arrived in the World Between?'

His stare is so intense, and I sense there is more behind his question than idle curiosity. The door opens, and a brownie brings in a tray of tea and small sandwiches. He places it on the low table in front of the sofa, then withdraws.

'Tea?' I ask, raising a frown from Percival. I suspect he will demand a response, but he breathes out and moves aside so I can pour.

By the time I hand him a mug, he is sitting on the sofa, an expectant look on his face. I sit beside him, take a sip of soothing chamomile, then tell him about my interview with the Dragon Queen, finishing with her expectation that I will take over royal duties.

I didn't know what to expect from Percival, but I definitely didn't expect him to have no reaction at all. He stares into his tea, not moving.

'Percival? Are you okay?' I reach out to take his cup as his head jerks up.

'We creatures have made a mess of things, have we not?' He looks away, and it's quiet in the room again.

The weight of Percival's sorrow hangs heavy in the air. I reach out and touch his shoulder. When he doesn't move away, I rub his arm.

'The past is the past,' I tell him. 'What is important now is how we move forward.'

My words are platitudes, but I hope they help.

Percival slowly shakes his head. 'I have been dwelling on the past since I arrived, and it has made me... melancholy. And you are right—we need to act. It really is time we helped Ariana understand that we must change if our world is to survive.'

The sprite's words are full of a determination and a sense of certainty that is new to my friend. Something has galvanised him into action.

'Percival, what's going on out there?'

While I sip my drink and nibble on sandwiches, Percival tells me of the rebellion brewing in every corner of the World Below. It seems Bernais Baaronson's council coup lit the fuse of a powder keg that has been threatening to explode for years.

The group I'd encountered in the World Between is just the tip of the iceberg. Wizards have defected from their order, the lesser creatures—or should I say the *cultivator* creatures—are standing against creator creature domination, and many in the villages have decided to stand with them.

'A slow shift back to the old ways, or the good old days, as the Baaronson's would have it, had been tolerated. When they forced the pace of change in Queen Ariana's absence, years of resentment boiled over, and now there will be civil war.

'Creatures want things to change, Pris, and they are willing to fight for it.' His gaze is full of determination.

Things really are a mess. It's not just about kicking out Bernais Baaronson and putting Queen Ariana back on the throne. The people of the World Below want change.

'I guess I shouldn't worry about being Queen because it doesn't sound like there'll be a throne for me to ascend to,' I say, my voice dry.

Percival snorts a laugh. 'Yes, I think that is the least of our worries. Drow and Mandor will arrive here soon with a petition to present to the Queen. It says something like,

"We will help restore you to the throne, but we want concessions."'

'You think she'll sign it?' I ask.

Percival shakes his head. 'I do not know. I would like to say yes because I know a young Ariana would have supported the sentiments. But a lot of water has passed under the bridge, and I am not sure where she sits—'

'Still on her throne, but somewhat restrained,' a familiar voice from the door interrupts. 'Excellent, you have tea.'

Euphemia sweeps by me, King Maddox trailing in her wake. She reaches down and places her hands around the teapot. I sense a whisper of magic, then she pours herself and Maddox a cup each. Euphemia sits beside Percival. I say nothing, waiting for them to speak as Maddox drifts over to the balcony doors, his gaze distant as he drinks.

'How is Ariana?' Percival asks.

Euphemia's chest rises and falls as she takes some deep breaths before responding. 'She will recover. She needs food and rest, but she should be back on her feet in a couple of days.'

Relief floods every fibre of my being, and I release a heavy breath. The Queen is alive. She will take back her throne and give her creatures the change they want.

'And then?' Percival asks.

'Then she and I must cleanse magic as we were supposed to do,' Maddox answers.

'What?' I demand, my blood running cold as the implications of this hit me. 'What about going to the Capitol and reclaiming her throne?'

Maddox's face tenses with stubborn resolve. 'You heard me, niece. The Queen of Dragons has demanded we uphold our side of the bargain and sort out the problem with magic once and for all. If we don't start work immediately, she will close off the World Between forever.'

'What about removing Bernais? What about my parents? What about the impending war?' Thoughts tumble from my mouth one after another.

Maddox runs a hand through his hair, accentuating the lines of weariness around his eyes. 'I believe you heard me. We must restore the flow of magic now or lose it forever.'

My jaw drops. Is magic more important than the loss of creature lives a war will bring? Perhaps my view is skewed by having grown up in a world without magic, but I think not.

Euphemia intervenes before I can argue my point. 'Pris, you must understand, dragons not only create magic, but they cannot survive without it. If we do not sort out the magical flow soon, they will close their borders to save themselves. The levels of magic in our worlds are so low that, when they do, magic will die here and in the World Above.'

The haunted look in my uncle's eyes reminds me that if magic dies out completely, the creatures locked in the Unseelie Court—the creatures he swore to protect—will be there for all eternity.

'Dammit!' I spit. Just when I see a way out of the mess, I get sucked even further into the mud. 'While you guys cleanse magic, we go to war. What happens if the Queen doesn't lead the creatures against Bernais? Will they accept her back as ruler once this is over?'

Maddox smiles, but it doesn't reach his eyes. 'The dragons suggest you should be her proxy while she cleanses the worlds. The Dragon Queen is impressed with you, niece.'

I'm not sure how to respond to that. It's exhausting always being the person everyone comes to. I just got out of school and haven't even had a chance to start my life, but now I'm expected to fix a problem that's been going on for centuries.

Percival places his hand on mine. 'Instead of looking at this as a death sentence, you could approach it as a once-in-a-lifetime opportunity to effect change.'

'Are you mad?' I hiss. 'No one is going to listen to me. They don't know who I am, and I'm not equipped for this.'

As I speak, a kernel of a thought forms in my mind. I know someone who has been fighting their whole life for the rights of others. Someone who the creatures of the World Below already know. I'm about to raise the idea when the doors burst open, admitting Snake and Drow.

'Snake, You're here.' I know I'm stating the obvious, but I'm so pleased to see him, I feel almost giddy with relief.

A nanosecond later, Drow demands, 'Have you initiated a coup?'

'What?' I look from one to the other, trying to make out what's going on.

A wry smile forms on Snake's lips. 'The Dragon Queen ordered us here because Queen Ariana has woken up. When we arrived, Ed'rathe told us to talk to you instead of the Queen.'

Percival slips off the sofa, holding his hands out in front of him as he tries to calm things down. 'I think you will find it is more to do with the Dragon Queen's orders than Pris's actions. In fact, we were about to discuss Pris's response, if you'd like to join us.'

Snake's eyes widen in surprise, but there is also concern in their depths, and all I want is to be alone with him to talk this through. Well, alone with him and Percival. Everyone else here has their own agendas, and none of them have my wellbeing at the centre.

'I'm sorry, but I need you all to leave—all of you except Snake and Percival.'

Drow voices his objection over Percival's head. 'But… but we have to—'

Euphemia rises from the couch and places her mug on the table. 'The princess has a lot to take in, and she has asked us to leave. The least we can do is give her space to think.'

Euphemia's glower stifles Drow's objections. I'd forgotten how empathetic Euphemia is. Her support warms my soul. Maddox follows the two of them out of the room. Once the door has closed behind them, Percival retakes his seat, and Snake, his eyes holding mine, crosses the room to stand in front of me.

He reaches out and cups my cheek, and I lean into his hand.

'Hey there, you,' he whispers quietly, and I feel some of the tension in my shoulders release.

I wrap my arms around his neck, needing the embrace. 'Hi back.'

His arms slip around my waist, and I feel him sigh against my hair.

After a moment, we step back from one another, and, hand in hand, we rejoin Percival on the sofa as Snake says, 'This mess is getting out of control.'

He sounds as weary as I feel.

***

There is a fragility about Pris that wasn't there when she left the caves this morning. Part of it will no doubt have come from the heavy magical energy in the air. It's almost suffocating.

I squeeze Pris's hand. 'How are you coping with all the magic swirling around?'

A smile tugs at her lips. 'Aeron taught me to create a shield.'

I draw a little magic to reach out and test the barrier. It's solid, and I'm suddenly very grateful to the Minotaur, although not so grateful that I've forgotten that he was planning to kill me not that long ago.

'So, Pris, what's going on?'

She closes her eyes and sinks back into the sofa, and it's Percival who answers my question.

'The dragons are demanding Queen Ariana and King Maddox fix magic in the two realms before doing anything about the political crisis facing us all.'

'And,' I prompt.

'And they want Pris to act as regent.'

Pris removes her hand, stands up, and makes her way to the window, leaning her forehead against the glass. I move to join her, but Percival shakes his head. I'm so pleased to have the old team back together, I heed his advice, and we wait in silence for her to speak.

'This isn't my problem to solve,' she finally says. 'Until a few weeks ago, I was happy living my life away from these centuries-old feuds and disagreements. If I had my way, Snake and I would walk out of here and leave you all to it.'

Feeling a sudden warmth inside at knowing she would choose me over the Crown, I respond in kind. 'Say the word, and we're outta here.'

'Huh, as if you could,' Percival says. 'Your parents did not bring either of you up to run away from a fight simply because it is not yours.'

Pris slowly releases a breath. 'No, they didn't, but they didn't encourage me to poke my nose into other's business either.'

'Still, here we are.' He crosses his legs, trying to appear casual. 'If you had carte blanche, what would you do to solve this little dilemma?' he asks.

Oh, he's good. I can see the cogs working in Pris's mind as she attempts to solve this puzzle.

'I don't know…. I've never lived here, so I'm not sure I'm qualified, but… perhaps using lessons from the World Above.…. Mmm…. History teaches us that countries run by an oligarchy or a dictatorship often do not treat minorities well.'

I get where she's going with this. 'The most stable societies let all adults have some say in the government.'

Pris turns from the window, her gaze now more thoughtful. 'Mum often comments on how many refugees flee their homes because, rather than listen to them, their government has persecuted them, and they no longer feel a part of the community.'

Pris is coming back to life before my eyes, and she's sweeping me along with her.

'Much like Verona and the creatures in the World Between.'

Pris nods. 'Yes. They feel the council doesn't speak for them.'

'As do many of the creatures who cultivate and care for our land,' Percival adds.

'Any solution we fight for must allow all creatures to have a say in who represents them,' Pris announces.

'I believe that *is* what Drow's petition suggests,' Percival says.

Pris takes a step towards us, her eyes bright with excitement. 'I would go one step further. I would see the council ruling the World Below and the Queen being perhaps one vote on that council.'

'What if the role of Queen weren't just ceremonial, but more like the Vice-President of the United States? She would have the ability to cast a deciding vote when the council is deadlocked,' Snake suggests.

'And if we separate the legal court and the royal court…,' Pris muses.

'Whoa, slow down,' Percival interjects. 'This is more of a long-term vision. I'm not sure the World Below is ready for such radical change.'

A frown draws Pris's brows together. 'You did ask what future I might imagine.'

I resist the urge to support her with a 'Yeah,' because I understand what Percival is doing. He has inspired Pris to take a position. Now he's probably wanting her to find something achievable she can lead people to embrace. Something Queen Ariana will be compelled to endorse when she's back in charge.

Pris's shoulders drop, and she turns away. 'They're only ideas. Anyway, it doesn't matter because I am not the heir to the throne. My mother is. And I believe she should be the one to take this on.'

'What?' Percival and I say together.

Pris's chin juts out as she raises her head. 'Everyone is so keen to push me onto the throne, but they've forgotten my mother is actually next in line.'

'But…,' Percival splutters.

'I know. She's locked in the palace. But that doesn't mean we can't find out what she wants to do.'

I beam at Pris, proud of the solution she has found to our problem. Percival still looks confused. Pris takes a seat between us and turns to him.

'This is the perfect solution, Percival. Queen Ariana is

part of the problem.' She holds up a hand. 'I get that she's your friend, but it's the truth. Even if she agrees to the petition, she has been so focussed on keeping magic alive that she has done very little to help creature-kind, which means many will question her true commitment to change.'

'I guess that might happen,' Percival reluctantly admits.

'Besides,' Pris continues, 'when this is over, her role will be to bring everyone together, including the elves. If my mother negotiates a deal and sets things in motion, then Queen Ariana can say she was forced into this position, and she will work with everyone to produce a compromise. She will be seen as the one healing the nation.'

Percival stares at his hands while he considers Pris's proposal. 'Can you explain to me why it has to be your mother and not you?'

Pris smiles wanly. 'Because she was born here. Because she left so she could be with my dad. Because this is what she's passionate about, and now I know why. And mostly because she will do it so much better than me.'

'How can she lead us all from captivity?' I ask.

Pris's brows draw into a frown. 'Well, obviously we use the dragons for communication—' she starts, then stops. 'Oh. Of course. This was what Gregor was talking about. The groups fighting Bernais are so diverse. We need someone to bring them together—a figurehead. A unifying force.'

'He was asking you?' Percival asks.

'He was asking *us*—Snake and me,' she tells him.

'It's because our quest has captured everyone's hearts,' I add. 'But—'

'You must do it, both of you,' Percival says with such conviction, it's difficult to argue with him. 'You're the future of our world.'

He is so earnest, I can't help but grin at him, ready to join him on the battlefield. Then I remember my promise to the Dragon Queen. 'I've sort of promised the dragons I will act as ambassador to them.'

Pris's and Percival's heads turn in unison 'What?'

'Gregor wanted me to act as poster boy for their cause, and he almost had me convinced. I wanted to talk to you first, Pris, 'cause I know you've been under pressure, but the dragons stepped in and offered me a solution. They want me to act as a go-between for the dissidents and the dragons.'

Pris frowns again. 'Percival, I thought the dragons didn't interfere in creature politics.'

Percival taps his finger on his leg and stares into the distance. 'It is unusual… but… I'm wondering if the state of magic has become so bad, they feel they have to inter-vene. I mean, if they are threatening to withdraw from the worlds… perhaps this is them showing they are giving us a chance.'

The room falls silent. The only noise is the tap-tap-tapping of Percival's finger against his leg. Finally, he says, 'I think the dragons deserve our consideration, and at the very least, they should be kept abreast of our activities.'

'I agree,' Pris says. 'Especially if we want them to aid our communication with my mother and one another.'

The two of them look at me as if waiting for my input. I agree with them, but I have reservations, mainly about my being the person placed in that role, but that is not my only concern.

'What is it, Snake?' Pris asks, quick to see my discomfort.

I suck in a breath, trying to relax before I voice my fears. 'I feel like events are controlling you and me again. You're going to be a spokesperson for your mother if she agrees to our plan, and I am going to be ambassador to the freaking dragons, for goodness sake. I want to say no, but I can't walk away either, even though every fibre of my being wants to return home.'

Pris reaches for my hand as Percival rises to his feet and begins pacing. Her fingers wrap around mine, and I draw some comfort from the gesture.

'Are you only staying because of us…. Because of me?' she whispers.

I shake my head. 'No—well yes, in part. But mostly I'm thinking about staying because I can't go back to my old life knowing what's happening here. If I do, then I am just as bad as the Baaronsons and their faction.'

Percival stops moving and turns to us. 'I feel sorry for the two of you, I really do, but I don't think this is exactly "happening" *to* you. I believe it's happening *because* of you. When Bernais took your parents, it was the beginning of his attack on the main power structure of our world. He believed it would crumble. Then the two of you came charging in to save your parents, putting a spanner in the works, so to speak.'

I turn the thought over in my mind as Pris says, 'Are you saying this coming war is our fault?'

Percival hides a cough that sounds suspiciously like a chuckle behind his hand. 'Well, I guess I am. If you and Snake had not come here, I believe Bernais would have succeeded in slowly relieving the Queen of her power. Instead, several very senior officials found themselves thrown together, trying to prevent Bernais from hurting you two. Keeping you safe and out of Bernais's clutches galvanised them into action, nudged them into working together to use the two of you to save the Queen. Your interference set all of this in motion.'

'And it was only the three of us who could have motivated those hiding out in the Unseelie Court to join the battle,' I add, understanding dawning.

Percival smiles. 'And your heroics inspired the discontented youth to stand up and fight, because if you could take on the establishment, so could they.'

I grimace as Pris's grip on my fingers tightens. Rather than soothing her concerns, Percival's theory has increased her anxiety level. I untangle her fingers and wrap an arm around her.

'Whether we're being buffeted by the winds of change or we're stirring them up, we're here now. If we work together, the three of us, we can at least channel the winds in a direction we're happy going in,' I say as I lean my head against hers.

'And when this is over? Where does that leave us all?' she asks.

'Hopefully together.'

She leans into me, and I want to stay holding her forever.

'So,' Percival starts, 'I'm going to go and make sure the proposal Drow has with him meets our needs and then figure out how we get it to Cecily.'

Pris pulls away from me. 'And I must talk with my mother and get her on board.'

'Do you want me to stay?' I ask.

'I want you to, but I think this is a conversation we'd best have on our own—well, on our own with our dragons.'

I rub her shoulder before reluctantly pushing myself to my feet. 'I'll leave you to it, then?'

She nods. 'Wish me luck.'

'You won't need it. This is a good plan.'

'But I don't feel good asking because—'

'You think you're using her to get out of doing this yourself?' I finish for her.

'Yes.' The word is a whisper.

'Do you honestly believe she's the best person to do this?' I ask. 'Because if you don't, there is still time for you to do it yourself. Percival and I will be here to support you if that's your decision.'

Her eyes slide to the side as she considers this. 'No, this is the right way to do it. I don't have what it takes to change the World Below—Mum does. It's like she's been training for this her whole life.' She looks at me, her eyes shining with wonder.

A smile tugs at the corner of my lips. 'Perhaps she has,' I tell her. 'But you'll never know unless you have that conversation.'

'Okay…. Something else to consider.' She grabs a hand as I turn to go. 'You're not leaving the maze, are you?' There is a note of panic in her voice.

'I'll be nearby,' I reassure her.

'Thank you,' she mouths as she shoos us both from the room.

CHAPTER 6

Who's Leading Who?

Percival opens the door, and Snake follows, then turns to me. 'Are you sure you want me to go? I can sit here in silent support.'

His mouth quirks upwards, and his half grin is so adorable, I almost change my mind. Before I allow myself the luxury of the distraction he would be, I shake my head. 'I appreciate the thought, but I think I need to do this alone.'

'Of course. Tell Am'ratha if you need me, and I'll come back.'

The door clicks shut behind him, and I allow myself a couple of minutes to clear my mind before reaching out to my dragon friend. Once our normal greetings have been dispensed with, I get straight to the point.

Am'ratha, if I wanted to talk to my mother, is there a way you and Am'rena can do that?

You mean other than our relaying your conversation? Am'ratha's tone is so dry, I imagine her raising a single eyebrow in disdain.

I think about it for a moment, then agree that that's exactly what I mean.

There is, but I will have to link my mind to yours, and Am'rena will have to link with your mother.

My mood lifts. Finally something is going in my favour. **Cool. Can we do that, then?**

Not so fast. If we do this, I will have full access to your mind—your thoughts, your memories, your dreams, your hopes, and your desires. No, don't answer immediately. Think about whether you are happy with anyone knowing that much about you.

But you can read my mind now.

True. But you can put up barriers, and I can choose whether to read your thoughts. I will have no choice if we do this.

Oh.

Yes, oh. And for this to work, your mother must agree to the same situation with her dragon. As they have only spent a short amount of time together since your mother left the World Below, they might feel uncomfortable being that close.

As with all magic, there is a downside. I've known Am'ratha long enough to know that my dragon friend will not rifle through my mind if we were to do this, but she would still be a part of me, a part of my consciousness.

Hold on a minute. If you pick up things from me and my private conversation during this process, do you have to report it back to your Queen?

That depends.

On what?

Well, everything is deemed private unless you

are threatening the World Between—that I would have no option but to act on.

I would never do anything like that, I reassure Am'ratha.

Not knowingly, Royal One.

Okay, just so we're clear.

I should be all right on that front, but the reasons for possibly not doing this are building. *Dammit.* I can't risk this conversation being misunderstood because someone else is filtering our words. Why don't they have phones here? I hope I'm doing the right thing and that it doesn't backfire on us.

Am'ratha, would you ask Am'rena if my mother with speak mind-to-mind with me?

As you wish, Royal One.

My mind goes quiet as Am'ratha chats with Am'rena. I use the bell on the table to summon a servant. He agrees to bring more tea and is just returning with a tray laden with a teapot and a tiered plate of sandwiches, savouries, and cakes when Am'ratha returns to my mind.

Royal One, your mother asks if this level of communication is necessary? Am'rena has been keeping her updated with news from our Queen and from Queen Ariana. She sends that it would have to be something surpassingly important for her to consider mind-merging with Am'rena.

Dammit. Of course it's important. I'm not exactly looking forward to this myself.

Perhaps rather than blaspheming, you could give her an idea of the purpose of the conversation, Am'ratha suggests, but rather than criticism, I sense amusement in her tone.

Given how often Am'ratha picks up on my thoughts, merging our minds might not be too challenging. My dragon friend's chuckle reverberates in my skull before she says, **You have no idea how difficult this will be for you. Another presence in your head is uncomfortable and disconcerting to say the least.**

My gut ties itself in knots as I think about Am'ratha having full access to me, and I wonder if maybe we could do this via the dragons.

Tell my mother this has to do with the future of the land. If that isn't important enough to take this step, then I don't know what is.

A sense of pride in my strength filters through the bond as Am'ratha leaves my mind. While I wait for Am'ratha to return, I pour myself some tea and nibble on a cake, my stomach churning too much to eat anything more.

They agree.

I slowly release my breath. **Good, now how do we do this?**

It is best if you lie down and make yourself comfortable.

Odd, but I guess I can do that. Before I stretch out on the sofa, I position my tea and the rest of my cake on the table. As I study the cornice work on the ceiling, I try to relax.

I am ready.

Without any warning, I feel tendrils of... *alienness* worm through my head. My first instinct is to fight them, push them out. It takes all my concentration to let them in. Just as my head feels like it's about to break apart, the movement stops. I'm pleased I'm lying down because the excess weight would have had me keeling over.

Then pain assaults me, like my mind has been flayed open, followed by the shouting of strange voices. As I open my mouth to scream for it to stop, I am suddenly in a...

void? The pressure is still in my head, and there is a roaring in my ears. It's like holding my breath underwater.

Breathe, Princess. That's it. Nice and slow.

I count in—one, two, three… and out. My heart rate slows, and the panic recedes.

Now, we will concentrate on the conversation. You must forget I am here. Doing both those things should keep the noise of my mind from intruding and overwhelming you.

Okay. The thought is a whisper.

Are you ready? Yes, I can tell you are. Please be quick, as the longer we are like this, the longer the side effects will last.

Side effects? Am'ratha, you didn't mention side effects.

Pris, is that you?

Mum? Mum's voice is so clear in my mind, I'm overwhelmed with longing to see her, to touch her. The pressure builds in my ears, and I remember Am'ratha's words—concentrate on the conversation.

Yes, Pris, I'm here. What is it you needed to talk about?

Are you okay?

Yes, your father and I are fine for the moment. Tell Snake his mother, Ginth, is also all right. Bernais's men surround the castle, but our defences have not been breached. But you didn't go to all this trouble for an update, Pris.

Although I am happy my and Snake's families are unharmed, the almost unbearable pressure in my head, along with my mother's tone, force me to get on with the main event. **No, Mum, I didn't. I guess you know Queen Ariana is awake.**

Yes.

And do you also know what the dragons want me to do?

Yes.

I pause for a moment, hoping my mother will say something like, 'Don't worry, Pris, this isn't your fight. We have a plan.' There is nothing.

We have another idea.

We?

Snake, Percival, and I. We believe we can win the coming battle if we pull all the factions fighting Bernais together, but we need your help.

Mmm, and what about Ariana and the Dragon Queen? What do they think?

Our plan involves more of an 'ask for forgiveness than permission' approach.

Okaaay. And what is my involvement in this?

Well, you're at the centre of it.

When Mum doesn't respond, I outline how we want her to agree to enact the constitutional changes that we will proclaim in her name to galvanise the forces should we win this war.

And what about our ruler, the actual Queen?

Percival is going to work on her. He says she always broadly agreed with a move to a more democratic form of government, so we're just providing her with cover.

I wait for her reaction.

And you're hoping that by the time Ariana is back on the throne, she won't be able to reverse the changes.

I grin. Mum always picks up on nuances. **Yes.**

Another silence. Maybe the delay is because Mum is keeping Dad in the loop.

And you are aware that if I do this, I am

accepting my place back in the royal line of succession, which means—

That I will also be in line for the throne? That we're making a commitment to giving up our lives and staying in the World Below?

When I discussed the solution with Percival and Snake, this hadn't seemed like a big thing. Talking to Mum about tearing our lives apart is next level.

Pris? Are you okay with that? Your father and I have always known this day might come, but we hadn't even had an opportunity to introduce you to your heritage before we were kidnapped.

She wants me to reassure her that keeping me from my family and my birthright was okay. I can't because the truth is, I'm still completely pissed that she and dad kept me in the dark and that I've had to feel my way blindfolded through this world.

We can talk about your parenting skills when this is over, Mum. In the meantime, we all have to do what is right for the creatures of this world and the World Above.

There is another pause, and this time I know for sure she is talking with Dad, possibly because my heightened senses are able to read her better—but more likely it's because Mum's tone of thought leads me to believe she's tiptoeing around me. Dad's always been better at handling me when I'm being 'emotional,' so they'll be strategising.

I've spoken with my mother, and she will never return to the World Below, so I am afraid if we want to keep the throne from Adina and Bernais, then you and I *will* have to step up.

The Dragon Queen as good as told me that.

Interesting. I must decide whether to take the reins and rule in a way you and I can agree on, or

whether I should do what I know Ariana would prefer....

What Ariana would prefer? Would she prefer to keep things as they are and potentially lose her Crown? I suppress the idea before it can take hold.

Mum, is there really any question?

I mentally cross my fingers, hoping I've called it correctly.

No, I guess not. It's just... we might send the realm into further turmoil.

It's already spinning out of control and splitting into factions. If we don't pull everyone towards a common goal, then Ariana won't have a realm to rule when she returns.

I sense Mum's tension through our bond, and it adds to the pressure in my head.

Mum, we're going to work with as many groups as we can out here to build a new base of support for the Crown. In order to do that, we have to be sure we can promise them real change —definite changed. This is the only way we have enough power and numbers to stand up to Bernais.

And if you do it in my name, you have legitimacy, and we have continuity of power should anything happen to one of us when you speak for me.

Yes.

Okay then, Pris. Let's do this. Am'rena will come and pick up the agreement for me to sign.

Relief almost overwhelms me, and for a second, I'm again aware of Am'ratha in my mind, before I concentrate on Mum and my dragon fades into the background.

Great. And Mum.

Yes?

We *are* going to have to talk about what you kept from me once this is over.

I know, hon. In the meantime, keep yourself safe so we can have that conversation.

You too.

Love you, Pris.

Love you, too, Mum.

That is as close as my mum gets to being mushy. If I'd known she'd been brought up as a royal princess, I would have understood her need to be proper earlier.

Are you ready? Am'ratha asks.

For what?

Suddenly, the pressure in my head recedes, and the room spins. I barely make it to the bathroom before my stomach empties. After, I sink to the ground and lean my head against the cool marble at the base of the basin, wondering how long it will take to get over the worst hangover ever.

⋯⋅•❥•⋅⋯

'For goodness sake, Snake, would you sit down,' Heart snaps. 'She'll come find us when she's ready.'

I scowl at my grandfather. He glowers back.

'Come and help Percival and me sort this agreement out,' Uncle Drow suggests. 'We could use your help.'

I close my eyes, praying for the strength to deal with my family. In the end, I take a seat at the table. It's been a long day. I'm tired, and I don't have the energy to argue.

'There is nothing in there that says it must be Queen Ariana who agrees to the terms,' Percival says absently, flicking pages. 'In fact, isn't Princess Cecily a better signatory because Queen Ariana is going to be recuperating or working on restoring magic for the foreseeable future?'

Drow drags a hand through his hair, causing it to stand on end, which gives him even more of a mad professor air. 'All the creatures thought the Queen was signing it.'

They have been going round and round this argument for the past half an hour, neither one giving an inch. My head is spinning, and I let out a groan. The three creatures around the table stare at me.

'What?' I snark.

Heart pats my hand, and guilt turns my stomach contents to acid.

'I just don't get it. Whoever signs the paper, the creatures will get a more democratic form of government if this works out. What does it matter whether it's Queen Ariana or Pris's mother who provides it?' I demand. 'Or whether Pris leads the army or doesn't?'

'But the Queen…,' Drow starts.

'Let me handle Ariana,' Percival says. 'And no one, not even the dragons, can object to Cecily becoming regent, as she is next in the line of succession. And no one can object to Pris acting in her mother's name if Cecily agrees to it. And if there are objections from the World Between, I'm sure Snake can manage those.'

My heart beats faster as I realise he's alluding to Princess Adina. He wants me to handle that viper? It didn't cross my mind that she might be there when I next meet with the Dragon Queen.

'This conversation might be moot if Pris can't get her mother to say yes,' I offer hopefully.

'Pris did get her mother onside,' a voice says from behind me.

I'm on my feet in a heartbeat, and my arms are around Pris seconds later.

'You look terrible,' I say, only half joking. She's grey, and her body trembles in my arms.

As I lead her to the table, I detect a trace of flowers and mint. Has she showered?

She sinks into a chair.

Percival pours her a glass of juice from the pitcher on the table and passes it to her. 'Here, drink this. It will help restore your equilibrium.'

Pris turns green as she picks up the glass. 'I can't.' She places it back on the table.

Percival nudges the drink closer. 'You can, and you should. I promise you will feel better with some sugar in your system.'

She takes a tentative sip, then a smile brightens her face, and she drinks the lot down before extending her glass for more. After she's drained her third glass, she appears done as she pushes the empty vessel away.

'Mum agreed to step up. She also agreed to the changes that will remodel the government of the World Below into a democratically elected council as soon as Bernais is ousted, followed by taking steps to move to a constitutional monarchy.'

'Then it is done,' Percival announces. 'We just need to get her to sign the document.'

Drow frowns. 'I really want to talk with the others about this… this change.'

Pris turns to me, eyebrows raised.

'Wait,' I mouth.

'Perhaps you could hold off on that until I have spoken to Queen Ariana. I have a meeting with her in the morning,' Percival suggests.

'A great idea,' Pris agrees. 'We could get together for lunch and make plans from there.'

Drow purses his lips as if preparing ready to disagree. Although he is getting what he wants for the various factions, he is such a stickler for detail, and not having the Queen endorse the treaty clearly does not sit well with him.

'Drow, Percival is going to get the Queen's approval for this plan, and that is as good as her signing the treaty,' I tell him.

He puffs out a sigh. 'I know, but so much could go wrong between winning the war and Ariana taking back control. There are other factions in the Capitol who can get to her and change her mind before she implements anything. We have walked this path before.'

Percival pats his hand. 'We won't let that happen, old friend.'

'Besides, don't we want to bring those factions on board once this is over?' Pris adds. 'Leaving them out will only provide them with an excuse not to support the changes.'

'And keeping Queen Ariana out of it means she hasn't allied with either side, and she becomes the perfect creature to negotiate the peace,' I finish up.

Drow looks at me, eyes wide with surprise.

'What? I have a brain and an education.'

Holding up his hands in surrender, Drow says, 'All right, all right. Your reasoning is sound. It's just that I haven't got anyone's agreement on the changes.

'Everyone trusts you to do the best for them,' Percival says.

'If that's settled, then? I'm exhausted.' Pris stands up, and her chair scrapes against the tiled floor. 'Aeron has kindly invited me to stay the night, and I'm turning in.'

She smiles at the others before capturing my eyes, and the message is clear—*Come with me.*

Heat rises in my cheeks. Everyone else probably gets the message, too, but I don't care. I take her hand and allow her to pull me to my feet.

'I'll escort you to your suite—you never know what might be lurking in the corridors,' I say as Heart mimes throwing up.

'I won't be long,' I tell my grandfather before following Pris from the room.

I've barely closed the door when Pris swings around, her eyes questioning. 'I won't be long?'

I tug her towards me, wrapping my arms around her. Was it only last night we were together? It seems like so long ago. Or perhaps that was a dream.

I rest my head against hers and say, 'I'm sorry, but I promised my grandfather that Ed'rathe and I would take him to visit his family.'

She stiffens in my arms. 'You're going? We're on the verge of war, and you're leaving me to face this alone?'

'This isn't just a family reunion. Heart's going to the deep Wyld Woods to convince the villages there to support the revolt against Bernais. Because of their distance from the Capitol, the villages have often ignored what is going on in the rest of the World Below, but Gregor thinks their numbers could change the tide in our favour.'

She relaxes. 'Sorry. I'm so emotionally strung out. I'd hoped we could be together tonight and… talk.'

I can't help the grin that lifts my mouth and my spirits. Mindful of the guard outside her room only two doors down, I whisper, 'Are you sure it's talking you want to do?'

Her laugh is breathless. She shifts in my arms and kisses my cheek. 'Although a repeat performance would be… nice… magic assaulted me for most of the day, then

I've been pulled through a magical ringer tonight. I think anything strenuous would break me. Besides, it's moot. You've other commitments.'

Standing there with her in my arms, I wish I hadn't told Heart we'd transport him into the woods. It's bad enough that escalating tensions mean I must report back to the Dragon Queen, if not tomorrow morning, then at least tomorrow afternoon, and can only spend a couple of hours with my family when I drop Heart off. Now I'm missing out on spending the night with Pris as well. It's a double whammy.

'I could come straight back—is that okay?'

'I'll probably be asleep….'

'But I'll be there when you wake up. And maybe we can talk for a while before the worlds interrupt us.'

'I'd like that,' she says, and my heart skips a little knowing she still wants to be with me.

She steps out of my arms and gives me a playful push away. 'Go on, then. The sooner you go, the sooner you can come back.'

I take a step towards her, unable to stop the smirk crossing my face. 'Or I could stay a moment longer for this.'

Leaning forward, I reach out and entwine my fingers in her hair before capturing her lips with mine. The kiss begins as gentle, but it is soon anything but.

'Snake,' Pris groans as the guard coughs into her hand.

I lean my forehead against hers and say, 'All right, visiting the family it is, then.'

It takes all my effort not to turn back as I open the door to Drow and Percival's suite. Once inside, I lean against the closed door. How can she do that to me? I was so sure I was in control there.

'Right, young man. Time to leave?' Heart says, passing me my jacket.

'Give me a moment,' I say, and he laughs.

'If I give you any time at all, you'll be down that corridor quicker than a flash, and I won't get out of here tonight.'

I take the jacket. He's right of course. And I curse him every step of our walk downstairs and out into the courtyard where Ed'rathe waits for us.

About time, Ed'rathe says. **I've been standing here forever.**

I had things to do.

I know. He manages to transmit a smirk with his words, and I am reminded I need to strengthen my wards.

The flight over the treetops to my great-grandparent's village is short, and we travel in silence. Ed'rathe lands in a field about a mile away before saying, **I will stay here. It will be dawn in four hours, so please do not be too long. Creatures scare easily with dragons around.**

I intend to be well gone before dawn, but I don't tell him that. **I'll be back in an hour.**

I hope it is not an hour like at the maze, he sends as he settles down to wait.

We enter the village via a different path to the one I took when I was last here, and we're much closer to the house my father grew up in. Halfway down the street, Heart stops and places a hand on my arm.

I pull up beside him. 'Is something wrong?'

The look he gives me is full of anguish. 'I'm not sure I can do this. I haven't seen them in over a hundred years… and I took their granddaughter from them.'

He swallows, and the gulp is audible in the night air. I take his hand in mine, each of the calluses on his fingers telling the story of the music he's played.

'I told you, Heart, they don't hold a grudge. They are sad they missed out on some things, but they understand the reasons.'

Heart's hand trembles in mine. 'Would you mind if I did this alone? I am sure they'd love to see you and you them. But I think this would be easier if I didn't have an audience the first time.'

I swallow my disappointment. Breaker and Keeper helped me through my first trial in The Minotaur's Maze, and I would love to have seen them again. However, this reunion with his parents is a huge step for Heart. I can give him the space he needs.

'Just initially, or should I save my reunion for when I come and pick you up?'

I'm pretty sure he'll choose the latter, but I'm hoping to at least say a quick hello.

He sends me a sheepish look from under greying brows. 'Would you mind?' Heart squeezes my hand. 'I'm asking a lot.'

'Not at all,' I tell him—a little white lie. 'I'll wait a ways down the street. If they don't throw you out after five minutes, Ed'rathe and I will head back to the maze.'

'Thank you,' Heart says, then straightens his clothes and smooths back his hair before making his way to the house at the end of the row.

As he raises his hand to knock, I slip into the shadow of a doorway. He bangs twice before I see the flicker of a candle in an upstairs window. Moments later the door creaks open, and I can hear the gasped 'Heart, you're home,' from my hiding place.

Tears well in my eyes as I watch Mender take his son in his arms and haul him inside. Once the door is closed behind them, I don't wait around. Heart is home.

Flipping through a book on creature magic, I make my way through the deserted corridors of the Minotaur's house back to our suite. I could have asked a brownie to bring me the book, but I wanted some time alone.

Drow is still going over the proposed contract. Without a doubt, he's triple-checking that we have not let down any faction in the rag-tag alliance.

'I've ordered cocoa for both of us,' he tells me without raising his head. 'I hope it will help me sleep.'

'I have my own methods of sending myself to sleep.' I hold up my book.

Curling up on the sofa, I am soon engrossed. A brownie brings in the cocoa, and I drink mine while I consider the chapter I've just read on how magic came into the World Below. We all know the story, but considering recent events, it is interesting to study it again.

'Percival, why are you frowning so intently?' Drow asks as he sinks into the sofa beside me.

'Magic? Power? I do not understand how creatures and humans can put these things above the welfare of others and their worlds.'

Drow chortles. 'So nothing deep and meaningful, then.'

I rub a hand over my face. 'My instincts tell me Bernais's control over the council is a grasp for power by a dying regime—except they control most of the military and the largest centre of population. They can also wield more magic than we can.'

'Do not forget, most creatures are too scared or cowered by years of mistreatment to stand up to them.'

I clasp my hands in my lap. 'Drow, I fear I am too old for this battle. I want to return to the grove and spend the last centuries of my life tending trees and spending time with Nisha.'

Drow quirks an eyebrow. 'What are your chances of being left to do that should we fail here?'

I'm saddened that his words ring so true. 'It is déjà vu. Or, if not a rerun, then we are about to fight the battle we were too scared to face all those years ago.'

Creases form around Drow's eyes as he smiles. 'Perhaps if we had had the courage back then… but we were young, and wounded, and we had so much still to learn.'

I rest my head against the back of the sofa. My purpose in studying history wasn't to evoke this sadness, but to find something to convince Queen Ariana that it's time for the elves to hand over power to the creatures of our world.

Will she consider it? Maybe if Elias, her cousin and chosen Chancellor, were here, she would listen to him. He had been the only one brave enough to stand by Ariana when we left, and he has earned her trust. Then again, at that time, he was recently betrothed, and perhaps he only stayed because he had more to lose than the rest of us?

I shoot a quick sideways glance at Drow. Once I had thought Drow would stay behind and help Elias. After all, his family were already advisors to the Crown. Then he had opted to follow Heart to the Unseelie Court.

'Drow?'

'Mmm.'

'Why did you decide to come back now?'

A brief look of worry crosses Drow's face, but it is gone so quickly, I am left wondering if I imagined it.

'Because everyone else was. Besides, what was the alternative? To get caught within a castle in stasis?'

I had forgotten about that. Still….

'There had to be a point when you were tempted to come home. What about when you heard about Ginth. Didn't you want to come back and advocate for her? Didn't Heart ask you to?'

Drow's fingers scratch against his growing stubble as he rakes a hand across his face. 'We talked about it. But Heart is still officially banished. And if I went alone, would I still hold any sway in a court I had deserted?'

'You would have had your family. They would have supported you.'

Drow sits forward, resting his arms on his knees. 'It is complicated, old friend. I am unsure if they would have welcomed me at court. He gulps as if the words are choking him. 'I am not sure *Elias* would have welcomed me.'

I study Drow carefully. His face and voice are guarded —then again, he has always been difficult to read when it comes to his feelings. He and Elias were once so close, the best of friends—then they grew apart. So many things had happened so close together when we dispersed, but had it actually been Elias's betrothal that had pulled apart the creatures who were once as close as brothers?

'Did something happen between you and Elias—something to do with you and Leesha?'

My friend's jaw tenses ever so imperceptibly, indicating I am getting close to the mark.

'Drow, did you and Leesha have a falling out? Or…?'

Oh my gosh, did Drow hold a torch for his best friend's betrothed and could no longer bear to be around the two of them? I thought everyone knew they had an arrangement. Once Leesha had produced two heirs, Elias would return to court, and she would have her own life in Essendore. The marriage had only ever been one of convenience.

Drow runs a hand through his already untidy hair, his brow furrowed the way it does when he's thinking. 'When I left the Capitol, I was so angry with Elias. Leesha had guessed our secret, and she gave Elias an ultimatum. Either he ended our friendship, or the engagement was off. She wanted no hint of impropriety.'

Hold on! Elias and Drow could no longer be together? Years of observing their friendship ran through my mind. How had I not seen this?

Drow is staring at me, his face showing concern. 'Percival? Are you all right? You didn't know, did you? I always thought you did. I hope....'

'Oh, Drow, it is nothing like that. I should have known, but I guess back then, I was so caught up in my own misery that I could not see anyone else's.'

'It is fine, Percival. We never made a big thing of it. I had always thought our lives would carry on as they had done forever. My family would never force me into a political union, but we hadn't counted on Elias's parents deciding he needed a family.'

Drow slumped and rested against the couch. 'In our youthful thoughtlessness, we thought Leesha would stay at the estate and we could continue to be together in the Capitol, sheltered from scrutiny by the guise of our friendship. We underestimated her, and I underestimated Elias's desire to be accepted.'

Drow is silent for so long, I think he's finished speaking. Then he says, almost as an afterthought, 'When Elias gave in to Leesha's demands, I thought my very soul would break. I could not be near him, so I exiled myself to the Unseelie Court. I guess part of me had hoped that amongst like-minded people, I could find someone who would mend my soul. But I could not stop thinking about

Elias, and I finally had to admit that while he lives and breathes, he will still hold my heart.'

I reach out and drop a hand on Drow's thigh to show…. I do not know. Perhaps solidarity.

'Now Elias is in real trouble, and I cannot let him face this alone. I have to do whatever I can to get him out of this alive. I've a lot to make up for.'

It never surprises me how much the world can change in a matter of minutes. Who knew my eternal bachelor friend had been in love with the same creature for hundreds of years and none of us knew—well, at least I *think* none of us knew.

'Drow, I do not know what to say,' I tell him.

'I do not need you to say anything. In fact I would prefer it if you kept this to yourself. Ariana is the only other creature who knows, and I would like it to stay that way. Although I have come back because I cannot bear to let Bernais ruin everything Elias has worked for, I have not come back for him.'

'Of course, Drow. Whatever you need from me, you have it.'

I let out a chuckle. 'I always thought you and Effie might… you know. How wrong I was.'

Drow is so filled with sadness at my words that I wish I had kept my thoughts to myself.

'You have to tell her,' I say.

He nods. 'I guess I owe her that. I had always hoped she would find someone and realise we are like brother and sister.'

We sit side by side in silence for some time, Drow lost in his thoughts and me with my mind racing. Was it any wonder Drow was so intent on making sure this agreement was perfect? He was hoping it would save the one he loves.

That made it even more imperative I convince Ariana to agree to our plan.

CHAPTER 7

The Burdens of Being a Hero

The palace is quiet as I creep back inside. Perhaps alerted by the swish of my footsteps on the marble floor, or maybe Pris has told her to expect me, the guard has the door open when I arrive at Pris's suite. We share a curt nod as I enter, then she closes the door softly behind me.

Pris had left one door slightly ajar to make it easy for me to find her room. At least I think it's her room. I hope they haven't given her a companion in my absence as I slip out of my shoes, heavy jacket, and top, and crawl into bed beside a sleeping female.

The figure snuffles and roles onto her back, and I'm relieved to find it *is* Pris. Moonlight from the window falls across her face, and my breath catches in my chest. She is so beautiful, my heart almost stops. For a brief moment, I consider waking her, but I'm exhausted, and she was not great when I left last night.

I move further down the bed and snuggle into Pris, her warm body moulding itself to mine.

'You came back,' she mumbles, a satisfied smile forming on her lips.

I kiss her hair. 'Yes.' I wrap an arm around her, and with a feeling of everything being right, I close my eyes and let sleep claim me.

When I open them, I'm assaulted with bright sunlight. Rubbing the sleep away, I reorientate myself. The bed beside me is empty. I run my hand over the sheet, and there's no trace of warmth at all. She must have been gone for a while.

The sheet slips down my body as I push myself into a sitting position, and just as I do, Pris enters carrying a tray.

When her eyes land on my bare chest, she grins. 'Good, you're awake. I thought you were going to sleep the day away. I've got breakfast for us.'

She scans my body, and heat rises to my cheeks. I stop myself from pulling the sheet back up. I've never felt insecure about my physique before, but in the stark morning light, all my imperfections are on display. Running a self-conscious hand through my hair, I catch a whiff of something not quite savoury.

'Can I grab a quick shower first?'

She nods towards the other door in the room as she places the tray on the end of the bed. 'There are guest pjs in there too.'

She's obviously taken advantage of all Aeron's hospitality. Her hair is still wet, and she's wearing a cream silk camisole and pyjama bottoms that highlight her curves. I shake my head and leap out of bed before my thoughts become physically obvious.

When I had suggested a shower, I didn't expect there to actually be one; baths are as good as it usually gets in the World Below. However, Aaron's guest suite has both options.

I choose the shower, and, while it's not hot, the water I release by pulling a chain is pleasantly warm. When I emerge from the bathroom a few minutes later, I'm refreshed and wearing pyjama bottoms similar to Pris's.

She has snuggled back under the duvet and placed the tray beside her, within easy reach of us both. I sit on the edge of the bed and slide my legs back under the covers. Once I'm settled and the tray stops moving, she pours us both mugs of coffee and leans back against the headboard of the oversized bed.

'We could fit my whole family in here with us,' she says dryly.

'Pris!' The thought of her parents seeing us like this is actually shocking.

She chuckles. 'I wasn't suggesting….. It was the size…. I mean—yuck!'

I grin as I take a sip of coffee, enjoying this little piece of normalcy. This is the life. Food on tap, Pris by my side, and no reason to leave the room. I reach for a croissant, take a huge bite of the buttery pastry, and stare out the window.

The sun is more than up. Have I slept most of the morning away? Fortunately, when the Dragon Queen sent me here yesterday, she had informed me that I would not be required back to appear at court this morning. If nothing has happened while I've been recharging my batteries, I may get away with spending most of the morning here before returning to report last night's events. Although I wouldn't stake my life on being left in peace for that long.

'Pris, what's the time?'

'Chill—it's only about nine. The sun rises early here.'

With a few more mouthfuls of coffee, my mind is firing again. 'What time is Percival's meeting with the Queen?'

'He was heading her way when the brownie brought the breakfast tray.' With her mug suspended in mid-air, Pris pauses, and a frown appears. 'It's crazy to think that it's my first breakfast in bed with someone, and we're casually talking about meeting with royalty.'

'Ah, it's the first time you've had breakfast in bed with a boy.' I tease, hoping to keep the mood light for a while longer.

Spots of pink colour her cheeks. I reach for her hand and give it a squeeze. Perhaps this isn't the right thing to tease her about.

'Soooo.' I draw the word out. 'When you imagined having breakfast in bed with me, was I shirtless?

She almost splutters out a mouthful of coffee but presses her lips closed. 'That's pretty bold, thinking I imagined this with you at all,' she says once she's swallowed.

Now we're back on track. 'I thought we might talk about how much you love me and how you want to spend the rest of your life with me,' I tease.

Next to me, Pris tenses. Man, I keep hitting bum notes today.

I sit up and turn so I'm facing her. 'I'm just messing with you, Pris. I wanted this time to be separate from what's going on out there. A little slice of normal in the madness.' Pris squeezes my hand, and I carry on. 'I guess when you're about to go to war, thinking about the future is not as easy.'

'That's why it's so important to grab on to those moments when we can.' Pris draws her bottom lip between her teeth, then releases it. 'This *is* new for me, Snake. And I can't tell whether what we have is real, or if it's because we were thrown together.'

It's like a physical blow to my gut. For me, I'm certain my feelings for Pris are real. Then again, this is not my first rodeo. I try to put myself in her place, and realise she might not have anything to compare this to.

Trying not to make too big a deal of this, I say as evenly as I can, 'Are you telling me you want this to stop?'

A troubled look crosses Pris's face. 'Hell no. What gave you that idea?'

I try not to show how relieved I am as I withdraw my hand, then take her mug from her and place it with mine on the tray. After putting everything on the floor, I settle back against the headboard and draw Pris into my arms, then rest my head on top of her hair.

'If this weren't going on, and we met in the World Above and had a date and ended up in bed together, the next morning we'd have breakfast, and then we'd talk—okay, we might do other things, but then we'd talk.'

She relaxes and leans into me. 'And what would we talk about?'

'We'd get to know each other a little better. Not the deep things that you and I already know about, but the little things, like, why are you studying law?'

'I'm not. Well, not yet.'

She's so practical. 'Just go with it,' I urge her.

The silence grows, and I wait to see if she's going to play along.

'I guess because of my parents. They brought me up with a strong sense of helping others. They're both lawyers, although their jobs are different, and I guess I see that as a starting point.'

'That's interesting. And what do you want to do after graduation?'

'I want to work with my mother, helping refugees and immigrants and minority groups.'

We're in the flow now.

'So you've always wanted to work with your mum, not your dad?'

'Yes. I mean, Dad's organisation does good work providing housing and assistance for those less well-off, but I've always felt more drawn towards human rights.'

I nod, wondering if she sees the parallels I do.

'What about you? Why physics?'

Before I answer, I consider whether bringing magic into this fantasy world will ruin the vibe. It'll remind us we're not in the World Above, and once we're back here, the real world would intrude.

'The long answer?'

'Yep.'

'The world is changing. Global warming is increasing, and consumerism has become toxic. I want to find ways to repair the damage to the environment, and studying physics is one way I can do that.'

Pris forces herself up so she can look at me, her eyes twinkling with amusement. 'So part of what we're doing now is what you were going to uni to achieve.'

I pull her back to my chest. 'Pot, meet kettle.'

Her laugh rumbles through her body. 'Ironic, isn't it?'

'It is.'

And now, we have broken the spell. We're back in the World Below, attempting to save the creature realm.

'If we get through this—'

'*When* we get through this,' I amend.

'Okay, when we get through this, do you want to go on a date?'

The laugh explodes out of me. 'Oh, yes, I want to go on a date and do all those things we've missed out on.'

'Good, so do I.' Pris tightens her hug. 'Do you think it will be here, or in the World Above?' The question is barely a whisper, almost as if Pris is unsure whether or not she should give it air.

She has just confirmed her place in the succession to the throne. Does she really think she can go back home?

'I mean, my mother and father had time in the World Above…,' she adds.

That's true. For a moment I allow myself to believe I can go back to my friends and the life I had above. It stirs up a strong desire, but the idea of going back feels wrong. I would have to leave my family behind again just when I've found them.

Fear winds icy tendrils around my heart. 'Do you want to go back?'

'I don't know. A part of me wants to, but I honestly don't know.'

I hold her close, and it almost feels like clinging to her, rather than drawing comfort from her presence. Do we have a future? I'm not ready to give up on the idea yet, and I hope she's not either.

'Snake? Have I ruined everything?' There is genuine distress in her voice, and all I want to do is ease it for her.

I'm doomed. This woman has stolen my heart and my common sense with it. Or has she? How can any of us make plans for a future that may not be there? Still, I can't lie to her.

'I don't know, Pris. My world has turned around, and I don't see myself going back to my old life. Yet, I've no idea what the future holds for me… for us. The only thing I'm certain of is, I am falling for you. And that has been the only good thing about these past few weeks. Whatever my future holds, I know I want you in it.'

There, I have laid my soul bare. Pris hugs me so tight, I almost can't breathe.

'Is it wrong to long for normal, for home? When I was

working towards getting Mum and Dad back and returning to our old lives, I had a goal and I could see a future. Now, I'm being swept along by events, and the only things that are constant, the only things stopping me from getting swept away, are you and Percival.'

I hate the despair in Pris's voice, and I want to make this better for her. Having grown up knowing I belonged to another world has given me a different perspective. Home has always been family for me, and now my family is down here.

Then again, if my mother decides she wants to return to the World Above, will that make me change my mind? I couldn't let her go alone. Dammit, it's not so simple, but we will not solve the future now.

'Don't tell me you think of Percival the same way you think of me?' I say in mock alarm, trying to lighten the tone again.

Pris slaps my leg. 'Snake! No! That's like fancying an uncle or some other family member.'

'Ah, so you still fancy me.'

Pris shimmies up my body, making it difficult for me to hold on to any playful thoughts. Then, when her mouth meets mine, all those thoughts are gone. As I run my hand along the length of her spine, a knock sounds at the door. We freeze.

'Who is it?' Pris asks.

'It's me, Maddox. We need to speak.'

'Seriously? Now?' I groan. Giving Snake a quick kiss, I roll off him but pause for a moment, torn between duty and wanting to continue what we'd started. I get up and scrabble around for the clothes left in the room for me last night, pulling on each piece as I find it. Clothed in loose tan linen trousers and a white linen shirt, I'm tidying my hair when I become aware Snake hasn't moved.

'You're not joining us?' I ask, a little impatiently. While I'm not sure how my uncle will react to my being with Snake so recently after he tried to have me marry his heir, I'm willing to risk his censure rather than face him alone.

Snake tilts his head to the side as if he's considering joining me. 'I'm not sure my appearance would impress King Maddox.' A wry smile tweaks his lips. 'Besides, I need a little longer before I make any sort of public appearance.'

It takes me a moment, but then my eyes drift to where the bunched sheet covers his lower half. 'Oh, okay. I guess I can do this alone.'

In a nanosecond Snake is alert and about to leap out of bed. 'Do what?'

'Whoa, slow down. I simply mean face my uncle. I've no idea what he wants, but none of our previous conversations were exactly comfortable.'

A knot twists in my stomach as I finish plaiting my hair. So far my uncle has tried to blackmail me into joining his court. When that didn't work, he upped the anti by trying to marry me off to his heir, who turned out to be a traitorous leech.

He redeemed himself by ordering my dragon to save me from a magical attack and transport me to the dragon court, but that doesn't mean I entirely trust him now. I haven't talked with him one-on-one since, but his wanting to see me can't be a good thing.

'You'll do fine,' Snake says. 'You've managed to thwart every one of his plans so far. But if you wait a moment, I can come with you.' He leans over the edge of the bed and reaches for his clothes.

The knot lessens somewhat at his words and offer of support. 'No, I'm okay,' I tell him rather more confidently than I feel. I take a deep breath before opening the door and entering the sitting room with a breezy, 'Good morning.'

Aeron stands up and returns my greeting. I reward him with a smile.

My uncle simply turns from his position on the sofa and studies me, his face an implacable mask.

Ugh, I hate all this court formality. I lower my head to my uncle, acknowledging him as my social superior, before asking, 'How can I help you two gentlemen?'

A slight grimace crosses my uncle's face. Maybe he's looking forward to this as much as I am.

'Please, take a seat.' He gestures to the sofa.

I pull out a chair from the table and sit facing King Maddox. His eyebrows rise a little, but he carries on.

'Queen Ariana asked me to talk with you in light of instructions we have received from the Dragon Queen.'

'So you and she have been scheming,' I say, unable to stop myself from needling him.

'You could say that.'

'We've been doing a little planning too,' I announce before he can say any more.

The King's lips almost form a smile before he schools his face back into disinterest. 'So I hear. Percival is talking with the Queen now. Whatever you have planned, I hope you remember she and I will be busy for the foreseeable future.'

'We've taken that into account,' I tell him.

He nods approvingly. 'Good. What I want to talk to you about is your new role…. Your royal role.'

My eyes flick from King Maddox to Aeron and back again. Dammit, if Maddox still thinks I'm going to be a part of his court, it will really throw a spanner in the works. And I can't believe Aeron is part of this—not after our conversation yesterday.

'Hear the King out.' Aeron's voice is low, but it still rumbles.

Maybe he's not thrown me to the wolves after all.

'Queen Ariana and I have come to an agreement about your royal status.' Maddox clears his throat, and I sit forward in my chair. Did my great-aunt take him to task? 'It seems you are already in line to sit on the throne of the World Below, and according to the Dragon Queen, this claim supersedes any from my court.'

Yes! I resist the urge to fist pump the air.

'We have made a mutual decision that you will assume the role of Ambassador to the Unseelie Court once it is fully reinstated, with the intention of fostering new relationships.'

'Did you now?' The old anger at being manipulated flares inside me. How is it that two people who don't even know me feel they have the right to decide my future?

I turn to Aeron for help. There is a sadness in his eyes as he opens his hands palms upward. Is he telling me that this is my time to take a stand? Hell, this is scary. I wish Snake were here.

I keep my features calm, relaxed. I don't want to come off as being a brat or even as being unreasonable, but I'm not going to let them move me round like a pawn on a chessboard.

'The courts exchanging ambassadors is a great idea,' I tell Maddox, 'but we're a long way from making appointments.'

Aeron smirks as Maddox's lips tighten. I'm pretty sure

he's suppressing a smile rather than showing displeasure. I decide to press my luck.

'I'm sure there's one thing we can sort now. I am not, and never will be, betrothed to Dinian.'

Maddox snorts out a rather un-kingly laugh. 'I think we can take that as a given, niece.'

There had been a small part of me that worried he might still expect me to marry his potential heir, even after Dinian had joined Bernais. To be fair, though, I would never have married the creepy elf. His sense of entitlement far outstrips any abilities he has as a ruler.

'Of course, Ariana and I will have to find you another suitable match.'

My fists clench, but then I catch the twinkle of amusement in Maddox's eyes. In our time in the Unseelie Court, Maddox had been every bit the epitome of the tyrannical king. Of course, he had just lost the love of his life, and his court was under threat. There is clearly another side to my uncle. Odd that it's appeared on the eve of a war that could decimate the World Below.

Aeron breaks the tension with a bark of laughter. 'You two are like two cocks in a ring, neither prepared to back down. Maddox, you know you will not marry Pris off any time soon. And Pris, you must know your great-aunt and uncle have more on their minds than your marital future.'

I turn my attention to the Minotaur. The more time I spend with Aeron, the more I appreciate what an accomplished political operator he is. In the past twenty-four hours, I've come to value his words almost as much as I would Snake's or Percival's.

I lean forward and pitch my voice low and neutral. 'Uncle Maddox, why are you really here?'

My uncle stares out the window, lost in his own thoughts. 'I am... not busy,' he finally says. 'I have spent so much time running my court, keeping everyone safe, and now I'm left… waiting for Ariana to recover enough to begin our work together.'

'You're bored?' I splutter. He's been teasing me all this time because he's bored? 'Have you spoken to the dragons about getting your court out of stasis?'

'Of course.' His tone is disdainful. 'The dragons believe it will take quite some time, maybe years, before magic builds up enough in the World Above to perform the spell to restore my home.'

He sounds defeated. He is a king without a court. And he's no doubt worried about his subjects caught inside. My old nanny, Susan, is probably there. I might not even be alive when she finally gets out.

'How many of your subjects are still inside?' I ask.

'In the end it was only the guards outside the room we were in. It seems Lady Susan had an evacuation plan and she got herself and the bulk of my followers away.'

Susan and the others made it out. That's a relief. I wonder where she is?

'Those left behind had volunteered to stay to make sure we were protected while we maintained the court barriers,' my uncle continues. 'When the dragons helped us escape, they were trapped.'

Those poor guards. I couldn't imagine being so devoted to a cause or a person that I would give up my life. Then again, isn't that exactly what I'm doing now—subjugating my wishes to the needs of the World Below? *No, don't think that. Be happy that most of the court got out before Snake, Euphemia, and Princess Petunia completed the stasis spell.*

Aeron clears his throat. 'Um, Maddox, you had some other reason for being here, did you not?'

Maddox frowns as he pulls his mind back to the present

'I did? Oh yes, of course. As I said before, Ariana and I

have been talking. She and I are unhappy with you wandering around the worlds alone, especially given your close ties with both royal families. The danger you face is very real, and we both feel you need greater protection.'

'You're kidding me, right?' I inject every ounce of disbelief possible in those words. 'You're worried now? After I've faced down a multitude of foes and extracted myself from several dangerous, life-threatening situations? Snake, Percival, and I have been fine, thank you very much.'

Maddox does not give in. 'As I understand it, the World Below is about to go to war. Your mother is already in a compromised position in the Capitol. As second in line to the throne, it is even more important that you remain well-guarded.'

I rush to my feet. 'You are not going to lock me up as if I'm some simpering princess,' I protest.

'Pris,' Aeron says, and I am reminded of his words about deciding what sort of princess I want to be.

Taking a couple of calming breaths, I start again.

'I may be a princess, but I am also central to what is going on in the World Below. Mum and the leaders of the revolt agreed to work together last night. Percival is speaking to Queen Ariana about it now. I am very much a part of their plan, and if we want a world we are all happy to live in after this, I must do my job.'

A smile plays at the edges of Maddox's lips. 'I do not remember saying we were going to lock you up, but merely that we are concerned for your safety.'

My anger deflates like a popped balloon as I hold his stare. I lower myself back into my chair. 'What are you suggesting?' I ask, feeling more rational now.

'We have asked Aeron if he will become your Royal

Guard until this is over, at which time Ariana will provide you with another.'

My eyes flick to Aeron, and he nods once, indicating he has agreed to this. My initial argument that I can defend myself stalls as I consider this option. It is true that the Minotaur is a mighty warrior, and his presence would make potential assailants think twice before attacking. However, there is another benefit to having Aeron by my side.

Well, there are a couple, really. He has proven to be an asset when it comes to politics. But even more, his presence in the meeting today has helped me react less and consider more. In short, he can help me become the princess I want to be.

'I agree—on one condition,' I say.

Uncle Maddox suppresses his surprise. 'And that would be?'

I turn to Aeron. 'If you are going to be around me all the time, then I would also like you as my advisor. We won't stand on ceremony, and you will give me your opinion whether I like it or not. Those are my terms.'

A Minotaur's grin is actually quite a fearsome thing to see, or it would have been if I hadn't seen the pride in his liquid brown eyes.

'I agree,' he says.

'And I guess I do, too, although I can see that is moot,' my uncle adds.

'Good, and the other thing?'

As I wait for an answer, King Maddox's cheeks actually redden. 'Well, umm, this relates to something I brought up before.' Maddox turns to Aeron for help.

'What Maddox is saying is that the dragons told Queen Ariana they are treating Snake as your consort. This is a breach of protocol for a proper heir, and she would like to meet with Snake to assess his suitability.'

My self-control flies out the window once more. 'Absolutely not! This is between Snake and me. Snake and the dragons too,' I amend. 'We are nowhere near the stage of anyone else needing to become involved.'

Maddox's eyes slide to the bedroom door, and it is my turn to redden. He has known Snake was in there all along.

'Oh, come on! We're not in Victorian times, no matter how much your court might like to pretend. Sleeping together is not a life commitment.'

'Actually,' Aeron says, 'In Victorian and Edwardian, times they were all at it all the—'

'Aeron,' Maddox rumbles.

The Minotaur grins at me, giving me courage.

'I appreciate I have royal responsibilities. So, I promise if Snake and I ever get to a stage where you and Queen Ariana need to become involved in "vetting" him, I will tell you. Then I'm sure he'd love to sit down and have a chat about his suitability as my consort,' I finish, mentally apologising to Snake for setting him up.

Before King Maddox can respond, the door opens, and Drow appears.

'Excellent, you're all here.' He scans the room. 'I was expecting—'

'Your nephew can join us momentarily,' Aeron says dryly.

Drow starts, then recovers himself. 'Queen Ariana has asked to meet with you and Snake, Pris.'

'If this is about Snake being here....'

Drow's eyes widen as a flush spreads across his cheeks. 'Ah... no. She wants to talk to you both about the agreement we made and your roles in the upcoming conflict.'

Queen Ariana closes her eyes and lies back against the pillows. Her grey-shot black hair is in a plait, and she wears a royal blue bedjacket, the sole evidence of her status. She is not as pale as she was when she was held in stasis in the centre of the maze, but she is not fully back to health yet either. Her skin is still a luminous white, and the fine lines around her eyes are a sign of the strain talking with me has put on her.

From her place in the garden, Al'kyla watches me through the patio doors with an eagle-eyed intensity. I promised her I would not weary the Queen, and I have tried not to. However, her realm is in turmoil, and discussing anything to do with its collapse would inevitably take a toll.

After outlining our proposal, I had thought we would discuss it. She had only stared thoughtfully at the wall, then called for a servant to fetch Snake and Pris.

I wring my hands as I pluck up the courage to ask her what she thinks.

A cool breeze ripples through the room, disturbing the cornflower blue curtains, and passes over my face. It must have disturbed the Queen, because she shifts restlessly in the yellow-damask-covered bed that almost swallows her and says, 'I am pleased to see you here on your own behalf, Percival, and not as Eleanora's messenger. How I have missed your incisive insights.' Queen Ariana clears her throat and reaches for a glass of water from the bedside table.

'Your Majesty is too kind,' I say, trying to mask my pleasure at her praise.

I've always been in awe of Petunia's sister. She is a little older, a little more aloof, and far more regal than her younger sibling. Truth be told, we all had a little bit of a crush on her, but she has only ever had eyes for Allard.

Fairburn, the head of the Queens Guard, appears in the doorway to the courtyard, startling me. His steps are so quiet, his sudden presence always seems to catch me off guard.

Queen Ariana finishes her water and leans back against the pillows. 'Is it done?'

He dips his head. 'It is. Are you sure this is for the best?'

'If we want to win, it has to be this way.'

The silence that follows fills the room with questions I cannot ask. What has Fairburn been organising? Why does the Queen want to see Pris and Snake? What does Queen Ariana think of the proposal? Will she accuse us of plotting treason? Is that what Fairburn has been organising? Our imprisonment?

'Percival, you look like you have eaten something disagreeable,' Fairburn says.

'Oh dear, Percival. You have had such a busy few weeks. I hope I have not overtaxed you.' Queen Ariana glances at Fairburn. 'Perhaps we should not have put things in motion without talking to everyone first.'

Something passes between the two creatures, and I get a sense that their relationship is more than that of guard and queen. Before I can explore this idea any further, the door beside me opens, admitting Snake and Pris.

They both look relaxed and well rested. They're dressed in the linen trousers and long-sleeved shirts most of Aeron's staff wear. Perhaps they both spent the night here. Holding hands, they step into the room and bow before the Queen. Behind them, a brownie appears with two more chairs and places them side by side near the foot of the bed.

'Snake Fieth, Priscilla Crown, I am so pleased to finally meet you,' Queen Ariana says. 'You may approach and be seated.'

Surprisingly, the two do as they are bid without any sarcastic quips or snarky remarks. Pris does slip a questioning glance my way as she takes the seat closest to me. I shrug, letting her know I have no idea what this is all about either.

'I believe you both know Fairburn,' the Queen continues.

I am not surprised when neither of the two acknowledge the centaur. It was he who broke the news that we had not completed our quest yet when we reached the middle of the maze. Fairburn assigning us the task of retrieving the King from the Unseelie Court to save Queen Ariana had not made him our friend.

Finally Snake breaks the silence. 'I guess you're happy now you have what you wanted.'

Fairburn shuffles a little but holds Snake's gaze. 'I will not apologise for doing what needed to be done to save my Queen.'

Snake shifts in his seat, dismissing the guard as he turns his attention to the Queen.

Queen Ariana studies the creatures in the room, and the air thrums with magic as she talks with her dragon.

'Peace, everyone. I am sure you have all done things you are not proud of while I have been gone. It was a trying time, and I take full responsibility for all actions carried out in my name. So, if you have a complaint, I am ready to hear it.'

It is Snake's turn to shuffle uncomfortably. While he may not have been happy about being moved from pillar to post, he would not raise such petty concerns with a creature so recently returned from the brink of death.

'Now that that is settled, and before we move on to more weighty matters, I want to thank the three of you for bringing Maddox here to help me. I know you were used by others, and it must have been frustrating. However, you could have backed out at any time, and you did not. For that, you have my gratitude.'

'You're welcome,' I say as Pris and Snake mumble similar sentiments.

'When things are settled in our realm, I will reward all of you, but I am not really in a position to do very much at the moment.' She smiles wryly. 'I acknowledge that I am thanking you one moment and then asking for more help the next.'

I stiffen with surprise. I am not sure I have another quest in me. Suddenly the mat in front of the fire of Eleanora's place in Wimbledon is very inviting. I push the thought away. I will not hide from my duty again.

Queen Ariana's laugh fills the silence. 'I am overwhelmed with your protestations of unqualified support.'

'With all due respect,' Pris starts as Queen Ariana laughs again.

'Usually that comment precedes something which shows a marked lack of respect,' the Queen says. 'In this room, here, today, I give you leave to speak freely. We do not know each other well enough to speak in courtly terms and still understand one another, and we do not have the time to rectify that.'

'Okay,' Pris says. 'We have not had such a great experience with members of your court, so we will wait and hear what you are asking before committing to anything.'

'Fair enough. Do you feel the same way, Snake? Percival?'

'Yes,' Snake says, but I hold back. Not that I do not agree with Pris, but I have a history of service to the Crown, and to Eleanora, that is difficult to set aside.

'Percival?' Queen Ariana asks.

If I do not stand up for myself and my beliefs now, when will I? 'I agree with Pris.'

There is a glimmer of a smile on Queen Ariana's lips. Does she approve?

'We know where we stand, then. So, let us get started. Percival, you and Drow, with the help of others, have worked on a near perfect response to the actions of the elven faction taking over the government.'

'Near perfect?' I ask, a little bewildered.

'Yes. I am not wild about being forced to move to a constitutional democracy, and with such a short timeline proposed. Nor am I happy about the implication that Cecily will take the Crown should I not fall into line.'

'It is not meant as a threat, Your Majesty. We offer it more as an option for you to step aside if you do not recover completely from your illness,' I say diplomatically. The worried look that crosses Queen Ariana's face has me regretting my words. 'I mean, uh, we weren't trying to depose you.'

The Queen composes herself. 'Relax, Percival. I will be fine, and I understand what you are saying. It is not that I disagree with what you are proposing. In fact, I have some sympathy with the ideals. When we were younger, Petunia and I often discussed how we hated our future being controlled by the actions of a long-ago ancestor who believed he should rule the world.'

I did not expect that. Neither Petunia nor Ariana had ever discussed this with us. Oh, they had talked about change and more equality, but not about how they felt about being part of the royal family.

'But that is neither here nor there. There are two problems I see with what you suggest. The first is that, although Petunia has stepped down from the line of succession, unless we have her on board, some factions could rally around her.'

I nod my understanding.

'But Grandmother isn't interested in taking the throne,' Pris interrupts.

'Unfortunately, what my sister does or doesn't want may not come into it,' the Queen says. Before Pris opens her mouth to object, Queen Ariana raises a hand. 'If I could finish?'

Pris nods for the Queen to continue.

'The second thing we must consider is the dragons. Al'kyla advises that I need to send representatives to the Dragon Queen to stop her from intervening in our affairs. Apparently, she has set some sort of deadline for me regaining control of my realm?'

'Yes,' Pris says. 'You have eight more days to do that, or the dragons will consider Adina's petition to have her family included in the line of succession.'

'That is what I understand you were told. What you may not know is that if Maddox and I cannot get magic flowing between the realms again, then the dragon realm will close itself off from the other worlds—meaning most of our magic will be lost forever.'

'We have heard,' Snake says.

'What you definitely do not know is that if we go to war to regain control of the World Below, magic will be affected. Instead of creating life, it will stop, and the worlds will begin to rot. While you fight, Maddox and I will work to ensure things do not get any worse than they are. If this battle is prolonged, he and I will not meet our commitment to the dragons, and that would devastate the world.

Already the climate is deteriorating in the World Above, and creatures there are becoming sick. Very soon we will see that reflected here in the World Below.'

The stunned look on Pris's face likely mirrors my own.

'The Dragon Queen mentioned it would affect magic but not what that meant, exactly,' Snake says.

War stops magic from being created and taints what is there. The taint likely will seep through to joined worlds, making the blight seem as nothing, so my Queen is worried, the dragon, Al'kyla, says to us all.

'Thank you Al'kyla. I can take it from here,' Queen Ariana says.

'Man, this is huge,' Pris says under her breath, releasing the tension in the room. 'We're damned if we let Bernais take control and damned if we fight to remove him.'

'Indeed,' I respond, marvelling at how I am still learning about the world around me after all these centuries. 'I guess it is a choice between the guaranteed slow death of magic in our land and risking it all in the hopes we can recover.'

I glance from Pris to Snake, seeking their permission to ask the big question. They both nod.

'How can we help you sort this out, Your Majesty?'

The smile on Queen Ariana's face is filled with sadness. 'I am desolate at having to ask more of you. Pris, it is your birthright to serve your people, but you are new to this. And Snake, you come from a family of advisors, but I am asking you to step up and take a role you would normally take centuries to grow into.'

Snake takes Pris's hand, 'We understand these are difficult times and that you must make difficult decisions.'

'Thank you. First, I need the two of you to ask the

Dragon Queen to remove her deadline. I suspect she will not because she will worry about an endless war and its impact on the worlds. When she refuses, I want you to have her confirm she will not give in to Adina's demands—no matter what—until after that deadline. You can tell her the request comes directly from me and would be seen as a personal favour. That should be enough to reassure her.'

Snake and Pris turn to each other, then back to the queen. 'We can do that,' Snake says.

'Then I need you both to meet with Petunia and have her agree to lead the army with Priscilla. As part of a united front, no one can rally dissent around her. She must also agree to relinquish her claim to the throne again when this is all done.'

'Sorry? You want me to lead the army?' Pris's eyes are wide with shock and apprehension.

Fairburn snorts. 'You'll be the figurehead. I will be the brains.'

'But who will protect the Queen?' The words are out of my mouth before my brain goes into action.

Queen Ariana leans over and pats my hand 'Thank you for your concern, Percival. I will have Maddox and our dragons. And this place is protected by Aeron's magic. If anyone gets through all of that, all will be lost anyway.'

My heart sinks at the thought of anyone attacking the Queen, but I will also be here to make sure she is all right. As if reading my mind, the Queen now turns to me.

'And you, my old friend—I have a special task for you. You must go with the others to the rebel camp and make sure my voice is heard, not just by Petunia, but by all the factions gathered there.'

'What? No, I am to stay here and advise you,' I protest, my head spinning as my plan is turned on its head. I am not to speak for 'lesser' creatures but to once again work for 'greater' creatures. 'Fairburn can speak for you.'

Queen Ariana shakes her head. 'No, Percival, he cannot. I have released him from his duties so he can lead the rebel forces. He has handed over his mantel to a Commander in the Capitol. You are a Dragon Friend, so Al'kyla can communicate with you if you both agree, and we can share information.'

'But Queen Ariana, my views are in opposition to yours. I want to fight for greater equality,' I protest again. I do not want to let the Queen down, but for once I want to stay true to myself.

'Perhaps we are not so far apart, Percival. Now that I know the time of the elves must come to an end, I think perhaps working with an advisor who sees things from a more egalitarian point of view is exactly what I need. I don't just want a yes-person. I want someone who can challenge me and others to make the best decisions for all creatures—and that creature is you.'

Queen Ariana squeezes my hand. 'Please help me with this, Percival. I know you want to convince me to work for equality for all creatures, but I am not against this. Your efforts will be better spent convincing others to take creator creatures seriously in the coming battle.'

With my free hand, I wipe a tear from my eye. How can I refuse her when she asks so prettily?

CHAPTER 8

Preparing for War

The enormity of what we are facing follows Pris, Percival, and me from the room. Part of me would like nothing more than to walk away from this problem that seems too big for us to solve, but the main part of me knows I am too committed to do that.

'It's not too late to run away,' I say under my breath, hoping to convince myself of the truth of the statement.

'We had our chance to say no, to back out,' Pris says when we're a few feet away, 'and we didn't, so we're in this to the end.'

'Mmm,' Percival says, clearly lost in thought.

Pris slips her hand into mine. 'It's not all doom and gloom. At least she agreed to our proposal, which means we might have a slim chance at a brighter future.'

I want not to be so grumpy about where we are, nor so scared that we'll muck it up and make things worse. She's only asking us to talk to the dragons, and I've been doing that anyway. 'I'm not looking forward to telling Princess Petunia what to do,' I say, attempting to lighten things up.

'Percival or I can talk to her. She'll probably take things better coming from one of us,' Pris concedes.

'And I guess in return, you'll want me to beg a favour from the Dragon Queen?' I don't quite pull the quip off.

Pris tugs on my hand, drawing me to a stop. When I turn to her, her face is set. 'What's your problem, Snake? This doesn't have to be hard. These are the same things we were sort of doing before we saw her.'

She's right, but our visit to the Queen changed things somehow. I close my eyes, unable to face Pris as I say, 'I don't know, Pris. I knew things were bad, that we're going to war, but having everything laid out like that? A few weeks ago, we were a couple of kids trying to find our parents. How can *we* fix this?'

Pris stares at me for a moment, then gently rubs my arm. 'I get where you're coming from. I'm scared too. I'm hanging on by a thread here, and the only things keeping me going are that I can't stand by and do nothing and also that we're not in this alone anymore.'

Her words strike a chord, reflecting perfectly what I feel. And it helps that she's scared too. She's so beautiful when she speaks from the heart like this, and I feel so connected to her. I only wish we could stay like this, in our own bubble. Unfortunately, she must have gathered where my thoughts were wandering, because she slaps my arm.

'Hey!' I protest.

Her blue eyes twinkle with mischief. She knows exactly what she's doing. 'Hey yourself. Mind on the job.'

I grin at her, and my mood lifts as I draw her arm through mine and follow Percival, who is now a few paces ahead.

'I'm sorry, I'm just having a moment. Let's put it down to my not looking forward to asking the Dragon Queen to forget her timeline. She's kinda scary.'

Pris shudders. 'No, she's full-on terrifying.'

Percival pauses. 'She would be easier to approach if we understood why she is paying close attention to the World Below now.' He taps a finger against his lips. 'We have had social upheaval before, and the problem with magic has been building for years....'

'Could it be because of the refugee creatures now being homed in her realm?' It seems like the most logical reason to me.

'Perhaps, but I feel there is more to it than that.'

The image of a sour-faced elf leaps to my mind. 'Perhaps Adina's petition to have her family recognised by the dragons has forced the issue?'

Before Percival can comment. a soldier rushes past us towards the vestibule.

Our eyes lock, then as one, we sprint after her, arriving just in time to hear her telling Aeron and Drow, 'Al'kyla says that the Royal Guard are holding strong for the moment, but the palace is essentially under siege.'

Drow is slowly shaking his head. 'The Royal Guard are intent on protecting Princess Irene as Royal Heir. If Bernais takes the palace, he can force Irene to stand down. That will cement his position as heir to the Crown, and the war will be over.'

'I do not believe that is his endgame,' Percival says. 'I think it is more likely he wants to remove Irene all together.'

Beside me, Pris gasps. She clearly had not understood the very real danger her mother is in. I wrap an arm around her and pull her close. 'We won't let that happen,' I whisper into her hair.

The Minotaur furrows his brow, and, deep in thought, he cups his chin with his thumb and forefinger. 'We get Fairburn back so he can take control, and then we can contact the rebels to urge them to take what forces they have and push forward.'

'But they are still waiting on some of the trained soldiers from the World Above to arrive. Without them, the army is basically a rag-tag bunch of civilians,' Drow says.

'I believe Fairborn has resigned his commission,' the guard says.

'What?' Drow splutters.

'It is true.' Percival says. 'He is going to lead the rebels.'

Drow runs a hand through his hair. 'I guess this just got real.'

Aeron claps a hand on my uncle's shoulder. 'It was real from the moment Bernais seized control.'

I understand how my uncle feels. Until now our actions were merely strategic moves on the chessboard, and the possibility of creatures dying in battle felt far away.

'Are you okay?' I ask Pris.

Leaning into me, she says. 'I guess so… or maybe not.' She shakes her head. 'Attacking the palace is now their endgame, and they want my mother dead. But my dad and your mum are there too.'

I am certain the worry and helplessness showing on her face are mirrored on mine. I hug her close as I turn to the others, almost too scared to ask, 'Aeron, how long can the palace hold out?'

The Minotaur's face twists into a grimace. 'That is like asking how long is a piece of string? Rest assured, the palace is constructed to withstand a siege.'

Pris takes a step forward. 'There's a but in there.'

Aeron nods. 'The palace will withstand a physical siege. However, it won't take Bernais long to figure that out.'

'And after what he did at the Unseelie Court, he will change tactics and use magic to attack it,' Pris finishes.

Remembering the magical attacks Grossman Green

and Giles Coronas led in Inverness turns my stomach. The thought of my mother and the rest of my family being caught up in that is terrifying.

'Don't look so worried,' Drow says from beside me. When had he moved? 'Cecily is strong in magic, and she has her dragon to help protect the castle.'

I think about Ed'rathe having been assigned to me because the dragons believe I am Pris's consort. 'Does Pris's father have a dragon?'

'No, I do not think so. Malachai and Cecily left the World Below before anything was official between the two of them,' Drow answers.

Pris's eyes narrow. 'Snake, let's add that to the list of things to talk about with the Dragon Queen. With Mum's being Queen Ariana's heir, Dad should have a dragon chosen to bond with him, even if he can't complete the bond while he is being held captive.'

'We were meant to be on our way to the World Between' 'Now that things have changed, should we still go?'

'It's even more important we follow through on our plans,' Percival says. 'If Adina can prove Bernais is more likely to take control of the realm without an all-out war, that may play well with the dragons.'

'And she will be in the Dragon Queen's ear at every opportunity,' Pris adds, her mouth curling with distaste.

'Indeed,' Percival finishes.

'And on that note,' Aeron says as he points at two bags. 'Queen Ariana requested formal court clothing for the two of you. I also had them pack some more everyday clothes and footwear.'

Pris flashes him a smile. 'Thank you, Aeron.' She turns to me. 'I guess we should say our goodbyes and be on our way.'

'Not so fast,' Aeron says, stepping between us. 'I am coming too.'

Pris blanches. 'What? I mean, why? I'll be with Am'ratha.'

Aeron folds heavily muscled arms across his chest. 'King Maddox and Queen Ariana asked me to protect you, and protect you I will.'

I chuckle, remembering how obstinate Aeron can be from our encounter in his Maze. Pris is also stubborn, but I don't like her chances of out-stubborning Aeron.

She blows out a huff. 'You can come... if Am'ratha is happy carrying you.'

Smart move.

Aeron's unsettling grin suggests Pris has been outmanoeuvred. 'King Maddox has already sorted that. The Dragon Queen has approved my accompanying you everywhere.'

Pris turns on her heel and stalks out. I roll my eyes at Percival and Drow. Although I'm pleased Pris has the Minotaur covering her back, I am smart enough not to let on.

'She has been through a lot, and she has much more to adjust to,' Percival says. 'We understand.'

I stand there, caught between following Pris and saying goodbye to Drow and Percival. We may not see each other again for some time, if at all, and the loss is already seeping into my soul. I have to say something, but if I do say goodbye, what is appropriate in this sort of situation?

Drow slips an arm over my shoulders. 'Let us not dwell on this. We all know what is coming, and none of us can predict what will happen. I'll just say, I'm pleased to have met you, Snake, and I hope I get to know you better once this is over.' He gives me a brief squeeze, then turns away.

I stare at Percival. If I am to stay at the Dragon Court

and he is to be with the army, he and I may well never see each other again. There is no way I can find the words to tell him what his friendship has meant to me these past months.

The sprite meets my gaze, a smile hovering at the edge of his lips. 'I know, Snake. There are no words.' He reaches out and clasps my hand in his. 'Until we meet again, my friend, in this world or the next.'

I withdraw my hand and drop to one knee before pulling Percival into a hug. For a moment, his body is stiff in my arms, and I think I've overstepped the mark. He relaxes and hugs me back. Then I rise, grab my bag from Aeron, and leave before the tears can fall from my eyes.

When I enter the courtyard, Pris is already on Am'ratha's back. Ed'rathe is waiting patiently, and his eyes twinkle with amusement as Aeron appears from behind me.

I do not know who is more displeased the Minotaur is joining us, my sister or the princess. Ed'rathe snorts in what I'm sure is a dragon version of a laugh.

I'm happy you find this so funny, I snap, then instantly regret it. This is not Ed'rathe's war. **I'm sorry, Ed'rathe, I didn't mean....**

It is all right. I was a little flippant, and I believe you have had bad news.

I nod, then climb onto the dragon's back, tucking the bag of clothes in front of me.

Back to my realm?

Yes. Pris is arranging to meet with your Queen, but we will need somewhere to change before we see her.

Ed'rathe launches into the sky, but not before I see the look of disapproval pass over Am'ratha's face as Aeron slips behind Pris. In contrast, the Minotaur's face glows with pure pleasure in anticipation of his first ever dragon ride.

It is arranged. You are to prepare for your audience with the Queen in one of the caverns near the court. I am to wait for you and then escort you inside. The dragon sounds proud.

Do you attend court often?

It is my first time. I hear the preen in his voice, and it makes me smile, eclipsing the dread pooling in my stomach.

The ride is short, and I'm soon inside a cool cavern at the entrance to the court, getting changed. Once again I am to wear the standard skintight black trousers tucked into knee-length boots, a ruffled white shirt, and a green tailed coat. Everything fits perfectly, and I luxuriate in the quality of the garments the Queen provided, happy not to magic something up of my own. I do use magic to tame my hair into something reasonable before joining Ed'rathe in the large cavernous space that joins our dressing rooms to the Queen's main court. He waits beside Am'ratha.

Where is Pris?

The tingle of magical communication pricks my skin seconds before a voice from just inside the opening says, 'Women's clothes take longer to put on, especially when there's no one else to help.'

Pris moves into view, holding up her hair. She turns her back to me. 'Can you finish doing these up?'

I fumble with the tiny pearl buttons closing the purple bodice of Pris's Edwardian-style dress. As my freezing fingers brush her neck, she shivers and, under the gaze of two dragons, I resist the urge to drop a kiss where her hair meets the nape.

'Thank you,' she says, dropping her hair back in place,

then smooths down the silk skirt of the dress before turning to Aeron. 'And thank goodness you chose something simple.'

'Nice to know I'm useful for something,' the Minotaur says sourly.

Pris places her hands on her hips. 'There was no way you were coming inside while I dressed.'

'I would have turned my back to you and guarded the door.'

'You could guard it just as well from outside.'

I intervene, saying, 'And no one was hurt, so all is well,' before turning to Am'ratha. 'Are they ready for us?'

We must wait for Princess Adina, Noble One.

I let out a heartfelt sigh. 'Must we really?'

Aeron's eyes flicker, and he smoothly positions himself beside Pris, standing at attention.

'Goodness, Priscilla, this is overkill, is it not?' A testy voice comes from behind me, and I cringe, awaiting the inevitable insult.

'Am'nera, Princess Adina,' Pris says, dropping her head in formal acknowledgement.

I nod at Am'nera but ignore Adina, showing her the same disdain she sends my way.

Bernais's mother sweeps past us, followed more sedately by Am'nera, who sends us a look of apology.

Aeron scowls at the elf's back as I hold out an arm for Pris to take. We follow our two dragon friends into court with Aeron guarding our rear, muttering under his breath about manners and what he would like to do to Adina.

Am'ratha and Ed'rathe block our view as we enter the vast cave, but they can't block out the murmurs rippling through the court as we progress towards the throne.

At first I think the excitement is because we are here, or perhaps they enjoy Adina's public displays. Then I catch a word here and there and realise it's Aeron causing the excited buzz. It's so good to have everyone's attention on someone else for a change.

Upon reaching the throne, our dragon friends lower their heads and move to the side. Pris curtsies and I bow, awaiting the Dragon Queen's leave to rise.

Aeron, Mighty Minotaur of legend, welcome to my court.

Oh my goddess, is the Dragon Queen fangirling over Aeron?

'I am honoured you have allowed me entrance. And, if I may say so, Your Majesty, you are looking particularly radiant today.'

Now she's giggling.

I quickly glance at Pris to find out if she's seeing this. She mouths, 'He's flirting with her,' and I choke back a laugh.

You are too kind.

'I beg to disagree. I merely state it like I see it.'

Pris's grip on my arm tightens as she tries to suppress her laughter and keep her balance. She's in danger of falling and causing an incident and, suddenly, the flirting isn't as amusing. Fortunately, Am'ratha steps in and saves us from a potentially embarrassing situation.

Your Majesty, Princess Priscilla and her consort bring a petition on behalf of Queen Ariana.

Oh, yes. Please rise.

I swear I can hear Pris's knees creak as she stands up. While we await permission to speak, Princess Adina steps forward and breaks protocol.

'Your Majesty, I—'

This audience has been granted to Princess Priscilla and Ambassador Fieth. Your role is to

watch and observe only, the Dragon Queen explains as if to a naughty child.

For a frightening moment, I think Adina is going to object, but she sees sense and steps back into the shadows.

What is it Queen Ariana wishes to petition me for?

Pris steps forward to respond.

'Your Majesty, Queen Ariana sends her greetings and wishes you to know she is healing well and should be able to return to cleansing magic in the next few days.

That is as it should be.

'Although her heart desires to see her realm settled, she is conscious of her duty and will comply with your request, but….' Pris pauses and takes a breath. 'She is aware it may take a little longer to sort out than the eight days she has left to return to her people and deal with the issues in the World Below.'

The room is still. Not a single whisper is heard. This is not good. I take the few steps forward to join Pris in front of the throne as she continues to speak.

'We appreciate you have been lenient with the creatures of the World Below and the World Above, especially as they failed to meet their commitments to you, but we are not simply asking for an extension. Princess Cecily will be governing the realm while Queen Ariana is busy.'

The Dragon Queen's eyes widen slightly, then almost pop out of her head as Adina rushes forward.

'No, you can't support this. Cecily has not lived in the World Below for years. She simply cannot succeed Ariana.' A sly smile forms on her lips. 'Besides, I hear Petunia is back. I bet she didn't agree to this.'

'Viper,' Pris hisses under her breath. I reach out and touch the back of her hand in warning. Schooling her face into a diplomatic mask, she says through gritted teeth,

'My grandmother has renounced her right to the Crown and is merely back to ensure my mother takes her rightful place.'

And what about you? the Dragon Queen asks.

Pris straightens her spine, turning regal before my eyes. 'I will be confirmed as second in line to the throne.'

Mmm, I see your family is working to rectify past wrongs and taking responsibility for securing the future wellbeing of the World Below, which is as it should be. However, my original ruling stands—if your family cannot sort out the rebellion in the World Below within the next eight days, then I will consider if granting Adina's petition will be better for our realms than the status quo. Or whether I should simply call my dragons home.

The cavern explodes with expressions of shock and disbelief.

'But you said you would give Bernais his dragon,' Adina yells.

SILENCE.

The command might have been imbued with a touch of magic, as there is an immediate hush throughout the room.

We have persevered with our centuries-old relationship despite recent betrayals as well as tainted magic entering our realm. It has come to a point where I must consider whether our relationship with your world provides any value.

I'm stunned into silence, but Pris doesn't cower or back down.

'I apologise for my ignorance, Your Majesty. Given that the other two realms have behaved with such bad faith, why do you still put up with us?

If I'd thought Aeron's smile scary, it is nothing compared to the one the Dragon Queen displays.

That is a fair question. Perhaps it is simply an indulgence, or perhaps it is because my dragons believe you can do better—that you can rise above your petty disputes and return to tending to your worlds.

'We *can* do better,' Pris says.

The Dragon Queen drops her head, and her voice is weary, **I hope you can, but you need to be better soon because my time of indulgence is at an end.**

The Dragon Queen's words reinforce for me how much I still have to learn about the World Below. The irony that earlier today, Maddox asked me to be an ambassador to his court is not lost on me as I'm given a lesson in inter-realm relations.

Why is the Dragon Queen staring at me? She expects me to respond. Heat rises to my cheeks, and I frantically search for something to say that won't sound stupid.

'Thank you for explaining things to me,' I start, playing for time. 'While I totally respect whatever decision you make, all I can do is thank you for your patience so far. And, I hope we can continue to work with you in the future, should that be what you desire.'

Then I remember Queen Ariana's other request.

'If I may, Your Majesty, Queen Ariana asked me to have you confirm that you will stick to your original time-line when it comes to considering Princess Adina's petition.'

As I wait for an answer, the air around me is chilly, and I worry I've gone too far.

It is only fair.

The Dragon Queen's tone is clipped, as if she's had enough of creature disputes. I bow and prepare to leave.

'Your father's dragon,' Snake whispers.

'Not the time,' I whisper back.

The Dragon Queen surprises us with a grin. **When will you two learn that if I can hear your unguarded thoughts, your whispers are like shouts to me?**

I cringe a little before forcing myself upright to talk with the Queen.

'With the succession confirmed and my mother becoming regent, we would like you to consider providing her consort with a dragon to bond with. Although I completely understand if that is out of the question, given what we discussed today.'

'You cannot do that,' Adina hisses.

The Dragon Queen turns her head away from Adina in dismissal.

While our agreement is in place, the consort can bond with a dragon. Ed'rathe, you were chosen to bond with the heir's consort. You have a choice. You can go to him now, or wait until Ambassador Fieth becomes an heir consort and finalise the bonding process with him.

Beside me, Snake pales, and the air around me buzzes with magic as he and Ed'rathe talk. Snake and I don't know what our future will be, so I'm almost certain he will encourage Ed'rathe to choose Dad. I understand how much Snake will miss Ed'rathe if he agrees. I couldn't imagine losing Am'ratha. I want to reach out to him, but I allow the two their private farewell.

'Please, Ed'rathe,' Snake begs out loud. 'It's not that I don't want you to stay, but I couldn't live with myself if you lost your position because of me.'

Ed'rathe stands tall and turns to face his queen. **I will stay. Rima is next in line. He will be honoured to become Ed'rima. You should send him to Prince Malachai.**

Snake brushes tears from his eyes, then catches his dragon friend watching him, concern written on his face. 'Thank you,' he mouths, and I feel the weight of another responsibility settle on Snake's shoulders.

'Thank you for your consideration,' I say to the Queen, aware of Adina snarling in the background. I ignore her. If it's good enough for the Dragon Queen to do this, then it's good enough for me.

It shall be as you request, Ed'rathe. This matter is closed.

The last was directed more at Aunt Adina, but we have all clearly been dismissed.

Aeron, perhaps we could have a private word.

It looks like not all of us are off the hook.

'Wait for me by the entrance, and stay close to Am'ratha,' Aeron demands, and we make our way to the exit of the audience chamber.

'Do you need any help changing?' Snake asks, and I am touched by his thoughtfulness.

Adina's furious gestures towards Am'nera catch my attention, causing Snake to move a little closer to me. She is clearly upset, and I am not in the least surprised when she storms off along the platform. Before she enters one of the caves, she turns and bellows, 'I will not allow my home to be ruled by half-breeds and interlopers.'

Before we can respond, she disappears. Nearby,

Am'nera grunts, then bobs her head politely in our direction before launching herself into flight.

'Am'ratha, how come Adina is not staying at the creature compound?' I ask, watching the dragon bank and fly over our heads.

Argh! My dragon manages to load that sound with a wealth of disdain. **She would not want to stay with such lowly creatures—that one has always thought more of herself than she should. To keep the peace, Al'kyla allowed her to use a guest room in the Queen's compound to keep distance between her and the other creatures claiming refuge.** Am'ratha tilts her head to the side. **You know, you may use a suite there. It is much better appointed.**

A chuckle bubbles from my belly. 'Am'ratha, are you teasing me?'

The dragon's stare is so unwavering that I think she might have been serious and now I've offended her.

Then her great shoulders rise, as if in imitation of a shrug. **Perhaps.**

'Thank you for the offer, but I would rather not have to listen to Adina's complaints this evening,' I inform her.

'What's that?' Snake asks, turning his attention back from Am'nera's retreating figure.

'Oh, Am'ratha is informing me we can stay in the royal quarters on this side of the mountains. Upside is the rooms are nicer. Downside is—'

'Adina,' Snake finishes for me. Pulling me into a hug he says, 'I think I prefer where we are, thank you.'

I snuggle in closer, allowing his body to warm me. 'How long do you think the Dragon Queen will keep Aeron?'

'I am here,' the Minotaur says. 'Have you not changed yet? You can't fly in that ridiculous dress.'

I glare at him. 'You told me to wait here.'

'Oh, I did too. Come on, then. Let's get you dressed, and then we can head to the rebel camp.'

Turning my head to take in the setting sun, I say, 'I think we'll stay here tonight, with Snake and the other refugees, rather than fly in the dark'

Darkness does not bother me, Am'ratha says.

Let's keep that to ourselves today, please.

Aeron raises his eyebrows. 'I guess we're staying to be safe, not so you can spend the night with young Fieth.'

'I'm JUST here,' Snake mutters as I wink at Aeron.

'Purely for safety reasons.' I tug Snake with me into the small changing room. He helps with my buttons, then dresses quickly, giving me space to change. As I pull on a warm top, I'm annoyed to see Aeron blocking the doorway, his back to me.

'So, Aeron, what did the Dragon Queen want with you?' I tease.

'Nosey.'

'Yes,' I reply. 'I am.'

I take a seat on the bench, then retrieve the boots from the bag and proceed to put them on. I wait a moment for them to adjust to my feet before standing up—I do love magic apparel. Aeron still hasn't answered.

I start stuffing clothes into the bag. 'You don't have to tell me....'

Aeron crosses from one side of the entrance to the other, then adjusts his jacket. 'She asked why I had involved myself in this conflict, given I am not of these worlds.'

I pause. *Should I ask what he said?* But instead, I simply tell him,'I'm done.'

Aeron half turns. 'Do you not want to know my answer?'

Of course I do, but I don't want Aeron to know that. 'If you want to tell me, I'll listen.'

His shoulders rise in a sort of nonchalant shrug. 'I have a pleasant life. I'm safe and secure, and I doubt very much that current events would threaten that.'

'That sounds more like a reason not to become involved.'

Aeron's lips curl into what I hope is a smile. 'It does, doesn't it. And, had my conversation with you yesterday not reminded me of my past, I would have forgotten how grateful I am for my life—and who I owe that life to.'

My eyebrows shoot up. 'Are you saying you are protecting me because you owe Fairglade a debt? I thought the King and Queen asked you to do it.'

With his grin widening, Aeron says, 'It is more that I am reminded why I chose to remain in the World Below. That in itself is reason enough to take some sort of action to save my home from certain disaster.'

'And protecting me?'

Aeron's grin fades, and his face softens, his huge brown eyes looking more cowlike than they had. 'When Fairburn and Maddox requested my services, they were asking me to commit to the future of our realm. Princess, you are our future. How could I refuse? And that is what I told the Dragon Queen.'

I'm speechless. The weight of Aeron's belief in me as the future of the realm is almost suffocating, ramping up the pressure of being the heir. My shoulders slump, and Aeron drops a meaty hand on my shoulder.

'Pris, my reason asks nothing more of you than you already agreed to give. Now, shake it off, and let's get ourselves to the guest quarters. After that meeting, I could do with a bowl of hot food and a cold tankard of ale.'

Aeron directs me past him and into the cold evening air, and my spirits lift a little seeing Snake is already atop Ed'rathe. At least I will spend tonight with him.

The trip across the canyon is short, and we do not waste time with long goodbyes. Am'ratha agrees to return a little after dawn before joining Ed'rathe in the sky. Pulling back the heavy inner hide curtain, we find the common room a study in chaos. There are creatures and bags and stuff everywhere. We attempt to sidle round the edge, but when the first creature spots Aeron, it's all on—calling to mind visions of rock stars being mobbed.

Snake tugs on my hand, and we try to slip away, but Aeron is having none of it. His strong fingers grasp my arm, and I'm going nowhere. He leans down and whispers frantically, 'Do not leave me to these…these… children.'

'Honestly, we have a war to fight, and you waste time clamouring over him?' The amused voice comes from behind the crowd. The "children" part to reveal the wizard Mandor.

Wait, he's not a wizard any more, is he?

Last time I saw the witch was when he set the final puzzle to get us into the maze, and he seems to have aged a decade since then. Maybe he aged when he gave up his powers. Or maybe that's what happens when you lead a rebellion. Given my role in things, I hope it's the former.

'Princess Priscilla, pleased to see you alive and well. Aeron, trust you to arrive and cause havoc with my well-organised relocation plans.'

'Old friend, it is my pleasure. But if you could point us in the direction of food, I'm sure we would be happy to leave you to it.'

The creatures rather reluctantly return to what they

were doing, and Mandor leads us into the dining room. 'We have eaten, but I'm sure there will be leftovers. Just ask—'

'Susan,' I exclaim as my family's ex-au pair emerges from the kitchen. I rush to her, dropping my bag on the way. My body slams into hers and familiar arms come around me. I hug her tightly, never wanting to loosen my grip.

'I thought I'd lost you forever,' I whisper. 'Then, when Uncle Maddox told me you were all right, I didn't get a chance to ask where you were.'

Susan moves so she can see Snake. 'Didn't you let Pris know I was okay?'

What? Snake knew?

'Sorry, Pris. Honestly there's been so much going on, it never occurred to me you didn't know.'

'Well, I'm here now, and I'm fine,' she says, her voice close by my ear.

I bury my face into her shoulder, and for a moment, I'm the girl I'd been before a strange gnome burst into my home. Relishing the sense of security, I'm reluctant to leave her embrace. My rumbling stomach eventually forces me to pull away.

Practical as ever, Susan says, 'Take a seat, and I'll get you all some food and drinks. Are you staying?' she asks Mandor.

He shakes his head. 'No, I have to oversee the evacuation. I'll pop back before I go.'

'Are Verona and Gregor still here?' Snake asks Mandor.

'No, sorry. They have gone on ahead to the mustering site to organise the arrivals,' Mandor responds. 'Can I pass on a message?'

Snake looks so forlorn. 'No, it's okay. It's just….'

'I understand, son. You want to be with them. They appreciate that we each have our own roles to play, and yours is to keep the dragons informed and neutral. The last thing we need is them deciding the Crown line is no longer capable of ruling the World Below. Then all we have worked for will fall apart.'

Snake forces a smile. 'So, no pressure, then?'

Mandor slaps him on the back. 'I'm sure you're up to the job.' He scans our group before he says, 'if there's nothing else?'

When no one speaks, he leaves us to find seats while Susan heads into the kitchen to get our food.

'Is everyone going?' I ask Snake as we sit, wondering if he will be alone here when I leave to see my grandmother.

'I'm not,' Susan says as she places a platter of bread on the table. 'I'm staying to set up hospital facilities. The Dragon Queen has agreed injured rebels can return here to heal after their initial treatment.'

She returns to the kitchen, and Snake wraps an arm around me.

'I'd be fine, even if Susan weren't here,' he tells me, and I lean into his shoulder.

'I know, I just wish—'

Snake places a finger over my lips. 'It'll be difficult, but we'll get through this. Remember, we're going to enjoy what time we have.' He removes his finger and presses a gentle kiss to my lips.

'Get a room, you two,' Aeron snorts, but is then distracted as Susan places a frothing tankard of ale in front of him. He greedily licks his lips and gulps half of it down in a single mouthful.

With our companion's attention directed elsewhere, I snuggle into Snake, brushing a kiss at the base of his neck where it meets his shoulder. He shivers. I'm pleased I decided to stay the night.

When Susan places bowls of spicy stew on the table in front of us, all thoughts of what might happen later are gone from my head as other appetites take over.

·· ◞ ··

Alyce portals me to a spot under the trees behind a huge white canvas tent, right beside Drow. From here all we can see are trees and white fabric. The only sign there's an army mustering at the base of the Essendore mountains is the incredible mixture of voices shouting, metal clanging, and feet marching that permeate the air.

'Thank you.' She is gone before I even finish the first word.

'She looked exhausted,' Drow says. 'I guess portalling skills are in demand now the army is mustering.'

'Which is why they should be taking more care,' I say, more than a little dourly.

'The Dragon Queen's arbitrary timeline is placing pressure on us all,' Drow says.

I worry we will achieve nothing if we run our scarce resources into the ground. Then again, creature-kind has been very good at focusing on our immediate needs, willing to sacrifice the future for a little ease in the present. Perhaps if we learn one thing from this debacle, it will be to think long term.

Alyce deposits Fairburn beside us before wandering off to find somewhere to eat and sleep.

'This is the first thing we will change,' Fairburn says, 'To have the back of the command tent so exposed is folly!'

We round the corner, and I stop short. In front of us are row upon row of tents in an array of colours and styles. While some are still being pitched, others are already set up with inhabitants gathered around shared fires.

To the right, a raggle-taggle of creatures is being drilled by an imposing dwarf who is almost as wide as he is high—and he is tall for one of his kind. The drilling creatures are a mix of races, but they have clearly had some sort of military training in the past because, although they wear civilian clothes, their form as they march is precise, like their muscles remember long ago commands.

'Come,' Fairburn says, 'We have little time to gawp. We need to find out what is happening in there.' He nods towards the wall of the command tent.

As we approach, two strong dwarf guards halt us.

'A little late for this,' Fairburn snaps. 'If we had wanted to, we could have obliterated your command when we arrived five minutes ago. You—' He points at the guard on the left. 'Go get a couple of creatures from that platoon and clear a space for the command and royal tents in the middle of the army. Anyone wishing to get to the leaders of this rebellion should have to fight through every soldier we have mustered to gain their chance.'

Recognising authority, although not perhaps knowing who Fairburn is, the guard salutes and leaps to action. The remaining guard is not so gullible.

'And who might you be to give orders?' he challenges the centaur.

'I am Fairburn, previously of the Queen's Guard, and I have come to offer my expertise.'

'F-f… Fairburn? C-c-c… Captain Fairburn?' the guard stammers, straightening his back.

Fairburn flicks a hand as if dismissing his title. 'Former. Now can we go in?'

'Of course, sir, but I warn you, it will not be what you are used to.'

Fairburn snorts. 'But I suspect it will be exactly what I am expecting, which is why I am here. Lead the way, soldier.'

The guard pushes open the tent flap and gestures for us to enter. If outside is organised chaos, inside is its disorganised sibling. Standing around a table, approximately thirty creatures are studying a map of the World Below. Everyone is talking, each raising their voice higher and higher to be heard over the others.

The only creatures I recognise are Thomas, Nathanial, and Gregor. The rest are strangers drawn from all races of creature-kind.

I catch Drow's eye, and he frowns, deepening the worry lines on his face. We both look at Fairburn to see how he is reacting. He remains in the doorway, arms folded over his heavily muscled chest. He appears to be waiting for something, but I do not know what. After some time passes, he clearly gets bored with this and yells, 'SILENCE,' in a tone used to being obeyed.

And obeyed it is. Every mouth in the room closes, and every eye turns to us. Expectation hangs heavy in the air. The creature opposite us opens his mouth to speak, but Fairburn raises a hand to silence him.

'We have two, maybe three, days before we engage the enemy, and you are standing here, arguing like a bunch of market traders haggling for the best price.'

A few of the creatures have the grace to blush. The one across from us stands taller and is not happy about having what authority he does have questioned by a stranger. Again, Fairburn does not give them a chance to speak.

'Firstly, there are too many cooks here. If you are not

the leader of the group you brought to muster, please leave.'

Some creatures come forward, and Fairburn moves to allow them to depart. A few look to their leaders for approval, and a couple throw rebellious glances our way. Fairburn is implacable. Eventually half the creatures in the room depart.

'Good. Now, have any of you had any military experience?'

No one moves.

A brief flicker of exasperation crosses the centaur's face. 'None of you have had any military training at all?'

One young creature, a goblin, perhaps, steps forward. 'I was part of the local guard until my brother passed and I was called home to run our vineyard.'

Fairburn's teeth flash the briefest smile. 'Excellent. And you are?'

'Brynn Bottas, sir.'

'Brynn you are now my Adjutant. If I am not around, then you will deal with everyone's concerns and questions.'

Finally the creature opposite can contain his ire no longer. 'And who are you to organise us so?' he splutters.

'I am the only one here with enough military experience to lead this force,' Fairburn says.

I lean into Drow and whisper, 'Why does he not introduce himself?'

Drow's grin is rather sardonic. 'He is so well known in the Capitol, he isn't aware that no one outside the city's confines has any idea who he is.'

Taking matters in hand, Drow steps forward. 'Elected leaders from the regions, may I introduce to you Fairburn, previous Captain of the Queen's Guard.'

Whispers circulate the room as eyes widen with shock. The creature who confronted Fairburn blanches. He quickly recovers and says, 'Well, sir, we welcome your leadership.'

Fairburn drops his head briefly, acknowledging the invitation and accepting it with the same gesture.

'You already know Drow, I suspect, as he has been working with Mandor to pull this alliance together. Once Mandor arrives, they will deal with any disputes you might have between yourselves. And this is Percival. He is here to represent the Queen's interests, but I want him to work alongside Brynn as my eyes and ears when I am otherwise engaged—that is if you accept me as your General.'

The last is less of a request and more of a statement. When no one objects, Fairburn seamlessly takes control.

'Right, our first order of business is to find out what we have to work with. I assume you have details of who has responded to the muster?'

One by one, the leaders step forward. Along with Thomas from the Wyld Woods and Brynn Bottas from the winemaking region of Avondale, there is: Angus Abernathy a dwarf from the mining region of Essendore, Toab Rowne, a gnome from the fishing region of Melliores, and Amelia Farrmer from the market garden region around the Capitol.

'We are still waiting for a response from the deep woods and there are still creatures arriving from the World Above. Also, Princess Petunia is here, and she brought a small contingent of soldiers,' Brynn advises. 'I believe they are drilling some of our recruits outside.'

'Thank you, Brynn,' Fairburn says, capturing Drow's eye. 'We must ask the World Above to send a representative to this war council.'

'I need to talk to Petunia on behalf of the Queen,' I whisper. 'Do you think I should go now?'

Drow shakes his head. 'I would wait until Fairburn

finishes. Especially now that he has given you a role as his adjutant.'

'Now, next item on the agenda. How many of your recruits have military experience? And do any of them have weapons?'

Angus Abernathy from the mines steps forward. 'All my people can wield swords. We must all be able to test what we make. We each brought our own weapon and a second sword to arm someone else. There is also a wagonload of 200 pikes arriving on the morrow.'

Fairburn's eyebrows rise. 'You have done us a great service, Angus. Thank you. Brynn and Percival, can you pull together a list of what else we have available from those who have their details with them?'

A few of the creatures separate from the group and wait by a smaller table containing paper and inkwells in the corner.

'Drow, would you mind scribing for me as I tour the camp with the rest of the representatives?'

'Of course,' Drow says and grabs a notebook and pencil from the table. 'Happy to be useful.'

And useful we are. Before I even have time to take a seat, the representative from Avondale starts listing their contributions. The sun has set when Brynn and I finally finish with our lists. It was immediately made apparent that our main issue is not the number of creatures gathered, but finding weapons for them and feeding them over the next few days.

After we have summarised everything in a report for Fairburn, I rise to my feet, stretch, then roll my shoulders. Every part of me aches from sitting for too long.

'If we are done here, I have a message from the Queen for her sister,' I say to Brynn as I tidy my workspace.

Their eyes widen as they study me with a newfound look of respect. 'You're more than a secretary, aren't you?'

I nod.

'Who exactly are you and the gnome you arrived with?'

I stop mid-action and consider how to answer their question. There are a myriad of possible responses, but which one is relevant in this context?

'I am Percival of the Wyld Woods, and the gnome is Drow—'

'Drow Fieth?' Brynn finishes, their voice tinged with awe. 'Gosh, wait until my friends hear I worked with creatures we learnt about in school.'

'Thanks,' I say dryly, 'Now I feel ancient.'

They grin at me. 'Well, Percival of the Wyld Woods, it has been an honour to work alongside one of the creatures who changed our world for the better. It gives me hope to know that we have you, and others like you, on our side.'

My ears tingle as heat rises from my neck to their tip. Who knew my coming out of hiding would be met with such welcoming support?

'Well… umm… thank you, I guess.'

'If you need to speak with Princess Petunia, then you'd—'

Brynn doesn't get to finish. The tent flap is flung open as Fairburn returns with the representatives and Mandor by his side.

I return to my seat while everyone crowds into the command space. While they quieten down, Drow places his notebook in front of Brynn.

'This is the command structure Fairburn has agreed to. Lieutenant Howden from Princess Petunia's forces is to be his second-in-command, and, well, you can see the rest. He wanted a copy made for each of the leaders.'

We make space for Drow at the table, and we each

begin copying what's on the page onto fresh sheets of paper. While we work, I listen to the discussion around the command table about splitting the volunteers into platoons, what weapons they will have, and how unarmed creatures will be assigned logistical support.

'Small well-armed groups will be more effective than large numbers for what I have in mind,' I hear Fairburn say. 'Now, I'm going to hand over to Mandor, as your signing of the accords that brought this group together is not a military issue.'

The centaur makes his way to our table in the back as the rest of the group gathers more tightly around the map. Drow joins them to answer any legal questions.

Fairburn taps my arm to get my attention. 'Percival, Brynn and I can finish here. Time for you to speak with Princess Petunia. Her agreement to this plan is critical.'

He does not need to tell me twice. I'm outside within moments, and I take my time walking the few paces to Petunia's tent, enjoying the fresh air and preparing myself for the interview ahead.

CHAPTER 9

It's Becoming Real

For some reason, I'm almost overcome with nerves outside the flap of Petunia's tent. I only saw her a couple of days ago. Could it be because then I saw her as a friend, but now I'm here for Ariana?

The guard stares down at me, an eyebrow raised. 'In or not?' he asks.

I square my shoulders. 'In.'

He slips between the opening. 'Your Highness, Percival of the Wyld Woods is here to see you.'

Petunia's voice drifts out. 'Oh, we don't stand on ceremony with Percival.' then I hear her say, 'Come in old friend,' a little louder.

Not a great start in my new official role. I step beneath the tent flap the guard holds up for me. 'Petunia, I am afraid this *is* a formal visit—Queen Ariana sent me.'

As my eyes adjust to the candlelit interior, I am aware of Petunia's eyes narrowing.

'Ariana sent an emissary? How so very her. I am surprised it is you, given our friendship. Then again, it must be something important to her if she is playing at this level of politics.'

Her words carry pain, making me feel uneasy. What have I walked into?

'I am an emissary to the military command. This is more of an… additional job… a one-off.'

Petunia gestures to the chair opposite her. 'All right. This is a little odd, but perhaps we can still talk as friends.'

I sit, my mind scrabbling for some safe footing. I had believed Petunia and Ariana were close, but I am getting the impression something has gone wrong.

'Tea?' Petunia asks.

I nod. 'Yes, please.'

Petunia rises and moves to the table, where she prepares the drink herself. This is a very different Petunia from the woman at the Unseelie Court. She is dressed in a brown woollen split skirt suitable for riding with a cotton shirt, and her feet are clad in boots. Gone is all the finery she wore in the Unseelie Court.

She returns with sturdy mugs of steaming tea. After passing one to me, she retakes her seat and waits patiently for me to start. I am even more reluctant to open my mouth now that I know there is something amiss between the sisters. What if I say the wrong thing?

'Percival?' Petunia prompts.

'Mother, did you know Howden is in the command tent?' a female voice asks as the tent flap rustles.

Moments later Princess Irene flops down in the seat between her mother and me.

'Did you really ask him to organise a force to breach the Capitol's defences?'

Petunia shakes her head as I ask her, 'How did you know about what Bernais is doing in the Capitol?'

'I sent Am'ralla to find out what she could. Did you

know the city is under martial law, and there is a curfew in force?'

'No, but I'm sure those in the command tent are aware,' I respond, wondering why I had not heard anything about this.

Petunia leans forward in her seat. 'Lesser creatures are being herded into ghettos, and anyone who resists the council is being imprisoned. They are being held at the hospital. I believe they are being drugged so they can't use their magic.'

I shudder at her words. If this is true, then it is grotesque.

'See? This is why I could not just stand by and do nothing. Lieutenant Howden and I devised a plan to get a small force inside the Capitol to free the prisoners.'

I cannot help the tut that escapes. Petunia scowls back.

'If Ariana cannot, will not step up. Someone has to take control,' she says.

'Petunia, if only you had attended the council, you would know Ariana *is* stepping up.' I wring my hands in frustration. 'This is what she was worried about, which is why I am here.'

Petunia does not hear me. She is on her feet, talking as she circles the tent. 'If she's taken charge, where is she, then? Still hiding behind her commitment to the dragons so she doesn't have to face up to the chaos she let develop in her realm?'

I hold my hands palms outward, trying to calm things down, but Princess Irene continues the tirade.

'You only have to look at the disparate forces outside to know things are not right in the World Below. Most of the creatures gathered here are rebels wanting to overthrow the Crown.'

Petunia turns to me. 'Percival, how did we not know

things were this unsettled in the World Below? We were remiss in staying away for so long, believing Ariana was handling everything. Now it is time for us to step up and sort this mess out.'

I place my tea on the side table between Irene and me, buying myself a little time to consider how to traverse the minefield in front of me.

As the silence grows, Petunia says, 'Just spit it out, Percival.'

'Petunia, have you considered asking how you might contribute to the coming war, rather than taking control?'

Petunia's face turns thunderous, telling me I have mis-stepped.

I run a hand through my hair, trying to clear the fog tiredness is creating in my brain. 'I am sorry, Petunia, that did not come out right. Let me start again.'

'Do you think I do not have the best interests of the creatures of the World Below and Above in mind when I take action?' Petunia asks tersely.

Perhaps I have gone too far to turn this around.

Princess Irene comes to my rescue. 'Perhaps we should hear him out, Mother.'

'Please, Petunia.' I'm not above begging at this stage. 'I have information you may not have, and I am sure you would like to be in possession of all the facts.'

Petunia's gaze is stony as she says, 'All right.'

I wring my hands together in my lap as I begin where I should have started a few minutes ago. 'While we were defending the Unseelie Court and Ariana was held in stasis, there were those in the World Below who were aware of what was coming and have been working behind the scenes. A young wizard called Gregor has been co-ordinating a group of young creatures who are tired of the slow pace of change.'

'I met Gregor earlier today,' Irene says. 'He has quite a force behind him, and they appear to be very anti-monarchy.'

I nod. 'It is true. They would like to see radical change. By the same token, there are those who have joined who prefer a more evolutionary approach to wrest control of the World Below from the elves.'

'How could Ariana let things get so bad?' Petunia whispers. 'Is there any way to come back from this?'

'Mandor and Drow believe so. In fact, at the moment, the leaders of various factions are signing an accord that will pull these disparate groups together.'

'How so?' Petunia asks.

I spend the next half an hour outlining the agreement made with Princess Cecily and the factions and describing how Queen Ariana has sent her support. Petunia and Irene allow me to finish before responding.

'If I understand this, you want me to allow my forces to work under Fairburn, and you want me to stand aside and let my granddaughter lead this rebellion?' Petunia summarises.

She was always good at cutting to the chase. In fact, I had often thought it was a shame she was the younger sister because she would have made a magnificent queen.

'Yes, Petunia. We need you to take a step back.'

'I have never met Priscilla, and she's only young. Why should we trust her to lead?' Irene asks.

'I *have* met her, and she has potential,' Petunia tells her daughter. 'But Percival, you and I both know Priscilla was not brought up to this role, and she was ambivalent about taking on royal duties when we were in the Unseelie Court. If it were Cecily here....'

I nod my understanding. 'Pris is not wild about this, but she realises it is her duty to stand beside Fairburn. And this is the second reason why Ariana wanted me to speak to you.' I cross my fingers, hoping Queen Ariana will forgive the small twisting of her words. I am sure she would have asked me to set this up had she had time to think of it. 'Pris cannot do this alone. She will need your support if she is to do a halfway decent job.'

Petunia sits back down, and my shoulders relax for the first time since I entered the tent. 'Well, I guess this was Cecily's destiny when I left the court. And Pris has always been next in line. And, I do intend to return to Urquhart Castle after this is over, so....'

Irene jumps to her feet and paces in front of us—she is so like her mother, it is uncanny.

'Mother, I can't believe you're thinking of doing this. Cecily brought her daughter up outside our world. There's no way she can lead this army. She should step aside and allow me to step up—at least I have military experience.'

'I did not know you wanted a royal role,' Petunia says, somewhat bewildered.

Irene stops in her tracks. 'You've never asked what I wanted to do. Wilfred is trained to take over the garrison, and his wife will take over your position. What is next for me at Loch Ness?'

The blank expression on Petunia's face tells me she really had not considered Irene's future.

'Besides, I don't want a royal role. I just want *a* role,' Irene finishes. Her tone is a touch sad—perhaps because it has taken a war for this to be brought to her mother's attention.

I cross my fingers again, hoping Ariana will support me on this as it plays out, and maybe it will be better received now Irene is searching for her place in the worlds.

'Ariana wondered, Petunia, if you would help her

strengthen relations with the Unseelie Court by becoming her ambassador there—once the court is restored, of course.'

Petunia draws her gaze from her daughter, stares blankly at me, then shakes her head. 'Well, it is about time she took a stance on that, but I am sorry. I am not the creature for the job.'

'Hold on, Mother. You've spent years saying the two courts should work more closely together. Now that it's happening, you opt out?'

Petunia is silent for a while, her gaze unfocused. When she speaks again, her words are considered and sad. 'It is not what I want to do, Irene. I was not happy to leave the Seelie Court, but it was impossible for me to stay. We have built a good life in the World Above since then, and I do not want to jeopardise it.'

'What if I want to go home to the World Below?'

'Then you should. Ariana would welcome you with open arms. In fact, *you* should help Pris. I am too old for this fighting nonsense. I'd be far happier working in the hospital tent with the witch sisters.'

'Mmm, I could do that.' A sparkle of excitement glints in her eyes, then her gaze turns to me. 'But I'll only help her if I think she is up to the job.'

Hold on, what is going on here? 'Queen Ariana wanted you to help Pris, Petunia. She knows you.'

'Oh, I'll help her with the nonmilitary things, but it would be good for Pris and Irene to get to know each other. Irene is an experienced soldier, and Pris can help Irene find a place in the World Below once this is over.'

'And the ambassadorship?'

'A discussion for another time, Percival.'

Do all emissaries lose control the way I did? Or *did* I?

My primary mission was to get Petunia to support Pris rather than strike out on her own or gather followers, and I did that. I stifle a yawn.

'Percival, you are almost asleep there. Have they allocated you a bed for tonight?'

'I will sort something out later. I want to go to the hospital tent and find Nisha,' I say, pushing myself to my feet. 'So, I will bid you all a good night.'

'Good night, Percival. Sleep well,' Petunia tells me, and I leave, feeling quite pleased with what I achieved during my short visit.

The hospital tent is busy, although they are only treating minor cuts and bruises at the moment. Effie and Genie are running some sort of clinic, while Ellie is reviewing paperwork with Nisha.

I watch the two of them. Their relationship has never been easy. I always worried Nisha resented my closeness to Ellie, who in turn harbours a deep sense of guilt about the time I spent away from Nisha. Seeing the two of them now, I wonder if I had been less selfish, would they have been friends?

Across the room, a creature groans, causing Ellie to half turn towards the noise. Spotting me in the doorway, she motions for me to come in.

'Percival. There you are. Nathanial told us to expect you sometime this evening.' Taking the sheaf of papers from Nisha, she says, 'I can finish these up. Why don't you find Percival a bed before he collapses.'

'If you are sure....'

'I am.' Ellie flaps her hands.

As Nisha slips an arm through mine, I mouth, 'Thank you,' to Ellie.

Outside the tent the cool air hits us, and Nisha leans into me so we might share our warmth.

'When I heard you were here, I hoped you would come and find me,' Nisha says, her voice a little tentative.

I pull her closer. 'Of course I would come. We have been apart too long, and I intend to make up for that.'

She leads us to a smaller shelter to the side of the medical tent. Pulling back the flap, Nisha enters, and I almost groan with relief when I spy the nest of blankets set on top of tree branches. It is a while since I have slept in the sprite style. I sink into the cocoon bed, pulling Nisha down with me.

Although we still have much to discuss about our future, my eyes flutter close and exhaustion seeps through my limbs. I whisper, 'Peaceful night's journey.'

Her breath warms my cheek as she returns the night-time wish, and I think that for all that is wrong in the world, this at least feels right.

⁘

A trickle of cool air seeps through a gap in the covers, and I snuggle into the warmth of Snake's body. He groans and wraps an arm around me, drawing me still closer. Sleeping two to a single bed does not make for the best night's sleep, but it'll do for the one night we are able to spend together before the crazy starts.

'Is it morning yet?' Snake mumbles.

'No, I don't think so. Go back to sleep.'

He nuzzles into my neck and is soon snoring gently. I attempt to relax, but sounds of creatures moving about in the hall make their way through the closed door. I'm awake.

I untangle myself from Snake's embrace, wrap the

blanket from the end of the bed around me, and head for the bathroom. By the time I return clean and dressed in warm clothing, Snake is up and dressing too.

He glances at me through his fringe as I enter, and the grin he sends my way has butterflies fluttering in my stomach. I step towards him and finish buttoning his shirt, stopping to consider if unbuttoning it is a better option. No. Last night was a gift. This morning would be a selfish indulgence.

While I grapple with the last button, he gently places his hand over mine. I lift my head, and he kisses my forehead.

'There's so much I want to say, but….' He closes his eyes for a moment. 'But it all seems so… unimportant.' His lips brush my cheek, and his breath tickles my ear as he says, 'Except maybe I think I'm falling in love with you.'

The words rock me to my core, and I resist the urge to pull away. As my heart pounds in my ears, my first thought is *This is too much.* Then I wrap my arms around Snake and bury my face in his shoulder. Perhaps it is not too much. I don't want to be anywhere else but where I am now. As he holds me, I sense he's waiting for a response, but although my heart screams tell him, my head warns me to wait and see what the next few days bring.

Snake loosens his hold on me. 'We should go get breakfast.'

I may not be able to tell him how I feel, but I'm not ready to let him go either. 'Not yet. I want one more minute of it being just us like this. Burrowing my face back into his neck, I breathe in the smell of him, hoping to hide from my responsibilities a little longer. Snake's arms tighten, and, to my surprise, I find tears leaking from my eyes.

'Hey, I didn't mean to make you cry,' he says, gently rubbing my back.

'You didn't,' I snuffle, and I feel the vibration in his chest as he chuckles. 'I mean, it's not what you said, I just feel so…. It's all too much.'

I take a step away from him. What I want to tell him is now clear in my head. Gazing at him through a haze of tears, I say, 'I think I'm crying for what might have been between us. You know, getting to know each other, drawing closer, allowing our feelings to grow.'

He takes my hands in his, and I worry he's going to say something before I've got everything out. I relax when he gives my hands a squeeze, signalling for me to go on.

'Instead, we have snatched moments with no guaranteed future, and I'm feeling the loss.'

Snake's mouth twists into a wry smile, and his eyes glisten with understanding. 'We have what we have, Pris, and I'm insanely grateful we have that much.'

I lean in a plant a soft kiss on his lips before letting go of one of his hands and turning us towards the door. 'Don't get me wrong, I would rather have this than nothing, but still….' I leave the rest unsaid because we both know what I mean. 'Come on, let's get some breakfast before Am'ratha calls and I have to leave on an empty stomach.'

Snake hesitates, then obviously decides food will serve us better than more words. By the time we reach the dining room, we are both ready to face what the day will bring.

If the corridors were quieter than we expected, the dining room is even more so. Only Susan is there, sitting at the table, cradling a cup of coffee.

'Where is everyone?' Snake asks as we take seats opposite her.

'The last of the refugees left a few minutes ago,' Susan says as George appears from the kitchen and places two plates of sausages and eggs in front of us.

'What? No choice?' I joke.

'Not much point in a big cook-up for only a few people,' he snarks before returning to the kitchen.

'He wanted to go with the others,' Susan says. 'It took a lot of persuading to have him remain here. We expect a lot of casualties, and someone will have to feed them.'

'So, they're all gone?' Snake asks before tucking into his meal.

'Yep. There's only the four of us here now—three when Pris leaves.' Susan stares into her mug.

I reach out and touch her hand. 'You wanted to go too.' It's a statement rather than a question.

Her head moves in an almost imperceptible nod. 'Yes, but I guess someone has to remain and prepare for casualties.'

'Wait, four of us? Where's Aeron?' My eyes scan the room even though there is no way the giant creature could hide anywhere in here.

George bangs the coffeepot on the table before taking a seat beside Susan. 'He went to the camp. Said you were safe here and he would meet you there.'

'So much for his needing to be by my side at all times,' I mutter. 'Guess that's only when it suits him.'

Our quiet breakfast serves as a stark contrast to the lively one I had last time I was here, highlighting the seriousness of the upcoming fight. All too soon, Am'ratha calls me to the ledge.

Back in our bedroom, I pull on my jacket and finish packing my bag. Snake watches me from the doorway, then escorts me outside.

It is as if the pall from the dining room follows us, or

maybe it's because the words we have to say are too over-whelming. Too personal. Too close to the bone. I place a hand on his chest as we stand between the two curtains.

Before he can say anything, I stand on tiptoes and kiss him. 'Let's not make this a thing,' I say.

He squeezes my arm in understanding. 'I don't know what the Dragon Queen expects of me, but I'll try to find you when I can. In the meantime, fly safe and be well.'

I nod curtly and turn away before he can see the tears forming. This is still goodbye, even if we don't say the words.

Princess. Am'ratha bows her head as I emerge. **Are you all right?**

What a loaded question. How do I answer that?

Ah, I see.

Am'ratha doesn't say anything more, but waves of sympathy travel through our bond, bringing more tears to my eyes. She waits until I am settled before taking to the sky. I turn my face to lessen the sting on my skin from the sharp, crisp air as we circle to leave the World Between. Catching sight of Snake standing on the ledge, I finally allow my tears to fall freely, fervently hoping this is not the last I will see of him.

Sensing my mood, Am'ratha leaves me to my thoughts as we fly. This is my first actual view of the world my fore-bears have ruled for centuries. My first impression is of a land sparsely populated. Settlements are small and spaced far apart, for the most part, with the occasional larger village.

It is also a land stuck in the past. There is no sign of electricity lines or motor vehicles. In fact, with only one main road in sight, there would be nothing for them to drive on. On the other hand, the air is clear, and I can see for miles.

While I have an excellent view, my eyesight can't match Am'ratha's, and as a range of mountains appears on the horizon, she suddenly banks.

Princess, there are men approaching the position of the rebel camp.

Are you sure? I mean, I can't see anything at all, let alone an army.

An invisibility spell hides it to most. I am able to see through the working. I count about ten groups of guards heading directly for the camp.

Am'ratha's revelation has me worried.

Can we still land nearby without alerting them to our presence?

She is silent as she rises high into the sky and circles what I assume is the encampment, which seems to be nestled in a clearing at the base of some mountains.

No, we cannot.

She ranges wider, and I can make out a larger force of guards heading our way.

How long before they join the others?

I would guess they are just over a day's march away, even if they use magic to move more quickly.

Wait, they can do that?

Some creatures, yes.

As we bank again, a group of about twenty men detach and take off at a jog, but I can see they are moving more quickly than should be possible. Could they be slowly bringing up troops to surround us? If we hadn't seen them, their attack would have taken us by surprise. More worryingly, although they couldn't hope to win against the number of creatures we have amassed, they could cripple our forces.

We need to alert Fairburn. Can you put me down close by?

Princess, you cannot make your way to camp through those guards. It is too dangerous.

Do you have another suggestion? I don't even try to keep the annoyance from my voice.

As we complete another circuit around the camp, a group of guards look up, clearly aware we are in the sky above them. I tense, sure they will send a magical attack our way.

Do not fear. From that distance, they will only see me—they cannot tell I carry a rider. Besides, they will not attack a dragon.

You seem sure of that.

There is a smile in Am'ratha's voice when she answers, **I am. Not only are dragons neutral, but they will not want to anger us lest we take a side in this fight.**

I am smart enough not to point out that they sort of have taken a side when they elected to support the status quo. Instead I say, **But that will not make it safe for us to land near the camp, will it?**

I have contacted Am'ralla. She is going to have Princess Petunia send a wizard to meet us behind the posting inn to take you to the camp.

Couldn't we have discussed options, like perhaps telling Fairburn what's happening? I send.

Am'ratha snorts at my sulky tone and doesn't deign to respond.

I'm sorry, I tell her once we've landed, hidden from the road by the posting inn. I dismount, allowing my dragon friend to crouch and rest while we wait for my wizard escort. **I want to be seen as a leader, not someone who needs rescuing.**

I rest a hand on her shoulder.

She snorts again. **We all have different skills and abilities. A good leader encourages those around them to use what they have.**

She's right, of course, and I know it. Before I have time to overthink it, a wizard appears. Holding a portal open, he gestures for me to hurry through.

Am'ratha?

I will stay close by with Am'ralla. She waits in a cave in the mountains.

Can you let Snake know what's happening? I ask as I step through the opening.

The portal closes as Am'ratha sends, **It will be done.**

Am'ratha ferries Pris away. All too soon they have disappeared from view, and I try not to focus on the possibility that this might be my last glimpse of the person who's captured my heart.

I need a distraction. Back in the kitchen, Susan and George are stirring rather foul-smelling pots of liquid.

'I hope that's not lunch,' I say, attempting a levity I don't feel.

Susan's nose wrinkles as she adds something to her pot, causing it to bubble. 'Fortunately for you, it's not. We're making up sleeping and pain draughts. If you want to help, you can decant the pot we made up before breakfast into the green bottles. It should be cool enough to handle.'

Happy to have something constructive to do, I do as I'm asked. Once I've finished and corked the bottles, there are two more pots cooling nearby.

'Those are to go in the blue bottles,' Susan instructs.

She takes the pot I have emptied to the sink and begins cleaning it. Over by the stove, George is stripping willow bark, preparing to distill another batch of pain tonic. The three of us continue working throughout the morning until we have no more ingredients left to process. The work is tedious, but it keeps my mind off Pris and the coming war.

George brings the last pot over and returns to his workspace with a bowl of steaming soapy water and begins scrubbing down. Susan moves the bottles I've filled into a cupboard at the back of the dining room as I finish emptying the last pot.

When the kitchen is clean and all the bottles stowed away, George makes a plate of sandwiches, and I put on the coffee.

'What's next?' I ask as we gather round the table to eat.

'Slow down, lad. Enjoy the break,' George says.

'I think Snake is trying not to miss the love of his life.' Susan winks at George, and they laugh as if they're sharing a huge joke.

I want to join in, but the truth is, I want to keep busy—*need* to keep busy so I don't miss Pris.

'Don't look so worried.' Susan pats my arm. 'We had a delivery of camp beds this morning, and they need to be set up in the dorm rooms.'

George groans, and Susan smiles at him. 'With three of us it should take no time at all.'

'I was planning to make some stocks for soups,' George protests.

Snake, are you there? Ed'rathe interrupts.

Yes, I'm here.

Can you be ready soon? The Queen has a job for us.

'Snake, are you all right?' Susan asks.

I focus back on the room. 'Just Ed'rathe. I'm afraid I won't have time to help with the beds.'

Susan flicks her hand as if to shoo me away. 'Go. I know you have work to do.'

Let me finish lunch, Ed'rathe, and I'll meet you out front.

Before I can take another bite of my sandwich, the air in the room goes cold, then shimmers. Next thing, an unknown creature appears on the other side of the table, my great-grandfather in tow.

I leap to my feet and am around the table in seconds. 'Mender,' I say, followed by, 'Why are you here? Is something wrong?'

The elderly gnome shifts the instrument case on his shoulder and draws me into a hug.

'Snake. It is so good to see you alive and well.' He turns to the stranger. 'Thanks for the ride, young creature. I can take it from here.'

The wizard draws a portal opening in the air and steps through without saying a word. Mender takes my arm and leads me back around the table, his face a picture of seriousness.

'What is it, Mender? Why are you here?'

My great-grandfather places his hand on my shoulder and urges me downwards. 'Sit, young Snake. Finish your food. There is nothing amiss. I have come to teach you.'

'W-what?' I stammer out as he leans his lute against the wall before pulling out the chair beside me.

'Yes, it was your grandfather's idea. He thought it might be useful for you to learn our family's magical secret.'

I am here, Snake.

'Wait. What secret?' My head is spinning. **Hold on, Ed'rathe.** I've gone from wondering what to do with myself to having everything thrown at me, and I'm finding it difficult to concentrate.

Mender chuckles, and Susan says, 'Snake, aren't you going to introduce us to your guest?'

I close my eyes, blocking out the world, and centre myself.

'Susan, George, this is my great-grandfather, Mender. Mender, I am afraid our reunion must wait. I have been called to work.'

Snake?

Coming.

Grandfather's eyes widen in surprise. 'I had heard you were ambassador to the Dragon Queen. Are you going to an audience?'

I shake my head. 'No. I'm not sure what I'll be doing, but my dragon friend is waiting for me.'

Mender's eyebrows shoot to his hairline. 'You have a dragon friend? Gosh, my family is rising through the ranks. I guess teaching you sleep magic can wait.'

I freeze halfway to my feet and drop back down into the chair. 'What? Hold on, you were going to teach me sleep magic? Is that even real? Or legal?'

Mender chuckles again. 'Semi-legal. We do not use it often, maybe to soothe a fretful child now and then, but I am assured this is something we might need in the coming days.'

Now I'm torn. I can't ignore the Dragon Queen's request, but wow…. sleep magic. That would be so cool.

Susan stands up and begins clearing the table. 'Snake, you need to go. I am sure Mender will be here when you get back.'

'Of course I will. Witch Lorin is not fetching me back until tomorrow morning. I'm told there is the possibility of a bed here?'

He turns to Susan, who in turn looks at me and grins. 'I assume there is a bed with unused bedding in your room?'

My face heats, as I'm well aware of what she's implying, and I mumble, 'Yes.'

'Good, now go. We'll keep Mender entertained while you do whatever it is you have to do.'

I push myself to my feet, grateful for Susan's pragmatic support and that Mender seems oblivious to her dig at me.

Mender places a hand on my arm and looks up at me, eyes twinkling. 'Wait. Would it be too much to ask to meet your dragon?'

It's sad that I have taken my friendship with Ed'rathe so much for granted that I've forgotten the awe and wonder dragon-kind inspires in others.

'Sure,' I say. 'Come with me to our room so I can grab a coat. You can leave your lute there.'

'And on the way, you can tell me why it's unusual for only one bed in your room to have been slept in,' Mender says, a cheeky grin crinkling his face.

I want to blot the next quarter of an hour from my mind, but I fear it's seared into my brain forever. Mender's questions about Pris and me create a new level of discomfort that is only superseded by my embarrassment as I translate a conversation between him and Ed'rathe—about me!

Your elder is a good creature, Ed'rathe informs me as we leave the World Between.

You're only saying that because he thought you were wonderful, and amazing, and awesome.

You say that as if you don't believe I am any of those things.

Ed'rathe manages to convey a little hurt in his words. I've gone too far with my teasing—after all, I *am* in awe of dragon-kind, and he has shown me nothing but friendship.

Dude, you are all of those things, and you know it. It's just me who sometimes forgets.

Ed'rathe grunts. Is he laughing at me? Before I can retaliate, my dragon friend chooses that moment to outline the Dragon Queen's orders.

We are to fly over the World Between, then report what is going on back to my Queen.

Can't she ask the other dragons who are out there with Pris? And don't Princess Petunia and Princess Cecily report to her?

Both sides protect those dragons, and they have special privileges. Reporting back activity relating to this war might affect their neutrality. However, if we fly over the World Below and happen to see things, we can tell the Queen.

Most of what I see as we fly is… well… nothing. There aren't even farmers in the fields, and the village streets are pretty empty. I guess creatures are lying low, or they have joined up to fight with one side or the other. This report will probably bore the Dragon Queen.

Look over there, Ed'rathe says as he banks right.

I can just make out uniformed creatures setting up shelters in the forest. When Ed'rathe straightens up, I study the surrounding area, searching for the object of their attention. I can't find anything.

What's going on? I ask.

The guards are encircling the rebel camp.

At first, I think he is kidding, but then I realise the camp is hidden from view. And, with that thought, fear for Pris takes over.

You must warn Am'ratha so she can get a message to Pris.

I cannot. We must not take a side in the coming battle.

I growl my frustration. **Then set me down, and I will warn them.**

Ignoring my request, Ed'rathe turns away from the forest and heads towards the Capitol.

Seriously, Ed'rathe. Put me down.

I am certain they know what is happening. They will have wards and scouts, and Pris and Am'ratha flew this way not so long ago. Besides, if their success in this endeavour relies on you and me, then they are doomed to fail.

How is he so calm? I fidget on his back, attempting to look back over my shoulder.

Please, be still. I do not want to have to pick your carcass up from the ground.

The reminder that I am flying stills me in my seat, and I resort to fuming.

I can sense your anger, but I assure you, all is well. The rebels have access to magic that allows them to see through the eyes of animals, and they will be using it to protect their position.

But we could help them by giving them a clearer picture of where the threat is coming from.

Not while you are with me and not using my mindspeak.

Is there a loophole there? I believe there is. Now my only thought is to get this mission over with so I can return to the World Between and alert the rebels.

In no time at all, Ed'rathe has us circling over the Capitol. The streets, much like the villages, are devoid of creatures. There are few guard patrols along the city's walls and fewer still on the ground. Has Bernais sent most of his force out to take on the rebels before they arrive at his doorstep? I really must warn Fairburn

Then all thoughts of the guards in the forest are driven from my mind as I see them—the hundreds, perhaps thousands, of uniformed humans camped out around the palace. This is why Bernais was able to send the governors' militias away—he has brought in mercenaries.

We know his plan. We can return home, Ed'rathe says.

Can we do another turn around—what the? My ears ring, and I grasp the side of one of Ed'rathe's scales as the mountains encircling the World Between appear beneath us.

When my balance is restored, I yell, 'What the hell was that?'

My Queen asked that we report back in a timely manner, Ed'rathe explains without answering my question at all.

I open my mouth to speak, but instead lean over to the side and lose my lunch.

Oh dear, time compression sometimes has this effect on mortals. Let me take you back to your quarters, and I shall report to the Dragon Queen for us both.

Time compression? You're kidding, right?

Ed'rathe settles on the ledge outside the creature guest quarters. As I attempt to get my breathing back under control, I slide off Ed'rathe, a little clumsier than normal. As a try to take an unsteady step, I find myself encased in a gentle pressure bubble preventing me from moving.

Wait. I will get someone to attend to you.

The call he bellows out almost splits my head in two. Susan appears moments later, followed closely by Mender. My legs buckle, one knee hitting the ground, and they help me to my feet and through the door as Ed'rathe says, **Rest for a while, and you will be fine.**

I'm not sure I'll ever be fine again. It feels like each part of my body is moving to a different rhythm—or perhaps operating in a different time?

'Apparently there is such a thing as time-shift magic?' I ask as my helpers lower me onto my bed.

'It's an urban myth,' Susan assures me, but my great-grandfather's brow wrinkles. 'There are old stories, myths even, that talk about dragon's compressing or warping time,' he informs me.

My stomach roils, and I close my eyes, certain it's no myth at all, but I don't have the capacity to argue with Susan and do what needs to be done to warn our forces.

'Susan, I need to speak to a rebel leader from the camp. Have you some way of contacting them?'

She pulls a blanket over my still-shaking form and says, 'You need to rest.'

'I will, but this is important. I have information they need.'

'All right, if you're certain?'

I nod, instantly regretting the movement.

'I will stay and care for him,' Mender says. Well, I think that's what he says, but his voice is drifting in and out.

My mind spins, and I try to catch hold of something that is just out of my reach… then I have it. Ed'rathe could have taken the flight over the World Below and reported back to the Dragon Queen himself. Although they had stuck to the letter of the law, they intended for me to have this knowledge and to pass it on.

Clarifying that thought leads me to another. The Dragon Queen would not have leaned this close to supporting us unless she was redressing a balance. Those humans should not be in the World Below. Does having them there breach some sort of agreement? No, that's not it. There are no laws against moving between the realms.

Then it hits me like a blow to the gut. There was only one way to get so many humans to agree to come to a magical realm, then follow the orders of mystical beings. Bernais and his cronies had done the unthinkable—they had bewitched mercenary soldiers from the World Above into our realm.

CHAPTER 10

The War Drums Beat

Standing alone outside the command tent amidst the whirlwind of activity, I swallow my disappointment and rejection. Fighters are being trained. Weapons and armour are being cleaned. Food is being cooked and clothes are being mended. Everyone is contributing to the war except me.

They already knew, Am'ratha.

I am not surprised, Princess. They have their own ways of finding out information. Do they have a plan?

They're working on it.

You are with them?

I close my eyes, blocking everything out and attempting to sort through the emotions that have been surging through me since I stormed out. There is anger, and frustration, and… if I'm honest, humiliation.

When they said they wanted me to lead them into battle, they meant me to be more of a poster girl than an actual leader.

There, I've said it. I'm not worthy of being included in

their planning. War and rebellion might be new to me, but I'm not totally useless in combat. Fairburn's rejection had stung. I may as well sit round in a pretty dress and smile all day.

Good. Now you have a job you can concentrate on.

That is the final straw. Being a pinup is not a job. How dare Fairburn tell me I can't fight either. I've been training in martial arts for most of my life.

Calm down. Your thoughts are being broadcast at full volume. He is right, though—you don't send the Queen or her representative into battle to be killed. If they get taken out, the army loses heart.

Dammit, there is a logic to that. Even though I'm not ready to let go of my anger, I try. I want to go back inside, but I'm worried if I don't get control of my emotions, I'll say or do something that will reinforce their opinion of me. That's why I had left in the first place.

I don't even know what a figurehead is supposed to do!

My tone is sulky. I sound like a spoilt child, and I'm annoyed at myself for falling back into this old pattern. I thought I had moved on from all this.

A figure slips through the tent opening and joins me. Percival. I almost sag with relief. He always knows how to bring the best out in me.

He gives me a knowing look. 'So, Princess, shall we go visit your grandmother? She has had more experience with this sort of thing, and there is no shame in asking for guidance.'

As he speaks, an elven woman dressed in guard leathers detaches herself from the nearby troop and heads our way. She looks familiar, but I can't place her—and that isn't good because she's someone I no doubt should be able to identify.

'Percival, they want your help moving the hospital,' she says, her voice displaying a slight Scottish burr.

Where do I know her from? Is it the Unseelie Court?

Percival's voice pulls me back into the conversation. 'I thought they were staying here.'

'Now that *they* know where we are, the wizards—sorry, witches—are moving the hospital to somewhere in Melliores tonight.

Percival's gaze drifts towards the tent emblazoned with a large red heart surrounded by black plants, then back to us, his brows drawing together. 'I was going to take Pris to visit Petunia.'

'I can do that.'

'If you are sure….'

'I am.'

I'm not. Something about this elf sets me on edge, and I don't want to be alone with her.

The elf places a hand between Percival's shoulder blades and gives him a gentle push. 'Besides, it's about time Princess Priscilla and I become acquainted.'

Percival throws a concerned glance over his shoulder, and I mouth, 'I'll be okay.'

I mean, who would attack me in the middle of the rebel encampment? Then again, this elf doesn't exactly seem friendly. Where is Aeron when you need him? I would feel a lot more confident dealing with this stranger if he were here.

Positioning herself directly in front of me and cutting off my view of Percival's retreating figure, the elf says, 'I am Princess Irene, your—'

'Aunt! That's who you remind me of—Mum.' It clicks, and now it's so obvious.

My aunt's response to my revelation is tart enough to curdle milk. 'I wouldn't know if I resemble Cecily, as *your* mother stayed behind with Queen Ariana when *my* mother left the World Below, and I have had little to do with her since then.'

Hurt and anger at having to answer for things outside of my control well up inside me. 'You knew where Mum has been. You could visit her. Talk to her. Write to her, even. I didn't know I had any family other than my parents until a few weeks ago,' I snap.

My aunt's brows form a disapproving frown.

Shame closely follows anger, and I take a deep breath. 'Look, I'm sorry. It's been quite a journey, getting to know my family and the magical realms.'

Rather than softening, the elf's gaze becomes even more stony, and her tone is scornful when she says, 'And everyone believes you capable of leading an army into battle.'

My jaw drops. I have met every challenge thrown at me these past weeks. Now, in the space of an hour, Fairburn's rejected me, and this... this *creature* is judging me and finding me wanting.

'You must feel so unprepared. Perhaps it is time to hand off to someone else.'

Although her words are consoling, I get the impression this is less about me and more about her.

Well, you know what? I've had enough.

Straightening my spine, I square my shoulders and meet her eyes. Does she want to lead the army? Is this some attempt to usurp Queen Ariana and my mother in retribution for an old grievance? My anger is bubbling below the surface, but I keep it locked down, careful to not let it show.

'I am sure my mother would be more than happy to step up and lead the army,' she finishes.

Okay, not her, but Grandmother. Is there something I'm missing?

'Queen Ariana doesn't want royal support becoming split between her and Grandmother.'

Irene's lips curl into a sneer. 'If she is so keen on family unity, why wouldn't she let Cecily live in the World Above with us? Maybe then we would have been better prepared to face this situation as a strong, united family.'

Well, this is something new to chew on. I assumed the Queen was putting the World Below first when she sent me here. Maybe I should have considered that she might have another, more personal, agenda.

'It is a bit of a mess,' I concede, my anger receding a little. I'm sick of raking over old history. It won't achieve anything. 'And I'm sure many mistakes were made in the past. But I guess we are where we are.'

Irene studies me for a long time, as if she's deciding something. 'True.'

'And as we're moving the troops tonight instead of tomorrow, we should save this family reunion stuff for later.'

Irene turns away. 'I guess we should go find Mother.'

I follow her, feeling like I've been tried and found wanting.

If my aunt's welcome was less than effusive, my grand-mother makes up for it.

'My darling Pris, I was so worried when I heard you were injured. Then, to have the Dragon Queen herself heal your wounds! You are blessed.'

I sit in an empty chair, surprised by the luxury of the tent she occupies in the middle of a battle camp. Although she is dressed in riding clothes, she still radiates royalty.

'I didn't feel blessed. All I felt was a whole lot of pain.'

She hands me a cup of tea, and I sip it gratefully while she and Irene settle.

'How is that young creature of yours doing? I hear he has his own dragon now. Does that mean you have something to tell me?'

My cup clatters on the table as I heavy-handedly place it down. 'No!'

Ignoring my outburst, Petunia turns to Irene. 'Snake Fieth is the gnome I told you about.'

For the first time since I met her, my aunt's eyes flash with approval. 'The one who helped place the Unseelie Court in stasis? Now *he* is someone I would like to meet.'

Unlike me, who merely convinced the King to leave his court and is clearly not up to much.

Something in my demeanour must have warned Petunia, and she turns back to me. 'So, if you are to be our leader, what do we have to work with? Can you ride a horse?'

Finally I have a chance to display my skills. 'Yes, I took lessons for a couple of years, but I haven't ridden since I started my A levels.'

Irene quirks a brow. 'Are we talking novice or competent?'

'Competent,' I respond, hoping her idea of competent and mine are the same.

Irene nods as Petunia asks, 'What about fighting?'

'What about it?' I ask, a little confused. 'Fairburn said I wasn't to fight.'

'You might not be in the thick of the battle, but we need to know whether you can defend yourself if you're isolated and attacked. It can devastate an army if their leader dies,' Irene explains as if speaking to a child.

'I know that,' I want to say, but I bite my tongue. 'I've studied martial arts since I started school.'

Irene frowns. 'What about weapons?'

'I have trained with a few, but I guess the most useful from horseback would be the Jian.' When Irene frowns, I explain, 'It's a double-edged straight sword.'

'Mmm… I think we could cover that.'

'How are your public speaking skills?' Grandmother asks, changing the subject.

I grin. Now we're talking.

For the next half an hour or so, Grandmother and I nut out some key phrases I can include in a rousing speech. When we're done, my grandmother excuses herself for a minute.

Irene takes this as an opportunity to study me thoughtfully. 'Better than I first thought, but I think I'll reserve judgement until I see you in action.'

'Just out of interest, what did you expect?' I ask, unsure how much my aunt knew about me.

'A spoilt, protected rich kid from London,' Irene says with a smirk, and I bark out a laugh.

Up until a few weeks ago, when I met Snake, that description would have been pretty accurate. In spite of her acerbic attitude, I find myself warming to my aunt. She's more like me and Mum than she'd like to think.

Grandmother returns with a sword in her hand. 'As I am to leave with the hospital crew, I think this will be more than suitable for you to use.'

She hands the sword and sheath to me as Irene gasps, 'No! Mother! It was Father's bride gift to you.'

Realising the weapon's importance, I shake my head. 'Irene should have it.'

It is Princess Petunia, not my grandmother, who responds. 'Symbols are important. This blade is known to be mine, and for you to wield it shows my support of you to everyone on both sides. I want it back, mind, because it will eventually go to Irene.'

Grandmother turns a questioning glance to Irene, who holds her mother's gaze then nods her consent.

Reluctantly I take the offered weapon. 'I will return it to you when I am done.'

'If you are able,' Irene adds, reminding me that this is no game we're playing. 'Come, we still have to find some suitable armour and a horse.'

I hug my grandmother goodbye, and she whispers in my ear, 'Be safe.' Then to Irene, she says, 'I am entrusting everything to you.'

Irene kisses her mother on the cheek. 'Goddess be with you.'

Thirty minutes later, I exit the armoury tent, tugging at my new leather armour. It is heavy and uncomfortable, and I can't get it to sit right. As it is similar to Irene's, I resist the urge to whine about it. I roll my shoulders again, and Irene pauses, studies me, then places her hand on the armour. The leather warms under her touch, but the armour now fits like a glove.

'Sorry, I forgot you aren't used to using magic. While all clothes are spelled to fit by their makers, you have to spell your own armour, as leatherworkers don't usually have the same skills.'

'Thank you,' I say, but Irene is already moving towards the makeshift field where the horses graze.

She calls over one of the creatures polishing tack and says, 'I believe there is a mount assigned to Princess Priscilla.'

The young female creature—a dwarf, I think, but can't be certain—nods. 'Yes, Princess. The dun-coloured one under the tree.' She points at a horse, who looks up as if she knows we're talking about her. To me, the creature says, 'She is strong and a little willful. If you let her know who is boss from the start, she will be fine.'

'Thank you,' I say.

Irene follows with 'She will be ready when we leave later on tonight?'

The creature nods. 'Of course.'

'Good.'

Irene turns and heads back towards the command tent.

'Thank you,' I say to the groom, and she smiles shyly at me.

'Her name is Gwen, and she's partial to an apple if you can find one.'

I smile back. 'I'll see what I can do.'

As I hurry to catch Irene up, Am'ratha sends, **She will not be as good to ride as me.**

You shouldn't be spying on me, I tease.

How else am I to protect you?

Fair point. And she might not be as comfortable to ride with as you, but she is a little bit less flashy.

I will take that as a compliment.

Gotta go. War council time.

I draw level with Irene as she reaches the command tent. It takes a moment for my eyes to adjust as we step inside, and before they do, a familiar voice beside me says, 'Well, it's about time you turned up.'

'Some guard you turned out to be,' I joke.

Aeron clutches his heart and moans, 'I have failed in my duty.'

Fairburn claps him on the shoulder. 'No, you haven't. Priscilla was never in any danger.'

Irene straightens by my side and says almost reverentially, 'I was with her, Mighty Warrior. Although I am not in your league, I am more than capable of defending my niece.'

To my surprise, Aeron bows. 'Ooh, am I in the presence of the legendary warrior elf, Irene? Your reputation in tournaments is celebrated across the lands.

I study my aunt with a newfound respect, and I'm shocked to see the tiniest bit of colour bloom on Irene's cheeks under Aeron's scrutiny.

'I am honoured to share the protection of Princess Priscilla with you.' Aeron bows again, and Irene giggles. Actually giggles!

I roll my eyes. *OMG, really.*

Aeron raises an eyebrow. 'I would keep silent if I were you, given what I have witnessed between you and your consort.'

'He's not my consort,' I respond automatically before my brain kicks into action.

Aeron winks, and I curse myself for having fallen for his ruse.

'Let us get this council underway before we descend to kindergarten level,' Fairburn says, much to my relief.

I smirk as I catch Aeron and Irene sharing admiring glances as we gather around the map table.

. . ◦ . ◦ ✦ . ◦ . . ◦

'I will not say goodbye,' Nisha says. She carries on packing a chest with bandages, keeping her back to me.

'But—'

'No, Percival. We have unfinished business, not the least of which is saying a final farewell to your father once this is over. I will not entertain the possibility that we will not see these things through.'

She has become so defiant, my bond mate. Where did this change come from? Is it hubris to wonder if my past decisions changed Nisha?

I am startled from my thoughts by a hand gently squeezing my arm.

'There is no use worrying about the path not taken. We are here now.'

She cups my cheek, and her brown eyes capture mine. 'Go help Eleanora with the carts. We will meet again on the other side.'

I lean into her and touch our foreheads together, mingling our breath. How could I have spent so much time apart from her? How did I bear it? Reluctantly, I draw away.

'Are you all right, old friend?' Ellie asks when I join her beside a loaded wagon.

'I am getting there, as the young people say. At the very least, I know where I am going.'

We cover the wagon, and as Ellie pulls the last tie tight, she turns to me and smiles. 'It seems odd for you to be so certain of your future when everything around you is falling apart. You never used to be this contrary.'

I consider her words. It is true I used to bend with the winds when I hid from the world. Now I am back and ready to lean into them when the cause is right. Still, this is not a conversation to be had on the eve of a civil war. It is too heavy, and we need lightness.

Pulling on a mock serious face, I tease, 'So... Mandor is not a wizard anymore.'

For a moment, she stops, and I fear she might ignore me. Then she says, 'Meaning?'

'Just saying.' *I really have spent far too much time with Pris and Snake!*

'I am trying hard not to think beyond the next few days, Percival. And I certainly do not want to be pining for what might have been.' She pats the side of the wagon and turns to me. 'I am not as hopeful for the future as you are, my friend.'

Sadness brings tears to my eyes. Working things out with Nisha has given me hope for the first time in a long while, and I am desolate that my friend does not feel the same—especially as she has kept me from despair for so many years. 'There is not even a little hope?'

Ellie gnaws at her lower lip. 'It has been such a long time, Percival. Perhaps we are beyond those feelings.'

'You will never know if you do not try. Soon the battle will be upon us, and it might be too late.' I hated saying the last, but given that we may not come through this, we cannot waste a single opportunity.

'Hark at you giving me relationship advice,' Ellie says, a twinkle in her eye.

I see the irony. She married two mortals, aged with them, and saw them through their deaths. Still, this is Mandor, the love of her life.

Ellie rubs her forehead. 'I can't do anything even if I wanted to. He is off in the deep Wyld Woods, searching for Heart and the creatures he promised to bring with him.'

It is almost as if by speaking Heart's name, she summoned him. He and a group of creatures bearing arms appear from nowhere, with Mandor trailing close behind. Ellie gasps in shock at this sudden appearance and then busies herself as if demonstrating she doesn't care. I know better, though.

'No excuse now,' I say to Ellie before moving to greet Heart. 'Pleased you could join us.'

Heart claps a hand on my shoulder. 'Can't stop now, old friend. I believe I have the solution to your problem. Lead me to the command tent.'

'Our problem?' I ask, somewhat confused as I nonetheless lead him to the centre of the encampment.

'Your ring-of-guards-around-the-camp problem,' Heart clarifies.

Behind us, Mandor calls for someone to take the new recruits to the food tent before he and Ellie follow us.

When she sees us approach, the guard outside the command centre flicks the flap open, and the entire command contingent turns as we enter.

Before anyone can utter so much as a word, Heart announces, 'I have a sleep spell that can solve your problem of how to sneak out of here tonight without alerting our enemies that anything is amiss.'

It was like someone hit the Pause button on a TV—the world stops while everyone takes it in.

'Well, a sleep spell,' Fairburn eventually says. 'That would indeed be very useful.' He turns to Brynn. 'Now that we might actually sneak out, we need to be certain no one does anything to tip our hand. Alert the surveillance teams to notify us immediately if they think the enemy is getting suspicious.'

Brynn leaves, and Fairburn calls everyone around the map.

'With the human mercenaries in the Capitol, it is essential the creature enemy forces surrounding us are committed to attacking our camp for as long as possible. We do not have the numbers to engage them as well as the human mercenaries should they join up. Right, let us go over the schedule one last time.'

One delegate swings a blackboard round, and we all

turn our attention to the details Fairburn summarises for us.

'At midnight we will begin moving the hospital to Melliores.' Fairburn's gaze turns my way.

'They are packed and ready to go,' I confirm.

'Excellent. Two hours later Percival and Drow will be portalled into the university at the heart of the Capitol to mobilise the students and security staff who have remained behind. We have been co-ordinating activities with them and training them to help us with some specific tasks.'

'Their most recent dispatch confirms they will be ready and waiting to receive their final orders,' Drow assures us.

'Good. The members of campus security will help us enter the Capitol through an assigned gate, and some students will be sent to rally creatures in the ghetto to create a demonstration to provide cover for our movements. Another group has been preparing to free our people who are being held captive. Once they have been dispatched, Percival and Drow will then set up our command post.'

Drow steps forward and spreads out a map of the city. 'There is a curfew in the Capitol, but our student friends are no doubt well versed in moving around after hours without being caught.'

There were a few laughs in the tent.

Drow smiles, then continues. 'The security guards will make their way to the Avondale gate and capture the enemy guards there. This is of upmost importance, as our best chance is to sneak into the city and battle the soldiers outside the palace. If we have to fight our way there, we will waste time and resources, which will allow Bernais to mount a defence.'

'Won't the guards hear us arrive outside the walls?' Pris asks.

'Our transport site is five minutes from our entry point. The first troop will immediately move into position in front of the gates and will be held in a sound bubble,' Fairburn explains. 'Once the gates are open, they will secure the area, then fan out around the walls, immobilising the other guard posts as they go. The rest of our force will make its way through the streets to their positions, ready to engage the humans surrounding the palace.'

'And the demonstration is timed to make enough noise to cover the sounds of their movements?' Pris asks.

Fairburn nods. 'That is the plan.'

Drow takes over again. 'As Fairburn touched on, we know from Princess Petunia's report that lesser creatures were rounded up and are being held in the suburbs behind the university in a sort of ghetto.'

'Shame,' someone near me hisses, and I have to agree.

'Indeed,' says Drow. 'We will send some students there under cover of darkness to encourage them to protest against their conditions once the curfew finishes at dawn. They should create enough noise and a big enough disturbance to cover our troops entering the city.'

Now it is my turn. 'Another contingent of students will be sent to free those being held in increature conditions at the hospital.'

It turns my stomach to even talk about creatures being held in stasis. Controlling creatures using spells or bewitching them is worse than murder. Some never fully recover.

'The more magically adept will break into the hospital and counter the spellwork keeping the prisoners docile. They will then bring those released back to the university, where we will see about getting them further help.'

Fairburn stands beside the blackboard. 'We hope to have all creatures released and either receiving medical attention or protesting by just past sunup. Soon after, we will have our forces in place. Once the sun rises, the witches left at the encampment will join the healers ready to deal with any casualties, and…. Well, let us say, all bets are off after that.'

Irene chuckles. 'It's a great plan, Fairburn, but will it hold up when we engage the enemy?'

'Perhaps, but probably not. That is why we are trying to move into place without the enemy knowing what we are doing,' Fairburn counters. 'It will give us the greatest chance of success.'

'Do we have contingencies?' Irene presses.

Fairburn's front hooves shuffle. 'Had we more time to plan, I am sure we could have had contingencies. However, not only do we not have much time, but the enemy encircling our camp has cut what little time we had in half. I am afraid we have one shot at ending this quickly, otherwise we will withdraw and fall back on guerrilla warfare to prevent the elven faction from consolidating their power.'

'No,' Pris says. 'We have one shot full stop. If we don't sort this out before the Dragon Queen's deadline, she will allow Bernais to ascend to the throne.'

The room falls silent as everyone contemplates the disaster this would be for our land.

'Then we had best not fail,' Fairburn says. His gaze rakes the room. 'Is there anything we have forgotten?'

No one speaks, but Heart is studying the map, a worried frown creasing his brow.

'Good, then with Heart's offer to spell the enemy to sleep—'

'Umm, about that,' Heart interrupts. 'I had no idea the area would be so big. I am going to need some help.'

Mmm, steak.

The thought permeates my consciousness and finally settles in my stomach, which rumbles loud enough to crash mountains, rousing me from sleep.

My room in the guest quarters in the World Between is empty and a little cool. How long have I been asleep? I was pretty groggy when the witch from the rebel camp questioned me about the human forces in the Capitol. Once she heard what I had to say, she had been keen to return to the camp as soon as possible, and I hadn't complained.

I push myself into a sitting position, and then I stretch and check myself out. I no longer feel like the world is spinning around me. Tentatively I swing my legs over the side of the bed and stand up. Yep, everything is good. My stomach grumbles, reminding me of why I am up and about at all.

As expected, Susan, Henry, and my great-grandfather are in the dining room. Henry has gone all out for dinner. A roast of beef sits between the creatures, slices of perfectly cooked meat steeping in aromatic juices. Roast vegetables are piled up on another plate sitting beside a large jug of gravy. There are even Yorkshire puds. I bite back a groan.

'Do not just stand there, boy,' Mender says, 'You of all of us could do with a hearty meal.'

I don't need a second invitation. Taking the seat beside Henry opposite my great-grandfather, I pile my plate high with food.

'This is amazing,' I tell the brownie as I stuff myself.

'It may be our last chance for a slap-up meal,' he tells

me, and although my stomach sinks at the thought of what is to come, I'm thankful for tonight.

'There's lemon meringue pie for dessert,' Susan tells me. 'So leave some space.'

This time I do groan. I can't remember when I last had a traditional, home-cooked meal this good.

When we're done eating the main meal, Mender says, 'Dessert can wait until you've learnt the sleep spell.'

Before I can argue, he drags me into the common room while Susan and Henry clear away the first course.

We sit by the fire, and Mender picks up the lute he brought.

'In the coming days, you may need this sleep spell, and we haven't much time for me to teach you,' Mender says, tuning the instrument. When he's done, he quietly strums a tune.

I try to concentrate on what he is playing, and I expect to start falling asleep, or at least yawn, but I don't feel any different.

'Grandfather, I don't think it's working,' I whisper, a little disappointed that it doesn't. I mean, how cool would it be to be able to do a sleep spell?

Mender chuckles but carries on playing. 'The spell has two parts. The first is the music, or the tune, really. The second is the intent. Much like the dynamics that turn a tune into a performance from the heart, you must concentrate on willing the subject to sleep.'

I nod my understanding. He is speaking my language, after all. With the fear of falling asleep while learning eliminated, I'm able to quickly pick up the tune. The base theme is Brahms's 'Lullaby.' There are a few added arpeggios, but it's essentially the same.

When he's run through it twice, Mender stops and hands the lute to me. I've only tried playing the instrument a few times, and it feels kind of awkward, but not completely unfamiliar. It's like a guitar, and I get the best sound by picking instead of strumming.

It takes me a few tries, but once I have the basics, Mender makes me play it a couple more times just to make sure—he's an exacting music teacher.

Finally he is happy, and he takes the instrument from me. 'Now is the telling part. If you have inherited the ability to use the sleep spell, I should be able to play it with intent and you will not fall asleep.'

'Wait, you mean there is a chance I may not be able to do this?' I ask, feeling the loss of a spell I never had.

'Yes, I am afraid not everyone with our blood can cast it.'

'That's a weird way of checking.'

Mender chuckles, his eyes twinkling with merriment. 'Or a very sensible way.'

'Sensible?'

'Yes. You can hardly use a spell if you fall asleep while casting it.'

Of course—it's so obvious.

'The trick is,' Mender says as he plays, 'to believe with your whole being that you want the listener to go to sleep. Any doubt or distractions, and it won't work.'

The music he is playing changes. The sound is fuller and encourages me to close my eyes and drift away with it. I concentrate, trying to work out what he's doing differently. Whatever it is, it's so subtle, I can't identify it.

He stops playing and smiles. 'Well, you've passed the first step.' He hands me the lute. 'Now for the second test. Susan,' he calls, raising his voice to be heard in the dining room. 'Would you mind being our guinea pig?'

Susan appears in the doorway. 'What?'

'Would you mind allowing Snake to sing you to sleep?'

'I have a lot to do….'

'I will only let him start to send you to sleep, then,' Mender reassures her. 'That way you'll wake up as soon as he stops playing.'

'Okay then.' Susan wipes her hands on her apron and takes a seat across from me.

Taking a deep breath, I play the tune through once for practice, then the second time, I will Susan to sleep.

She stifles a yawn but is otherwise unaffected. A frown appears between Mender's brows.

'I could feel your intent, but it did not change the timbre of the music as much as it should.'

'So, you're saying, once more, with feeling,' I joke.

Mender nods solemnly. 'Yes, please.'

I try again. Then once more. Then again. My desperation lends the music a sharpness that counteracts my will, and the most I get from Susan is another yawn.

Mender rubs a hand across his brow. 'I do not understand it. I have never had this much trouble teaching one of my blood this spell.'

'Perhaps it's just that Snake is tired,' Susan offers. 'He's had a bit of a day.'

'Yes… that could be it.' Mender's tone is not convincing. 'We can try again—'

Mender stops mid-sentence as the air shimmers, and Mandor appears behind Susan.

'Good, you're both here. We need your help at the camp.'

'Snake and I?' Susan asks.

'No, Snake and Mender. We need them to play their sleep spell.'

'But I only agreed to teach Heart and Snake the spell. I am too old to involve myself in war,' Mender says.

'And I am presently serving the Dragon Queen,' I add. 'I can't go anywhere without her permission.'

Mandor frowns. 'This is really important. We are surrounded, and this is the only way we can see to move our troops into position without alerting the enemy that we are leaving.' He runs a hand through his dark hair, a forlorn look crossing his face. 'Is there any way you….'

Mender lets out a breath. 'I guess if this is all you will ask of me, then I could lend a hand.'

They turn to me. No one has mentioned that I can't actually complete the spell yet, so I don't either. No need to worry about that until I have permission to help.

'Okay, let me talk with Ed'rathe.' I look down at my crumpled clothes. 'And I'll get my gear as well.'

Back in my room, I grab a change of clothes as I contact Ed'rathe and explain the situation. He agrees to speak with the Dragon Queen on my behalf. He comes back before I've even pulled on my boots.

The Dragon Queen allows you leave until tomorrow morning. I am to wait with Am'ralla and Am'ratha and bring you back tomorrow.

You don't need to come until tomorrow.

That is too far away if something happens to you.

Oh. I hadn't thought this might be dangerous. **Can you thank the Dragon Queen for me?** I ask and grab my jacket. **For letting me go and sending you.**

There is one commitment the Dragon Queen asks for. She says if she calls for you, you must return immediately.

Of course. Nothing ever comes without strings in the World Between. **As she commands.**

I sense Ed'rathe leave, and I head back to the

communal room. Mender has returned his lute to its bag and is waiting while Mandor talks with Susan. I hover in the doorway, a mess of uncertainty. I can't do this.

It's not nerves. Well, it sort of is, because this will be dangerous. I mean, I literally can't do this. I can't make the sleep spell work, and even if I could, I don't have an instrument to play on.

Mender must have sensed my concern. He steps towards me, takes my arm, and moves me back into the hallway.

'I know what you're thinking,' he says, 'and I don't want your inability to complete the spell to put you off. You were close, and I have an idea on how it might work for you.'

I hold up my hand. 'It doesn't matter, Mender. I don't have an instrument. The lute you gave me is in the Unseelie Court along with all my other possessions.'

Great-Grandfather claps a hand on my shoulder. 'Impatient imp, that was what I was going to tell you. You are competent with a lute, but it is not your natural instrument. However, you sang for my people when you were in the Minotaur's Maze, and your voice is as good an instrument as any.'

My nose wrinkles with distaste. My voice is not an instrument—it's an accompaniment. It complements the music I play.

'All right,' he allows, 'it is not an optimal solution, but you could try.'

He is so positive I can do this, I don't have the heart to let him down. Besides, if I go to the camp, at the very least I'll get to see Pris one more time before the battle.

'Are we ready?' Mandor calls.

I suck in a breath, 'As ready as I'll ever be.'

By the time we return to the fireside, Mandor has opened a portal.

'One at a time?' I ask.

Mandor shakes his head. 'We have modified the spell, and we can now hold the doorway open long enough for more than one person to travel at a time.'

'Good luck,' Susan calls as we step through to a clearing in front of a large tent.

To the left is a large fire, and I spot Drow and Heart sitting together on a log, both eating from wooden bowls.

'Go join them. You have some time before you're need-ed,' Mandor says before disappearing into the tent.

My heart races as I locate Pris sitting on the other side of the fire. She is sharing a log with Aeron and a female elf I feel I should know. I make my way directly to her, and as if sensing my presence, Pris glances up, and smiles a welcome as she reaches to pull me down beside her.

I lean in and whisper, 'I've missed you.'

She chuckles. 'You only saw me this morning.'

'And that was too long apart.'

I wrap an arm around her and pull her closer as I study the rest of the group.

'Where's Percival?' I whisper.

Aeron leans round Pris and responds, 'Saying his good-byes to Nisha.' His smile suggests more than a simple goodbye, and I turn to Pris, my eyes wide.

Her eyes darken with emotion. 'They've been getting on really well. It's so lovely.'

I'm not sure whether I find that comforting or disturb-ing, like thinking about your parents being intimate is. The only way I can deal with it is to push the thought from my mind.

I nod towards Aeron, who is following the familiar elf

as she speaks while looking up at him with doe eyes. I lean in close to Pris to speak into her ear again. 'What's their deal?'

She chuckles. 'It appears Aeron has a crush on my Aunt Irene.'

'That's Princess Irene? Wow, she's supposed to be this amazing warrior woman.'

Pris's voice is tinged with exasperation when she says, 'Great—everyone has a crush on my legendary aunt. Perhaps she should be the one leading the army.'

I pull Pris in and kiss her cheek. 'She's got nothing on you.'

She relaxes into me. 'Good recovery. And timely, too, as I was considering whether or not to show you what I found for you.'

I rest my head on hers. 'You have a present for me?'

'Sort of. Heart was telling us about the spell you guys are going to play and that you need instruments. We sent a witch to get a lute for him from Mender's shop.'

'And you got one for me too?'

'No, we did one better.' Pris looks up at me, her lips curling into a smile. 'Percival has been working with a crea-ture called Brynn. They mentioned their brother brought a guitar back from the World Above and they said you could use it. We sent a witch to get it for you.'

As if by magic, a goblin appears beside me with a rather beautiful acoustic guitar in their hand. 'I hope you can play this, as my brother certainly could not,' they say, holding out the instrument.

I leap to my feet, gratitude filling me as my fingers curl around the neck of the guitar. 'Thank you for loaning this to me,' I say. 'Tell your brother I will take good care of it.'

Brynn stares at the ground. 'My brother has passed to

the other side. I would be honoured if you would take this.' He chokes up at the end, and I reach out and squeeze his arm.

'What is your brother's name?'

'Gareth.' Brynn's voice is little more than a whisper.

'I will sing the sleep song in Gareth's name, and together we will fight for creature freedom.'

The gnome looks up, tears glistening in their eyes. 'Thank you.'

'Come, join us.' I gesture to the fire, and Brynn takes a place on the other side of Irene.

I lean against the log Pris sits on and tune the guitar. It has a beautiful, rich tone, and my fingers fly along the strings as if I've been playing this guitar all my life. I play the sleep spell through a couple of times, and I connect with the piece in a way I couldn't when playing it on the lute. Just to test things out, I send a little intent into the last few bars, and a few of the creatures around the fire yawn.

From across the blaze, Mender's eyes meet mine, and he sends a nod. For the first time, I believe I might actually be able to help our forces move.

Reluctant to put the guitar down, I strum a few chords, thinking about what I might play to capture the mood tonight. Mandor and Eleanor join us.

'The hospital group are safely in Melliores,' Eleanora announces.

Percival appears from the darkness and takes a seat beside Drow. My uncle places an arm around his friend's shoulders. Percival has been Pris's and my rock since we started on this quest. He was there for us even when we didn't know he was. This is the first time I have seen him so forlorn.

This more than anything brings home the enormity of what we face tomorrow. Yet here we all are, supporting each other through this, and in that moment, I so want to believe that everything we are giving up will be worth it.

Almost as though my fingers are moving of their own accord, they find the notes for Rachel Platten's 'Fight Song,' and the lyrics rouse everyone. By the last chorus, they're all singing along.

When the words are done, I carry on playing the tune. It then drifts into Bob Marley's 'Redemption Song.' When I sing the chorus, Pris and Irene join me.

Eleanora and Mandor stand and leave the fire, hand in hand.

'Do not do anything I wouldn't do,' Drow teases.

'Leave them alone,' Pris says, and Drow bows his head like a naughty child.

'Are they back together?' I ask.

Pris slips down the log and lays her head on my shoulder. 'Perhaps they are simply taking time to be together before tomorrow.'

I lean the guitar against the back of the log and wrap an arm around Pris. She nestles into my side, and I catch sight of Aeron and Irene sneaking into the dark.

'Creatures and humans alike crave connection at times like this. It may be for one night, and that is fine. For something longer term, you have to make a choice to be together and keep choosing to be together,' I muse.

The crackle of the fire fills the air as we're distracted by our thoughts. As I drift off I whisper in Pris's ear, 'I choose us.'

❧

'I choose us.'

At least, I think that's what Snake whispers as he falls asleep. My heart flutters at the words, and I feel I can face anything tomorrow… no, *today*.

While I'm worrying that I should respond in some way, Snake's snores ruffle my hair, so he's clearly not waiting for me to do so. Still, I should say something, but what?

In his arms, I am at home, but is that enough? Can I make that leap and choose us—choose him too? I can't bring myself to say the words. Instead, I watch the flames and try to sleep until, sometime after two, Brynn stirs.

'I guess it's time,' they say.

I nudge Snake. 'Time to go.'

He looks so young, rubbing the sleep from his eyes, and I want nothing more than to take him in my arms and run away somewhere this war cannot reach us. Leaning in, he kisses the end of my nose, and I press my forehead to his.

'Stay safe,' I whisper. 'I couldn't bear it if….' I can't finish the sentence.

He pulls me close. There is nothing more to say. Aeron emerges from the darkness and helps me to my feet.

From beside him, Irene asks, 'Have you got your speech?'

I nod as they draw me away. I send one last glance over my shoulder to find Snake's eyes following me. 'Goddess, please don't let that be the last time I see him,' I whisper into the night.

In Grandmother's quarters, Irene helps me into my armour. I attempt to block out my worries and fears by going over my speech in my head. When I'm ready, Aeron pulls back the curtain, and I almost throw up when I see the number of soldiers assembled outside.

Irene places a hand in the small of my back and gives me a gentle shove. 'If it were easy, anyone could do it.' She escorts me out and adds, 'Remember, Fairburn has arranged for a muffling spell, so speak loud and clear for those at the back.'

Aeron helps me onto my horse so I will be high enough for everyone to see me. Then he grabs the bridle to ensure my mount doesn't spook. I sit up straight in the saddle to survey the crowd, and I almost lose my nerve there and then. All these creatures are about to face death, and I don't want to let them down.

I suck in a deep breath, and find Snake who, along with Heart and Mender, is leaving. Snake looks back over his shoulder, and his gaze finds me. For a second, we connect, then Heart tugs his arm, and he's gone. I suck in a breath and tell myself, *They're prepared to give their lives for this, so this is the least I can do for these creatures.*

In the soldiers' faces, I see a mixture of hope, and fear, and determination. Suddenly, the speech I'd prepared seems inadequate. I shove the paper in my pocket and lean my hands on the pommel.

'I was going to give you a rousing speech about how we will win this war, defeat the council, and everything will get better,' I start. 'And while I do hope for all that, the words did not come from my heart.'

Unrest ripples through the ranks.

I'm losing them.

'What I want you to remember today as we fight our common foe is that we are all here for a reason. Your reason may be different to that of the creature standing beside you, or you might have come here together to fight for a particular cause. Whatever your reason for being here, we are all putting our lives on the line because we believe it is time for change in the World Below—time for all creatures to be heard.'

The crowd is silent now, and I frantically attempt to remember the ending of my planned speech. My mind goes blank. I look down and catch Aeron's eye, and I get a piece of divine inspiration.

'If a mere girl without magic from the World Above can defeat a Minotaur in his very own maze, then this creature army can topple mountains.' I hold my fist in the air. 'To victory!'

Crickets. You could hear a pin drop. Even hearing that would be better than the dead silence that fills the air. Then, as if a wave ripples through the soldiers, their fists pump the air. 'To victory!'

I get very little time to bask in my success. All too soon the troops are moving, and Aeron sends me a mock hurt look. 'Did you have to tell them about beating me. My reputation will be in tatters. What will Irene think?'

Over Aeron's head, my aunt winks, clearly amused.

'I think she'll be fine,' I tell the Minotaur as he moves my horse beside Irene's.

We wait for some signal from outside the dome that our watchers are asleep, then Mandor and two other witches open a portal wide enough for three horses to ride through. Behind them are three other witches to take over when they tire.

Ahead of us, the witches who will perform the sound suppression spells move forward, followed by Fairburn and the first wave. Our group moves behind, and seconds later, we're close to the Capitol walls. Fairburn is already urging his group forward—the advance party who will clear the way into the city.

Irene, Aeron, and I wait with the war council as the rest of our forces come through the opening. As the last of the troops emerge, a murmur ripples through the ranks.

I lean across to Irene. 'What is it?'

'It seems like there were fewer guards to send to sleep than we expected.'

'Is that a problem?' I ask.

My aunt waits until the portal closes before answering, 'I don't know. Then again, that's the problem with battle plans. They only hold up until first contact, and we're past that point now.'

With trembling hands, I play the first notes of the sleep spell, loading it with intent and playing it through. It sounds eerie in the night air, and it's like the trees around me rustle in time.

Erina, the witch assigned to portal me back to camp should anything go wrong, gives me a thumbs-down.

What have I done wrong? It was working around the fire. Then again, I was relaxed, no one was relying on me, and no one would shoot me if they figured out what I was doing. How am I supposed to do this? How can I possibly block out everything else and concentrate on sending someone, anyone to sleep?

'Once more, with feeling,' I whisper as I close my eyes and bring up the vision of us sitting round the fire a couple of hours ago.

I start playing and humming the tune, wishing I could send my friends all to sleep where they would be safe. I send a little 'louder' spell along with the intent and carry on. Finally, I open my eyes and search for Erina. She sends a thumbs-up. Relief surges through me, encouraging me to play the song with more conviction. I even sing the words of the original lullaby under my breath.

'Lay thee down now to rest, may thy slumber be blessed....'

The bushes behind me rustle, and I stop. Erina returns and circumnavigates the plant, her sword at the ready. Chuckling under her breath, she returns to me. 'One of their scouts. He's completely out of it.'

I nod and carry on playing until Erina stands in front of me and chops her hand in a stop motion. When I'm no longer playing, she removes the plugs from her ears.

'Our watcher signalled that our section's all asleep.'

I lay the guitar in my lap. 'I expected that to be more difficult. Or at least take a little longer.'

'It *should* have been more difficult,' the guard says from behind Erina. 'Yesterday afternoon, there were three guard platoons in this section. Tonight, there are only perhaps fifty creatures in total.'

Erina chews her lip, considering our options. Should we check for more guards or return to camp? 'Is it possible some guards moved to another section, perhaps expecting us to head for the road?'

The guard shrugs. 'That's possible. However, it is not our problem. Our orders were to spell anyone in our section asleep, then return.'

I stare expectantly at Erina, who takes a moment to react, then opens a portal back to camp. Just as I'm about to step through, there is a noise above, and a dragon drops into the clearing in front of us.

'Oh my goddess,' the guard says, his jaw dropping at the sight of the enormous creature.

Noble One, you are called to the Dragon Queen's Court.

What? Now? We're just about to—

You promised, Snake. And she would not send me unless it was important.

I turn to Erina. 'Unfortunately, duty calls. I must return to the World Between.'

'You're going to the Dragon Realm?' the guard asks, assessing me with a newfound respect.

If the dragon being there wasn't enough, the guard is struck dumb as Ed'rathe crouches to allow me up.

I am afraid we must compress time, my dragon friend informs me as he leaps to the sky.

My dinner prepares to make its way from my stomach at the thought. **But if we do that, I'll be in no condition to talk to the Queen until perhaps tomorrow afternoon.**

Let me worry about that, he responds.

We land on the ledge outside the Dragon Queen's audience chamber seconds later. The only thing keeping me on Ed'rathe's back is his magic. The world swims around me, and I am about to lose the fight to save my dinner. Then a wash of healing magic sweeps over me, and the nausea is gone.

'So...' I turn to Ed'rathe once I reach the ground. 'You can cure sickness from time compression?'

I'm certain his face darkens, perhaps in a blush, but it's difficult to tell with dragons.

I was not given leave to heal you last time.

Right as I'm about to answer, Am'ratha comes flying down with Pris riding along. Am'nera, with the familiar figure of Adina on her back, follows closely behind. There's an old elf lord with them. It is clear from his resemblance to Bernais that this is Magnus Baaronson, the notorious elf responsible for transfiguring Percival. I feel the bile rise in my throat at his presence.

'So, time compression is a thing,' Pris says as she joins

me, slipping her hand into mine so we can enter the hall as a united front.

I grimace. 'Yeah, it's not really my thing, though.'

She sends a side glance. 'You've done it before? When?'

'Later,' I say as the three dragons lead the way in, followed by the Baaronsons, who sweep past us as if we are beneath their notice.

'This is going to be a blast,' I say, wondering what the Dragon Queen could be thinking, calling this meeting now.

The audience chamber is deserted. Then again, it is the wee small hours before dawn. Our dragons lead us directly to the throne, and the Dragon Queen does not stand on ceremony.

There is to be war in your realm. Creature will fight creature, and there will be deaths. Some of you are prepared to go to extremes, perhaps even beyond the pale, to achieve victory. I wanted to take this opportunity to bring you here to broker a peace before it is too late. The Dragon Queen's tone is weary, and she pauses. Is she expecting someone to respond? No one does.

What is at stake here is more than the leadership of the World Below—it is the natural balance between all the worlds. On the one hand, I have two regents working day and night to restore that balance as fast as they can. On the other, I have thousands of creatures threatening to pull that all apart. Can we not spend a little time here and negotiate peace?

The Dragon Queen trains her fathomless eyes on each of us, ramming home her message. I'm guessing now is the time to speak. I tug at Pris's hand, pulling her back so we can talk privately as Magnus Baaronson steps forward.

'You cannot be serious about peace. Not when you bring me here with a dark elf and a half-breed gnome. They represent all that is wrong with our world, and they must be stamped out of existence. If we achieve nothing else with this war, we will ensure the purity of our races.'

'At the cost of draining magic from our world?' Pris splutters.

Magnus Baaronson does not turn our way. 'Then so be it.'

'This is madness,' Pris whispers. 'There is no negotiating with zealots.'

I give her hand a squeeze, urging her to try.

Pris turns slowly to the Dragon Queen and bows her head. 'Your Majesty, I am sorry to say we cannot negotiate with anyone denying the rights of so many inhabitants of the World Below.'

Then, although it may tear families and communities apart and destroy magic in the World Below forever, it will be war.

'It was always going to be,' Magnus Baaronson says with a sneer, then turns on his heel and stalks from the room without waiting to be dismissed.

Adina tuts, then drags her eyes from her husband's back. 'If that is all, Your Majesty?'

Go.

Adina follows her husband, but Am'nera waits. The Dragon Queen and she are clearly talking, but their conversation is not for our ears. Soon after, she follows her bonded one out.

Priscilla, Am'ratha will take you back and make sure you are ready to fight. She will remain nearby until this is over. She cannot aid you in the battle, but she will ensure you remain as safe as possible.

'Thank you, Your Majesty.'

May your goddess go with you.

Pris and Am'ratha are dismissed, leaving Ed'rathe and me with the Dragon Queen.

Have you done what is required of you?

'Yes, Your Majesty.'

Good, then you and Ed'rathe can go. Your task is now to report on the progress of the war.

No. I can't watch my friends risk their lives while I do nothing. 'You don't need me to do that. Ed'rathe can keep you appraised. Let me fight.'

I swear the Dragon Queen tuts at me as if I'm being a willful child. Then I remember—Ed'rathe can report to the Dragon Queen, but he can't report to our Commanders. I will be in a position to provide information that could change the tide of the battle.

Something else that could change the tide of the battle would be having Queen Ariana and King Maddox join us. It's a shame the Dragon Queen will not consider…. Hold on, why did the Queen leave it to the eleventh hour to try and broker a peace? What changed?

'Your Majesty, if I may, can I ask you something?'

You may. I might not answer, but you will not be punished for your question.

'You seem worried about magic in the worlds. Are things not going well with Queen Ariana and King Maddox?'

Mmmm. You are very clever, Sneak Thief. Priscilla has chosen wisely.

It is not exactly an answer, but it tells me what I need to know.

'Can't Cecily be brought from the palace to help Ariana?'

Ariana wants to make amends for the mess she

has created by saving magic for her people. She will not release her position as guardian. It may kill her, but she refuses to leave a mess for Cecily to clean up.

This is worse than I imagined.

There is little you can do about it, young gnome. You can only tread the path you are on.

'Thank you for sharing this with me, Your Majesty. And thank you for your consideration these past few days.'

You are welcome. I hope it has shown you that there are options for your future. Your family has served the worlds for generations, and there is no reason why you, too, cannot find a way to do so.

The Dragon Queen's eyes close, and I am clearly dismissed. For a being who doesn't want to become involved in the affairs of other realms, she certainly spends a lot of energy nudging creatures into positions she wants them in.

One of the Dragon Queen's eyes opens. Dammit, I forgot she can hear thoughts. I bow and leave before I can think anything else that might get me into trouble. Pris and Am'ratha are waiting for us outside.

'Are you able to tell me what she wanted you for?' Pris asks.

'She wants me to observe the battle,' I respond, not voicing my suspicions as to why she wants me there, as it's best not to acknowledge it in any way.

On the other hand, I don't think there's anything stopping me from letting her know about Queen Ariana, but this may not be the motivation she needs going into battle. Then again, the shock of finding out later could have an equally bad impact.

She leans in and kisses my cheek. 'Goddess be with you today.'

'And with you,' I say even though I really want to beg her to stay.

I draw in a breath. We can put it off no longer. Time to go to war. She quickly mounts, and a nanosecond later, she and Am'ratha vanish from view.

From our vantage point to the side of the main gathering, Drow and I watch Pris give her speech. I was so worried about her, but she has come through. While not a conventional battle cry, it comes from her heart, and its impact is felt by everyone.

'I feel like a proud parent,' I say to Drow, and he laughs.

'Yes, it would appear your protégée has graduated. Now, can we go? We have a lot to organise in a short time.'

I nod, and the witch assigned to us opens a portal into the library at the university. The room is both different and familiar. I run my hand over the table where Drow and I had prepared my case for transformation reversal. I can still picture us sitting there, so full of hope and passion.

The library is empty. We had sent messages, anticipating the university activists to be waiting for our arrival. Through the stacks, I hear snoring. Perhaps we are not alone after all.

We wend our way through the corridors of books until we arrive at the front desk. Sprawled across it is a sleeping figure hidden under voluminous white hair. At our approach, the creature snuffles and turns, and I can almost make out the features of the university's head librarian.

'Jasper. Jasper!' Drow calls.

No response.

Drow strides over and shakes the elderly elf awake. Jasper rubs his eyes and glares at us. 'No need to be so rough.' He brushes his hair back from his face, then breaks into a grin. 'Oh, it is yourself, Drow. And you, too, Percival. Wait a moment.'

The librarian picks up an ornate bell and shakes it. There is no sound to be heard in the library, but somewhere in the halls, it will be ringing.

'We are so few now that we cannot waste resources waiting around for the likes of you to appear. Those you have requested to meet will arrive—'

Jasper's last words are drowned out by the scrape of wood on wood.

'I must get that door sorted,' Jasper says ruefully as about half a dozen young creatures barge into the room. Upon spotting Drow and me, they pull up and study us with wary eyes. My goodness, did Drow and I ever look that young? A male gnome follows behind them, entering at a more sedate pace.

'Are you sure this is them?' a tall, thin female with jet black hair asks Jasper.

'Oh, aye, this is them,' the librarian confirms.

The creature's eyes widen. 'I expected... I don't know... someone a little more... imposing.'

'Sorry to disappoint.' My tone of voice is as dour as I feel. 'Regardless of how uninspiring we are, we do have orders for you, and we have little time to waste.'

I catch Drow's eyes, and he's grinning. I'm pleased he finds this amusing.

'Right,' he starts. 'Let's get the lie of the land.'

He leads the way back to the large central table and draws out a map of the Capitol and surrounds from the tube he carried. We spelled it to show our troops, and he and I will update it as the battle progresses. A couple of the creatures provide books to stop the edges from curling.

'As you can see, our forces are already amassing outside the city. Do we have the head of campus security here?'

The gnome steps forward. 'I am he. My people are waiting by the entrance to the sewers for your orders.'

'Percival, if you would do the honours?'

I draw the gnome aside and hand him Fairburn's signed orders. 'The goal is to neutralise the guards at the Avondale Gate, keeping casualties to a minimum. Then you are to open the gates and let our forces in.'

The gnome nods once. 'Consider it done.'

He leaves more quickly than he entered. I return to the table and squeeze in beside Drow. Someone has helped him add the student teams to the map. In addition to our forces outside the gate, there is a team by the sewers and a couple of other groups congregating in the dining hall.

Once our creatures come in contact with enemy forces, they will send word via magical paper planes, and we will have a complete picture of the battle. Couriers will also drop in and out to provide updates and carry information back to Fairburn and the other leaders as the battle progresses. We hope no one will realise we are co-ordinating things from here, so Drow and I should remain safe.

Drow has finished setting up the map and has checked all the spells are in place. He is now briefing the students who will be sneaking into the ghetto.

'The idea is, you will mobilise the creatures and they in turn will take responsibility for spreading the word. Remember, they are to amass in groups large enough that the small number of guards will not want to stop them, and they are to be ready to move at sunup,' Drow explains.

'What if the guards call for reinforcements? Shouldn't they be ready to fight just in case?' a small gnome asks.

'That is why they are to wait until dawn before they move. By that time our forward platoons should have immobilised the main guard posts around the walls. Bernais will have been informed that we are attacking the Capitol and will be reluctant to release anyone from the palace precinct,' Drow explains.

'And please remind the lesser creatures to disperse when our army arrives. They are there to create a diversion, not to take part in the actual fighting,' I remind them.

They repeat their orders, and Drow says, 'Do not forget to send a note if you encounter enemy soldiers. The more information we have, the better this will go today.'

They pat their pockets to show they have the spelled paper, salute, then scamper off.

There are two leaders left, the tall female creature and her shorter male companion.

'You are leading the expedition to free the prisoners being held in the hospital?' Drow asks.

'Yes. We pulled together a group of the strongest magic workers in the senior class, along with a couple of witches who, like me, specialise in dismantling spells cast by others.'

'Excellent,' Drow says. 'I believe you have figured out a way to enter, but we have not been told about your strategy for extracting the prisoners. They will be weakened and disoriented due to insufficient sustenance, so you may need assistance.

The girl grins, and I would not want to be on the receiving end of her malice.

'Oh, we're not getting them out. We plan to hold the building and get the creatures back on their feet there.'

'How are you going to manage that with so few in your team?' I ask, worried we might have to change their plan on the fly, and we do not have much time.

'We expect there will be some attempt to take back the building because some of the most vocal and connected creatures working against the council are being held in there, and at the very least, they would be useful hostages,' the girl explains.

'That is why we targeted the release of these creatures as being of the utmost importance,' Drow says. 'We think Bernais will attempt to regain control of the building. That is why we had asked for a plan to remove the prisoners and bring them here.'

There is that grin again. It really is most off-putting.

'That is a poor plan for several reasons.' The female holds up her hands and begins counting off. 'First, it would draw attention here, and the council may find out this is our command centre. Second, there are too many opportunities for ambushes if we move the prisoners. Third, some prisoners will need time before they're moved—time that we would have to defend the building and support an evacuation. And, finally, the hospital is easier to defend than the university.'

Drow is nodding, clearly impressed by this logic. 'It could work. How do you propose to hold the building and care for the prisoners with so few creatures?'

'The council has done most of the work for us. They have sealed the windows and closed off all but two of the doors. Once we have disabled the guards and sent them packing, our strongest magicians will seal the final two doors. After that, most of our efforts will be spent ensuring the wards remain strong, except for a few creatures who will head to the roof with some nasty little surprises we have been gathering. We aim to hunker down and wait the war out.'

'Nasty surprises?' I ask.

The grin is now almost gleeful. 'One student from the

World Above got us a recipe for something called a Molotov cocktail.'

Drow and I share a look. 'I think she has defence covered,' I say.

'Defence is good, but what about caring for the prisoners?' Drow asks.

'Felix here is part of the Fieth clan, and they have a formidable network of creatures who are good at.... shall we say, working in the shadows. They have been gathering food and medical supplies and storing them in the sewers beneath the building. When we have control, they will begin bringing up supplies. I believe they also have some volunteer medical professionals who will assist once our spell breakers have worked their magic.'

Drow raises his eyebrows, and I nod my approval. I am impressed with the plan and how organised they are. I turn to Felix. 'And your family.... They are happy to be involved?'

Tears well in the young gnome's eyes. 'Some of my family are being held by the council, and still more are stuck inside the palace. We can't do anything about those in the palace, but at least they are not being tortured. We will do anything to get our creatures out of the council's grasp.'

Apart from the trembling of his bottom lip, Felix is stoic and shows a firm resolve. Snake's grandfather, the Fieth, would be proud of his young relation.

'We can find nothing to object to with this change of plan,' Drow says. 'You may proceed. Good luck.'

'We will not fail,' the girl says.

'If you do not mind me asking,' I say to her, 'What is your name?'

Again that grin. It reminds me of someone. 'I am Renata. You know my uncle, Mandor.'

I try to hide my shock, and she laughs. 'Everyone tells me I am a lot like him.'

'Indeed,' I say. 'He would be proud of you.'

For the first time, her sang-froid waivers, showing how young she still is. 'Thank you.'

When the two have gone, Drow and I watch the map and trace the departure of our young warriors.

'They should be in class, not undertaking missions that could end their lives,' Drow says, weariness tinging his voice.

'We all do what we must in times like this.' Jasper's voice drifts through the stacks, and he follows soon after it, a tray with steaming mugs of coffee and a pile of sandwiches preceding him. 'If you consider the consequences of not overthrowing this corrupt council, you will understand why they are taking such risks.'

The tray thumps down on the table beside the map. 'Make time to take sustenance now, because when the action starts you will need all your energy,' he instructs.

We do as he bids while watching the map. Jasper keeps the coffee flowing, and we adjust the map as spelled paper brings us written updates from the creature ghetto. As time marches on and we have not heard from the prison or from the contingent sent to open the gates, my anxiety rises, making my stomach knot. The only consolation is that we can still see them moving on the map.

Finally, a note arrives from the gates. There has been a setback, but they'll keep us informed.

'Oh well,' Drow says as he updates the map. 'It would not be a proper battle if everything went to plan.'

'Please, Goddess,' I pray, 'Help them get through the gates. If they do not, all will be lost.'

May the goddess be with you this day, Am'ratha tells me before flying off to find a place where she can watch the battle that is close enough for her to rescue me should she need to.

I am still a little wobbly from the time compression even though Am'ratha swears she healed me, and my ears are still ringing from her lecture on the many reasons I should keep out of the fighting today.

The air is heavy with tension as I make my way through the army. From half-heard conversations, I gleaned it was partially battle nerves, but there is also growing concern that it was almost sunrise and we weren't moving.

Irene and Aeron are laughing like hyenas when I reach the front of the forces. I'm about to snap that this is not the time and place for jokes before it hits me—this actually *is* the time and place. Seeing their leaders so relaxed will only boost the confidence of the soldiers.

I reach up and scratch my mount's neck. 'Aeron, what's going on? Why are we still here?'

Irene leans in and whispers, 'Do not react, and laugh like we're sharing a joke. It's because the scouts have not called us forward.'

I grin inanely at her and hide my mouth as if I'm stifling a giggle.

'And why am I acting like a half-wit?'

'It's crucial that we appear unbothered by the fact that dawn is breaking and we are not inside the Capitol.' Aeron speaks close by my ear as he pretends to adjust my horse's tack.

'What do we do?' I ask.

At that moment the head of my grandmother's forces rides over.

'Is it time, Howden?' Irene asks.

'It is, Princess. If we don't go now, we will lose the cover of darkness. We must trust that by the time we reach the gates, Fairburn will have everything in hand.'

'Right you are,' my aunt says, hauling herself up onto her horse.

Aeron helps me up, then takes his position between Irene and me. Howden glances over his shoulder to ensure we're all ready, then leads us forward.

We don't have any magic workers to muffle the sounds like Fairburn's troops do, and I am surprised by the roar that moving so many soldiers makes. Darkness may still hide our exact numbers, but anyone awake on this side of the city will be in no doubt that we are coming.

Fairburn's troops wait in the shadows of the wall, and we approach them at a right angle. When we halt, the noise coming from inside the city makes it clear that Bernais's guards are fighting to keep the gates closed.

'We may need to blast our way in,' Howden says to Fairburn.

The centaur nods. This option is far from perfect because it will reveal our presence and allow Bernais to position his troops to mount a better defence. Fairburn is about to give the order when one side of the gate swings open.

As I release the breath I was holding, a voice inside the walls yells, 'Sound the warning.'

Into the night air, the single clang of a bell rings before a body falls from atop the guard tower. It is like the world holds a breath, wondering of that single clang has signalled the death knell to our plans.

Ignoring the interruption, Fairburn rallies his team to action. 'Take the other guard posts. We don't want anyone coming in behind our forces.'

As they scatter along pre-arranged routes, the Commander of our forces turns to Howden and says, 'Your path to the palace may not be as straight as we would have wished,' before following his troops.

'Right-o,' Howden says, 'We're going with plan B, the three-pronged approach. Irene.'

'Group one, to me,' she commands and swings to the right. Aeron and I follow, to make our way round the city walls towards the palace's delivery entrance. Group two is to go the long way round to the servants' entrance to the left, leaving the main force to take the most direct route to the palace.

'Why was this plan B?' I whisper. 'I mean, surely a single point of attack would be bad tactics.'

'Normally,' Irene says. 'However, the original plan moved our forces directly to the palace under a spell of silence, and we would have fanned out once we got there. This way will take longer. We don't have enough creatures able to use muffling spells on all three groups, and we're at greater risk of ambush because our forces are split.'

And this is why Irene is in charge.

Footsteps and the clink of metal on metal fill the air as we slink through the shadows. I strain my ears for any sign that the demonstration has started so we can pick up the pace. As the sun turns the sky pink, shouts ring out from closer to the palace, and Irene gives the order to speed up.

'I'm not sure that is the demonstration—it sounds more like a skirmish. Maybe they're barricading the roads,' Aeron says, hefting his mighty sword.

I draw my weapon as Irene commands, 'Eyes about.'

A handful of creatures peel off and scout ahead while everyone else prepares to fight.

A couple of turns later, we encounter several open doors. Aeron checks each dwelling before we pass, ensuring we are not ambushed from behind. When he returns to my side, he says, 'They are empty, and not just of creatures. They've been stripped bare.'

'Why would they do that? Are they leaving the city?' I ask.

Aeron barks a laugh, and when we turn the next corner, I understand the joke. Under the watchful gaze of a handful of soldiers, a stream of men, women and children are carrying furniture to a makeshift barricade.

The female gnome at the back of the line turns and screams when she sees us. She drops the wooden kitchen chair she's carrying, grabs two children, and disappears down a side alley. More civilians follow her as the guards scramble over the makeshift structure blocking the road.

Irene calls, 'Halt. Take positions.'

Aeron bustles me backwards as some of the troops melt into doorways along the street. Still others break away down the alley, and I can just make out shadowy figures climbing to rooftops.

'What are you doing?' I ask as Aeron leads my horse back around the corner.

'Keeping you out of range. We do not know what weapons they have, and I do not want to give them a clear shot if their human mercenaries have brought guns with them.'

'Oh, I hadn't thought of that.'

'Let Irene and her people clear the way. Then we can move forward.'

'I can't stay back here and let others fight for me,' I

protest, a power struggle between fear and embarrassment going on in my head.

Aeron maintains a tight hold on the horse's reins. 'Most of these creatures fight for Irene as part of the Loch Ness battalion. They have this under control, and you will only get in their way.'

I nudge my mount forward so I can at least see what is happening while trying to find the right words to convince Aeron to let me join in. Before I form a coherent thought, arrows rain down on the defenders behind the barricades, and the air fills with their screams.

The soldiers in the doorways make their way towards the barricade under cover of the eaves. Instead of climbing over, as I would have done, they dismantle the structure piece by piece.

They are fast and efficient, and it is only a matter of minutes before Irene emerges from the alley and calls her troop back to her. We join the back of the procession through the gap in the barricade.

I've watched battles in movies and seen the aftermath of war on the news, but nothing could prepare me for how much blood runs over the cobbles. Nor for the tang of iron on the air or the smell of bodily fluids released from injured and dying creatures.

Although my gorge rises in my throat, I force myself to imprint the scene on my mind. I helped make the decision to fight today, and I am partially responsible for every wound, lost limb, and death that occurs as a result of that.

Irene dispatches a handful of soldiers to check for survivors to be taken prisoner or transported to the hospital. I don't like their chances of finding anyone alive, but it still has to be done.

'Does it get any easier?' I ask Aeron.

The Minotaur raises sad eyes to meet my horrified ones

and shakes his shaggy head. 'Never. And it should not. If that happened, making the decision to go to war would be too simple.'

Would I have been so cavalier about going into battle if I had known what today would be like? Or would I have spent more time focusing on a diplomatic solution? It is difficult to say. But one thing I *can* say is, I don't want to see anything like this ever again.

As the sun shines brightly in the clear blue sky, shouts of creature protests ring through the air. I shake off my shock and heartbreak over the death that is all around me. We are in this now, for better or worse, and the only way is forward.

CHAPTER 12

War is Messy

E d'rathe glides downwards and gently settles on the clifftop. Am'ratha lifts her purple head, and the tingle in the air tells me the siblings are talking.

Am'ratha says Pris is back in place and that we have missed nothing.

'Thank you, Am'ratha.'

She blinks twice, then drops her head to rest it on her front paws, her gaze directed back towards the Capitol. The dragon on the other side of Am'ratha turns her head, appraises me, then turns away. I get the impression this unknown dragon has dismissed me as unimportant, and that irks me.

Do not mind Am'rena. Princess Cecily has forbidden any rescue attempts, and she has been sitting here brooding for days.

The pre-dawn light glints off the green dragon's scales as she opens an eye. **I do not need your pity, youngling. Save it for those who fight today.**

'I meant no disrespect. I was merely thinking how difficult it is to stand by while someone you care for risks themselves.'

Her eyes widen as if in surprise. **Yes, Snake, I see you do understand. But sometimes knowing you are nearby is worth something to those we love.**

Now it is my turn to be surprised. It hadn't occurred to me that knowing we are here might provide a comfort for those who are in the midst of battle.

Someone has to rescue them if things go wrong. Ed'rathe's tone is dry.

The sun peeks over the horizon, turning the sky pink. Birds in the nearby trees sing in the morning until unfamiliar sounds carried on the wind silence them. It has begun.

Ed'rathe lowers his head. **Come, Snake, it is time.**

With some trepidation, I climb onto Ed'rathe's back. When I'm settled, the dragon takes off out to sea, then turns back around and heads towards the Capitol. I know very little about the battle plans except that once the mercenaries have been engaged, the palace guard are to join in and create a second front.

In the palace courtyard, a mass of creatures is chanting and taunting the human mercenaries. The soldiers hold their positions but seem a little perplexed.

We circle wider and find three columns of soldiers wending their way towards the palace—one group fighting through a barricade to reach their destination.

Back at the palace, the mercenaries are being reinforced while the rest of their number pull apart their makeshift camp in the palace grounds. They are clearly aware this protest is the precursor to something bigger and are preparing for it.

While the grounds are a hive of activity, the palace is strangely quiet. On a balcony stands a lone centaur watching the action, but there is no sign the Queen's Guard are even up. Did the message not get through?

Ed'rathe, can you ask Am'rena if Cecily got the messages about the plans for today?

The air sings with magic, and the conversation between dragons goes on for much longer than I anticipated.

She says Cecily will not commit their force until they are certain we will win. Guard Captain Georgio advised that to strip the palace of its protections would be a disaster should we lose.

Really? Creatures are putting their lives on the line, and they are protecting themselves?

Even though these creatures are also keeping my mother and the Fieth family members taking refuge in the palace safe, their lack of action puts everyone else at greater risk, and that makes me angry.

They are only doing their job, Noble One. The palace guard's primary aim is to keep the royal line safe.

I huff because I can see the logic. Still, don't they understand that if they don't engage, all will be lost?

Ed'rathe banks again, and as he does, I make out a small group—mercenaries, judging from their dress—climbing the palace walls. There are not enough of them to take on the might of the Queen's Guard, but there are enough for an assassination attempt on Princess Cecily.

Let me down, Ed'rathe.

I can tell Am'rena about the men.

We don't know what they're up to, and I don't want to give the palace guards any excuse not to join the main battle.

I cannot help you if you leave me, and you cannot help the main forces from there.

True, I won't be able to follow the battle, but I must make sure Princess Cecily is okay. Also, it might help to remind her personally what is at stake today.

I have to do this, Ed'rathe.

My dragon's response is to take me out of sight of the climbing soldiers and lower me towards a balcony round the corner. I ignore the long drop to the ground three stories below, and I'm grateful Ed'rathe uses his magic to ensure I land safely on the balcony after sliding down his leg.

I will continue to circle. Come back here if you need me to pick you up.

After wandering through the empty suite in the dawn light, bumping into sofas and tables as I go, I fumble for the doorknob, then stick my head into the corridor.

To my right I make out two centaur-like figures guarding a stairwell. My immediate thought is to call them, but in the time it takes to explain who I am and why I'm here, the mercenaries will be long gone. I can always call for help if I need them. What am I saying? Of course I'll need them. I can't fight five men alone.

Ahead of me, the sounds of boots trying to creep across a stone floor attracts my attention. Crouching, I duck my head around the corner and quickly pull back. There aren't only five men, but more like twenty standing in the hallway, consulting a map by torchlight.

There is no way two guards and I can take on this amount of people. Or can we? Mender said singing the sleep spell should work. I guess I'm about to find out if that's true.

I crouch down and start singing the spell in a soft voice, filling it with intention and using a direction spell to send my voice along the corridor.

One of the soldiers glances over his shoulder. 'Hey, what's that?'

The others turn. Two of them rush towards me, and my voice cracks a little and I lose the melody.

There's no time for subtle now. I stand up, take a deep breath and bellow out the words, willing the soldiers to sleep as if my life depends on it. And it just might because the entire group is now bearing down on me, and they'll be here any second.

The lead soldier is about four steps away, drawing his sword, ready to attack, when the weapon slips from his grasp, and he drops to the ground. The man behind him falls over the prone body and is asleep before he hits the floor.

In a split second, the spell starts to take hold, and I can actually see the other soldiers' eyes droop. Slowly they crumple one by one, except for the three at the back. They act quickly and stuff their fingers in their ears. As their mates fall around them, they stride towards me.

From behind me the clatter of hooves on stone bolsters, my resolve and I force more intent into my song. It only slows the two men and one woman, but it's buying me some time for the cavalry to arrive. As two centaurs push past me, I drop to the floor, exhaustion pulling me under. The next thing I know, I'm being nudged by a hoof.

'Oi, you, up.'

I stare up into the brown eyes of a centaur guard whose face is way too close to mine for comfort.

'He doesn't smell like the others. He's creature, not human,' he says to the other guard.

'I think he was the one singing,' his female companion says.

'Were you?'

Again that intense stare.

'Yes, a sleep spell. Did you get them all? I think they were trying to get to Princess Cecily.'

'Well, obviously. But what are *you* doing here?'

'I need to talk with the princess?'

The centaur stands back and snuffles. 'Huh, you and thousands of others.'

Shaking my head to clear the magic hangover, I search for inspiration in the fog of my brain before crossing my fingers and saying, 'But I *really* need to speak with her. I have a message from the Dragon Queen.'

Okay, the Queen didn't specifically ask me to update Princess Cecily with what was happening with her aunt, but they don't know that.

Again the centaur snuffles, which I'm thinking is him laughing, but I can't be certain. His companion sniffs the air.

'Hermes, I think we might have to at least take this one to Georgio. He has the smell of the Fieth about him, and I think one of them was with the dragons. Can't you smell that other scent?'

Hermes shakes his head. 'Sorry, hay fever, my nose isn't working at its best.'

Okay, maybe not laughing.

'All right, Fiamma, but it's on your head. I can't take any more kitchen duty.'

'You all right managing this lot. I already called for backup to help take them to the dungeons.' She nods towards the shackled men.

Hermes tests the restraints and assures her he can deal with them. Fiamma leads me past the mostly sleeping soldiers.

'How did you get them tied up so fast?' I ask.

'We centaurs have little magic, but we can transport a few chains from the dungeon when we need to.' She looks towards the stairs where another couple of centaurs appear. 'And send a message for help.'

'Hey, can you wake them before you go?' Hermes asks.

I smile ruefully. 'Sorry, mate, I was only taught the sleeping spell.'

'Try a bucket of water,' Fiamma calls over her shoulder, laughing to herself at the thought.

Out the library window, the Capitol stretches out towards the horizon. Ignoring the occasional shouts and clanging of metal and the empty courtyard, it feels like I'm studying here again. I rub a hand over my weary eyes and return to the table.

Jasper is asleep, his head resting on his arms. I gather the teacups and consider heading to the kitchen to make a fresh brew. Drow is gazing at the map, magical notes piled up beside him, and I'm distracted from my task.

'What is the matter?' I ask.

He points at a building close to the university. 'Renata and her group arrived a little while ago, but I have not received an update. I fear for them. And see here. We broke into three groups, so we are following plan B, but no one has informed me of the reason or let me know about enemy forces'

I place the cups on the table and move until I am beside my friend. 'We cannot worry about every deviation from the plan. We were aware it would not be a walk in the park and that changes would have to be made. That is why we maintain the map—so the Commanders can send for an overview and adjust their tactics.'

The paper plane updates have allowed Drow to spell in the opposition forces, and it is clear we have taken a number of captives.

'Where are we holding the enemy soldiers?'

Drow raises a weary head. 'We had planned to use the main guardhouse, but it is already full. I have sent word to bring the overflow to the university refectory.'

A knot of worry tugs in my stomach at these words. 'Was that wise? It may turn attention our way.'

Running a hand through already messy hair, Drow's gaze returns to the map. 'It was the only area within our control large enough to accommodate the numbers. They will be in chains and have guards with them. Besides, there is no way for prisoners to find out we are here.'

It all sounds reasonable, but worry claws at my gut. The map is a study in chaos and does nothing to soothe me.

'What does that mean?' I point at a swirling pattern outside the city walls.

Drow's brows draw together. 'I have no idea. It appeared there about ten minutes ago.'

'It is not something you spelled in from the dispatches?'

He shakes his head. 'No. But I did spell the map to pick up any seriously bad weather or large groups of creatures in the area.'

The knot pulls tighter. 'And the sky is clear... so, a group of creatures?'

'Mmm... perhaps. Or maybe livestock?'

I shake my head. Large herds of animals do not just wander around the World Below untended. And why would they be heading for the Capitol? There were no markets being held, with mercenaries camped out in the palace square.

'We will monitor it, and I'll send a message to Fairburn so he's aware.'

Drow picks up a clean sheet of paper and begins writing. We're so engrossed in the message that it takes a moment for us to realise a portal has opened into the room. It is only Jasper sitting bolt upright that alerts us.

Eleanora, Eugenia, and Euphemia step through the opening, followed by the half dozen witches who had remained with them at the campsite. Mandor is last through, and he closes the portal.

'I thought you were going on to the hospital with Mender and Heart,' I say to the witch sisters.

'We were,' Genie starts.

'Until we checked on the soldiers we'd sent to sleep before leaving,' Effie adds.

'Yes, we thought rather than let them join up with their friends, we'd take as many of them prisoner as we could with the handcuffs and shackles we had,' Mandor says as he joins us, 'but we found there were far fewer than our earlier reports had indicated.'

Drow stops writing, 'How many fewer?'

The witches look at one another.

'Perhaps less than half of what was counted earlier in the day,' Mandor says, and the others nod their agreement.

Drow and I lock eyes, then we both look at the map and the swirling mass moving closer to the Capitol gates. 'Is it possible surrounding our camp was a feint intending to force us to move before we were fully ready?' Drow asks, voicing my own concerns.

'We need to find out what that is,' I add.

'Alyce,' Mandor calls, and a witch steps forward. 'Go to the guard tower nearest to there and find out what is causing this disturbance.'

The room is silent while we wait for the young witch to return. Minutes later our worst fears are confirmed.

'It's the guards we saw heading to our camp yesterday. They must have turned around and headed back at a quick magic-assisted march when night fell,' she informs us.

'And I'll bet our missing guards from the perimeter are not far behind them,' Eleanora comments.

Jasper leans over for a better view. 'Looks like our creatures will be caught between them and the human soldiers.'

'Not if the Queen's Guard in the palace attack the mercenaries from behind,' I say, although a little doubt is worming its way into my confident tone. We should have had a note by now, telling us the guards have left the palace.

Effie has drifted over to the window. 'Worrying will not help, the die is cast, and we must now wait to see the outcome. Percival? Who is that coming into the courtyard —they look like prisoners.'

I join Effie, and Ellie and Genie cram in behind us.

'They are prisoners. Drow says we ran out of space in the guard quarters.'

'You can no longer stay here unprotected,' Ellie asserts, and her sisters mumble agreement. 'We'll send a message to the hospital that we're staying unless they desperately need us.'

'But you did not want to fight,' I protest.

'Defending you is not fighting,' Genie tells me.

We continue to watch the string of prisoners make their way into the building to the right, while in the background, Mandor gives instructions to the other witches. Once the prisoners vanish and the witches have left to deliver news of the new danger, we resume our positions at the table and witness the enemy's rear guard entering the city.

⸻

For the moment before we enter the square in front of the palace, it's like I'm watching something out of a movie. Hordes of creatures are shouting at the human mercenaries who are attempting to fend them off without breaking their lines. The soldiers are being forced backwards until they can move no more. It's like they've hit a brick wall, and perhaps they have.

'Have the Queen's Guard set up a shield around the palace? Is that how they've been keeping safe?' I ask Aeron.

His huge shoulders rise in a shrug. 'It could be them, but could be us. Centaurs have little magic, so they cannot protect the entire palace. But I guess they could put up a targeted shield to slow down an attacking force.'

Irene signals that the other groups have arrived at the square, then sends one of her scouts to clear the area. Some creatures who have been protesting head for the streets, but others want to join the battle and are creating chaos.

In the confusion, a group of mercenaries surrounds some protestors and takes them hostage, then order the other creatures to leave or the hostages die. To prevent panic, Fairburn sends in a group of trained creatures on a rescue mission. Then it is all on.

We surge forward into the marketplace to support the initial troops as the scared protestors flee towards the emptying streets. The area is so crowded, Irene orders us to get off our horses and send them back out of the arena.

I've experienced fighting before, have even fought for my survival, but nothing can prepare you for confronting an adversary in battle. My ears ring from the noise, and my stomach roils from the smells—and not just blood either.

A few minutes in, my energy is draining fast, and my sword feels twice the size—and I'm only at the edge of the fighting, helping the protestors away from danger. There is no way to conserve energy when you are under constant attack, and I can't fight like this for long.

Beside me Aeron roars, and I half turn to see blood streaming down Irene's arm from a gash. Aeron makes his way to her, and I follow in his wake. By the time we arrive, she has bound her wound and is ready to fight again.

I glance towards the palace, hoping that by now they have sent out a force of guards to aid us. The building is eerily quiet.

'Get Irene to safety,' I order Aeron.

'No, I am fine. I've had worse in training. But you should get Pris out of here,' the princess tells the Minotaur.

I glare at her as she glares back. And the only reason we're not cut down is that Aeron is protecting both of us.

Irene pinches the bridge of her nose and closes her eyes. Finally she says, 'All right, we protect each other.'

I don't know what that means, but I get the idea when Aeron and Irene turn shoulder to shoulder, leaving a space for me to create a triangle. They have me angled towards the back of the fighting, protecting their backs, but Aeron hasn't carried me away, so I'm not complaining.

Am'ratha?

Princess, concentrate on the fight.

I grit my teeth and parry a blow from a mercenary who

looks even younger than me. He's swept away by the crush of creatures still moving to the streets.

I need you to find out from Am'nera what's happening with the Royal Guard. We really need them.

All right.

There is a long silence. Then it stretches for even longer.

Am'ratha?

She is still talking with your mother.

Still talking? What's there to discuss? **Tell her to tell my mother to look out the window. If she doesn't want the creatures fighting for her to be wiped out in a single battle, then she should send out—**

'We're trapped!' a cry rings out.

Before my mind can process that, a blast comes out of nowhere and fells a creature beside me.

'They're using magic against us.' Aeron bellows.

'Who is?' I'm confused. That attack came from behind. Oh my goddess, we've been outflanked.

Am'ratha, get my mother! Now!

Then a shockwave sweeps over the marketplace, and in its wake, everyone holds still.

'Was that another magic attack?' I ask Aeron.

'I have no idea what that was, but it was nothing good.'

CHAPTER 13

All Or Nothing

'While I appreciate your help in foiling the enemy incursion this morning, the head of my guard and Ariana's chief advisor, Elias, have made it clear that if we were to lose the battle today having committed our forces to the fray, we might as well give up now. I promised to hold the throne for Aunt Ariana, so I must follow their advice.'

Although the woman in front of me is wearing jeans and a denim shirt, she is no less regal. She is definitely Petunia's daughter, and I can see where Pris gets her haughtiness from.

'That's the whole point,' I argue. 'Today is an all-or-nothing situation. And if you don't help, it will definitely be nothing.'

'I am aware of the knife edge we are on, and I am not standing idly by. Elias and Georgio are watching proceedings, and the guard is ready to go on their command.'

This isn't working. Telling her about Queen Ariana sacrificing herself for magic had only made Princess Cecily more determined to stay out of the battle today. What will make her change her mind?

'Pris is down there fighting.'

Cecily barely flinches, but something changes in her eyes. There was also a gasp from the creature standing by the door—Pris's father. The princess draws her bottom lip between her teeth, and it's so reminiscent of Pris when she's worried that it almost breaks my heart.

'And the Dragon Queen will not let this battle turn into a prolonged war without intervening.'

Before Princess Cecily can respond, a wave of power travels through the room, then it's as if the whole world stands still. When it is over, no one moves.

> *We mourn the loss,*
> *The Worlds all weep,*
> *Her memory safe,*
> *The dragons will keep.*

The haunting words rumble through my very bones, and a sadness pulses in my chest like a heartbeat.

'What was that?' I whisper.

Princess Cecily places her hand on my arm. 'You heard that?'

I nod as I realise many in the room did not.

'It was a dragon sending.' Princess Cecily pauses as though listening to someone, then adds, 'Am'rena says Queen Ariana is dead.'

Gasps ripple around the room.

A taller, slimmer version of King Maddox moves to Princess… *Queen* Cecily's side.

'Malachai?' The word is a question.

In response, he wraps an arm around her. 'It was inevitable this day would arrive when you retained your position in the line of succession. It is no longer enough to keep the seat warm for Queen Ariana. Now *you* must decide what is right for the realm.'

She doesn't even wait a heartbeat before beckoning over a youngling dressed in palace livery. 'Tell Georgio it is time to release the guards.'

'Thank you,' I say, my entire body sagging with relief before it dawns on me that I am now in the presence of the Queen of the World Below. 'Your Majesty, I have much to do on behalf of the Dragon Queen—'

'You may go, Snake.' She gives my arm a squeeze. 'And stay safe.'

'I will, ma'am,' I respond before hurrying from the room.

Ed'rathe, I am ready.

I meet the dragon at the agreed place and find it's harder to climb up than it was to get down. Thank goodness for dragon magic, or it would be impossible. Ed'rathe takes to the skies, sweeping over the chaos in the courtyard. I can't see Pris anywhere, and worry churns my stomach.

Am'ratha would tell me if she is in danger, and you would see my sister dragon fly to her rescue.

That is a little comforting. Hold on, do they think of danger as mortal peril or wounded? I can't bear to think of either.

Let's go a little wider and see what's happening in the rest of the Capitol, I say.

Ed'rathe banks to the left and takes me out towards the university. As we sweep over the streets, my gaze is drawn to a group of about thirty creatures skulking in the shadows about five minutes out from the main university buildings.'

No, that's not good. Drow and Percival are the only ones there, and we will lose our command centre if they are captured. I tap on Ed'rathe's scales.

Can you set me down in the university courtyard?

I feel rather than hear him sigh.

It is safer for you if we are together.

I can't let anything happen to my uncle and my friend. If there is a chance I can stop it....

I understand.

Ed'rathe sweeps around and gently drops to the ground. My feet have not quite found purchase when Ed'rathe snorts a warning, and I look up to find we're surrounded by armed creatures.

'Grossman, what luck. We come to ensure the students stay out of the battle, and we find ourselves a couple of traitors,' a familiar creature says.

Ed'rathe tenses beside me, and I can't believe Giles Coronas would be stupid enough to attack a dragon. As Grossman Green steps from behind Giles's left shoulder, his face twists into a mask of fear, and I worry that the elf may just be that stupid.

I hold up my hands in a placating gesture. 'Now, Giles, while I am a legitimate target, you don't want to start anything with the dragons.'

The elf sneers, and the malice in his eyes sends shivers down my spine. 'I've studied enough dragon lore to know that you and he are in some way bonded, and to get to you, I must go through him.'

I don't want Ed'rathe getting involved in this. 'I'll send him away.'

'He won't go. He will stay and defend you to the death

if he must,' Giles spits. 'And the best thing is… if I ask even one of my creatures to not join the fight, he will not use his dragon fire in case he hurts them.'

Ed'rathe?

He is right, Noble One. I cannot return home head held high if I desert you.

And the dragon fire thing?

That is also correct. It would shame me to hurt an innocent bystander, and dragon fire is not a precise weapon. But I am still a formidable foe without it.

Resting a hand on his flank, I consider my options. I'm sure Ed'rathe can fight well, but the courtyard is not big enough for him to move with ease.

My gaze falls on Grossman Greene. The goblin has been strangely quiet. He shakes his head as if he's urging me not to fight. Why would he do that? The air pops beside me, and I jump with fright when Mandor, Eleanora, and Euphemia appear.

'I think this evens up the odds a little, don't you?' Eleanora grins with a ferocity I never thought I would see on the normally caring witch's face.

Giles sneers. 'You have no weapons!'

Pop.

Eugenia appears with an array of swords and parcels them out. There is even one for me, although I have no idea how to use it.

'Where?' I ask.

Eugenia winks. 'The university mess hall has an amazing display of ancient weapons. I don't know how sharp they are after all this time, so you might want to tend to the blade before we begin.'

There is a hum of magic as the others do as she

suggests, but I think it's better if mine remains blunt so I don't inadvertently cut someone in my ineptitude.

If you position yourself near my flank, then I can use teeth and claws to protect your back.

I tell the others what Ed'rathe suggests, and we're just getting into position when the fighting begins. Grossman comes straight for me, sword in front, and it doesn't take me long to realise he's as incompetent at this as I am. After one ringing blow, my sword slips from my hand, and I think I'm done for. Then, as if he's evening up the odds, Grossman lets go of his own weapon and comes at me fists swinging.

I centre myself, ready for impact, then pull back my arm and land a satisfying punch to his jaw. As our struggle continues, I catch a glimpse of the scene around me, and it's not good. My team all have injuries, some more serious than others. Mandor is working hard to keep Giles at bay, but the elf is ferocious in his determination to beat us. This fighting for your life thing is terrifying, and the scene doesn't cut away when it gets too messy.

No one is going near Ed'rathe—I guess the wrath of a dragon is something to be feared after all. Still, even though Ed'rathe has our backs, we are outnumbered, and we're tiring. If something doesn't happen soon, then we're done for.

My distraction costs me as Grossman lands a blow that sets my ears ringing. I shake my head to clear it, but there appear to be more creatures in front of me than there were before. My head swims, and I'm not sure if it's a reaction to the blow or the certainty I'm about to die.

'Keep fighting, you ninny,' a familiar voice yells in my ear as Verona pushes Grossman out of the way. 'Where's your sword?'

I glance at the ground and duck one of Grossman's swings as I bend to pick up the useless item.

There's a groan, and Grossman stumbles back, a sword sticking out of his shoulder. Blood stains his shirt red, and the smell of warm iron hits me, sending my head swimming, and it's all I can do to remain on my feet.

Ed'rathe roars, and the earth shakes. Grossman loses his balance and collapses, and I scan the area as Gregor and several other students close in on the rebels.

'It's over,' Gregor shouts. 'Drop your weapons.'

Most of the enemy does as he commands, but a few around Giles stand back to back, ready to fight till the end.

'You,! What are you doing here?' Giles snarls, pushing through his followers as his daughter moves to stand beside Gregor.

'I know you won't understand, Father, but I'm doing what's right,' Verona says.

'You're besotted with him, and he's turned your head.' Spittle flies from Giles's mouth as his eyes spin wildly. 'Can't you see this madness between you and him is what we are trying to stop?'

He's lost it, and he's going to do something stupid. At that exact moment, Giles leaps forward, sword aimed at Gregor's heart.

What happens next is so fast, it's a blur of arms and weapons. Then Giles falls to the ground, a sword in his side. Verona drops to her knees, tears streaming down her face, her hands empty.

'Dad.' Her voice is full of pain and regret.

Behind her, Gregor clutches his stomach and blood seeps through his fingers. He stares at his wound as if he can't believe it's there before collapsing silently behind her.

I'm so transfixed by the scene, I almost don't hear

Mandor say, 'Snake, it's safe. We can take it from here, Ed'rathe.'

I do feel cold air as Ed'rathe shuffles away. **Do you want to come with me?**

I survey the devastation and shudder as Verona's scream of anguish when she sees Gregor on the ground cuts me to the core. **No, Ed'rathe, I think I am needed here now, unless the Dragon Queen still wants something from me.**

I will be above, watching. Should she need you, I will find you.

'Prisoners are being held in the refectory,' Mandor says, his voice cutting through the murmurs echoing in the courtyard.

Ed'rathe launches into the sky, and I reach down and pull Grossman to his feet. He groans in pain, but he will live. I'm not so sure about Giles and Gregor. Effie and Genie are tending to them, but their wounds are serious.

'Wait. Wait,' Grossman says.

I pause. 'What?'

'Your princess still owes me,' he pleads.

Anger washes over me, and he winces as I squeeze his arm. He's going to ask me to let him go. He's going to get away with this. 'You want me to release you, don't you?'

His head drops. 'No, I have done some bad things, and I must pay for what I did... helped do. I have a wife and children in the World Above. It is them I worry about. I did it for the gold, to take care of them. Please, make sure they stay safe.'

I don't know what disgusts me more—the thought that creatures would support Bernais and the council because they endorse their racist beliefs or that someone could support them for money alone.

Either way, Grossman's family should not have to suffer

for his actions. And Pris does owe him for letting us go from Wistman's Woods.

'I'll do what I can,' I say, pulling him after the others.

⋅⋅•⋅⋅

We mourn the loss,
The Worlds all weep,
Her memory safe,
The dragons will keep.

I repeat the words under my breath, and beside me Irene stiffens.

'What?' I ask over my shoulder, unwilling to take my eyes off the enemy even though no one is moving.

'A Dragon Bonded is dead,' Irene says, 'That's the dragon lament for one they consider to be of their own.'

Queen Ariana is with the ancestors, Am'ratha sends.

No! I didn't know her well, but she was my great-aunt, and the World Below will miss her. And it couldn't happen at a worse time. Or perhaps it isn't as bad as it might have been. The Queen hadn't signed the agreement, and many on our side saw her as part of the problem.

However, I bet there are some followers of Bernais who are excited about this because now they have a chance to claim the throne.

The clash of sword meeting sword rings out in the silence, then it is all on again. Aeron, Irene, and I carry on fighting in our small circle. Irene's wound hinders her, but she is still better at this than I am.

Minutes or perhaps hours later, a shout goes up, and

everyone turns towards the palace as if drawn by an invisible force. I can just make out a figure on the balcony. 'Mum?'

Aeron bellows, 'Long live Queen Cecily!'

Others follow suit, followed by gasps and murmurs as creatures on both sides realise what this means; Queen Ariana is dead and Queen Cecily now sits on the throne. Seconds later a thundering fills the air as figures pour around the palace like a wave.

The centurion royal guard are finally joining the fight. My spirits soar as I see the fear on the mercenary soldiers' faces. They look like they want to run, but there is nowhere to go.

As the fighting begins again, a shout rings through the square. Somewhere above me, a dragon I know lands on the building directly across from the palace. Two figures descend—Adina and her son, Bernais. He waves, and our opponents cheer—even the mercenaries are shouting their support. Then again, being under a curse, they probably have no say in the matter.

Suddenly the fighting becomes more intense as dragons take to the sky above us, ready to protect their bonded creatures.

Get to a safe place, and I will pick you up.

Am'ratha's voice distracts me, and I take a nick to my forearm.

No. I am staying here.

You are now heir to the throne, and I cannot protect you in amongst that.

As if in concert with Am'ratha, Irene commands Aeron to get the heir to the throne out of the square. Before I can protest, Aeron picks me up and throws me over his shoulder. He slices his way through the crowd, and I do my best to protect his back from my ungainly position.

We almost make it. Struggling through the edge of the fighting a sword comes out of nowhere and slices across Aaron's back, finding exposed flesh where the minotaur's armour has moved as I fought.

Aeron staggers a few steps into a side street, then drops to the ground. I roll to the side and pull my legs out from under his bulky form. 'Aeron!' I scramble back to his side, rip at my shirt, and apply pressure to the wound. Blood seeps through the fabric as panic surges inside me.

Am'ratha, come find me. Aeron is down.

The window is cool as I lean my forehead against it. I itch to be down there helping my friends fight. A hand squeezes my shoulder as if in sympathy, but I do not take my eyes from the scene below.

'We are too old and not warrior enough to launch ourselves into that,' Jasper says.

'I know, and we have an important job to do here,' I respond wearily.

'Or not.' Drow's voice comes from behind us as he stares at the map, a paper plane message in his hand.

We rejoin him at the table, and I study the map. Nothing is different. What has changed for Drow?

'What's going on?' I ask as a dragon shadow appears over the palace and the site of the battle in front.

'I believe this is the endgame,' Drow says.

As if his words are portents, the library door crashes open, and King Maddox appears. Although he is moving fast, his face is ashen and his eyes dull.

'Come quick, we must go and protect Cecily and Malachai,' he commands.

'But the map...,' I say lamely.

'Go. I can keep the map updated,' Jasper says.

Drow doesn't need to be told twice, but I pause. 'Ed'ruven can't take all of us.'

Maddox grabs my hand and starts dragging me out of the room. 'Then it is a good thing the Dragon Queen sent along Ed'rima, my brother's Dragon Bonded. As you a Dragon Friend, he will allow you to ride him.'

My heart almost stops in my chest. I have not had much luck riding dragons, and that was with someone else on back with me. My mouth is dry as Maddox pushes open the door to the roof, and I see the silver dragon lounging beside the midnight black Ed'ruven.

King Maddox and Drow are already seated when I take my first steps towards the dragon who has offered to take me to the palace.

Hello, Dragon Friend. I have heard much about you, and I am honoured to escort you to the palace.

He stays down as I tentatively climb onto his back.

It is my honour entirely, I tell him even though I am quaking in my boots.

The dragon chortles. **Do not be afraid. I will use magic to ensure you stay safe. There will be no... accidents.**

Thank you.

Even though I trust his words, I grip the scale in front of me tightly as we fly over the city. He descends to the main palace balcony and uses magic to place me safely by the doors. When my feet touch the ground, my shoulders sag with relief.

Thank you, my friend.

As he and Ed'ruven take to the skies, I look across the marketplace below and at the dragon perching on the roof of the building opposite. A quick 'far-see' spell shows me Bernais, Adina, and Magnus Baaronson watching the proceedings.

As if in response to our arrival, Adina and Bernais climb onto Am'nera's back. As the dragon takes to the sky, Am'rena appears from nowhere, screeching a warning, determined to protect her new Queen.

I do not get to watch the battle play out because King Maddox again grabs my hand and pulls me into a crowded room. There is Cecily, surrounded by people all yabbering at her. Before I can intervene and rescue her, the door opposite opens, and Malachai strides in, followed by Elias, who overtakes the King Consort and commands, 'Quiet. QUIET!'

Miraculously the crowd parts to let him through. He takes Cecily's arm and leads her to the throne to the right of the balcony doors.

'The throne is not just a sign of office. It also makes sure petitioners cannot surround you,' I hear him tell the Queen as he helps her sit. 'Now, one at a time, please.'

Elias spies us by the window and motions us forward. 'Make way for the Queen's advisors,' he orders, and the creatures part to make way for us.

Before we can take a single step, a shout rings out from behind me. 'How dare you sit on my throne.' Fury and disdain drip from the words.

Everyone's attention shifts to the balcony. I can see nothing through the throng of taller creatures, but I know that voice—Bernais Baaronson. How did he get by Am'rena?

'Make way for the true King,' a woman's voice bellows.

Adina is with him. Of course Am'rena could do nothing that might hurt the Dragon Bonded.

The creatures who had previously crowded around Queen Cecily draw back to the edge of the room, leaving Bernais and Adina to continue confronting Cecily and Elias. In a split second, Maddox and Malachai take their place in front of the throne, brandishing their swords.

Surprisingly, there are a couple of courtiers lining up with Bernais. Had the palace harboured traitors all along, or are these courtiers merely bending with the prevailing wind? They don't have their swords out, so they're clearly not that committed to Bernais's cause.

'Now, now,' Adina is saying, 'there is no need to fight. Cecily, come down from there and let Bernais take his rightful place.'

The princess is speaking as though to a child. I cannot believe she thinks this will work.

'Really, Aunt Adina, this is not a fight between cousins. This is a matter of state, and the line of succession is a matter of public record. I may not have been crowned, but I am Queen.' Cecily's voice is confident as she embraces the role of ruler.

'You have no right to the Crown. You gave it up when you chose that dark elf over your people, cousin,' Bernais responds, clearly trying to goad Cecily.

'Interesting that you choose that as your bone of contention, not that I left the World Below,' Cecily says. 'Can you not see that the era of elven dominance is drawing to a close, and no amount of bloodshed will prevent it?'

'It is you who are wrong,' Bernais says, lunging forward just as Adina moves, arm outstretched.

'No, Bernais,' she says, but she is too late. He pushes

past her, and in his fury, his sword slices through her clothing, drawing blood.

The room freezes as Adina clutches her wound, her eyes wide on her son. She sways, then falls to the floor as if in slow motion. Bernais does not pause or hesitate. He screams and carries his attack forward, facing the two dark elves he so despises alone.

As Bernais leaves his mother behind, a figure detaches itself from the handful of courtiers to help Adina. It is Ginth fo Drefin, Snake's mother. Drow steps forward to help her escort Adina to a couch as a servant leaves to find someone to tend to the elf princess's wounds.

Back in the centre of the room, King Maddox is forcing Bernais away from the throne. 'I will not let a Baaronson make me cower this time.'

King Maddox's face is a mask of anger, and each clash of swords pushes Bernais back a step.

Bernais is a picture of righteous fury. 'How dare you think you have the right to decide who sits on our throne.' Disdain is threaded through each word as he spits them out. 'When I am King, we will return to the old ways, and abominations such as you will be banished from the land.'

Gasps fill the room, and the creatures who had stood behind Bernais use the distraction of the fight to melt back into the crowd.

'You don't get it, do you?' Maddox counters. 'The time of Seelie Elves setting the rules is over.'

As if the goddess hears his words and acts, Bernais slips on the blood on the floor and falls to one knee.

'I will never accept that,' Bernais chokes out as he tries to regain his feet.

Before he can rise, Maddox has his sword pointed at the elf's throat. 'Give me an excuse, any excuse, to finish this,' he says with a sneer.

Bernais locks eyes with the King of the Unseelie Court. 'Do it,' he dares him.

A ripple of fear runs through the courtiers. Most of them want to see Bernais defeated, but few of them are prepared to witness his cold-blooded murder.

'Maddox, no.' Cecily pushes past Malachai. 'He must stand trial for his actions. It is the only way we can start healing.'

For a moment I think he's going to ignore her. Then he nods. 'Spoken like a true Queen, sister.'

Malachai steps forward and takes Bernais's weapon, and King Maddox moves his sword a little away. 'Someone get a guard to take this creature to the dungeons.'

I'm so engrossed in the scene that my heart nearly leaps from my chest when I feel cold steel at my throat.

'I think not. Not if you want this sprite to continue breathing.'

CHAPTER 14

After the Heat of Battle

The sound of that voice sends terror through to my very soul. The pain of my transformation knots my joints, and I sweat as if my body is attempting to return to its natural state but cannot.

'Step away from my son and allow him to bring my wife to me.'

The voice is as commanding as ever, and it turns my insides to water. Fury at his plans being thwarted rolls off him in waves.

Cecily sends me a compassionate look, and I know what she is going to say before the words leave her lips. 'You know I cannot do that, Uncle. It is time to stop fighting and to work together to heal our world's wounds.'

Magnus's grip tightens, and I cringe as a sticky substance dribbles under my shirt collar. *My blood?*

'Isn't this poetic, sprite! I finally get to finish what I started. It will give me great pleasure to sever your life force.'

'No! Please, Uncle Magnus. I don't want my first act as

Queen to be prosecuting you for murder.' There is real distress in Cecily's voice, but there is also determination.

'Then don't. Stop this nonsense and throw your support behind Bernais.'

Cecily holds out her hand towards her uncle. 'No matter how much I don't want to see Percival hurt, I can't. It's not what Ariana would want. It's not what I want. And, more importantly, it's not what most creatures want. It is time for us to all work together to mend the rifts between us for the good of our world.'

'Never. We will not accept the dilution of our race or see our land devolve into chaos. If you will not join us, Cecily, then you leave me no choice.'

The blade pushes more firmly against my throat, and I send up a silent goodbye. This is my end, and rather than sending off my father's spirit, I will join him soon. While I'm not happy at the thought, I am grateful that I at least repaired things with Nisha before this moment came.

The sharp edge of the knife cuts into my skin, and I tense, then my body is shoved forward, and I am falling to the ground. My knees crack against the polished stone, my hands landing in a pool of blood, and I do a body check. Where is it coming from?

I turn my head and find myself staring into Magnus's lifeless eyes. Blood oozes from a slash across his throat, and I sag with relief. As I haul myself to my feet, I am helped by King Maddox, who has a satisfied grin on his face.

'You know, I have wanted to do that since I arrived in the World Below. He treated me as less than when I first arrived here—me, a prince of my people.'

'Arrest him! He murdered my father,' Bernais is calling to the guards who have finally arrived.

This is where I see Cecily, who I have known since she was a child, come fully into her new position.

'Halt.'

The guards pause mid-way to King Maddox.

'Bernais is a traitor. He is to be taken to the dungeons to await trial.'

The Guard Captain motions for two of her creatures to take Bernais into custody.

'What about Governor Baaronson's attacker?'

'Magnus threatened Percival's life. King Maddox saved him and ended a threat to us all.' Cecily's eyes rake the room, daring anyone to refute her claims.

Only Adina moves. On uncertain feet, clutching at her side, she crosses the floor and kneels beside her husband. The room holds its breath as we prepare for her grief.

'How typical of you, Magnus,' Adina snarls, surprising us all. 'You make yourself the centre of attention, follow it up with a grand gesture, then leave it for me to clean up your mess and take the heat. Well, I won't do it.'

We're all stunned by the disdain and anger in her voice. Then, before anyone can react, she grabs Magnus's knife and plunges it into her stomach.

The entire room draws in a breath in shock as Bernais grief is displayed for all to hear. 'Mother, no!'

'Is there a healer in the room?' Queen Cecily calls as the guards move to the two figures on the floor.

They are quick, but not quick enough. The lifeless body of Princess Adina rests beside her husband, her eyes locked on the son she risked everything for.

The world stops again as another Dragon Bonded dies.

The second shock wave occurs as I leave the refectory, the last of the prisoners finally under guard. My intention had been to head to the control room, as I had just received an update from Ed'rathe.

> ***We mourn the loss,***
> ***The Worlds all weep,***
> ***Her memory safe,***
> ***The dragons will keep.***

I collapse against the cold, hard wall as the words ring in my head.

Ed'rathe? What's happening?

Everyone in the square is staring at the palace. Am'nera and Am'ratha are missing.

No. It can't have been Pris. Please don't let it have been Pris.

The witch sisters join me in the hallway.

'Another death of a bonded princess?' Euphemia asks.

I nod, unable to trust my voice.

Noble One, the Dragon Queen calls you back.

What? No! I have to find Pris.

Eleanora rubs my arm. 'Snake, what is it? You've gone white as a sheet. Is it Pris?'

I shake my head. 'I don't know, nor does Ed'rathe. The Dragon Queen wants me.'

'Then you must go,' Eleanora says decisively.

'But... Pris?'

I can't do it. I can't leave when I don't know what's happened to her.

'Who ever has died, you cannot do much about it now,' Eugenia says. 'Go to the Dragon Queen, and we will do what we can to find Pris.'

Shouts from the courtyard tell me Ed'rathe has likely

landed. Euphemia gives me a gentle shove. 'Go. We have things covered here.'

As Ed'rathe flies over the city, my heart is breaking, and I can't breathe. There are still some minor skirmishes, but the fighting has mostly stopped. I search for Pris, and I think I see Am'ratha in a corner of the palace square, but we are so high, I'm not sure which dragon it is.

We travel to the World Between by conventional flight, and it takes forever. I just want to finish this and go back to the World Below to find Pris. Even though I know I have to accept the possibility of losing her one way or the other once this is over, her death is the worst of the two options.

By the time we reach the landing space, tears stream from my eyes. My sense of loss is so strong, I can't bear it. It is all I can do to pull myself together as Ed'rathe leads me into the audience chamber.

The dragons gathered in the cavern are sombre. With two Dragon Bonded dead, the court is in mourning, or so Ed'rathe tells me. He also warns me that today is not the day to test the Dragon Queen's patience.

Bearing that in mind, I bow before the monarch, and I wait for her to speak even though every fibre of my being wants to be gone from here.

It is done, Noble One. The fate of the World Between has been decided.

Really?

Queen Ariana was successful in her quest to restore magic, giving her body to the flow in the end. Cecily will be brought before me and confirmed as Queen in her place. Her commitment to cleansing the flow will return to a biannual event—midsummer and midwinter. She will be joined by King Maddox. In return, I will restore his court.

If all is well, then why am I here? I should be out looking for Pris. I don't even know if she's okay.

Ed'rathe drops his head and nudges me, reminding me that I have perhaps been a bit too bold.

In spite of your bad manners, I have an offer for you. I would like you to be my envoy to the new Queen, and, perhaps more importantly, to the new council she will form.

I'm confused both by the request and the urgency. Couldn't this have waited? However, mindful of Ed'rathe's advice, I choose my next words carefully.

While I am honoured, do you really need a creature to speak with the Queen? You can talk directly to her through her dragon.

Ed'rathe shifts beside me, reminding me not to go too far.

In the past that is what I have done, but my words are only for the ruler. If I have a creature speak for me, then everyone hears and can take dragon-kind's wishes into account when they make decisions.

I tilt my head to the side, my fears for Pris momentarily eclipsed. That is actually an important distinction, given the changes that are likely to happen in the World Below.

Ahh, and you need me to agree now because Queen Cecily will be listening closely to her advisors even as we speak.

See, I knew you were the right creature for the job.

I am honoured, but this is not the future I had planned. Once this was over, I intended to return to studying magic.

I appreciate your concerns. You would not

need to spend all your time at court. You would only be required to attend council sessions, giving you time to continue your studies.

That is more appealing.

And, as an incentive, I would allow you to bond fully with Ed'rathe.

Really? I place a hand on the dragon's flank. He has given up so much to remain with me. This would be my way to pay him back for not bonding with Pris's dad.

Perhaps I could study magic at the university in the World Below? Drow would be able to help me sort that out. It would also be an opportunity for me to spend more time with my family.

What about my mother? She would be alone in the World Above. Then again, I would have to move away to attend university there—would this be any different?

Life is difficult as an adult when you have to balance so many competing interests, the Dragon Queen says, interrupting my tumbling thoughts. **And you have been through so much. What say we start on a trial basis?**

But what about Ed'rathe? It would be unfair to keep him waiting about his position while we find out if this will work.

I think that as this is a new initiative, I could allow the full bonding to take place as a reward for your service to creature and dragon-kind.

I laugh. **And I am more likely to take the job if I am bonded to my friend.**

The Dragon Queen bares her teeth in what I hope is a smile and not a sign that she is about to eat me. **I see we understand each other. Now, Ed'rathe, perhaps it is time to cement your formal bond before Snake Fieth changes his mind.**

A shiver of pleasure comes down the bond from Ed'rathe as he bows his head. **As you command, Your Majesty.**

I follow him from the audience cavern, excited about the possibilities the future offers, pleased to have cemented my friendship with Ed'rathe, but unable to fully appreciate it because of my gnawing worry about Pris.

·· ·✦· ··

'Do you have to push so hard?' Aeron groans.

'Do you want to die?' I snap back. 'Medic,' I yell at the top of my lungs.

'What's that supposed to do?' Aeron mutters. 'You already called your dragon, I presume.'

'What makes you say that?'

He looks over my shoulder into the square. I half turn and find Am'ratha peeking around the corner.

'I thought you said you couldn't land.'

It seems when a dragon wants to land somewhere, creatures move out of their way.

'I'll bet they do,' I say, frantically looking round for someone to help me get Aeron on Am'ratha's back.

'Can you help me get him up?' I ask her.

Aeron grabs my wrist. 'Are you trying to kill me?'

'I thought you said your wound wasn't too bad.'

'I meant I am not dead yet, but I will be if you try to get me onto her.'

'What should I do, then?' I ask, anger rising. 'I can't let you stay here either.'

I have contacted Princess Petunia via Am'ralla.

She is sending a healer as soon as she can find a witch to open a portal.

'Thank you. And thank you for protecting us while we wait,' I tell Am'ratha.

Princess, I have not been protecting you. Most of the fighting has stopped. Did you not feel the change in the air?

'I heard another Dragon Bonded was lost, but I've been too busy taking care of Aeron to worry about who it was and what it meant for the war.'

A ruler has been named.

Hold on, a Dragon Bonded lost, and a ruler named? My panic comes back full force. 'Am'ratha, is my mother all right? And Snake? Is he Dragon Bonded yet?'

I am sorry, Princess. Dragons are mourning, the Dragon Queen is busy, and no one will answer me.

When we were fighting, I had been frightened for my life, but now I'm frantic. Is Mum okay? Has Snake survived the battle? Is Bernais now King?

I search around desperately, trying to find someone to ask or to look after Aeron while I find out what is going on. No, I can't leave him. He is only like this because he was trying to protect me.

Am'ratha, I need you—

The air a few meters away crackles and seems to shimmer, almost vibrating and a loud *pop* follows it.

A portal opens up across the street, and Nisha steps through, followed by a couple of dwarves.

'Princess, I can take over from here,' the sprite tells me as she makes her way to my side.

Able to be relieved of my duties, I suddenly have no desire to go. I can't leave Aeron, and I am not really sure I want to know the outcome of today's battles. If Bernais is King, perhaps I will be better off at the hospital.

Beneath my palm, Aeron's breathing is becoming shallow. Nisha gently nudges my hand aside. 'Let me help him, Princess.'

I push to my feet, and a dwarf leads me away so Nisha can deal with his wound.

'He has lost a lot of blood. Where is that stretcher?'

The other dwarf lays down the stretcher beside the Minotaur, and I can't help the thought that Aeron will break that in a heartbeat. Then again, this is the realm of magic. They levitate Aeron onto the stretcher and start moving him to the portal.

I go to follow, but Nisha places a restraining hand on my arm.

'No, Princess. If you come, he will worry more about you than himself. He needs time to heal, and you have responsibilities here.'

I want so much to argue with her, but she is right.

'But he will be alone.' I can't bear the thought of that.

Nisha's lips curve into a knowing smile. 'Princess Irene arrived just as I was leaving. I am most certain he will not be alone.'

I hesitate. They both took care of me. Shouldn't I be there for them? No, I would only be in the way. Nisha squeezes my arm, then follows the others through the portal.

Princess, I believe we should go to the palace.

If Bernais is King, then is this over—or are our forces regrouping? If we won, where am I meant to be? Irene or Aeron would know. Or Percival.

We should go to the palace, she repeats.

'Do you have any more information?'

I believe everything will become clear once we are there.

With no strong alternative coming to mind, I decide to trust Am'ratha. 'Okay.'

I pick up my sword, and for the first time I take in the blood covering my hands and sleeves—Aeron's blood. 'Please be all right.' I freeze, not seeing anything but the stains.

Princess? Pris? We should go.

I sheath my sword, then use a little of what I know of magic to remove what blood I can. It's not the best, but it no longer appears as if I've been ruthlessly slaying creatures with my bare hands.

Am'ratha rises gently, then banks around, giving me a bird's-eye view of the square. Creatures have dropped where they stood, all facing the palace. Some have wounds being tended to by their fellows, and every now and then, a portal appears to transport the more badly wounded to the hospital.

Creatures in pairs are carrying soldiers to the edge of the marketplace. At first I think it is to make transportation to the hospital easier. Then I work out that they are the bodies of the dead. There are so many of them. Tears well in my eyes as I think of all the souls lost today.

Am'ratha hovers over a balcony at the front of the palace, then lands. I wipe away the tears before slipping down her foreleg.

I will wait on the roof, she tells me.

I'm so tired and hollow inside and worried about what I might inside. How nice it would be to ask her to come in with me so I don't have to face what is waiting for me alone. Instead, I say, 'Thank you for staying close and being there when I needed you.'

She inclines her head in acknowledgement, and I step

through the doors into what appears to be a large reception room. To my right, there is a throne, and in front of it is something on the floor covered by what looks to be a large curtain. I shudder at the crimson blood soaking through the material—there are bodies under there.

A centaur who would rival Fairburn in stature and magnetism is talking to two human guards by the open door across from me. They have hold of a prisoner. It takes a moment for me to register that the creature they are holding is Bernais.

'Take me into custody if you must, but my parents deserve justice,' he is saying to the guards.

I glance back at the bodies. Are those his parents under there? I almost sag with relief. Adina was Dragon Bonded. My mother must still be alive.

I'm brought back to the present by the sound of voices in the room to my left. The guard by the door is so preoccupied with the drama going on, I am able to slip by them and stand in the shadows by the door as I assess the lie of the land. This room is smaller and cosier, studded with groups of chairs and couches. Standing by the fireplace, my mother is talking to a majestic female centaur.

'All the mercenaries you rounded up are to be taken back to the World Above, and they are to have their memories of this place wiped. You will need to take a healing witch with you. See if you can find Eugenia. It would be best if it were she, as they will be her responsibility to check on later.'

'Yes, Your Majesty.'

Although I'm used to seeing my mother take control of things, hearing her called Your Majesty is a whole new level of weird.

'And what about the governors' guards?' the centaur asks.

'As we have discussed, regional governors will no longer be able to keep standing armies. The current guards are to be offered places in a to-be-formed Council Guard. The alternative is banishment.'

The Royal Guard salutes and leaves. Seconds later the door she left through opens to admit Elias, who is followed in by Snake. He's alive and unhurt. I'm sure I'm grinning stupidly as I receive the second lot of good news this evening. However, this is not how I wanted Snake to be introduced to my parents. I take a step forward as the guard says, 'Your Majesty, may I present Snake Fieth, ambassador for the Dragon Queen.'

What? Snake is still ambassador? When did that happen? Does that mean he's staying?

From the back of the room, I watch him bow to my mother.

'Am'rena told me of your appointment, and that you have been brought up to speed on where we are. We welcome you as a representative from the World Between. I am sure you will be a great asset to the new council and to me in the meantime.'

Snake grins, and my heart melts. 'I'm not sure how this is going to work, but I am told my first duty is to escort you to the Dragon Court for you to affirm your commitment to maintaining the flow of magic.'

'Of course. Once we have things stabilised here, it will be my priority.'

The adrenalin leaves my body as the realisation that this is finally over hits me. My father, King Maddox, Glinth, and Drow join Mum and Snake, and I suddenly feel on the outside looking in. They have all moved on and accepted the changes this war has brought about. My head is spinning and I need time to think..., to regroup.

I quietly escape the room and head back to the

balcony. As I watch the chaos below slowly return to order, I can't believe this whole adventure is really over. Someone moves in beside me, and I stiffen, wiping away the tears gathering in my eyes.

Percival clears his throat, a sound I know well, and I relax.

'I nearly died today,' he says.

'Me too. Wait, you were supposed to be at the command post.'

'I was, but I flew alone on a dragon to get here.'

The laugh escapes, and I can't stop giggling. It's good to be alive. I drop an arm around Percival's shoulders and give him a hug. 'I'm pleased you survived that trauma. Wait, how did you get that cut on your throat?'

'It is nothing. A story for another day.'

I study my friend, and the light I had started to let in blinks out. 'Percival, what is it?'

'Drow and I sent a small group of creatures to rescue the prisoners in the hospital, and we haven't heard back from them. I am afraid they are dead.'

'Oh, Percival.' I hug him again, picturing the bodies piling up around the market square in my mind.

'I can't believe I sent them to die.'

The reality that we both sent creatures to their death sobers me. My part in this will never leave me. 'So much about this is messed up, Percival. I believe we did what we had to.'

He is silent.

'And that doesn't make any of this any easier,' I say.

We stand together, watching the sun set over the battleground below us, so lost in our thoughts, neither of us hears someone approach from behind.

'Excuse me, Percival.'

We both jump at the noise, then turn as one.

'Alyce, have you any news?' Percival asks, and the hope in his voice brings tears to my eyes.

'The prisoners and their rescuers remained holed up in the hospital building throughout the fighting. They are all being taken to the hospital in Melliores. Would you like me to take you there?'

Percival looks towards the room where the new leaders of the World Below are making plans, then back at Alyce.

'Percival, I am sure the witches and Nisha have things under control in Melliores. Perhaps you could go and tell Mother and Drow the good news that the last of our people have been accounted for.'

'And what about you?' he asks.

I finally allow myself to smile. 'I have some other creatures I need to hug.'

CHAPTER 15

Counting the Dead

Why everyone gets excited about riding dragons is beyond me. What is wrong with a horse and carriage? Or, better still, why doesn't someone invent a type of car like they have in the World Above? Now that magic is fixed, it should be possible. I think I should suggest it to someone—maybe Mandor.

'Percival, can you quit wriggling? You'll have us both off in a minute,' Snake hisses in my ear.

As if I would let him fall.

'You did once,' Snake reminds Ed'rathe.

How was I to know he would turn into a cat? The dragon's tone is sulky.

'I have forgiven you, Ed'rathe, and I trust you to keep me safe. It is just that this is not a sprite's natural habitat.'

See, Snake?

It is like riding with children. My only consolation is that none of the other riders with us appear any happier about this trip to the World Between.

In front of us, Cecily has Mandor on her dragon. He is upset that the Dragon Queen has cast a spell preventing unauthorised portals being opened into the World Between. When he muttered something to Snake about bringing it up today, Cecily mentioned something about the World Below regulating portals too. He went quiet after that.

El'ruven is tucked in behind us. After Queen Ariana's death, he took over as leader of the bonded ones and is taking his new duty of care seriously. Never one who enjoyed additional passengers, he even deigned to take Drow with Maddox without too much grumbling. Drow had initially refused to come, saying he was not officially a councillor. Cecily insisted he did to ensure any dragon requirements are enshrined in our new constitution.

I heave a sigh of relief as we touch down in front of the Dragon Queen's audience chamber. After a little preening, our procession enters with Queen Cecily and King Maddox at the head. As a mark of the occasion, the Dragon Queen is standing on all fours as she awaits us. I rather wish she had stayed lying down, as she is even more formidable when upright.

The Dragon Queen adjusts her glamour as we approach. Even so, she radiates an almost crippling amount of power.

Welcome Queen Cecily, King Maddox. And welcome to your guests.

'Thank you for allowing them to accompany us, Your Highness,' Queen Cecily says. 'I believe Ambassador Fieth informed you of the proposed changes in the World Below, and from now on the creature responsible for maintaining magic will need to be agreed to by the ruling council.'

The gaze the Queen sends our way is intense. **Do you mean to say that in the future that it will not be a King or Queen?**

'Your Majesty, we propose that any creature with

magical abilities can be considered for the role in the future,' Cecily suggests.

Mmm. You would still require my endorsement—

'Of course, Your Majesty. In fact, our intention is for both courts to work more closely with you to ensure a growth in magic in all the realms.'

Then I guess this is the way it will be. And where is Princess Priscilla today?

'She begs your forgiveness, but she is spending some time with friends and family who were injured in the recent war.'

I guess that is acceptable. Come forward, Queen Cecily and King Maddox.

The two rulers take a step forward.

Do you both swear to maintain the flow of magic between the worlds?

'I do,' Cecily says.

King Maddox hesitates.

Is there a problem?

'No, Your Majesty. I do so swear. But I am wondering why you would take my word for it when I so recently let you and Queen Ariana down.'

Yes, well, you can thank El'ruven for that. He explained the pressure you were under, and he believes you have learnt your lesson.

'I have, Your Majesty. And thank you for trusting me.'

I do not trust you. I trust El'ruven. He has vouched for you and your commitment to the Unseelie Court. It is for this reason, and as a deathbed boon to Queen Ariana, that I will bring the court back into time. Do not let either of them down.

I smother a grin. The Dragon Queen is a canny creature. Perhaps the one creature alive who Maddox cares about more than himself is his bonded dragon. He would not lightly do anything that would hurt El'ruven—not even if it were only to hurt his reputation and standing in the Court of the World Between.

'I will not, Your Majesty.'

The official swearing over, the Dragon Queen lowers herself onto her rock and eyes the two monarchs. **What will happen in the World Below now?**

It is Queen Cecily who answers. 'Elias is finalising details for the state day of mourning for the casualties of war tomorrow and the funeral of Queen Ariana two days later. Two days after that, my coronation and the signing of our new constitution. Then the real work will begin.'

You have a busy time ahead. And what about you, King Maddox? Will there be changes in your court?

'I believe it might be time to shake things up a little, but nothing so drastic as in the World Below. I currently have no heir, and I have been thinking of holding an election.'

I catch Drow's eye. He shakes his head. He had no idea King Maddox was planning this either.

Then we had best set about retrieving your court.

'We have a few days yet, Your Majesty. I would like to see Cecily safely on the throne before I leave for the World Above.

Of course. Thank you all for your time today, and may all our realms prosper.

And with those words, we are dismissed.

Percival, please stay.

The others continue to file out, and I appreciate the Dragon Queen's words are for me alone.

'Your Majesty?' I ask, stepping forward from the shadows.

I think it is time.

'Time for—'

The rest of my words are stolen from me as every cell in my body explodes in pain. Heat whips up my spine, burning through my veins and spreading out to every limb. The torment goes on until I think I can bear it no longer, then it suddenly stops, and I fall to the ground. Through my exhaustion I experience a bliss that has been a memory for too long. I am me again.

Thank you.

You are welcome, Dragon Friend.

I lean back against Am'ratha and watch Aeron and Irene choose their weapons.

'Are you sure you should be doing this?' I say as they test bows and choose their arrows.

'How else are we to find out who is the best archer?' Aeron asks.

'One arrow each at ten, then twenty, then thirty paces,' Irene says, ignoring me altogether.

I try again. 'Aeron, you still have stitches in your side, and Nisha will have your guts if you burst them.'

Following Irene's lead, the Minotaur tests the string of his crossbow and tries to hide his wince of pain.

They are going to do this regardless of what you say, Am'ratha sends, her tone amused.

I sigh. 'I just wish they would both rest a while and allow themselves to recover.'

It is not in their natures. They both need to be doing something.

'I know how they feel.'

Shading my eyes, I watch Irene line up and pull back her bow. The shot she releases flies smoothly through the air and lands dead centre in the bull's-eye.

'Nice.'

'Your foot was not behind the line,' Aeron complains.

'Rubbish, you're just worried you can't do better,' my aunt counters.

'And we are not going to find out today.' Nisha's voice comes from behind Am'ratha.

I scramble to my feet in time to see the sprite striding towards the Minotaur. Instead of his usual bravado, Aeron kicks a hoof through the dirt, and he reminds me of a child caught doing something they know they shouldn't.

'I did not use my medical and magical skills to heal you only to have you undo my good work,' Nisha lectures, and Aeron's head drops.

'I'm sorry, Nisha. I got carried away in the moment. It won't happen again.'

'And as for you—' Nisha turns to Irene. 'If you are encouraging this foolishness, then you are ready to be discharged. Princess Priscilla, perhaps you would be good enough to escort the princess back to the palace with you?'

I place a hand on Am'ratha's side. **Are you okay with that?**

I do not want to court Nisha's displeasure, do you?

I chuckle under my breath. **No.** 'We are happy to escort Irene to the palace.'

'Excellent. Thank you, Princess. Aeron, if you will accompany me, I will check your wound. If it is healing well, then there is plenty to busy yourself with in the hospital where I can keep an eye on you.'

As Nisha leads the Minotaur away, he glances back over his shoulder and mouths, 'See you soon for the rematch.'

Irene laughs. 'Name the time,' she tells him.

'You shouldn't encourage him,' I say to Irene as she joins us.

'As if that would stop him getting into trouble,' she says gruffly, but there is real affection in her voice.

'True. Do you have anything you need to get before we leave?'

Irene shakes her head. 'Mum took my armour away when she visited, and I am wearing the only clothes I have here. I'm sure I can sort myself out when we get to the palace.'

'Okay,' I say. 'You know your mother is in her old suite of rooms, and she is ready for you to join her.'

Irene's face twists into a grimace.

'What's wrong?' I ask.

'Is it ungrateful to say I feel like I've gone out and forged my own path, and now I'm returning home to Mum, and it just doesn't feel right?'

I bark out a laugh. 'I couldn't have put it better myself. I mean, it's nice to be back with family and to be safe, but I can't return to the way things were.'

Irene is nodding as I speak. 'And you can't because you are not the same.'

'Exactly. And, even worse, my parents haven't even noticed the change.'

'So, my wise and thoughtful niece, what do we do about this?' Irene's tone is playful, but her question strikes a chord.

I lean my cheek against Am'ratha's scales and draw

strength and resolve from the contact. 'I think we should make a pact. We will not fall back into our old lives. Instead, we will seek out new challenges.'

Irene stares into the distance, and I'm worrying I read this situation all wrong when a smile forms on her face. 'You are wise beyond your years, Pris. And I have an idea where I can make a difference. We need to get back so I can talk to King Maddox.'

'I'm pleased for you. Now all I need to do is find my niche,' I say as I climb up to position myself behind Am'ratha's neck.

As Irene joins me, Am'ratha says, **You are in a new world. You need time to find your role. It will come.**

The confidence I sense through our bond gives me hope that like Snake and Irene, I, too, will find my place in the magical worlds.

· · ◡ · ·

The state day of mourning is the first time I've had to myself since the end of the war. During the day, I've had one meeting after another, and at night, I'm often called to the World Between to update the Queen and receive my instructions. I've barely had a moment to breathe, let alone spend any time with Pris, and the time we're apart is making me more and more desperate to see her.

Some nights I fall exhausted into bed in the room I've been assigned at the palace. Others I sleep in a room in the royal quarters in the World Between, only to be woken before dawn so I can be flown back to the palace. Thank goodness the palace brownies have taken me under their wing and kept me in clean clothes, otherwise I would have spent the whole time in the same outfit.

Now I finally have a day off, and the Fieth has called a Cruinniú Teaghlaigh—some sort of family meeting I have to go to. I tried to wrangle an invite for Pris because we'd organised a picnic together. I'm still waiting to hear back from my grandparents, so I take that as a no. Pris is having breakfast with her parents, and I have to resort to cancelling with a note.

At a loose end, I decide to walk, but I still arrive at the family home on the outskirts of the Capitol early enough to spend time with my mother—another creature I have spent little time with lately. Mum, Heart, and Mender are staying in the guest suite, and they are all in the small sitting room when I am shown in. Taking in their formal dress, I ask, 'Are you all going to the gathering?'

'Ginth is family, so we are apparently family by extension,' Mender says. 'So it would be rude not to.'

'And how does dad feel about your going?' The words are out before I have a chance to appreciate how abrupt the question is.

Heart claps me on the back. 'Not subtle at all, Snake.'

'Sorry, Mum, it's just that….'

'I know, Snake. Now that you've found I wasn't exactly truthful about the past, you're wondering about your dad and me and perhaps what my plans are?'

I lean back in the chair, making as if I don't mind if she doesn't answer, but in reality, I'm still struggling with the secrets Mum kept about her mixed heritage and what really happened with my father. Then again, if I've learnt anything over the past few months, it's that life doesn't go to plan and we all have our secrets. And maybe also that we don't have the right to know everything about our parents.

'Well, I'm staying in the World Below for a while. I want to spend some time with Dad and his family. He's going back to the village to take over the music shop from Mender, and I will be returning with them.'

'Oh.' I don't know what to say. It's irrational, but I feel abandoned even though I would have been leaving home myself this year. Then again, she will be closer than she would have been if she returned to the World Above. 'What will you do all day?'

She taps the side of her nose. 'I have something lined up. 'Mum laughs and leans over and ruffles my hair. 'You look like I just said I was abandoning you forever to do something nefarious. But it's just for a while, and I promise you I won't be doing anything illegal—there will be no more Bad Fairies turning up on my doorstep. Besides, you have a dragon. You can come and check up on me any time.'

'And I hope you do,' Mender interrupts.

'This is a big thing for me, Snake. I had a lot of time to think when I was a prisoner. It's time I stopped blaming everyone else for the horrid things in my life and start taking control. I can do that best if I spend some time finding out who I really am.'

'I get that, sort of,' I say.

'And Princess Petunia has promised that when I'm ready, she will arrange an introduction to my mother's family. When I meet them, do you want to come with me?

I'd almost forgotten I had another set of grandparents out there somewhere. 'That might be nice,' I tell her, not sure if it will be. Pris didn't have much fun meeting all of her family.

'And as for your father and me, we're friends. If there is more than that, well... we'll see with time.'

The door opens, and a young gnome pops a head in.

'Sorry about the tea, Ginth, but the Fieth's called everyone to the main room,' she says.

I bite back a sigh. I can't even get a decent cup of tea before going to yet another meeting.

My young relation leads us through corridors cut into a living tree. As I did last time I was here, I run my hand over the wood and believe I can almost feel my ancestors embrace me.

In the main room, I find a space beside my uncle Earth and his wife, Glisth. They are the only members of my Fieth family who have always been there for me. Earth hugs me, and Glisth passes me a steaming cup of coffee and a hefty slice of banana cake. She shows her love through food, and for once, I am grateful for it.

I have time to eat most of the cake before the Fieth calls the room to order. There must be about fifty or more gnomes over the age of thirteen here. I had no idea the immediate family was so large.

When we are silent, the Fieth rises to his feet. 'Before we head out into the garden to the children and the feast we have prepared for this day, I have an announcement. This war we fought has shown me I am too old and too tired to run this family. Chroma and I are retiring to the Wyld Woods to live the rest of our days in peace.'

The Fieth holds up his hand to forestall any comments. 'Save your words for later. I will hear you all out. We have a house with many bedrooms picked out. Ginth is coming with us to help us set up and to spend some time with her extended family. After a month or so, I am sure we would love to have visitors, but not before then.'

The room is so silent, you could hear a pin drop.

Beside my grandfather, my father hauls himself to his feet. 'I have a big shadow to fill, but I am happy the first task he set me is a happy one. Let the feasting begin.'

I wait for everyone else to leave before asking Earth, 'Are you and Dad going to stand for the new council? I know Queen Cecily asked Dad to represent the gnomes on the interim one.'

Earth shakes his head. 'Glisth and I are happy in Mawnan. We will return home after the coronation and carry on supporting the creatures in the World Above as best we can.'

'What about Dad?'

Earth glances up, then takes Glisth's hand. 'You'd best ask him, lad. Come, my darling. Let us go and eat before there is nothing left but pickings.'

I stand up to let them past before turning to my father.

'Goodness, son, you have grown since we last saw each other. Trouble seems to agree with you.'

In spite of the warmth radiating from him and the love I find in his eyes, I still feel awkward around my father. 'It has been a difficult time,' I say.

'And it will not be any easier in the months to come.'

'So, are you going to take the position on the interim council?' I ask. It will be odd working with my father, but it might also give us an opportunity to get to know each other better.

'No, son, I am not. The time of the Fieths supporting the monarchy is over. It is time we look to the needs of our own race.'

I have to admit, I'm a little disappointed. 'But can't you do that on the council?'

'Drow is making sure gnomes will have their say, and we will definitely be well represented—I have been speaking with Mender about that. Maybe it is time for the gnomes in the Wyld Woods to stand up.'

'But what will you do?'

'I will be learning the family business and maybe

looking at some changes. Some of our less… aboveboard activities no longer seem appropriate in light of Queen Cecily's intentions.'

'You mean her declaration that any gnome who wishes can be unbound?'

'Exactly. I am putting the Fieth resources at the disposal of the council to identify gnomes and organise the transition.'

'Won't that mean we will simply be elves?' I ask.

'I thought so, too, but apparently not. Even though our magic will be unbound, genetically we will still be different, and we have developed our own distinct culture, so we will still be a separate race,' my father explains.

'Good. I really don't see myself as an elf,' I say, and I mean it. When I first found out I had elf blood in my veins, I didn't know how to take it. I believed I didn't fit in anywhere. However, when Queen Cecily made her announcement, it clarified my thinking. I am a gnome and proud of it.

My father rests a hand on my shoulder. 'You have a room here, and I would like you to move back home and spend time with your family when you're not working at the palace.'

The offer is heartfelt, and I'm surprisingly pleased by it. Part of me wants to accept, but I have already made other plans.

'Drow has introduced me to Professor Xander—he specialises in the study of magic at the university—and he has accepted me as a part-time student. Drow also organised a shared suite for me in the dorms there so I will have more time to study'

Sadness passes across my father's eyes, but he pastes a smile on his face.

'I am pleased for you and proud of you, son. You will still have your room here should you need it.'

'Thank you. I am sure there will be weekends where I will want to escape duties and study and just be a gnome.'

'And you will be more than welcome.' He drapes his arm around me and says, 'Come, they can't actually start the feast until I'm there.'

⌣

'Not only did you keep a whole other world from me, but when I finally turned up here after leading an army to rescue you, you were so busy ruling the realm, you didn't even think to ask if I was alive or dead.'

I've been avoiding this conversation with my parents ever since we reunited because I wasn't sure how to approach it, and my parents have clearly been waiting for me to raise the subject.

So, I've decided on a jokey approach, but I don't quite hit the right note. Instead, I sound kinda hurt and angry. I think Mum senses this isn't easy, because there's no lecture for being childish. Instead, she hands me the strawberry jam I can't quite reach, then takes a sip of her coffee before responding.

'We *had* planned a holiday to Scotland after your graduation, and we were going to stay with Mum and Dad at Urquhart Castle. The idea was to ease you in gently by introducing you to my family first.'

'We thought Maddox and the Unseelie Court might be a bit much for your introduction to the magical world,' my father explains dryly.

I'm not ready to let them off the hook yet. 'Did you

really tell Uncle Maddox I would join the court when I was older?'

He stops buttering his toast and glances up, surprise clear in his widening eyes. 'No, of course not. I did say that when your mother and I had to retire from the World Above at the end of a human's natural life, we would likely go to the Unseelie Court because I was not welcome in the World Below.'

'Oh.'

'And before you ask again,' my mother says, 'Am'rena was in constant contact with Am'ratha. I had asked her to help protect you.'

They have an answer for everything, but I'm still angry with them.

Mum places a hand over mine where it rests on the table. 'We tried to protect you from the worst aspects of the World Below long after you were capable of facing them, and for that, I am sorry. I'm also sorry that we were not the ones to introduce you to our extended family. And even more sorry that this meant so many of them kept things from you when telling you would have been a better choice.'

Dad leans around Mum. 'Yes, so much would have been easier for you if they had taken it as our wishes in normal circumstances rather than a royal edict to be obeyed even in extreme situations.'

Their eyes show genuine sorrow, and I can't hold them responsible for what others have done, no matter how much I want to.

'There's still something else bugging you, isn't there?' Mum asks, releasing my hand and turning so her attention is fully on me. 'You have seen how busy things are around here. If we don't deal with it now, I'm not sure when we'll have time together again as a family.

She is right. Best to get everything into the open. 'I feel like a spare wheel. You guys have all been so busy, and I haven't been doing anything.

Mum's brows draw together. 'You've had a tough few months while we lazed in luxury. Your father and I thought you would enjoy the break and a chance to catch up with Susan.'

'But I've hardly even seen her. She is busy with Irene and Uncle Maddox setting up the embassy for the Unseelie Court.'

'And to visit Aeron at the hospital,' my dad adds.

'He's healing well, and is already up and about, helping the orderlies out.'

'And spending time with Verona Coronas. I hear she isn't in a good way,' he finishes.

'She can't bear to be here now without Gregor, so has been spending time with Eleanora and her daughter, making plans for creature support in London. Everyone is busy.' I know I sound like a spoilt child, but I am not built for doing nothing.

'So what you telling me is that you're bored,' my mother says, a touch of impatience in her voice.

'Yes, I am, but it's not just that,' I add quickly when I see her frown deepen. 'I've spent weeks championing change in the World Below, only to find that now I have achieved it, I'm no longer needed.'

'Perhaps it's time,' Dad says.

'Time for what?'

'Time for you to return home and begin university as planned,' he says.

I stare at my parents in disbelief. 'You're kidding, right? I can't simply go back and pretend none of this ever happened.'

'We thought you would want a bit of normalcy after this?' Mum says.

Dad follows with 'This isn't anything to do with young Snake, is it?'

My glare hardens. My parents are treating me like the Pris they left behind. She would have wanted home comforts and would have been swayed by her friend, but I am no longer that person. How I wish Percival and Snake were here. They see me as I am, and that always gives me confidence.

My mother's voice breaks into my tumultuous thoughts. 'How do you see things moving forward?'

I shake my head. 'What?'

'I want to know what you would want to do if you could choose anything.' she says.

I want to spend time with Snake, really getting to know him and finding out if what I feel is real. I don't say this, though. Not only would my practical parents wonder what had got into me, but my whole life can't be about what Snake wants. So I take a breath and wait for the answer to come to me.

'I am heir to the throne, which I believe you are turning into a constitutional monarchy.'

'For starters,' Mum responds.

'There is a lot I need to learn about this world, given I didn't grow up here.'

She nods. 'That is also true.'

'So, I think I should stay.'

'Doing what?' my father intervenes. 'You know long term we won't countenance you sitting around all day.'

As if I had even considered that an option.

'What are you going to be doing?' I ask him, sure he would never be a King Consort who spends his time accompanying Mum and making sure she was okay.

'I'm going to work with your uncle and a professor at

the university, Xander, contacting the other magical realms and reopening lines of communication that were broken when the elves took over the World Below.'

'You're planning something bigger, though,' I say, suddenly interested.

He grins. 'Professor Xander has a special interest in magic, and we want to see if we can improve magic in our realm and rekindle magic in the World Above. We want to learn from other communities where magic still flourishes both in the creature and human realms.'

Dad's eyes sparkle with excitement, and I'm energised by his enthusiasm. 'Oh, that sounds huge.'

'It is.'

I know I only have to ask, and Dad would include me in his project in a heartbeat. It's amazing, but it's really not my thing.

Mum leans forward. 'You were going to study law. Can we find you something around that?'

'Isn't Drow Fieth leading the group drafting the constitution and reviewing the laws to see which ones will need to be changed?' Dad asks.

Mum chews her bottom lip. 'He is, but Pris is nowhere ready to work on redrafting laws.'

Dad shifts in his seat, suddenly excited about something. 'Drow has a team working for him on the legal side. He doesn't need anyone else for that. But I overheard him and the Chancellor of the University discussing his teaching a new class on constitutional law. He might want someone to help him co-ordinate his two roles until the university term starts—a PA, so to speak.'

Now I'm interested. Drow is a legal mastermind. Even being around him doing menial work for a while would teach me so much.

'I could go and talk to him,' I say.

My father beams. 'I know you're all grown up and saved our bacon, but I didn't like the idea of you being so far away in the World Above.'

I grin. My dad comes across all tough, but he's a marshmallow at heart.

'What about you and your young man?' Mum asks, and my bubble of joy bursts.

'I'm not sure he's my young man anymore. We haven't really spoken since the day of the battle. Every time we try to catch up, he gets called away.'

'These things have a way of sorting themselves out for the better,' Mum says, and that cryptic comment tears at my heart.

We have not been apart for long, but we have not spent enough time together for Mum and Dad to understand how the past few months have changed me. I am no longer their little girl, and what I feel for Snake is no teen crush.

So, I will work with Drow for the moment, if he will have me, until I find what I want to do. And I will not leave my future with Snake to chance. And, in time, Mum and Dad will come to know the adult me.

CHAPTER 16

Where to From Here?

Being Drow's assistant is a mixed blessing. I'm learning so much, but he is ultra-organised and wants things done just so. Like right now, he has me reorganising the papers in his files in the correct order in front of the whole interim council.

I understand that he wants to lay his hand on any document at a moment's notice, but this proceeding is a formality. On the top of every individual's file is their signed confession and their agreement to their punishment, so they're hardly likely to object to anything now.

When I'd mentioned this to Drow a couple of minutes ago, I'd earned a withering glare that then had me worried that he regretted bringing me on board.

'If we always do things the right way every time, we do not have to guess whether or not they will be correct this time,' he had told me.

I hand him back the files just as the conspirators enter the room. They arrange themselves around the lower end of the oval table, facing the members of the interim council. There are a few specialists and assistants like myself and Drow sitting around the walls. When the room falls silent, my mother begins.

'You have all signed confessions attesting to your treasonous actions. And, in consultation with your representatives, we have agreed that there will be no public trials.'

When I'd heard this, I was beyond surprised, especially as Bernais Baaronson was more than happy to live his life in the spotlight. However, Grossman Greene, the elven councillors, and the other governors had persuaded their leader to agree to a private hearing and sentencing.

'In a perfect world,' my mother continues, pulling me back into the room, 'I could trust that, now the line of succession is in place, you will work with us for the good of the worlds.'

Bernais leans forward in his seat, his eyes challenging my mother, but his tone is even when he speaks. 'You will pull our land apart with these changes. The very heart of elven society is here in this room. Elves are the strongest magic users and have been protecting our people for years.'

'I believe you are wrong in your thinking, Bernais. Your view of the world does not acknowledge the contribution all creatures make to our community,' my mother responds.

Tensing, I await an outburst from the creature who has dictated the course of my life with his bigotry and hatred of other creatures.

Instead of railing against my mother, he slumps back in his seat. 'You won the war, and, as history shows, the victor is always right and the looser is always evil.'

Mum runs a hand through her hair, signalling to those who know her well that she is uncomfortable. 'I wish life were that black and white, cousin, but it is lived in the grey. There are many, some of whom are around this table, who would have liked nothing better than for all of you to be executed publicly for the damage you have brought to our realm.'

Some of the accused gasp, and a few mutter objections. However, Mum holds up her hand before any of the traitors can protest. 'Others of us choose to believe that you were trying to fix some very real problems in the World Below, just perhaps not in the way your fellow creatures appreciated. It is for this reason we have agreed on the following sentence for your treasonous actions.'

This is Drow's cue. He stands up and reads from the signed declaration. 'For your actions against creature-kind, each of you will lose your title and rank. You will be magically bound to your lands for a period of fifty years. Your families will go unpunished, except that because you have lost your titles, you cannot pass them on to your heirs.'

'Fifty years is a long time,' one of the advocates says.

'Not long enough,' Snake mutters under his breath.

'Perhaps,' Drow says, 'but the council deems that by then, the coming changes in the World Below will have been around for long enough that any trouble you stir up will fall on deaf ears.' He takes his seat, and Mum continues.

'The council removed your titles from the rolls. If you attempt to break the spell keeping you on your lands, then you will be banished from this world and your lands sold. The gold will be deposited so you can use it to fund your life elsewhere.'

'This all seems so civilised,' Grossman says, before quickly adding, 'Not that I'm complaining. But it would have been easier to execute us?'

I know the answer to this because I'd asked Drow the same question. This was before I understood that he considered himself my mentor and, as such, I would never get another answer out of him again.

'You already know why,' he'd said.

'Is this some kind of a test?'

'Perhaps.'

It had taken a while, but I finally came up with something from my history classes at school. 'Because they would be martyrs. And, as martyrs, they could be a rallying point for their followers.'

'Very good,' Drow had said, and I'd beamed with pride.

However, this was not the answer my mother gave to Grossman. Her response was more positive.

'We all want what is best for the World Below, and the new government does not wish to punish those who offer alternative points of view. For our new council to work, we must welcome questions and opposition. Therefore, your sentence is not for treason but for promoting hate and violence against other creatures, hence the lighter sentence. This sends a message that, while we appreciate differing opinions, we strongly oppose violence.

Grossman Green nods at my mother, then turns to Snake. 'Thank you,' he mouths, and I wonder what that is about.

As Bernais and his followers are led from the room, I lean forward and whisper to Snake, 'If you're free, perhaps we could get some lunch somewhere private.'

He grins at me. 'As it happens—'

'Drow would like to go over the details of the interim governing document—he prefers we don't call it a constitution—before we all formally sign it tomorrow,' my mother interrupts.

I shoot a withering look at my mentor, who does not

appear the least apologetic. 'You do not have to stay for this if you have something better to do,' he says.

'But *I* do,' Snake mutters.

I sigh and sit back in my chair as servers bring in food and beverages so we can work through lunch, Snake leans over and rubs my leg in sympathy. Sometimes helping to right the world can be so frustrating.

Running a finger around under the high collar of my suit jacket, I groan inwardly—I can't believe I'm dressed like a stuffed turkey again. Drow assures me I look the part of an ambassador in the long brocade jacket over a white linen shirt and slim fitting trousers, but the whole thing is itchy and uncomfortable. I guess the coronation of a queen will not happen every day, but today I'm even more aware that by remaining here, I'm giving up jeans and T-shirts for the foreseeable future.

Although I could have taken a position on the dais as a member of the interim council and representative of the Dragon Queen, I chose to stand with my father—the Fieth and titular head of the gnomes. We have a front-row view, but at least no one is staring at us.

Along the back of the dais, the Royal Guard has arranged itself. It is odd not to see Fairburn there. Rumour has it, the death of his Queen devastated him, and after her funeral, he retired to Aeron's property to mourn.

Speaking of Aeron, he stands among the guards. It seems he has decided to stay in the Capitol and continue to guard Pris. When I catch his eye, he sends me a hip-level finger wave. Georgio glares it him. Aeron grins back, not scared of the newly appointed Guard Captain in the least. A trumpet sounds, and Aeron immediately stands at attention—he'd never let Pris down by fooling about.

The Royal family walk in procession from the back of the room, led by the Queen and King Consort. Princess Petunia follows them with an elf I assume is her husband, Duke Anatola. Theirs was an arranged marriage, but the story goes that after he arrived from the mountains of Russia, they were soon besotted with each other.

Escorting Princess Irene is her brother, Prince Wilfred. The two look so alike, they could almost be twins. Next in line is King Maddox, proudly walking beside Pris, his head held high as he escorts her to the dais. She is so beautiful, she takes my breath away. Although she'll no doubt hate being dressed for the occasion as much as I do, she looks every bit the princess in her deep purple Edwardian-style dress and her hair piled on top of her head.

As she passes by, I catch a glimpse of her footwear and grin. Underneath her dress, she is wearing the World Below version of a trainer. As I applaud her personal style, the ache inside me grows. I worry she is now too far out of my reach. Maybe it's a blessing we have spent little time alone together because she couldn't tell me it's over, which grants me extra time to emotionally prepare for the hurt that's bound to come. My father drops an arm over my shoulders, and I'm grateful for his silent support.

I am so focused on Pris, I almost miss Elias's entrance. He had been Chancellor for so long, it is easy to forget he is a prince. He is accompanied by a stunning elven woman and two elven girls around my age. The girls are wearing simple outfits, and their facial expressions show their displeasure at being on display.

Once the royal party is in place, the interim council files in from a side door. Percival sends me a meaningful stare, and I grin back. This is a World Below celebration, and the Dragon Queen agreed with me that as a representative of the World Between, I should take a back seat.

When everyone is on the dais, Queen Cecily steps forward and stands in front of the throne. Elias and Percival take the trappings of office from servants, then join her. Elias places the crown on her head, and Percival hands her the staff of justice.

Then Elias says something that I am sure is meaningful, and so does Queen Cecily, but my eyes are all for Pris, and I don't hear a word of it. In fact I don't hear anything until Pris steps forward.

'I formally introduce my daughter, Princess Priscilla, heir to the throne.'

Pris takes her place to the right of the throne. Then Princess Petunia steps forward.

'I formally and irrevocably renounce my place in the succession of the throne of the World Below and my allegiance to the Seelie Court. Although a part of my heart will always remain here, I do this to support my husband, the Keeper of the Pathway for the Unseelie Court.'

'Know that you and your husband will always be welcome in the Seelie Court, Aunt.'

Princess—no, just plain Petunia now—returns to her place by her husband.

Princess Irene now steps forward. 'I formally and irrevocably renounce my place in the throne's succession of the World Below, and my allegiance to the Seelie Court. I grew up in the Unseelie Court and hope to best serve both our worlds in my role as an ambassador for them here in the World Below.'

The ex-princess joins her mother.

'I now formally introduce my brother, Prince Wilfred

and my cousin, Prince Elias, second and third in line to the throne, respectively.'

The two princes join Pris.

'And finally, I formally introduce you to my cousins, Princesses Ember and Eloise. They are the last of the line of royal blood and will be fourth and fifth in the line of succession.'

'Who are they?' I whisper to my father.

'Elias's twin daughters. They have always preferred a life away from court, so I cannot imagine they are enjoying this.'

The newly crowned Queen takes her seat on the throne, and there ends the formal announcements. Although the council had wanted Queen Cecily to renounce the Baaronson family line verbally and declare they have been removed forever from the line of succession, she had decided that declaring who was included in the line was enough for this gathering. The formal disinheritance was a matter of written record and would have to do.

A priest of the goddess enters and formally blesses the royal family, then wishes Queen Cecily a long and prosperous rule. Once he has cleared the stage, Queen Cecily stands up. The room is silent. This is the first time most of those here have heard her speak, and there is much riding on her words, as she wants to begin bringing the creatures of the World Below together.

'This is odd for all of us,' she starts, and there is a ripple of displeasure round the room.

'This is not how a Queen speaks to her subjects,' I hear the woman behind me whisper.

In my head, I tell her that this opening is the point. Queen Cecily aims to be a ruler like no other.

'I believed I had hundreds of years before I would be

called to the throne, and many of you thought I would never be here at all.'

The room falls silent again.

'I come to this position after a civil war—however brief —that has torn not only our realm but families apart— mine included. My job will be to rebuild our world so it is better able to weather the storms of progress in the future. To do that we must ensure every adult creature has a say in how that is done. I will not be ruling with absolute authority, guided by a council. I will chair a council of elected representatives who will make decisions on your behalf.'

Despite the rumours, the surprised looks in the room confirm that the idea is unsettling to many. And if they find that confronting, the next part about creature equality is going to blow their minds.

A loud *crash!* echoes through the cavernous space.

Every head turns to the back of the room—to the source of the interruption. A tall, imperious, supercilious figure moves into the aisle between the seats and saunters towards the dais. From the corner of my eye, I clock the guards moving closer to the royal family while still others leave the dais. The identity of the intruder has my hackles rising.

The strutting peacock stops when he recognises me. 'I see you didn't make the cut, Snake. What a shame. Guess that leaves the way open for me.'

He turns his attention to Queen Cecily and says, 'Hello, Mother-in-Law.'

No one moves. The audacity of this unknown elf has them all frozen in place.

Queen Cecily raises a disdainful eyebrow. 'Do I know you?'

'You have not yet had the pleasure, but I am here to

rectify that. I am Lord Dinian, Heir to the Unseelie Court, and betrothed of Princess Priscilla.'

A growl rises from the pit of my stomach, and it is all I can do not to leap over my father and wring the neck of that duplicitous creep. Where had he come from? And how did he get in here? I might not kill him, but I can't just stand here and let him preen.

As I slowly rise to my feet, I glance at Pris. Her lips are curled with distaste, and her fists are clenched as though she'd like nothing better than to punch that smug look from Dinian's face. She can't do anything from where she is, but I can.

'Dinian, I thought you would have grown a spine by now, but you've obviously been hiding while the rest of us have been fighting for what we believe in.'

'My court is the *Unseelie Court*. I saw no reason to get involved in your little squabble.'

Ugh, he's so… so…

King Maddox steps forward. 'Dinian, this is not the time or the place. Let us retire where we can discuss things in private.'

Dinian pulls out a gun and points it at Pris. 'No, Maddox. I will not listen to your honeyed words again. I. Am. Owed. Her.'

I launch myself forward, placing my body between Pris and that gun, then stare at the weapon and freeze. I didn't think this through. I have no plan.

Mandor appears from nowhere, and before the elf can use the weapon he's pointing, the witch opens a portal. Dinian half turns at the noise, and Aeron moves with a blur of speed. He pushes Dinian through the opening, which Mandor snaps shut behind him.

In the meantime the guards have bustled the royal party from the dais. It seems the formal part of the proceedings are over. Not exactly the ending we expected, but Queen Cecily still has a chance to win over hearts and minds at the reception. And I might get some time with Pris—once I manage to get my pounding heart under control.

Unfortunately, Pris, Aeron, Mandor, and Maddox are not in the reception rooms when we arrive. I join Irene and Petunia, introducing them to my father. As Drow enters, I scan the room again for Pris. Irene leans in and says, 'She won't be coming. She has gone with the others to sort out young Dinian.'

Yet another opportunity gone. Although my head is starting to tell me we're not meant to be, my heart refuses to move on.

· ·ᐧ ᴗ ᴧ· ·

Standing between Eleanora and Nisha, I watch the great and the good of creature society enter the ballroom. As a sprite, I stand tall and proud to be part of this moment in our history even though I think our inclusion is long over-due. There are a few brownies, sprites, pixies, and gnomes here, but too few compared to elves, witches, goblins, and dwarves. This will change. I will see to that—I promised the grove I would.

Ed'rima had dropped me at the grove after our audi-ence with the Dragon Queen. She insisted I needed time to recover, although my thoughts were of singing my father's spirit to rest—and of course testing my ability to be at one with the forest.

It was odd being in the grove without Nisha, who still had work to do in the Capitol, but the gap her presence left was more than filled by the grove itself—my home sang to me for the first time in hundreds of years. Tears form in my eyes even now as I remember the joy rushing through me.

The elders soon swept my plans aside. 'We are pleased you are back with us and able to commune.'

'Thank you,' I had said. 'I hope to bring Nisha back and settle here once the new government is in place.'

'And you would be welcome, but we want you to consider a different option. You have been in the world for some time now and know how it works, yet you also know what it means to be a sprite. We would like you to put yourself forward for election to the new council.'

My first thought had been to reject their request, but my brother Emrys had taken me aside. 'Our father foresaw this, and the spirits of the grove sense it is right. Please, think about it.'

Nisha's hand on my arm draws me from my thoughts. 'Surely you should do something other than stand here daydreaming.'

'Perhaps, but let us simply enjoy being here for a while before I do my duty and greet the members of the court.'

She smiles at me, and my heart leaps. My time in the grove was nothing compared to last night. Ed'rima had come and taken me back to the palace so I could prepare for today. When I entered the rooms I had been allocated, I found Nisha had transformed the bedroom into a grove away from home.

She had removed my bed and replaced it with trees. All right, the trees are in pots, and the moss around the base will require a lot of upkeep and will probably have to be changed frequently, but it is a grove. And in that grove, I can sleep in sprite form and recharge my energy.

Last night, bathed in candlelight and connected with

the trees, Nisha and I had finally cemented our bond—and it was life altering. Being fully bonded is a transformation like no other. It is not that we became one, but that we became three. There is Nisha, there is me, and there is us. When we choose, we open the connection our bond created and share our essence, and we are one.

The memory brings a smile to my lips until Nisha digs me in the ribs and whispers, 'If you are going to think inappropriate thoughts, then perhaps it is time we mingled.'

Eleanora chokes back a laugh, but she schools her face as Queen Cecily heads our way, leading the two newly anointed Princesses of the Royal Blood.

'Eleanora, Percival, and Nisha, may I present Princess Ember and Princess Eloise.'

'Please,' Princess Ember says, colour infusing her cheeks, 'just Ember will do.'

'It is a pleasure to meet you, Princess Eloise and... Ember,' I smile kindly at the princess. She reminds me a little of Pris when I first met her.

As we form a group, the two princesses position themselves near Nisha.

Queen Cecily starts, 'The twins are studying healing at the university and asked especially to be introduced to you, Nisha.'

It is my bonded mate's turn to colour. She is not used to being the centre of attention and though she no longer shies away from it, nor does she court it.

Princess Ember steps closer. 'We have been told that you might have time on your hands now that your patients have been moved to the hospital in the Capitol. So... Eloise and I thought you might consider teaching a semester class in sprite healing techniques. We have already spoken to the Head of Faculty, and he is quite excited by the idea.'

Nisha takes my hand and through our bond asks, **What do you think, Percival? Should I do this?**

Not used to having her in my head, I'm also not sure I am in a position to advise her. She loves the grove, but from the way she helped during the war, it is clear she has so much to offer the wider world. Perhaps this would be good for her.

You would make a wonderful teacher, but it is up to you. We think there will not be full elections for perhaps ten or so months, so I will be in the Capitol longer than a semester.

Nisha nods at me, but still chooses her words carefully before answering, 'I would be honoured to take up such a role, but I have other commitments. I am training two students in the grove, and I cannot leave them for that long.'

'I would be happy to sponsor them for entry into the university. That way they could continue to study,' Queen Cecily says.

A ghost of a smile hovers at the edge of Nisha's mouth, telling me that this is only part of her plan.

'That is very generous of you, Your Majesty, but I am afraid I could not ask such young sprites to spend so much time away from the grove. The Capitol is not a healthy place for our kind to live.'

Queen Cecily taps her lips in thought. 'I believe you have transformed your quarters into a sort of grove.'

'That is merely a stop gap, Your Highness. For sprites to feel welcome and at home in the Capitol, we really need our own grove here. It would also help me better teach the healing practices of our kind.'

Queen Cecily smiles, appreciating how deftly Nisha has handled the situation.

'Cousin Cecily, this is such a great idea. Ember and I would love to help Healer Nisha establish a grove in the Capitol,' Princess Eloise gushes.

Now Queen Cecily is grinning. 'I am going to like having you around, Nisha, although I sense I am going to have to watch myself. I will discuss this with the interim council, but I am sure we will be able to accommodate your request. The Capitol should have a place for all creatures to feel at home and supported.'

As Queen Cecily leads her cousins away, I lean close to Nisha and say, 'I'm not sure I am the best one of the two of us to be sitting on the interim council. You are a much better politician'

Nisha smiles a shy smile. 'I think the creatures of the Capitol should watch out for both of us. Together we will ensure sprites are seen in this new world we are making.'

CHAPTER 17

Beginnings and Endings

Eugenia's second-story apartment overlooks a leafy square in the Witch's district. Normally, it is more of an office cum dormitory. Tonight it is alight with candles, and a large circular dining table laden with food fills the room. The wine has been flowing, as has the conversation as the three witch sisters, Drow, Heart, Mandor, Nisha, and myself eat, drink, and celebrate our being together.

As Drow and Genie clear away the last course, I study the usually spartan room, noting little changes here and there. I am sure that painting on the wall used to be in Ellie's bedroom in Wimbledon. And that armchair by the window definitely was not here last time I visited.

'Ellie?'

'Mmm?' my friend responds, not taking her eyes from the pie Drow is carrying into the room.

'Have you something you wish to tell me?'

A cheeky grin transforms Ellie's face as she turns towards me. 'Perhaps.'

'Is it something about your staying in the World Below?' I guess.

She barks out a laugh. 'You are too observant, old friend. Yes, I am staying.'

'But what about your role as the Witch of Wimbledon? Who will look after creatures in London?' Eleanora has been The Witch of Wimbledon for so long, I cannot see anyone else ever filling her kitchen.

'Mae has been training for years. She is ready,' Ellie says.

'Won't she be busy, what with the shop and—'

'And filling your pocket with cake?' Ellie teases.

It is true, I had set up a small portal back to a room in Ellie's house accessed via my trouser pocket. Mae is good enough to ensure it is always stocked with cake and tea. However, that was not what I meant.

'And your grandson,' I say a little tartly.

'Mae is going to be working with Verona. Unbeknown to me, the two have been talking about setting up a creature way station in London for years. The health food shop in Wimbledon will be a contact point, and Verona wants to turn the elven house in Grosvenor Square into a kind of hostel,' Ellie explains.

I suddenly feel very old. 'It seems the younger generation have it all in hand.'

'They do. And that frees me up for some new challenges.' Ellie passes me a plate filled with apple pie and ice-cream.

I place the dessert in front of me, sneak a quick glance Mandor's way, then ask, 'And do those plans include anyone else?'

Ellie eats some pie before answering, her face thoughtful. 'Possibly, or yes, and depending on why you're asking. I will work with Cecily and Mandor to find places for the ex-wizards who do not want to return to the order.'

I raise an eyebrow. 'I thought the order would disband because the new constitution allows any creature to study and use higher magic.'

Ellie shakes her head. 'No, some like the quiet of the Wizard Order, and some are not happy that the study and use of higher magic outside of the order will have to be licensed. So, a few are returning and taking their vows.'

'And I take it from your new role, not all of them want to study higher magic with Mandor to get a licence?'

'No, not all of them, especially the younger ex-wizards born into the order. We want to find a place for all of them. In fact, one of them, Alyce, is going to the World Above with Genie, isn't she?' Ellie turns to her sister.

Genie looks up from her dessert, swallows her mouthful, and says, 'What? Alyce? Yes, I am pleased she is coming with me to train as the new Hag in the Bog, as Pris once called me.'

Effie joins the conversation. 'And you'll find one for me too, won't you?'

I do not believe what I am hearing. 'You are all retiring? But you are in the prime of your lives.'

Effie barks out a laugh. 'Retiring from our roles in the World Above, but we're not going out to pasture yet. When I've trained a replacement, I will work with Petunia setting up a community where human magic workers can live in peace. Loch Ness is so remote—it's a perfect place for them to gather. Maddox has agreed to support us as part of his efforts to improve the creation of magic in the World Above.'

'So you won't return to the World Below?' I ask.

Effie's eyes drift to Drow, then back to me. 'There is

nothing here for me. At least not now that Drow and Elias have rekindled their friendship.'

My eyes widen, and Effie's mouth twists into a sad smile. How long has she known?

'Oh, Effie…,'

'I have always known his heart lay elsewhere, just not where until recently. So, although I may visit sometimes, I will pledge myself to the Unseelie Court,' Effie says.

'And what will you do when you retire?' I ask Genie to give Effie some space.

My witch friend beams. 'I am going to do what I always wanted to. I am going home to help Mamma tend to magic in the Wyld Woods.'

'And keep an eye on Bernais,' Drow adds.

Genie nods. 'Yes, that too.'

There is a lull in the proceedings, and Mandor chooses that moment to push back his chair and stand up. 'Who knew when we fought the blight and challenged the council that we would end up here, hundreds of years later, having finally achieved what we once set out to do? I toast us, my friends, and I toast the World Below—may we in the World Below finally be as one.'

We raise our glasses and drink, and I can't help but think that this really is the end of something. It's a beginning, too, but it is the end of our youthful dreams as we step up and take on the mantel of community elders.

As if we all sense the mood has changed, the evening winds up. Nisha and I say our goodbyes, and, feeling a little melancholy, I suggest we walk home via the university.

As we enter the courtyard, the ancient oaks whisper to me. A welcoming hum fills my ears, and tears fill my eyes as I send soothing greetings back. As always I feel sad that the song of the trees in the Capitol is but a shadow of the music their counterparts make in the grove.

A long time ago, in what seems to be another lifetime, I came here and listened to the song of the oaks, and it almost broke my heart. When I had attempted to commune with the trees, it had almost crushed my spirit. I place my hand against the trunk of the closest tree, letting it know I am here and it is loved. I smile as the tree returns my affection.

Nisha appears oblivious to the ancient oaks and our shared emotions as she studies the buildings surrounding us. 'I never studied here like you, yet I will begin teaching students next week,' she says, amazement and excitement glinting in her eyes.

'You are a great healer, but I am sure you are an even better teacher.'

She turns to me. 'I want to teach, Percival. In my bones, I feel this is right for me. If I stay after this semester to teach and help sprites who want a future in the Capitol, will that work for you? Will it work for the life we wish to build?'

She has had a calling, and she is asking if I will support her. Part of me desperately wants to go home to the grove, to make up for lost time with my family and to find a role there. However, the elders and the grove wish a different path for me.

'If you want to be here, Nisha, then we will be here.'

'You will stand for council?'

'I will.'

'And together we will make a difference for sprite-kind.'

The song of the trees is thrumming through me now, as if agreeing with our decision. I take Nisha's hand and place it beside mine on the wood. She closes her eyes and we become one as we change and merge with the trees. Moving from tree to tree, we begin the process of healing.

After closing the leather straps on the bag containing the clothing and supplies my father and mother had thoughtfully provided for me, I lean the neck of the guitar Brynn allowed me to keep on top of it before turning to my father.

'I guess that's it, then.'

'I hope you left something here just in case you want to stay the occasional night,' Dad says, clearly trying to keep the tone casual, but he is unable to hide the hope in his eyes.

I smile. 'Of course. Everyone has made it clear that Sunday dinners are an open invitation, and I'm sure I'll need something decent to eat if most of my meals are coming from the university canteen.'

Dad's brows draw into a frown. 'You don't have to eat there. I have opened an account for you. There's enough in there to cover fees and some spending money too.'

I flush and fiddle with the straps on my bag. My father has been trying for years to find ways to support my mother and me, so I know this means a lot to him. I give him this moment and keep the fact the dragons are paying me a salary to myself.

'Thank you,' I say. 'It'll take a weight off my mind. Professor Xander suggested I apply for the position of his research assistant to cover fees, but I was wondering how I was going to fit that in with my duties at court.'

My father beams, and I'm pleased I kept my mouth shut.

A face appears over my father's shoulder. Dad steps

aside, and Drow enters. 'The carriage is downstairs, if you're ready.'

I nod briefly, but I'm not. Over the past couple of months, I have done so much, grown up so much, but this is too like leaving home for the first time. My palms are sweaty, and I'm suddenly finding it hard to breathe.

As if sensing my unease, Dad picks up the guitar, leaving the bag for me, and leads the way downstairs. Drow follows, catching us up at the door. I'm almost relieved to find Earth and Glisth standing outside, waiting for us.

'I always imagined this day would happen in the World Above,' Earth says, wiping a tear from his eye.

Glisth draws me into a hug, then hands me a paper bag. I catch a whiff of chocolate, and my stomach rumbles appreciatively. 'A little something to tide you over until Sunday.'

Drow places my luggage in the horse-drawn carriage and follows it inside.

'Bye, Dad.' I give him a quick hug, then get inside before I lose my nerve.

Dad leans his head in through the window. 'We are here if you need us.'

Drow snorts. 'He will have me close by should he run into trouble.'

Dad and I exchange a knowing glance. For all his best intentions, Drow is often too caught up in his own world to remember where he is, let alone care for someone else.

The ride to the university is short. In fact, I could easily have walked it except Drow had rented a carriage to take his books and offered me a lift. As he had been so good about arranging rooms for me at the last minute, I felt I had to accept.

I regret my decision as soon as we arrive. The few

students mingling in the courtyard stop what they are doing and watch our progress. They follow the carriage to the main entrance to see what is going on. So much for staying under the radar here.

Oblivious to the stir we're causing, Drow sweeps through the vestibule, then up a flight of stairs, and I follow in his wake. 'These rooms belong to those with places sponsored by the Crown,' Drow tells me. 'Nisha's trainees will have the suite beside yours.' He points at a door as we pass before stopping at the next one and opening it. 'You know, this is the very same suite Eleanora and Percival had when they attended the university.

'Cool,' I say, stepping inside. 'I so want Percival's room.'

Opposite me are two sets of windows overlooking the courtyard with a small dining table set between them. To the left is a sofa and two armchairs in front of a fireplace. On the far side of the fireplace is a door, and there is another directly opposite.

'His was on the right,' Drow tells me. 'And it looks like your roommate is not here yet, so the room is all yours.'

I cross the room and open the door to peek inside. As I do, a porter arrives with my bags and bundles past Drow.

'It looks like you're set, Snake, and I had best go and settle in. I need to be ready for classes starting tomorrow, and I still have so much to do. Do you want me to come back and take you to the dining room for dinner?'

'Will you be eating there?'

'Goodness no. I will dine in my rooms.'

'Then I will be fine.'

Drow seems reluctant to leave. 'I am sure your room-mate should arrive soon. I expected them to be here already. They are cutting it a bit fine.'

'Drow, go. I'll be okay.'

My uncle turns somewhat reluctantly. 'I will.. um, check on you later?'

'All right,' I say as he shuts the door behind him.

Returning to my room, I look out the small window into the courtyard. It is strangely comforting that Percival probably stood here and did the same thing.

I unpack my belongings and set up my desk, and the bell still hasn't rung for dinner. I pick up the guitar, strum a few chords, tune it, then strum again. Before I know it, I'm playing the Extreme song 'More Than Words'— a song I associate with Pris.

Alone in this room, I indulge my sense of loss and allow myself to mourn the closeness we once had and are never likely to have again. I let myself have this quiet moment to admit how much I miss her.

I'm running so late. My meeting with Mum and Dad took longer than I'd anticipated, but I wanted to get things sorted today. It had taken a while, but they finally agreed in principle to my setting up a legal-aid clinic for the creator creatures who can't afford lawyers, provided I get Drow to supervise it.

The idea had come to me as I listened to yet another creature gush over Drow and Percival and how they had changed the law on behalf of creator creatures centuries ago. It saddened me to think little had changed for them since then. It turns out finding my calling in the World Below was as simple as listening and applying a World Above solution.

As I push open the door, the sounds of a song drift my

way. I close my eyes and allow a little hope to enter my heart. Hope that I haven't left it too late. Hope that he still plays this song for me.

I wait for the music to finish, then drop my bag on the floor. Before I can make it across the room, the door to the right opens.

'Hi, I'm....'

'Snake Fieth, pleased to meet you. I'm Priscilla Crown, but you can call me Pris.'

He runs his hand through his hair, which is a little long —just the way I like it—and smiles tentatively. 'I know who you are. I thought you were my roommate.'

His eyes drift to the bag on the floor, then widen a little as they return to me.

'Hope you don't mind. I pulled some strings with Drow. You know Percival—'

'And Eleanora used to share here.'

'I bags Perc—' I peer past him through to the bedroom. 'You already have, haven't you. Now I'm stuck with Eleanora's room. She's probably booby-trapped it especially for me. I knew I should have gotten here sooner.'

Snake is silent. He just stands there staring at me. Am I too late? He's changed his mind these past few days. I tried to find time to talk with him, to let him know what I'm thinking, but it was like the universe was always working against us, keeping us apart.

'You pulled strings with Drow?' His voice is quiet and even, and it's maddening because it gives nothing away.

'Yes. He's sponsoring me to study creature law here. He and Mum thought it would be useful in case I become Queen—if they can't find some way to get me out of it before then.'

Is it that? The whole royal thing again? Dammit, if I don't want to do it, how can I expect Snake to take it on?

Maybe I can convince him it won't impact us. I step towards him. He doesn't move away, but he looks… bemused.

'So, you're staying in the World Below? I thought….'

Blast all of this, it's too much like a trite romance novel. Will they, won't they? This could go on forever, and I won't wait that long.

'I thought you said you chose me. Then you turned up as the Dragon Queen's representative to the council, and I thought you had decided on a different path. Then my mother reminded me of how difficult it is to turn the Queen of Dragons down and said that I should give you a chance to explain. Then things got away from us, and there never seemed to be any time to talk. And I was aware that I never said the words back to you and that you probably thought I didn't care. And my whole future was up in the air, and my family thought I might want to go back home, but I knew you would be staying, and, well….'

Goddess, I'm blabbering like a fool. I suck in air and try to calm my racing heart. 'I heard you were going to be staying in these rooms, and I pulled some strings, and here I am.'

'Tell him the words, Pris,' says a voice from the other side of the door.

'Aeron, you said you'd wait in your room across the hall until I called you,' I groan in exasperation.

Snake stares at the door, a smile tugging at the corner of his lips. 'Aeron's here?'

'Yeah, Mum insisted I have a guard, and he volunteered.'

'He'll blend right in,' Snake jokes.

I smile, the tension leaving me a little. 'He wanted to stay in the Capitol. Something to do with an ex-princess he's sweet on.'

'That's private,' comes a shout through the door.

'If you don't want to hear me talking about you, you should have done what we agreed in the first place.'

Seconds later, a door slams, and I laugh. Not that Aeron's absence makes this whole situation easy. It's just so much harder with an audience.

I turn back to Snake, trying to read his expression, worrying I've said too much. I'll wait for him to make the next move.

He does, sort of. He takes a couple of steps and picks up my bag and carries it towards the other bedroom door, and I follow. As we pass the window, I make out the figures of two dragons perched on top of the opposite building. Really, is nothing private?

Snake opens the door and says, 'We'd best check for booby traps.'

I flick my hand in a go-away motion, knowing full well the dragons can see me with their extra keen eyes.

I follow Snake into a spartan room containing only a plain wooden bed, chest of drawers, desk, chair, and wardrobe. I have nothing with me to make it more homely, but I guess we all have to start somewhere.

'Dinner will be soon. I'll let you get unpacked.'

Snake moves to pass me, and I grab his arm, spinning him around to face me. If he wants to be friends, I will work with that, but I have to at least try for more. Aeron is right, I have to say the words.

'Snake, I choose us. I. Choose. Us.'

Time freezes, and I am not sure which way this will go. A moan rises from inside Snake, and I don't know exactly how it happens, but I'm in his arms and pulled tightly against his chest. As his lips press to mine, I have one thought—I am home.

We should give them privacy now, Ed'rathe.

You should teach the princess better shielding. Every dragon in the realms will know they fully bonded today.

Come, it is time to return home. They will call us of they need us.

Am'ratha takes to the sky. With one last glance at the embracing couple, her brother joins her.

THE END

Acknowledgments

The World Below has been a wild ride. Starting with the USA Today Bestselling Realm of Darkness Boxset containing The World Below, through to this mammoth last book in the series, I've fallen in love with the characters in this series, and I shall miss them terribly.

I couldn't have done this without an amazing support team, starting with Creating Ink, especially Sali Benbow-Powers. Then there's the team at Hot Tree Editing, and McKinley Hellennes Krantz for improving my story telling and making it more readable.

As always, my love and thanks to my moral support Jim, and my son Sam for putting up with me when I hide away to finish a book. Without them I wouldn't eat and I'd miss every deadline. And to Trouble and Lola for keeping me company when I write.

Finally, thank you for reading my musings. If you've enjoyed these books please leave a review on your favourite book site.

Vivienne has been writing books since she was fifteen years old, but only friends and family were allowed to read them. Forced to give up work because of family commitments she was encouraged by friends and family to finally put some of her writing out there for others to read.

Born in Invercargill (New Zealand), she has lived in; Dunedin (New Zealand), London (England), Petersfield (England) and currently lives with her husband and son, their dog Trouble and cat Lola in North Sydney (Australia).

When not reading or writing she can be found walking, crocheting, knitting and watching movies.

For future releases and current news you can find Vivienne at www.viviennelfraser.com.au where you can also join my newsletter.

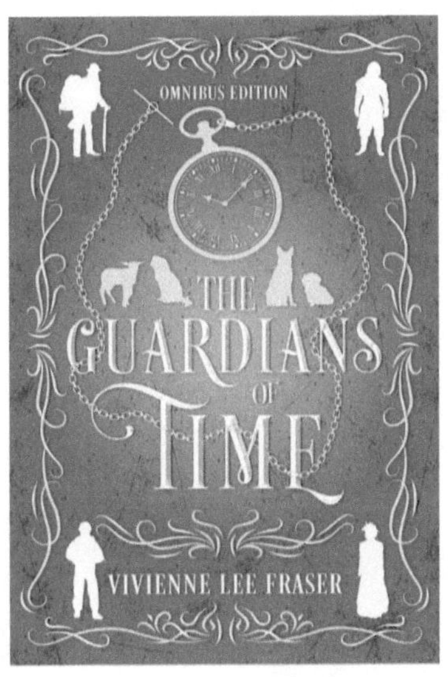

In the shadows between history and time a secret war is waging—
a war where the stakes are the future of humanity.

On one side are the Time Fixers, often called the Time Wreckers
by their enemies. They believe fixing past wrongs will pave the
way for humanity's salvation.

On the other side are the Time Guardians, who fight for history
to remain as it has always has been, believing humankind will
find a way to save themselves.

Time Guardian Sigma has pulled together a team of would-be
guardians to help him keep history in line; John the pragmatist,
feisty Barabal, Alain the inquisitive, and Stanislaus the loyal.

As his team portal through time foiling Time Fixer plots, Sigma is

worried they may be winning battles, but they are losing the war
—and that's not just because Time Fixer Isolde has been getting
inside his head.

Will the Time Guardian's win the war? Will humanity survive the
battle? More importantly, will Sigma be there at the end?

Centuries ago prophets predicted the rise of a great wizard and a formidable warrior who would save the people of their land. Now an invasion fleet is heading for Aria, is it time for the Wizard and the Warrior to arise and save them all? Runaway bride Aliah wants to be more than someone's wife. Fleeing his destiny, Seamus has no idea what he wants from his future. Thrown together by fate, the two journey to the nation's capital; one to warn the king of an impending invasion, the other to do the unthinkable—train to be a wizard. Their chance encounter takes them on a wild adventure where they must face their pasts and decide their future, all while helping Aria prepare to defend itself.

However, fate has not finished with Seamus and Aliah. In an unexpected twist, they are placed at the very centre of the conflict facing their home, and must decide whether or not to take up the challenge. With the gods on their side, it should be easy for Aliah and Seamus to identify and locate the real power behind the invasion and find a way to defeat him; all while pulling together a support team and having mid-night lessons to learn how to use their newly acquired magical tokens. Well, it would be if the gods weren't hiding more than they shared. Aria's future hangs in the balance, can two runaways tip the scales?